# GUIDE ME HOME

# Praise for
## *Guide Me Home*

"Quite simply, I loved this story from page one until the end. Rebekah Hardin is truly one of Kim Vogel Sawyer's most lovable heroines. Kim has created a story that lovingly depicts the people, land, and culture of Appalachia. *Guide Me Home* is a tale of love and hope and faith that will hold your heart long after you reach the end."

—Laurie Alice Eakes, author of *The Mountain Midwife,* 2016
Rita Finalist

"Kim Vogel Sawyer's characters light up the pages in this deeply moving story of misplaced guilt, ambition, and dreams. I found myself quickly turning pages to find out how Devlin and Reb would resolve their differences in class and culture. And Kim didn't disappoint. As I read the last page, I felt as if I too had been guided home."

—Pam Hillman, author of *Stealing Jake*

"Just when I thought Kim Vogel Sawyer's novels couldn't get any better, *Guide Me Home* fell into my lap, and I was once again amazed by her marvelous resourcefulness. I've read several of Kim's books, so I can say with honesty that this is one of her finest. It is a poignant story of faith, family, and endearing romance. If you are a fan of historical romance rich with descriptive detail, you will love *Guide Me Home.*"

—Sharlene MacLaren, author of the *Tennessee Dreams* series
and the *River of Hope* series

"Kim Vogel Sawyer has expertly crafted a novel that's rich in both God's truths and American history. I thoroughly enjoyed this dynamic story. It's been wonderfully researched and delves into the concept of watching our words and the consequences that can unfold when we don't. But Kim doesn't leave readers there, suffering in guilt. Through compelling characters, she illustrates God's infinite grace and love's healing powers. Readers will not be disappointed!"

—Andrea Boeshaar, author of the acclaimed Shenandoah
Valley Saga

# GUIDE ME HOME

# Kim Vogel Sawyer

A NOVEL

WATERBROOK
PRESS

GUIDE ME HOME

All Scripture quotations are taken from the King James Version.

The characters and events in this book are fictional, and any resemblance to actual persons or events is coincidental.

Trade Paperback ISBN 978-0-307-73139-5
eBook ISBN 978-0-307-73140-1

Published in the United States by WaterBrook, an imprint of the Crown Publishing Group, a division of Penguin Random House LLC, New York.

WATERBROOK® and its deer colophon are registered trademarks of Penguin Random House LLC.

Library of Congress Cataloging-in-Publication Data
Names: Sawyer, Kim Vogel, author.
Title: Guide me home : a novel / Kim Vogel Sawyer.
Description: First Edition. | Colorado Springs, Colorado : WaterBrook Press, 2016.
Identifiers: LCCN 2016010328 (print) | LCCN 2016004747 (ebook) | ISBN 9780307731401
   (electronic) | ISBN 9780307731395 (paperback) | ISBN 9780307731401 (ebook)
Subjects: | BISAC: FICTION / Christian / Historical. | FICTION / Christian / Romance. | FICTION
   / Romance / Historical. | GSAFD: Christian fiction. | Love stories. | Historical fiction.
Classification: LCC PS3619.A97 (print) | LCC PS3619.A97 G85 2016 (ebook) | DDC 813/.6—dc23
LC record available at http://lccn.loc.gov/2016004747

Printed in the United States of America
2016—First Edition

10  9  8  7  6  5  4  3  2  1

*In memory of my grandparents,*
*Henry and Elizabeth Klaassen Voth and Lillian Miller Vogel,*
*with thanks for giving my parents a legacy of faith.*

For thou art my lamp, O LORD:
and the LORD will lighten my darkness.

2 SAMUEL 22:29

# ONE

*Good Spring, Kentucky*
*Mid-April 1907*

*Rebekah Hardin*

Rebekah awakened to birdsong, the most perfect way in the world to start a new day. She smiled as she stretched, rolled over, and poked her feet from beneath the soft, old patchwork quilt that always made her think of Jacob's coat of many colors.

On the other side of the bed, Cissy stirred and groaned. "Aw, Bek, can'tcha ever lay still 'til Mama hollers? You always wake everybody up before we're ready. An' it's Saturday. Don't even gotta get up for school."

The rustle of dried corn shucks and murmurs carried from the other two beds crowded in the drafty room, proving she—or maybe Cissy—had disturbed her youngest sisters, too. Rebekah sent an apologetic look across their bleary-eyed faces, although with the shutters latched up tight, she doubted they would recognize her remorse in the still-deep shadows.

"Shh," she crooned. "Drop on back to sleep." She sat still as a mouse until all six tousled heads returned to the pillows and six pairs of eyes slid shut. Then she tiptoed across the unstained pine floorboards through thin ribbons of light sneaking between cracks where chinking had crumbled. The planked door's rusty hinges squeaked, earning another low growl from Cissy, but Rebekah ignored the complaint. Cissy was always grumpy in the morning.

She crossed the threshold into the main room of her family's century-old cabin and settled the door in its frame. Mama, never one to laze in the morning, was already at the fireplace, stirring last night's coals to life.

Rebekah aimed a hopeful smile at her mother. "Morning, Mama."

She didn't look up. "Fetch me some wood."

Rebekah stifled a sigh. "Yes'm." Mama's morning crankiness was harder to bear than Cissy's. Rebekah lifted the crossbar to the back door and stepped off the flat rock serving as a stoop onto the dewy grass. She left the door standing wide to let the sweet spring breeze fill the house. Now that winter was past, maybe Mama's spirits would lift. Rebekah missed her mother's smile and the musical, girlish giggle that invited everyone to join in.

"Gal!"

She paused at the edge of the stoop, shivering in her nightgown. But not because of the chill morning air.

"Close that door. You'll let flies in."

It was too early for flies and Rebekah knew it. But she closed the door anyway. Mama must not be ready yet to cast off her winter doldrums. Rebekah turned her pleading gaze to the pink sky visible above the towering trees.

*Please, God, bring Mama her joy again soon.*

As always, talking to the One who'd created all the beauty coming to life in the forest around her family's simple cabin restored Rebekah's happy mood. She hop-skipped across the cool, damp grass on bare feet to the woodshed tucked at the edge of the clustered pine and aspen trees. When she emerged only minutes later, the pink sky had faded to a blue as pale as a robin's egg. Mama would wake the children soon. She'd better hurry with the firewood.

She balanced the armload of wood against her chest and stepped onto the stoop. The dry, weathered bark bit into her flesh through the thin fabric of her nightgown. Eager to dump the wood into the box beside their stone fireplace, she carefully extended one hand toward the pull string. But before she tugged, a voice from inside the cabin froze her in place.

"Nell, I'm worn out with you. This mopin' has gotta stop."

Chills exploded across Rebekah's scalp and traveled down her spine. Never had she heard Daddy speak so harshly to Mama. Daddy was the kindest, most patient person she knew. She stood quivering, afraid to enter the room lest he bark sharp words at her for interrupting.

"Don't you think I want to stop, Festus?" Mama's words choked out. "I'm weary of feelin' sad inside. I tell myself every day it's plumb foolish to pine so over our boy. Four babies I've buried in them woods behind our house. Each of 'em left a gnawin' ache inside o' me, but I overcame it 'cause they nary took a breath nor tasted life, just went straight to Jesus's arms. I could bear them goin' away from me 'cause the Lord giveth an' He taketh, an' He knows best. But Andy . . ."

Her mother's anguished, strangled sob tore a ragged hole in Rebekah's soul. Sympathetic tears flooded her eyes, making the grain in the wood door blur.

"I suckled that boy at my breast. I watched him grow. For fifteen years he was ours, Festus, makin' us laugh an' makin' us worry an' lettin' us dream o' the man he'd be someday. 'Twas two years ago today we buried all our dreams for him when we put his body in the ground."

Mama's voice became muffled, and Rebekah knew Daddy had pulled her against his shoulder the way he always did when one of his gals needed comfort. Even so, she made out every one of her mother's pain-filled words.

"If he had a decent headstone—somethin' carved with his name an' the dates of his time here on earth—then maybe I could put him to rest. But only a wood cross? Two sticks bound with twine? It'll rot and fall away an' nobody'll know a boy named Andy once tormented his sisters an' brought his mama bouquets of star chickweed an' claimed he'd be just like his daddy when he grew up. I want him to have more, Festus. He needs more."

"I'd give him more if I could, darlin'." Daddy sounded old. Defeated. "Soon as I scrape up twenty-six dollars that don't need spent on somethin' else—"

Rebekah groaned. They'd never have twenty-six dollars at one time that didn't need spending elsewhere.

"—I'll go to Bowlin' Green an' get him a fine marker with his name, the record of every day he lived, an' even a verse carved in pretty writin'."

"A . . . a verse? Can I choose it?" Mama sounded so hopeful Rebekah found herself holding her breath in anticipation of Daddy's answer.

"Any verse you want, Nell. I promise."

Rebekah's bare toes ached from the cold seeping from the stone beneath her feet. Her arms ached with the weight of the logs. But mostly her heart ached for the loss her mama couldn't overcome. She closed her eyes against the deep sting of remorse. *Oh, dear God, I didn't mean it. If it's true that You giveth and taketh, like Mama said, You could've given Andy life that day.* She gulped, sending an accusatory look skyward. *Why'd You take him away from Mama? You should've taken me instead.*

The door snapped open, and Daddy nearly plowed straight into her. He stopped short, his brows low and mouth set in a tight line. "Gal, what're you doin'? Get in here an' bring your mama that firewood. The house has a chill."

Rebekah had a chill, too, caused by Daddy's frosty treatment. "I'm sorry, Daddy."

He stepped aside long enough to let her pass. Then he stormed out, leaving the door open behind him. Rebekah didn't need to watch to know he was heading to the woods. To the little clearing where a twig fence encircled the graves of those in her family who'd gone before—Granny and Granddad Hardin, Uncle Fenway, Uncle Birch, Aunt Sal, all the babies who left Mama's body already empty of life. And Andy.

Agony writhed through her middle. The babes never lived. Granny and Granddad and her aunt and uncles enjoyed good, long lives. But Andy? He had no place inside that fence under the cold ground.

"Gimme some good kindlin' pieces." Mama swiped her eyes with her faded calico apron and held her hand toward Rebekah. "These coals're about to die clean away."

Rebekah dropped the full load into the firebox, then picked out the two skinniest chunks. Mama laid them in an X over the blinking coals and, on her hands and knees, gently blew until a tiny lick of flame rose up and tickled the underside of one log. Within minutes a dozen tongues danced around the logs, growing into a blaze. Mama layered in more wood, one piece at a time. Soon the fire snapped and writhed. Rebekah watched, mesmerized by the warmth and light emerging from a glowing coal, a pair of sticks, and Mama's breath.

Mama sat back on her heels, sighed, and gave Rebekah a weary look. "Get the young uns up. All o' you get dressed. Breakfast'll be on soon enough, an' then we can set to the chores. Heap to be done now that spring time's arrivin'."

Rebekah had lost her appetite for their customary cornmeal mush flavored with the molasses Daddy rendered every winter, but she hurried to the room she shared with her sisters and did as her mother bade.

Their dresses from yesterday lay at the foot of their beds, waiting another day's wearing. Rebekah dressed quickly and then said, "C'mere, Little Nellie." The littlest Hardin scooted off the bed and scuffed across the floor, still yawning. She stood complacently and allowed Rebekah to manipulate her limbs as if she were a large rag doll.

Twelve-year-old Della scrambled into her blue-checked dress, topped it with a feed-sack apron still bearing a faded round stamp advertising Superior Egg Pellets, and offered to help five-year-old Trudy with her buttons. Trudy poked out her tummy and linked her hands behind her back, giving Della easy access.

Cissy reached over and grabbed Della's wrist. "She's never gonna learn to dress herself if you keep doin' it for her. Heavens to Betsy, she'll be startin' school next term. You gonna write her name on the papers an' do her cipherin' for her, too?"

Trudy's lower lip puckered. Plump tears quivered on her thick lashes.

Rebekah glanced up from tying the strings on Little Nellie's apron. "Leave them be, Cissy."

Cissy huffed, but she flounced to the other side of the bed and tossed a mint-green dress over her tattered pantaloons. Della shot Rebekah a thank-you smile and continued fastening the buttons on Trudy's well-patched frock. Eleven-year-old Jessie and eight-year-old Tabitha began squabbling over their lone hairbrush, and Rebekah ended the disagreement by taking it for her own use. Both girls fussed until Cissy snapped at them to stop or she'd bang their heads together. They scurried to the far side of the room, away from her. Rebekah ran the brush through her long, thick hair, chuckling to herself.

The morning routine was familiar, comfortable despite the frenzied bustling of seven people in a small space. She'd had the chance to leave last year when Calvin Adwell asked her to marry up with him. She almost said yes, too, because at twenty years old she was fast gaining old-maid status among the folks of Good Spring. Even among her family, if Cissy was considered a reliable source. After thinking it over, though, she'd said no. Not because she disliked Cal. He was a nice enough fellow, handsome enough to not make her squirm. But if she was going to spend her life with somebody, she wanted more than nice enough and handsome enough. She wanted what she'd always seen between her mama and daddy—sparks that never needed somebody puffing at them to make them flare up again, sparks that didn't die even when hardships came along.

"Ain't you done brushin' yet, Bek?" Cissy's fretful voice cut into Rebekah's reflections. "Gimme that thing or none of us are gettin' outta here anytime soon."

Rebekah handed her sister the hairbrush. She gathered her heavy hair into her hands and twisted the strands into one thick braid. As usual, it ended off center and fell across her left shoulder. She tied the end with a piece of string and then aimed a stern frown on the oldest of her younger sisters. "Cissy, I'm gonna help Mama put breakfast on the table. Get everybody's hair braided, then hurry on out. Don't leave us waiting on you. It's chore day." Cissy was prone to drift away in daydreams, but Mama wasn't up to Cissy's thoughtlessness today—not the way she was hurting over Andy.

"I know, I know." Cissy glared at her image in the cracked mirror hanging from a nail in the wall and smacked the brush through her tangled lengths. "Just once, though, couldn't we do somethin' fun on a Saturday instead o' doin' chores? Couldn't we hitch up the mule an' drive over to Sutherland Pass, maybe choose some fabric for a new dress or ribbons for our hair?"

Trudy crowded near, looking up at Cissy with shining eyes. "Or striped candy sticks."

"Candy," Little Nellie echoed, wonder blooming on her cherubic face.

"An' gumdrops!" Tabitha added. The trio of little girls licked their lips as if tasting the sweet treats.

"Yeah." Cissy turned her glare on Rebekah. "We didn't even get candy in our Christmas stockings this year. Just nuts an' some ol' wrinkly apples." She thrust the hairbrush into Della's hands. "Just once couldn't we have somethin' special?"

Rebekah pinched a strand of Cissy's hair, which was two shades lighter than that of the other Hardin sisters, between her fingers and gave a gentle tug. "Special costs money, Cissy. Extra money is rare. Daddy and Mama would love to treat us to something special, but times being what they are, they can't. So we have to be patient and understanding."

Cissy jerked free. She folded her arms over her chest and pursed her full lips into a pout. "Ain't fair, Bek. Why can't we be like them families that go to the hotel an' pay to climb down inside Mammoth Cave?"

Rebekah cringed. How could Cissy forget the pain that cave had caused their family? She started to command her sister to never mention Mammoth Cave again, but Cissy hurried on.

"Those folks seem to have money to do whatever they please." She slapped at a patch sewn to the skirt of her faded dress. "You wouldn't see none o' the girls from those families wearin' worn-out hand-me-downs an' tyin' their braids with old shoelaces."

Her tawny-brown eyes pensive, Tabitha caught Rebekah's hand and swung it. "You reckon those girls do chores all day on Saturday, Bek?"

Cissy was planting seeds of rebellion in the little girls' heads. Rebekah needed to snatch them out before they took root. "Chores are part of everybody's life, Tabby. Otherwise nothing would get done."

Cissy snorted. "Betcha they all have maids an' such to do their work." She tossed her thick ponytail over her shoulder. "I'm tellin' you right now, I ain't gonna spend my life pickin' hornworms off tobacco leaves. I'm gonna have money—lots of it. An' I'm gonna wear store-bought dresses an' let my maid scrub the floor an' cook my meals."

The younger girls gazed at Cissy in open-mouthed fascination. Rebekah stepped between them and Cissy and snapped out a snide question. "And just where are you planning to get all this money, Miss High-and-Mighty?"

A wicked gleam entered Cissy's eyes. "There's ways. But I ain't gonna tell you what they are." She flounced out of the room.

Jessie put her fists on her hips and cocked her head. "What's she talkin' about, Bek?"

Rebekah shook her head at the eleven-year-old. "Never you mind. Cissy's always full of ideas that don't come to much." She sent a frown across the assembly of freckled faces. "Tabitha, why haven't you put on an apron? Get one from the trunk. Trudy, come here and I'll braid your hair. Della, put that brush to use on Little Nellie's tangled mess. If we don't get to the table soon, Mama's gonna throw our breakfast out the back door to the chickens."

To her relief, her sisters obeyed without argument. While she plaited Trudy's fine, soft hair, she pondered Cissy's declaration, "There's ways." Rebekah had found one way—selling the mushrooms that sprouted at the mouth of the cave on their property to the cook at the Mammoth Cave Hotel. He paid her five cents a pound for the white mushrooms. Daddy was always happy to drop the coins into the old coffee tin that held their savings, no matter how paltry the amount. Maybe there were other ways she could bring home money from some of the rich guests who stayed at the cave's hotel and paid to tour the cave's dozens of tunnels.

The bedroom door burst open. Cissy scowled into the room. "You gals comin' or not? Mama's about to have a conniption fit."

Rebekah waved her arms the way a mother hen flapped her wings and herded her little sisters out the door. "Come on now, let's go."

Daddy, wearing familiar striped overalls and a homespun blue cotton shirt with the sleeves rolled above his elbows, already waited in the chair at the head of their Granddaddy-built plank table. Cissy, Della, and Jessie clambered onto the bench on his left, and Rebekah slid in with Little Nellie, Trudy, and Tabitha on Daddy's right. Mama thumped the kettle, its bottom blackened from hanging over the fire, onto the table and then sagged into the remaining chair. Everyone joined hands and Daddy asked a blessing on the meal.

At Daddy's "amen," Mama jammed a wooden spoon into the kettle. "Hand me your bowls. It's comin' up on eight o'clock already. Mornin'll be gone before we know."

While Rebekah ate, a plan formulated in her head. After breakfast she'd take Daddy aside and ask him about talking to the cave owner about some sort of job beyond selling mushrooms. Her heart gave a hopeful flutter. If she snagged a job—a decent, good-paying job—she could maybe buy the headstone Mama wanted so badly for Andy. Then maybe, just maybe, their smiling, humming, ever-peaceful mama would come back to them.

# TWO

*Rebekah*

Before Rebekah's mush was half gone, Daddy pushed his empty bowl aside, swiped his mouth with the back of his hand, and stood. "Thanks for breakfast, Nell." Every day, every meal, Daddy thanked Mama for the food.

Mama nodded. "Did you get your fill?" Her customary question.

"To the top." His customary answer.

Across the table, Cissy rolled her eyes. Rebekah knew what her sister was thinking—*Why can't things be different?* But Rebekah liked the familiar routine. Liked the security it offered. Even if she had to quench her thirst for learning by borrowing books from the library wagon that rolled through their community twice a month, she was satisfied with her simple life. Except for Andy no longer being in it.

Daddy cleared his throat. "Jessie, help your mama with the dishes." His gaze shifted as he addressed his gals by turn. "Cissy an' Della, you two get the hoes from the toolshed an' chop all the weeds from the garden plot for your mama. We'll need to be puttin' seeds in the ground before long. Tabitha, the floors need a sweepin' an' scrubbin'—you give 'em a good one. Even in the corners." His expression turned tender when it fell on Trudy and Little Nellie. "Leastuns, you drag all the quilts an' beddin' off the beds an' make a pile by the fireplace—help your mama with the washin' today. Can you do it?"

Trudy swung her feet and beamed with importance. "I can do it, Daddy."

"Do it, Daddy," Little Nellie added.

"Good."

Cissy sent a sour look across the table. "What about Rebekah? What's she gonna do today?"

Daddy settled his gaze on Rebekah. "I'm fixin' to get my ax an' head to the woods. I could use your help draggin' back some good firewood logs."

Rebekah bounced up so quickly she almost knocked Little Nellie, who'd been resting her cheek on her big sister's arm, from the bench. "Sure, Daddy."

He chuckled—a low, comforting rumble. "Finish your breakfast. Can't give a full mornin's work unless your stomach's been filled."

Rebekah bent forward and spooned up the last of her mush in two big bites. She grabbed the bowl, carried it to the dry sink, and dropped it in the wash bin. She held her hands outward and smiled at her father. "Ready."

He shook his head, his lips curving into an amused grin. "If you're goin' in the woods, you're gonna need shoes, gal."

Grimacing at her forgetfulness, Rebekah dashed into her bedroom and fished from under the bed the brown lace-up shoes Mama had found in one of the charity barrels city folks donated to the church. She forced her feet into the shafts without loosening the laces, tied a quick bow at the top, and darted back into the main room.

Daddy waited by the back door. "Ready now?"

She lifted the hem of her skirt and tapped the scuffed toes of her shoes together.

"Let's go then."

Rebekah trailed Daddy past their dried-up garden plot, past the corncrib and tobacco barn, and into the woods. She could hardly believe her luck. Most Saturdays she worked alongside Mama tidying the cabin, plunging their sheets and blankets in a tub of sudsy water, then tossing them over bushes to dry. A morning in the woods with Daddy was a treat. Smelling the perfume of new, uncurling leaves instead of lye soap, enjoying Daddy's cheerful whistle and the chatter of squirrels instead of Mama's deep sighs and her sisters' squabbling. And best of all, she'd have him all to herself for a long talk.

Daddy lifted a pine bough and held it up so Rebekah could duck under. He let it go, releasing the sweet scent of pine along with little droplets of moisture. She turned and walked backward in front of him, studying his whiskery face. They were far enough from the cabin no one would overhear, but was he in a mood to listen?

"Gal, you're gonna knock yourself on your backside movin' like a crab."

She grinned. Daddy had visited the ocean once when he was young, and he never tired of sharing about the rolling sea and the funny little creatures he'd chased along the shore. His teasing let her know it was safe to talk about something serious like a job. And Andy.

She reached for his hand, the way she used to when she was no bigger than Little Nellie, and he caught hold. "Daddy, I heard you an' Mama this morning."

His fingers tightened. "Thought so by the look on your face when I opened the door." He carried her hand to his chest and chafed her knuckles against the rough fabric of his overall bib. "I'm sorry I snapped at you. I wasn't upset with you, gal."

"It's all right, Daddy. I worry about Mama, too."

The path narrowed. He released her and took the lead.

Following close on his heels, she gathered her courage and spoke to the straps crisscrossing his broad back. "I'd sure like to help get that marker for Andy."

Daddy's steps faltered, forcing Rebekah to slow her pace. Then he set off again, his stride long and his feet thudding on the hard ground. "I shouldn't 've made that promise to your mama. Not when I know deep down I can't keep it. How will I get the money? We spend it fast as it comes in. I got nothing of value to sell except the land, an' I won't never part with that. Not with our family's bones planted in the soil." He spoke soft, so soft she barely heard him over the crunch of their feet on dried pine needles and the wind's whisper through the tree branches. "No, I won't be able to keep that promise, no matter how much I want to. But Nell needs somethin' to hold on to. Some little hope to keep her heart beatin' 'til the Lord finally heals all the hurt she's got inside."

Rebekah grabbed the X on Daddy's back and drew him to a stop. He turned, his brows pulled into a puzzled frown. "Gal, why're you tuggin' on me?"

"'Cause I need you to listen."

"To what?"

She straightened to her full height—two inches taller than Mama but still a good six inches shorter than Daddy. She looked her father directly in the eyes. "I want to help you keep your promise to Mama. I want to buy that fancy headstone with Andy's name and a verse carved into it."

Daddy's frown changed to such a look of sorrow Rebekah experienced the sting of tears. He gripped her shoulders. "Gal, you gotta stop blamin' yourself for Andy's dyin'."

*Would you get lost? You're the biggest pest in the world!* She closed her eyes, willing away the memory of the last words she said to her brother. She'd been trying to read, and his pestering had kept her from focusing on the beautiful story of Jane Eyre. How could she have let a storybook hold such importance?

Daddy gave her a little shake. "That boy with his active mind was always seekin' adventures. He did a fool thing. Ain't nobody to blame except Andy himself."

Rebekah wished she could blame Andy. She opened her eyes and aimed her best pleading look at her father. "If I can get him that headstone, it'll ease my conscience."

Daddy sighed. He released Rebekah and ran his hand through his graying hair. "Where do you think you're gonna get enough money for a headstone?"

She hung her head. The idea that had made so much sense that morning now seemed as foolish as Andy's decision to explore the cave two years ago. "With a . . . a job."

"Where?"

"At Mammoth Cave."

"Doin' what?"

He hadn't said no. Rebekah jerked her gaze upward again. "I don't know. Working in the hotel, cleaning rooms or doing laundry. Or maybe in the kitchen. I could wash dishes and such."

Daddy sighed. "Lord knows you're a comfort to your mama an' me, almost bein' a second mother to your sisters. But why don't you set your thoughts on doin' all those chores in a house o' your own?" He cupped Rebekah's face, his calluses rough yet somehow soothing. "Cal Adwell hasn't started sparkin' some other girl yet. He's still set on you. You could—"

She stepped away from Daddy's hands. "I don't want to marry Cal Adwell."

"Then who?"

"I don't know yet. But somebody . . . more."

Daddy shook his head. "You sound like Cissy, always thinkin' some prince on a white horse is gonna ride in an' carry her away." He tapped the end of Rebekah's nose with his finger. "I blame you for that, seein' how you're the one always takin' books off the library wagon an' readin' 'em to your sisters. But I figured you knew those stories weren't for real."

"I'm not waiting on a prince, Daddy. I'm waiting for my Festus Hardin."

The corners of his eyes crinkled with his tender smile. "Well, now, that's about the nicest thing any o' my gals ever said to me." He hung his head. "Truth be told, someone with a mind sharp as yours deserves to go to one o' those city colleges. To maybe be a schoolteacher or even somebody like the library lady—somebody who helps others learn."

A lump of longing filled Rebekah's throat. But farmers like her daddy couldn't send their children to such places. Besides, after how she'd treated Andy, she didn't deserve to go to college or do even more reading. She swallowed the desire.

Daddy angled a weak grin at her and winked. "Seein' as how you'll likely stay right here in our hollow, I'd like you to set your sights some higher than a squatter's son who mostly never has two nickels to rub together."

Rebekah recognized the regret beneath his teasing. She dove at him, wrapping her arms around his middle and burrowing her face against his chest. "There's no man better than you, Daddy. And until I find one who's worthy of standing in your shadow, I want to do what I can to make Mama happy."

He rested his cheek on the top of her head. "Aw, gal . . ."

"Della and Jessie are big enough to help with the tobacco crop. You won't miss me in the field. If I get a job at the hotel, I can bring home money every week. We'll put it in the can—every penny of it. In no time you'll be able to buy a nice marker for Andy's grave." Still holding tightly to his waist, she tipped her head back and gazed up at her father. "Please say yes. Let me do this for Mama. For Andy. Please, Daddy?"

*Lexington, Kentucky*
*Devlin Bale*

"I won't beg." Devlin slipped his hands into his trouser pockets and met his father's gaze without flinching. The university students said Father could wither a person with his steely glower, but Devlin knew that his father was more bark than bite. Even so, he'd carefully chosen the day and time to approach Father with his idea.

Saturday—no classes, no students knocking at his door, hardly any activity at all on the sprawling campus. Early morning, before Father had started grading papers or planning lessons for the coming week's studies in American history or political science. Consequently Father couldn't claim distractions or other duties. He had no choice but to listen. And, as Devlin anticipated, he had listened. Now Devlin waited for the answer.

"Don't stand there like a soldier on guard. Sit."

Devlin swallowed a chuckle. So Father wanted a conversation. That meant he wouldn't give a blunt no in response. A positive sign. Devlin dragged a straight-backed chair across the thick carpet to Father's desk and dropped onto the sturdy seat. He placed his hands on his knees, forcing himself not to bounce his legs in impatience. "What do you think?"

"I think your mother will have a few choice words if I approve your taking off instead of spending your last summer under our roof."

Devlin cleared his throat. "Not just the summer, Father. The remainder of this semester as well." He'd already brought his trunks down from the attic and begun sorting through his clothes and belongings. The moment he received permission to go, he'd be ready to board the train.

Father's frown deepened. "Professor Scholes approved this harebrained plan of yours?"

"He didn't call it harebrained, Father." Devlin took care to maintain an even tone although Father's derision stirred defensiveness. "The map of Mammoth Cave on record here at the university was drawn in 1845 by an uneducated slave. Many more tunnels have been discovered in the past six decades, but no American cartographer has taken the time to create a new map."

Excitement quivered through him, bringing him to the edge of his seat. His left leg bounced despite the firm grip of his fingers over his kneecap. "Professor Scholes says it's a perfect senior project for my land surveyor degree. He even offered to talk to my other professors and obtain their approval for early dismissal so I can dedicate a full four months to it."

Father grimaced. "Four months under the ground? Devlin, you've lost your mind."

Devlin laughed. "I'd come up to eat and sleep."

Father waved one hand, his familiar gesture of dismissing his son's words. "You know my meaning. Even if the cave is miles long, as purported by the owners, you wouldn't require a third of a year's time to survey and record it."

Devlin's leg stilled. He slid on the seat until his spine met the chair's back. "Suppose I told you I had an . . . ulterior motive for surveying Mammoth Cave."

Father sat back in his well-oiled chair and folded his arms over his chest. The gold chain looped across his vest front draped over his arm and glinted in the overhead electric light. "Such as?"

"I'm aware that you want to run for a seat in the Senate in the next election."

Father's gaze narrowed, his thick brows pulling into a V.

"It will take something special to unseat either Blackburn or McCreary in our Democratic state, but money talks to both Republicans and Democrats."

"Devlin, you sound like a politician, speaking in circles."

He raised one hand. "Listen to me, Father. Right now Mammoth Cave is in the hands of a private owner. All the revenue from tourists flocking to the cave goes directly into his bank account, and rumor has it he's become a very wealthy man, thanks to the fascination people hold for the remarkable cave. The revenue will only increase now that people can reach it by steamboat." He leaned forward slightly, unable to hold his stiff pose with so much adrenaline coursing through his veins. "What if the money flowed into the nation's coffers instead?"

Father continued to scowl, but a glint in his blue-gray eyes changed his expression from fierce to intrigued.

"While I'm surveying the cave, I could also survey the surrounding acres. Scope out a section of ground suitable for a national park. People will continue to visit Mammoth Cave, they'll continue to pay the fees to explore the tunnels, but the money will no longer benefit a single owner." Devlin leaned closer to Father until his elbows met his knees. He gripped his hands together and gazed fervently into his father's stoic face. "The man responsible for generating such a change would be held in great esteem by our country's leaders. A seat in the Senate could become his, and he would have an opportunity to further influence Kentucky and the entire United States."

Someone passed by in the hallway, the sound of footsteps on the hardwood floor creeping beneath the closed door. Father didn't even blink at the distraction. Devlin listened to the soft *tick-tick* of the arched clock centered on the fireplace mantel and allowed his father to consider the possible positive ramifications of his plans.

At the age of twenty-two years, most young men wouldn't ask permission for such an excursion. But Devlin held too much respect for his parents to go willingly against their wishes. If Father refused, Devlin would set aside his plan and seek a different senior project. A different means of supporting his father in the next Senate election. But he couldn't help hoping that Father would agree. It would do Devlin no harm to be known as a senator's son.

Father cleared his throat and sat up, lowering his arms so quickly the gold chain quivered against the brocade of his vest. "Although it's hard to fathom, considering she isn't allowed to register, your mother is a stauncher Republican than I am. Give her your argument at the dinner table this evening. If she has no qualms about you pursuing this project, I will grant my approval as well."

If Devlin were still an excitable ten-year-old, he would leap into the air and whoop with glee. But he'd left those boyhood days behind. So he rose, offered a humble bow of his head, and said with perfect decorum, "Thank you, Father.

I'll let you return to your work now." He left his father's office, exited Barker Hall, and made his way across the greening expanse of grass to their family's horse and carriage.

The gelding stood with its head low, drowsing within the traces, but when Devlin climbed upon the driver's seat, it raised up and released a snort. Devlin picked up the reins, sent a quick look in every direction to be certain he had no witnesses, and finally let his elation explode. "Yee-haw!"

The exclamation pierced the peaceful morning. The gelding bolted forward in surprise. Devlin's feet left the foot bed and he nearly flipped over the back of the seat, but he only laughed. Who cared if his dignity got dented? Mother wouldn't stand in the way of Father's political ambitions. His trip to Mammoth Cave was as good as confirmed.

# THREE

*Rebekah*

Monday morning, after waving good-bye to Cissy, Della, Jessie, and Tabitha, who entered the schoolhouse with varying degrees of eagerness, Rebekah set off for the rambling hotel on the Mammoth Cave property. The mushrooms she'd gathered over the weekend filled Mama's largest basket. She expected a full fifty cents from the cook today. The weight of the plump white orbs made the wood handle cut into her wrist, so she cradled the basket against her ribs instead as she made her way up the road.

Excitement trembled in her belly. After she delivered the mushrooms, she would talk to the hotel's owner and ask about taking a job. Mama had fussed a bit, but Daddy took her aside and spoke to her in hushed tones. When he finished, she told Rebekah to do as she pleased—not with any joy, but Rebekah would accept resignation if it meant earning money for her brother's headstone. And after a fine marker stood at Andy's grave, she'd keep working. The money could pay for other things. New shoes for all of them, real glass windows for their cabin instead of shutters that locked away the sun along with the cold air, a pretty store-bought dress and hair ribbons for Cissy, books—books they could keep forever and read again and again—for all the little girls . . .

She imagined Christmas, the overflowing stockings, the smiles and laughter, all because Rebekah earned a wage. She gave a little skip to hurry her steps. The sooner she reached the hotel, the sooner she could claim a job, and the sooner she could start making restitution to her family for stealing Andy away from them.

The rattle of a wagon's wheels and the chatter of at least a dozen voices captured Rebekah's attention. She moved to the edge of the road, ducking a bit to keep drooping branches from grabbing her hair. One of the hotel's transport wagons, pulled by four cream-colored horses, rounded the bend. She recognized the driver, Tolly Sandford, by his top hat. He was a lanky, older black man who'd lived in one of the little cabins behind the cave's hotel for as long as Rebekah could remember. He grinned and tipped his hat as he guided the horses past her.

Rebekah couldn't wave in return with her hands holding the heavy basket, but she bobbed her head and smiled. Several of the people seated on the built-in benches in the back of the wagon called hellos and waved at her, too. Her heart filling, she smiled at all of them. Cissy had claimed the people who came to the cave would be snooty and look down their noses at the employees. She couldn't wait to tell Cissy how she'd been greeted. The enthusiastic waves and cheerful hellos rang in her memory as she set off once again.

Clouds gathered, covering the sun and throwing a shadow over the road. Rebekah glanced skyward, worrying her lip between her teeth. Would it rain today? Ordinarily she didn't mind getting wet—as Mama teasingly said, she wasn't made of sugar so she wouldn't melt. But out of respect for the hotel owner's position of importance, she'd fashioned her hair in an upswept twist instead of her everyday braid and donned her best dress, the one with some of Granny's fine hand-tatted lace at the collars and cuffs. The lace rolled up when it got wet and looked like a long, skinny caterpillar instead of delicate loops and swirls. She didn't want the hotel's owner to see her with bedraggled hair and a caterpillar circling her neck.

*Hold back the rain until I'm all done at the estate, Lord, please?*

Just in case God decided He'd rather let those clouds send down rain right away, she tucked the basket under one arm, lifted her skirt, and ran the remaining distance. The door to the kitchen stood open in invitation, and Rebekah stepped inside without bothering to knock. The smell of fresh-baked bread and simmering meat made her mouth water. If the food tasted as good as it smelled, the guests would have a fine meal for lunch today.

She located the cook behind a long, high table, using a butcher knife to chop potatoes into chunks. She crossed to him and set the basket at the end of the table. "Good morning, Mr. Cooper."

He glanced at her without breaking the knife's rhythm. "Morning to you, Miss Hardin. More mushrooms to sell?"

"Yes, sir." She lifted the toweling she'd used to cover the mushrooms and grinned. "A full basket today."

He used the knife to slide the chopped potato pieces into a large kettle. "Lyle! Weigh Miss Hardin's mushrooms." One of the kitchen workers bustled over, took the basket, and hurried away. Mr. Cooper grabbed another potato from a bowl, whacked it into slices, and began dicing again.

Rebekah rested her fingertips on the edge of the worktable, well away from Mr. Cooper's knife, and gathered her courage. "Mr. Cooper, where would I find Mr. Renshaw?"

"In the manager's office inside the main entrance if he's on the property."

If? "Isn't he here every day?"

The cook paused and pinned Rebekah with a bemused look. "A live-in trustee runs the cave, Miss Hardin. No need for Renshaw to dally here all day."

"Oh." Rebekah's spirits sank. She chewed the inside of her lip. "Well, then, where would I find the trustee?"

Mr. Cooper set his knife to work. "Likely selling tour tickets or checking in guests." He smacked the batch of diced potatoes into the kettle, clunked the kettle onto the massive stove, and then glowered at Rebekah. "You thinking you'll get more money for your mushrooms if you pester Mr. Renshaw or Mr. Janin? Because I can tell you I've got full rein over the kitchen. I do the buying of produce and such."

She gaped at him, stunned by his gruffness. Heat flooded her face, and she held one hand to him. "I don't want to talk to somebody about my mushrooms. I need a job."

The stern lines in the man's face relaxed. "A job?"

Rebekah nodded. "Yes, sir. I appreciate you buying the mushrooms. I—I hope to keep selling them to you." If she hadn't insulted him so much he didn't want them anymore. "But I need a way to make more money than I can with the mushrooms. Do you know if they're hiring hotel maids or servers for the dining room?"

Lyle returned with Rebekah's basket, now empty. "Ten an' a half pounds, Mr. Cooper."

The cook aimed a scowl at the young man. "With the basket or without?"

"Without."

"That scale always weighs a little light. Let's call it eleven pounds. Get Miss Hardin fifty-five cents."

"Yes, sir!" Lyle darted off again.

Rebekah's heart expanded. She must not have offended the cook after all. "Thank you."

Mr. Cooper shrugged. He dumped several peeled carrots onto the work surface. "That's the least I can do, considering I have to tell you the only hiring Mr. Janin is doing right now is for a guide."

"You mean for the tours?"

"What else would I mean?" He lined up the carrots and began turning the lengths into thin slices with smooth chops of the knife. "One of the longtime guides died a week ago, so they'll need to replace him. But I don't know of any other positions open here on the estate."

She hugged herself. After losing her only brother to the cave, she had no desire to lead others into those dark, cool caverns. But if no other position was available, she didn't have any choice. "Do you know what the job pays?"

Mr. Cooper's hand stilled. He gawked at her for several seconds and then burst out laughing. "Miss Hardin, you can't apply to be a guide."

"Why not?"

Lyle sidled up and plopped two twenty-five-cent pieces and a nickel on the table. He grinned, too. "Guides are men." His brazen gaze traveled across Rebekah's skirt and upswept hair. "You're not a man, that's for sure."

"Get back to work." At the cook's brusque demand, Lyle trotted off. Mr. Cooper wiped his hand over his face, removing the glint of humor. "Lyle's right. Only men take folks on the tours."

Rebekah frowned. She'd seen several women in the wagon heading for the cave. "But why?"

The cook folded his arms over his chest and leaned against the table. "'Cause it's the way it's always been, I guess." He blew out a short breath and reached again for his knife. "I'm sorry, but there aren't any jobs open right now for a young lady. Chances are there won't be for a while. Mr. Janin's already hired for the spring and summer seasons, and he always has a list of women waiting to fill any position that opens unexpectedly."

Rebekah blinked rapidly, fighting tears. "Oh."

He bumped her chin with his fist. "But I'll tell him to add your name to the list, and I'll even let him know I think you'd be a good worker, all right?"

Rebekah forced a smile. "All right. Thank you, Mr. Cooper."

He offered one more quick smile and then turned his attention back to chopping vegetables.

With a sigh, Rebekah pocketed the coins and left the kitchen. She stepped from the warm room into chilly, moist air. Those clouds would let loose any time now. She needed to hurry home. But somehow she couldn't convince her legs to move faster than a snail's pace.

She'd set her hopes high, so sure she'd find a job and would be able to buy the marker for Andy. She'd gotten Daddy's hopes up, too. How could she tell him she'd failed? Her chest felt tight and heavy, the way it had the day they laid Andy in his grave. Losing the chance to buy the headstone and all the other things she let herself dream about was like burying her brother all over again.

Fat raindrops began to fall from the sky as she reached the edge of her yard. She ran the last few feet and gave a lithe leap onto the porch just ahead of the real soaking rain. The slanting porch roof would hold back any water from entering the cabin, so she left the door open to let in light as she stepped over the threshold.

"Mama, I'm back. I—" She stopped and looked around in confusion. The cabin was empty. Where was everybody? A slip of paper waited in the middle of the table. She crossed the floor and picked up the sheet.

*Dear Bek, Daddy and me tuk the leastuns to Susan Lindseys to trade a gallon of sorghum for black walnuts. Spring soup in the kettul. Back soon. Mama.*

She dropped the note on the table and sighed. Mama's flavorful wild greens and ham soup, a treat this time of year, held no appeal. She wanted to talk to Daddy. "Back soon," the note said, but with the rain coming down in buckets, she didn't expect Daddy to leave the Lindsey place until he could be sure the little girls wouldn't get soaked to the skin. Trudy had always been prone to colds. Spring colds could linger a long time, and they didn't have spare money for doctoring. She likely wouldn't see them for an hour or two.

She flicked a glance around the room, shivering. How could this cabin, her only home, seem so forbidding when everyone was gone? She opened the shutters on the front windows to let in as much light as possible. Then she hung Mama's basket on its hook, clanked the coins into the money can, and went to her bedroom and changed out of her good dress into one of her work dresses. As she exited her bedroom, a flash of lightning briefly lit the cabin's main room, and her gaze collided with the ladder hung high on the back wall.

Thunder boomed and her heart double-thudded. She hugged herself, uncertain whether the thunder or the ladder had caused the gallop in her chest. She slowly crossed the floor while rain pelted the roof and a cool breeze snaked in to chill her bare feet and arms. She stood up on tiptoe and slid her finger along one side rail. She wrinkled her nose. Sticky cobwebs collected between the rungs, proof of its long time going unused.

She remembered the day Daddy put it on the wall. The same day they'd buried Andy. He'd pounded in nails and hung it high so none of his gals could bring it down. Rebekah asked him why he didn't take it out to the shed, use it to climb up on the roof or to reach the fruit in one of the cherry trees growing in the woods nearby. She could still see the stunned look on Daddy's face, hear his pained reply.

*"It's Andy's ladder."*

She sank back onto her heels, nodding in agreement with the memory. Andy had built the ladder himself to gain access to the small loft, his own little space away from his sisters. He'd go up there, pull the ladder in behind him, and then make faces at them from the opening. Daddy never used Andy's ladder. Mama never let anybody go into the loft. As far as Rebekah knew, Andy's trunk of clothes, his mattress, and the quilt Granny Hardin had sewn for him when he was no higher than Daddy's knees were all still up there, untouched, a silent testimony that at one time a boy had lived there.

Another slice of lightning flashed through the open windows, and a rattling crash of thunder chased it. The sound jolted Rebekah forward. She rose on tiptoes again, pushing the heels of her hands against the ladder's rail. The ladder flipped from the nails and clattered to the floor. Quickly, before she could change her mind, she snagged the end and propped it against the opening carved in the ceiling to give access to the loft. Then, her heart pounding harder than the raindrops that pelted the roof, she gripped her skirt in one hand and climbed upward on trembling legs.

Her head and shoulders entered the dark, airless space. She paused, shivering, waiting for her eyes to adjust enough to find what she wanted. If Daddy or Mama were here, they'd screech at her in protest. But they weren't here. She could enter Andy's private space, open his trunk, gather up some of his clothes, use them to— Her thoughts froze, her pulse pounding. Could she really wear her dead brother's clothes?

Wind shrieked. Lightning crashed. Thunder boomed. Nature itself seemed to scream at her to make up her mind. Lyle's comment—*"Guides are men"*—swooped through her mind, followed by Mr. Cooper's apologetic reply: *"There aren't any jobs open right now for a young lady."* She had no choice. If she wanted the job, she'd have to be a man. Or, at the very least, make them think she was a man.

She scrambled into the loft and eased her way across the rafters on her hands and knees to the trunk tucked beneath the eaves. She squeaked it out far enough to lift the lid. Tears flooded her eyes when she reached inside and encountered Andy's shirts, britches, boots. With a vicious swipe of her hand, she removed the tears and then rolled the clothes around the boots. Then, cradling the wad against her aching chest with one arm, she inched her way backward and crawled down the ladder.

Her feet met the floor. Her entire body shook—from fear, from excitement, or from guilt? Maybe all three. She scampered to the bedroom and shoved the clothes under the mattress on her side of the bed. They created a lump, but hopefully Cissy wouldn't notice if the shutters were closed and the room stayed dark.

As she left the bedroom, something brought her to a halt. She tipped her head, pondering what was different. Oh, yes. It was quiet. The storm had blown over. Daddy, Mama, and the littlest girls would come home now. She pulled the ladder from the opening and, after three tries, secured it on the nails again. She winced, realizing how many of the cobwebs she'd knocked loose. She hoped nobody noticed.

A fresh scent flooded the cabin. She turned, and her bare toes met a band of sunlight that flowed across the floor from the open door. A smile—a genuine, thankful smile—pulled at her lips. It was as if God Almighty Himself brought the rainstorm to keep her folks away long enough for her to retrieve those things from Andy's room. The sun felt like His approval.

She stepped to the edge of the porch, aimed her smile at the sky, and whispered, "Thank You."

# FOUR

*Cissy*

The family gathered around the table for supper. Mama came last, carrying a platter of cornbread. Cissy sighed. Cornbread. Again. They should have cornstalks growing out of their ears with all the cornbread they planted in their bellies.

"Let's pray," Daddy said, and he bowed his head.

Cissy folded her hands and rolled her gaze to the ceiling, holding back a sigh, while Daddy thanked the Lord for the refreshing rain and for the fine supper Mama had prepared. Fine supper? Cissy wrinkled her nose. The pot in the middle of the table was full of black-eyed peas. Black-eyed peas smelled bad—like old tar—and they tasted like dirt. If her stomach hadn't been growling for the past two hours, she'd skip supper and go pore over the photographs in the *Vogue* magazine her friend Pansy let her borrow.

"Amen."

Cissy snagged a square of cornbread and grabbed the pitcher of sorghum syrup. She drowned the mealy wedge with the thick honey-colored sweetnin'.

"Not so much." Daddy reached for the pitcher. "Leave some for your sisters."

Cissy pursed her lips. What would it be like to be the only child, like Pansy, who never had to share anything with a whole herd of pesky little sisters?

Daddy drizzled his cornbread and then turned to Rebekah. "How'd things go at the cave estate this mornin'?"

Rebekah spooned black-eyed peas onto Little Nellie's plate. "I didn't get to talk to the owner because he wasn't there. So . . ." She shrugged, flicking a smile that looked strained. "I guess I'll have to go back again tomorrow."

Cissy frowned. "Why're you talkin' to the owner? I thought the cook bought the mushrooms."

Daddy squeezed Cissy's wrist. "Your sister's tryin' to take a job over there, earn a little extra money."

Cissy yanked her hand free. "How come she gets to take a job at the cave?"

"'Cause she's done with school." Daddy spoke calm and kind, like he always did, but a hint of warning glittered in his eyes.

Cissy decided to ignore the warning. "Who's gonna do her chores here at home when she's off at the Mammoth Cave estate?"

"I reckon you an' the other gals'll hafta fill in. You'd be doin' that anyways if your sister found herself a beau."

Cissy thumped her fist on the table. "That ain't fair. Bek gets to do everything."

Mama scowled. "Cissy, settle yourself down."

"Yeah." Della aimed a sour look at Cissy. "You're bumpin' me with your bony elbow."

Cissy jabbed Della in the ribs. Hard. Her sister yelped.

"Cissy!" Mama and Daddy said at the same time.

Cissy didn't care. She snorted. "She asked for it. Della's such a baby."

"I am not!"

"'Nough talkin' now." Daddy pointed at their plates. "You girls eat. When you're done, you'll do the dishes for your mama."

Cissy gawked at her father. "It's Jessie's turn to wash the supper dishes."

Daddy's eyebrows rose. "You'll be takin' her turn. It'll make up for your tomfoolery."

Della frowned, but she bent over her plate and forked a bite of peas.

Cissy fisted her fork and battled the temptation to stab it into the tabletop. "But I got cipherin' to finish after supper." And a magazine to examine before the sunlight all faded away. She'd promised to bring it back to Pansy tomorrow.

"Then you'd better set to eatin' so you'll have time to get to it when the dishes're done."

Cissy stifled a growl. Her appetite was gone, but she knew she'd be half starved by morning if she didn't clean her plate. She seethed in silence while her family chattered about the rain and Bek's fifty-five cents and other things she didn't care about even one smidgen. She forced down every bit of the sodden cornbread and dirt-tasting peas, and then she flounced to the dry sink and clanked her tin plate and cup into the washbasin.

She glanced at the table. Might be a while before everybody finished up. She could sneak a peek or two at that copy of *Vogue*. She started for the bedroom.

"Cissy?"

She stopped and looked at Daddy. Would he relent and tell her to do her cipherin'?

"Since you're done, take the bucket to the creek. Might as well get the wash water to heatin'."

With a huff of aggravation, Cissy pranced out the back door. She snatched the bucket from its hook and stomped across the yard, muttering as she went. "Cissy, get the wash water. Cissy, don't pester your sisters. Cissy, straighten up. Cissy, mind your manners." She swung the bucket by its rope handle, whacking bushes and drooping pine limbs as she went. By the time she reached the creek, she'd spent most of her fury. She dropped to her knees and started to plunge the bucket into the clear, sun-speckled water. But she caught a glimpse of her reflection and sat still as a mouse, staring at the tight-lipped face peering back at her.

The water gently flowed, making the image waver, but she examined her hair, long and straight and woven into a pair of thick red-brown braids. Her wide eyes, blue green with thick black lashes. Her face, full cheeked with a tiny cleft in her chin. Pansy called Cissy pretty, and gazing at herself, Cissy had to agree. She didn't look much like her sisters, though, who all had wavy hair as dark brown as a pine cone's center, eyes the color of maple syrup, and heart-shaped faces.

"Maybe I was a foundling," she told her image. "Took in by Mama an' Daddy 'stead o' bein' born to 'em like all the others. Maybe that's why I always feel so restless inside, always wantin' to escape."

She didn't know where the thought came from, but once it entered her head it stuck. If she was a foundling, it would explain why she didn't look like her sisters. And why she didn't act like her sisters. Her sisters were all content to wear homespun dresses and mind Daddy and be good girls. She stirred the surface of the water with her fingertips. Her reflection chopped into pieces like a puzzle dumped on the table. "And that's just about how I feel . . . all chopped up an' befuddled. I surely ain't a real Hardin down deep. I must be a—"

"Cissy!" Mama's fretful voice echoed through the trees.

She lurched upright. "Comin'!" She swooped the bucket through the creek and then trotted up the pathway, the rope biting into her palm and water sloshing over the bucket's rim to splash her foot. As she passed along the sun-and-shade-striped pathway, she thought about Rebekah getting to take a job at the cave estate because she'd finished her schooling. Well, Bek wasn't the only one who was done with school.

The teacher would close the schoolhouse doors in less than a month so youngsters could help their folks with the spring planting. She'd turned fifteen last January, so she was old enough to leave school if she wanted. And she wanted. So that meant she'd be footloose and free from studies in just a few more weeks.

She aimed a smug grin at a squirrel scolding from the tip of a tree branch. "I ain't gonna spend my break pokin' seeds in the ground or choppin' out weeds with a rusty hoe. I'm gonna get me a job at the cave estates an' make money like Bek. While I'm workin', I'll meet up with boys from rich families, an' I'll tease an' flirt an' make 'em all fall in love with me. Then one of 'em will take me away from Good Spring to a big city where I can live like a queen an' never have to do chores again."

The plan strong in her mind, she hurried her feet toward home.

## Rebekah

Rebekah hugged the rolled bundle of clothes to her ribs and slowly made her way across the deeply shadowed ground toward the old tobacco barn. Only a sliver of moon hung in a sky so black she couldn't make out the shape of tree branches against the dark backdrop. Even the stars were only pinpricks of light, too dim to provide guidance. She hoped she wouldn't walk directly into the barn wall. Painted black, it hid well in the thick nighttime shadows.

A hoot owl released a throaty call. Its wings pounded seemingly right over her head. She instinctively gasped, ducked, and then froze in place. Chills broke out all over her body followed by a wave of heat. She gripped Andy's clothes so tightly the heels of his boots dug into her stomach. Had she awakened anyone? She stood still as a scarecrow, hunched over, holding her breath, listening, hoping.

Daddy didn't appear at the back door, shotgun in hand.

No little sister called her name.

She let her breath release in a slow exhale as she straightened her spine. She was safe.

Squinting, straining to make out the shape of the barn, she eased forward on bare feet. The cold, soggy ground sent shivers all the way up her frame to the top of her head. Cool wind, damp from the day's rain, tossed a strand of hair across her cheek, and she pushed it behind her ear with an impatient thrust. Then she stopped again, her hand beside her cheek. Her hair! She swallowed a groan. She'd never fool anybody into thinking she was a boy with hair hanging almost to her waist. Why hadn't she thought about her hair before now?

Closing her eyes, she hung her head. *Lord, my family needs the money I can make. There's no job open except for a guide. You gave me the chance to get some of Andy's clothes and put the whole plan in my head. Why didn't You remind me about my hair?* But it wasn't God's fault. She'd have to think of something.

If she went back inside and climbed into her bed, she'd surely wake Cissy. And her feet were muddy and wet—no sense soiling the sheets. She'd sleep in the tobacco barn, the way she'd intended. Maybe by morning she'd have some idea of what to do with her hair.

"Here, chick-chick-chick. Here, chick-chick-chick."

Rebekah sat up. Bits of hay and dried tobacco leaves flew in an arc beside her. A muscle in her neck cramped, and she winced. She rubbed the spot, her mind scrambling to understand why she was in the tobacco barn.

"Here, chick-chick. C'mon now, I don't got all day to stand here feedin' you." Mama's voice carried across the yard and crept through the cracks in the barn's wall. Rebekah moved on hands and knees to the wall and peered through a knothole.

Pink rays of dawn fell over Mama and their small flock of chickens. Mama scooped handfuls of feed from her apron, which she used as a pouch, and scattered it. The chickens pecked, clucking and flapping their wings. Mama laughed and Rebekah smiled. What a pleasant sound. Mama shook her head. "Greedy cluckers, that's what you are. Oughta make you search for grubs an' such 'stead o' spoilin' you so." She tossed another handful.

The back door popped open, and Jessie stepped onto the stoop. "Mama, Rebekah ain't in her bed."

Mama lifted her head and scanned the yard. Rebekah held her breath and went stiff, certain her mother would see right through the wall to her hiding place. Mama's gaze skimmed on past the tobacco barn and over to Jessie. "She's prob'ly set off already for the cave estate—tryin' to catch the owner soon as he shows up over there."

Jessie frowned. "Little Nellie's fussin' for her. Wants Bek to do her braids."

"Tell Cissy or Della to do up Little Nellie's hair. It don't have to be Rebekah doin' everything."

"Yes, ma'am." Jessie went back inside.

Mama gave her apron a flick, swished her palms together, and headed inside, too.

Relief turned Rebekah's muscles into liquid. She turned and sagged against the wall, closing her eyes for a moment and letting full wakefulness come over her slow and easy. Her plan to be off the property before anybody else woke up hadn't worked so well. Who knew she'd sleep so hard and sound on the barn floor with nothing but an old horse blanket for a bed? But now she needed to hurry and scat. After breakfast, the bigger girls would head for school, Daddy would trek off to their small field over the knoll, and Mama would be in and out with the littlest girls.

She pushed upright and tossed her nightgown over her head. She grabbed up Andy's shirt. In the pale morning light she recognized the green-and-yellow-plaid shirt Mama had sewed him for his last Christmas. Her hands began to shake. Could she wear this?

She set her jaw at a determined angle. Yes, she could. She had to. She gave herself a little shove and jammed her arms into the sleeves, then buttoned it all the way to the top. She stepped into his britches. Both the shirt and the britches were baggy, but that was best. No sense in calling attention to her feminine form with snug-fitting clothes. She'd use a piece of twine through the belt loops to keep the pants from sliding over her hips.

She sent her gaze down her length. The pant legs ended a good four inches above her ankles. She stared at her feet and skinny ankles, chewing the inside of her lip. Then she shifted her attention to Andy's boots. Thick, clunky things with worn toes and broken laces. But the shafts were at least six inches high. She could tuck the britches into the boots and nobody would know the legs were too short. She plopped onto her bottom and pulled the boots over her feet. Grunting a bit, she wrapped the shaft around the fabric. Bulky. Uncomfortable. But it would have to do.

She stood and took a step. Her feet slid, and she grabbed an upright beam to catch her balance. She glared down at the boots, but her withering stare didn't shrink them any. They stayed three sizes too big. A chuckle threatened as a memory surfaced—Daddy saying if Andy grew into his feet, he'd likely be as tall as Goliath.

Her nose stung. She sniffed hard and made herself stop remembering. She'd find some rags to stuff into the toes. And once she got her feet figured out, she'd turn her thoughts to how to fix the top end of her body. Her hair was straggling in her face, a constant reminder of the problem it created.

A large wooden trunk with Great-Granddaddy's name, "Cyrus Hardin," and "Kentucky, USA" carved into the lid crouched in the corner of the barn. Daddy kept all kinds of odds and ends in the trunk. There'd be rags, too. She scuffed across the floor and raised the lid. Sure enough, a tangled wad of rags lay on top of the heap. She fished out the ones with the worst holes since they'd be missed the least, and then she started to close the lid again. But something caught her eye. A curl of something brown. Worn. Leathery. Her heart leaped.

With a little cry of elation she pushed aside the mouse-eaten quilt they used for picnics and yanked out Great-Granddaddy Hardin's hat. She angled it toward a pale shaft of light sneaking between slats high on the wall and examined it, her pulse galloping faster than a stampeding horse. It was mouse chewed on one side of the brim, misshapen, and sweat stained, but the crown was intact.

She put it on and fingered it all the way around, a smile pulling on her lips. If she piled her hair up on top of her head and then tugged the brim over her ears, wouldn't it look as if she had short hair? Very short hair, like a man? Sure it would. She wanted to whoop in delight, but she gave the hat a toss in the air instead. While the hat bounced across the hard ground, she bent over and gathered her hair into a tail. She twisted it as tight as new rope and wound it into a coil on top of her head. Then she jammed Great-Granddaddy's hat over the coil and stood.

For a moment she was afraid to move. Would it stay in place? She shook her head a bit. The hat didn't fall off. She scuffed around the floor with turtle-slow steps. No slipping. She gave a few bounces on her heels. It still stayed in place. Happiness danced through her middle, and her feet followed suit, stirring up dried bits of tobacco leaves with a little jig. She giggled, clamped her hands over her mouth, and swallowed the joyous sound.

She was ready. Now to snag that job.

# FIVE

## Tolly Sandford

T olly opened the door to his cabin and tossed the water from his washbasin into the yard. The water splattered right at the feet of a boy dressed in his pappy's hat and boots. The boy came to a halt, his body arching like lightning had struck his toes, and Tolly couldn't hold back a hoot of laughter.

He plunked the basin on the stand inside the door and stepped off the stoop, his hand extended toward the startled boy. "Sorry 'bout that, young fella." The boy stuck out his hand—a very slender hand—and Tolly gave it a firm shake, chuckling. "If you ain't had your weekly bath yet, you can claim that sprinkle I just gave ya an' avoid the washtub."

The boy's lips twitched into a funny half grin. "That's all right." His voice sounded gravelly, like he wasn't fully woke up yet. He jammed his hand in the pocket of his britches and poked his toe against the ground, hanging his head low. "No harm done."

Tolly figured not. A little water never hurt nobody. He pinched his beard and gave the boy a head-to-toe look. He'd seen this one somewhere before. "You ain't stayin' at the hotel with yo' family, is you?"

"No, sir."

"You live somewheres 'round here?"

"Yes, sir."

This was one tongue-tied youngster. If he didn't have something to hide, Tolly would turn cartwheels for the next batch of guests. Wouldn't that be a sight to behold? Balling his hands on his hips, Tolly barked in his sternest voice, "You'd best not be sneakin' 'round, thinkin' you're gonna go explorin' in the cave. Mistuh Janin, he cracks down hard on them who don't pay fo' tickets."

The boy's head snapped up. "I'm not going to sneak into the cave. I came for a job."

"A job, huh? Doin' what?"

"Being a guide."

Tolly snorted. He couldn't help it. This one looked scared of his own shadow. And he wanted to take folks through dark caverns and narrow passageways where spiders crept along the walls and bats swooped out of nowhere? "You must be joshin' me."

The boy bit his lower lip and blinked several times. If Tolly wasn't mistaken, the kid was trying not to cry. This was one peculiar boy. But the reaction stirred Tolly's sympathy. The Lord called on His followers to be loving to folks, and Tolly tried to follow well. He gentled his tone. "How you know we's needin' anothuh guide?"

"The cook—Mr. Cooper—told me so."

Just like that Tolly knew who stood before him. Not a boy at all, but the oldest of the Hardin girls, the one who delivered mushrooms to the hotel kitchen, the one who'd fallen across the new grave and—

His knees went weak, and he turned his face away so she wouldn't see the moisture filling his eyes. If he lived to be a hundred, he'd never forget finding her brother crumpled like a pile of rags at the bottom of a ravine. He'd never forget this girl's sorrow. Hadn't he vowed then and there to do whatever he could to help the family? But he hadn't got the chance. Not until now.

"All right . . . boy. What be yo' name?"

"Reb—" She gulped. "Reb Hardin."

Least she hadn't straight-out lied to him. But what should he do? Trekking through the cave could be treacherous. A guide had to keep the folks who were taking the tour safe. Safe from the cave. Safe from themselves. In every group there was one or two who thought they'd be just fine exploring on their own. If somebody got stubborn on her, this slip of a girl wouldn't have much authority.

He ought to snatch the sorry-looking old hat off her head. Let her know he saw right through her pretense. Send her back to her mama. But that family must be hurting. Hurting over their loss. *Lawd Almighty, what'm I s'posed to tell this here gal?*

He jerked his attention to the girl who stood in the morning sunshine all decked out in men's gear. "You got any experience in cavin'?"

She shrugged. "There's a cave on our property. Just a small one. But I'm in and out of it nearly every day."

"You ain't squeamish 'bout spiders an' such?"

Her face went white and she grimaced. But quick as a firefly's flash she straightened her shoulders and lifted her chin. "I'm a lot bigger than they are."

Tolly laughed. Her adamant statement didn't match the disgust on her face. "That's true enough." He looked her up and down again. Tall compared to most girls, coming all the way to his chin. But scrawny as a beanpole. Still, she had tenacity. He saw it in the tilt of her chin and the way she stood without fidgeting while he took his going-over. And even after her brother got lost and died in the cave, she was still willing to go on in and traipse around. So she must be braver than she looked.

He stared straight in her eyes and folded his arms over his chest. "Why you want to be a guide?"

Her chin quivered briefly. "I need the money."

"What fo'?" If she said something frivolous, he'd send her home, no matter how much he owed the family.

"To buy a decent headstone."

Tolly swallowed hard. "Who that stone be fo'?"

She swallowed, too. "My mama."

He squinted at her. Far as he knew, her mama was still living. "You sure?"

"Yes, sir."

Maybe her mama was sick, even at death's door. *I gots to help this family, Lawd. What would You have me do?* On the tail of his prayer came the answer. He'd keep this one safe while she earned a wage. And he'd finally get to repair his dented conscience at the same time. Still, he wouldn't break any rules.

He barked, "Guides gotta be at least eighteen years old. How old're you?"

"Twenty last February."

So he could tell Mr. Janin she was old enough. He pushed his hands into his pockets and rocked on his heels. "Lemme tell you somethin', Reb Hardin. I growed up right here at Mammoth Cave. Been trailin' my pappy through the tunnels from the time I was big enough to leave crawlin' behind—more'n fifty years now. Seein' as how I's right at home in the cave, Mr. Janin put me in charge of assignin' guides an' helpuhs."

Her eyes widened. Her lips turned white around the edges. He was scaring her—making her worry. But she didn't turn away from him.

"See, we never send only one guide in with a group. One leads 'em all, an' anothuh goes behind, makes sure they all stay togethuh. I's a lead guide. You'd be goin' behind. So you'd be a helpuh, not a guide." He narrowed his gaze. "You still thinkin' you want the job?"

She nodded so fast he was surprised she didn't lose her old, battered hat.

"All right then. I'll let Mr. Janin know to add Reb Hardin to the books."

Her face lit. "When do I start?"

He scratched his cheek. He could use her today. He'd taken a group by himself yesterday and spent the whole tour nervous as a cat with deaf kittens, worrying somebody might fall behind. But it'd take a day or so to get everything squared away with Mr. Janin. And he ought to take her on the tour by herself a time or two before trusting her with guests. "Come back tomorruh mo'nin', but meet me at the mouth o' the cave. You an' me'll follow the trail by our lonesome—get you familiar wit' the short tour since that's the one I lead. Soon as I think you's ready to keep a group movin', you'll start drawin' the wage."

"I'll be there at daybreak tomorrow."

"You'll be there all by yo'self 'cause I's gonna eat my breakfast fuhst."

"Yes, sir." She thrust her hand at him. "Thank you."

He shook her hand. "You's welcome." He pulled in a breath. If she was a boy, her cheeks wouldn't still be smooth as silk at twenty. He gripped her hand hard and lowered his voice so nobody would overhear. "Reb, on yo' way ovuh here tomorrow, stop along the road an' smear some dirt on yo' face. Seein' as how there ain't no othuh way fo' you to have a whisker shadow like othuh . . . fellas . . . yo' age."

## Rebekah

The shrewd glimmer in the older black man's eyes sped Rebekah's pulse. She yanked her hand from his tight grasp and pressed her palm to her chest. "You—you know?"

He gave a slow nod, his dark eyes never shifting away from hers.

"How?"

"Kinda hard to fo'get somebody you seen sobbin' ovuh her brothuh's grave."

Rebekah stepped back, memories rising up to taunt her.

"But, Reb?" He pinned her with a serious look. "I don't aim to let it make no diff'rence."

She gazed at him in open-mouthed amazement. He'd still hire her?

As if he'd heard her inner question, he bobbed his head and spoke in a low, raspy voice. "I reckon I owe ya."

"Why?"

His dark eyes narrowed, his lips went tight for a moment. "I know that cave like the back o' my hand. When yo' brothuh went wanderin' an' got hisself lost, I knowed I'd be able to find him wherevuh he landed, so I promised yo' mammy I'd bring her boy out. An' I did. But not alive like she expected me to." He sighed again, his shoulders rising and falling as if he tried to dislodge a mighty weight. "No 'mount o' money'll bring yo' brothuh back again. But if it'll ease yo' family's burdens fo' you to earn money fo' a headstone, then I can sign you on."

Mr. Sandford's kindness astounded her. His sense of responsibility humbled her. She swallowed a knot of worry. "You—you won't get into trouble, will you, if other folks figure out I'm not a boy?"

A smile rounded his full cheeks and painted starbursts at the corners of his eyes. "See now, here's the thing. Ain't no writ-down rule that says only fellas can be guides. Oh, now, we allus done it that way. Just makes good sense. Whole lot easier to move 'round in there with britches on 'stead o' skirts. Folks is more likely to listen if some man tell them to stay on the trail. So it'd be best to have you gussyin' up like a fella 'stead of a girl. But I ain't breakin' no rule. Othuhwise I wouldn't take you on. But like I says, I owes yo' family."

He tipped his head to the side and seemed to study her. "Did ya know guides live right here on the estate?" He gestured to the row of cabins. "Hank Dauber—he's the one who took sick ovuh the wintuh an' done passed just last week—lived in that'n next to mine. Now it's sittin' there empty. Mr. Janin'll prob'ly tell you to move in."

"Oh." She hadn't considered living away from home. What would Daddy say? "Um, do I have to?"

Mr. Sandford's forehead puckered. "I reckon not, but it'll make things a mite easier on ya, not havin' to go back an' forth. An' the pay's twelve dollahs a month plus victuals. Almost seems like throwin' away part o' yo' pay if you don't stay on the grounds, take yo' meals an' such here." He leaned in, waggling his eyebrows. "Place o' yo' own. Three meals a day. Ol' Coop, he's a right fine cook. You won't go hungry."

Rebekah nibbled her lip. If she didn't eat at home, it would mean more food going into her sisters' bellies. The thought of a whole cabin to herself appealed to her. And frightened her, too. Sharing a room with so many others, she'd often yearned for privacy, but she'd never been completely alone. Would she pine for her parents and sisters?

He patted her on the shoulder. "You think on it. But to ease yo' mind, the guides an' helpuhs, they's all trustwuhthy men. You don't gots to worry about any of 'em pesterin' ya. 'Specially with me so close." He stepped up on the cabin's stoop and waved his arm at her, the way Mama tried to shoo the chickens when they followed too close on her heels. "You skedaddle now—go tell yo' pappy 'bout yo' new job." He closed the door behind him.

Rebekah stood for several minutes, absorbing everything Mr. Sandford had told her. He wanted her to keep wearing britches, and it didn't matter that she wasn't a boy. The job included a cabin all to herself and three meals a day cooked by somebody else, and best of all it paid twelve dollars a month. Her pulse stuttered and her mouth went dry. Twelve dollars? She'd never seen twelve dollars in one place before. Her mind scrambled through the things they could do with so much money.

Eagerness to tell Daddy about their good fortune propelled her feet into motion. She dashed through the woods for home.

## SIX

*Rebekah*

Rebekah burst from the thick growth behind their small field and half jogged, half stumbled across the uneven ground to her father. "Daddy! Daddy!"

He jerked his gaze in her direction. His body jolted. He brought the hand plow to a stop and gaped at her. "Re—Rebekah? Is that you, gal?"

She'd forgotten about her clothes. With a laugh she popped Great-Granddaddy's hat from her head. Her hair spilled around her shoulders. She threw her arms wide. "It's me!" Her chest ached and her muscles quivered from her run through the woods, but she couldn't resist spinning a circle that made her tangled locks fly out like the skirt on a woman's fancy ball dress.

Daddy caught her arm and gave a firm yank that halted her dance and sent Great-Granddaddy's hat rolling across the ground. He bounced his gaze up and down her frame, his face flushing red and his eyes snapping with fury. "What do you think you're doin' paradin' around like that? Has Nell seen you?"

She'd expected surprise. Maybe even curiosity. But his anger stunned her so thoroughly she lost her ability to think clearly. She stared at him mutely.

"I asked you a question, gal!"

She frantically gathered up her hair and braided it while she answered. "No, Daddy. Nobody's seen me. Well, except for you and Tolly Sandford at the cave estate."

Daddy's jaw dropped. "You went to the cave dressed like . . . like that? Where'd you get those clothes?"

Rebekah hung her head and dug one toe in the ground. "From Andy's trunk."

He grabbed her chin and lifted her face. His fingers bit into her skin and his glare pierced her heart. "Gal, you better start explainin' yourself 'cause I'm about to come undone like I ain't come undone since Cissy went swimmin' in the altogether with the Davis boys."

Rebekah gulped. She wasn't ten years old like Cissy had been, so it wasn't likely Daddy would cut a switch, but seeing him so angry made her stomach tremble. How she hated displeasing him. "R-remember last night at supper I told you I'd need to go back to the cave today because I didn't get to see the estate manager?"

He nodded.

"Well, Mr. Cooper—he's the cook for the hotel—told me the only job open was for a guide. And that the guides are always men. So I figured to get a job there I'd have to be a"—she gulped again—"man."

Daddy dropped his hand and took a step back. "So you stole clothes from your brother's trunk an' lit out early this mornin' like some sneaky thief." His flat voice didn't hide his disapproval. The words stung worse than any switch could.

Tears filled her eyes. "I didn't think of it as stealing."

He drew his hand down his face. He stared outward, somewhere beyond her shoulder. Suddenly he seemed very old and very, very tired. "Gal, I always thought you was the sensible one o' the lot. Now I'm wonderin' if you got any sense at all."

She jolted forward and grabbed his arm. "Daddy, listen. Mr. Sandford—you remember him, he found Andy in . . . in the cave. He saw right off that I'm a girl. But he hired me anyway. He said there's no rule against a girl being a guide, but I'd need to wear britches because it's safer for me when I'm taking people on tours. And he said the guides get paid twelve dollars a month. Twelve whole dollars, Daddy! Why, you'd have the money for Andy's marker in no time at all."

Daddy's stony expression didn't change.

Rebekah went on as if he'd expressed enthusiasm. "Guess what else? I get to live right there on the estate in my own little cabin and eat my meals at the hotel. So all the money they pay me can go right to you and Mama." She waited several minutes, but he didn't look at her. Didn't say anything. She wrung her hands. "I'm supposed to go back again tomorrow morning so Mr. Sandford can show me through the cave, get me familiar with the tour. But I won't go if you"—she pulled in a breath, almost afraid to finish her sentence—"tell me I can't."

Slowly Daddy shifted his gaze until his blue eyes met hers. "How old are you now, gal?"

"Twenty, Daddy."

He looked down, shaking his head. "A woman growed, for sure."

For reasons she didn't understand, the statement made her want to cry.

"Old enough to choose to marry up or not. Old enough to decide to take a job . . . or not."

He was letting her choose. She dove at him and wrapped her arms around his middle. Despite the chill morning air, the bib of his striped twill overalls was warm beneath her cheek. He already smelled of sweat and soil—better than any dandy's cologne. "Thank you, Daddy."

He caught her by the arms and set her aside. "But you ain't gonna go to work in your brother's clothes. If your mama sees you comin' up the yard in Andy's shirt an' britches, she'll likely faint dead away. So you change into a dress, gal, you hear me?"

"Yes, sir."

"Then head over to the preacher's house. Well-meanin' ladies from the city churches are always sendin' barrels o' clothes for us poor folks. Ask to pick through the barrels an' find some shirts an' britches an' such. Leave those things you're wearin' now in the toolshed. I'll see they get put back in Andy's trunk."

Rebekah nodded. "I'll do that. And, Daddy?" Unblinking, she gazed into his weary face. "I'm sorry I made you angry. I only wanted to help."

He grabbed her in a hug so tight it stole her breath. "I know, gal. I know. But when I seen you come runnin' that way, for a minute I thought—" He gulped. His hold tightened briefly, then he patted her shoulders and let her go.

"Make sure your mama doesn't see you in that getup. Not so sure her heart could take it."

## Cissy

She couldn't take it! Cissy smacked the plates onto the table. How unfair that Rebekah got to take a job at the cave. Plus, starting tomorrow, she'd be staying at the estate, not even coming home to help ready the little girls for bed or get them up in the morning or help with first-thing and last-thing chores every day. So who'd be stuck with all that? Cissy, that's who. She stomped one bare foot against the floorboards and growled under her breath.

"What's the matter, Cissy?" Tabitha looked up from laying out the spoons and forks. "Your foot go to sleep?"

Cissy scowled at her sister. "What're you talkin' about?"

"You done this." Tabitha imitated her foot-stomp. "I do that when my foot's gone to sleep. Wakes it up again. Did your—"

"Just shut up, Tabby."

The little girl's brown eyes flew wide. "You ain't s'posed to say 'shut up.' Mama'll put lye soap on your tongue when I tell her."

Cissy rounded the table in a flash and grabbed Tabitha by one of her braids. "You better not tell, you little brat, or I'll put spiders in your nightgown while you're sleepin'." Tabitha was more scared of spiders than anything. Except maybe of Cissy.

Tabitha wriggled. "Lemme go, Cissy. I won't tell."

"Good." Cissy yanked Tabitha's braid, making her sister yelp, before releasing it. "See that you don't."

The girls continued setting the table, Cissy with tightly crunched lips and Tabitha with her lower lip quivering. Cissy sent glowering looks meant to tell Tabitha to get that quiver under control before everyone else came in from their chores. If Mama asked why Tabby was all a-pucker, and Tabby told, Cissy'd gather up a dozen spiders.

Mama and Little Nellie hurried in as Cissy and Tabitha finished. Tabitha aimed a pathetic look at Mama, but Mama went straight to the fireplace and picked up the stick she used to shift the blackened kettle to and away from the fire, not even looking at Tabby as she went. "Cissy, fetch me a dipperful of water. This's about bubbled itself dry."

Cissy deliberately bumped Tabitha with her elbow as she moved to the water bucket. She carried the dripping dipper to the fireplace and gave it to Mama, wincing as the heat reached out and singed her. "Here." She scuttled backward while Mama stirred the cool water into the pot, making steam rise from the boiled greens. How did Mama stay so close to the flame without turning into a melted puddle? Lucky Rebekah, getting to eat in the hotel dining room instead of having to cook over burning logs in an old rock fireplace. The jealousy flared up higher and hotter than the dancing flames.

She eased close again. "Mama, since Rebekah's gonna be workin' at the cave, could I maybe—"

Mama rose and stepped past Cissy. "Gal, I haven't got time to talk right now. Gotta get supper on the table. Your daddy'll be in any minute now, an' them peas ain't even been seasoned yet."

Black-eyed peas again? Bet Rebekah wouldn't be eating black-eyed peas in the estate dining room. Cissy trailed Mama to the cellar door. "Then can I ask you after supper?"

Mama pulled the door open and stepped onto the ladder leading downward. "After supper I'm gonna be checkin' Rebekah's things, makin' sure they're all mended, then helpin' her pack for her move to the estate. Gonna be a busy evenin'." She inched down the ladder and disappeared in the shadows below.

Cissy huffed. Mama used to sing ballads while she stitched. She hadn't done it in a long time, but if she could stitch and sing, then she could stitch and talk. If she wanted to. Cissy bent over and called into the gray hole. "We could talk while you're stitchin'."

Mama reappeared cradling two onions and a small crock with a layer of hardened fat hiding its contents. She handed up the things to Cissy and then climbed the ladder, her face set in a scowl. "Why're you pesterin' me? Can't you see I'm busy? An' don't you got chores to see to?" She dropped the trapdoor into place and planted her fists on her hips. "I gotta tell you, your daddy an' me are plumb fed up with your lazy ways. If you're fixin' to weasel your way out of helpin' take over your big sister's chores, then you best save your breath 'cause—"

Cissy thumped the crock and the onions onto the table. "Never mind. Didn't really wanna talk to you anyway." She headed for the door.

"Cissy Rose, don't you take on out o' here. I need your help with—"

Cissy charged across the yard right through the flock of chickens. Hens cackled and scattered. She used the side of her foot to nudge one that pecked in the dirt instead of getting out of her way.

Daddy, with Della, Jessie, and Trudy trailing him, stepped from the trees. He shot a frown at her. "Cissy, you bend even one feather on that chicken an' I promise I'll wear you out."

Cissy growled and angled her path to avoid the stupid cluck.

"Where you goin', gal?"

She ignored Daddy and darted straight into the outhouse, the only place she knew for sure nobody would follow. She turned the little strip of wood to block the door, plopped onto the warped seat next to the hole, and snatched up the raggedy Sears, Roebuck catalog. She ran her thumb along the pages again and again, but the *riff-riff* didn't cover up the voices from her family out in the yard.

"Where'd that girl get to?" Mama, all put out.

"Closed herself in the outhouse." Daddy, short of patience.

"Cissy told me 'shut up,' an' she pulled my hair an' pushed me." Tabitha, whiny and put upon.

Cissy scanned the small space for spiders.

"What's gotten into that gal?" Mama, probably shaking her head at Daddy.

"Daddy, I gotta make water." Trudy, sounding close to tears.

Cissy rolled her eyes. Trudy didn't need to make water. She just wanted Cissy to come out so she could watch Mama and Daddy holler at her. Trudy was a spoiled baby. Her and Tabitha both.

A fist thumped the door, rattling it in its frame. "Cissy, you hurry up in there, you hear? Your mama needs your help, an' Trudy needs the outhouse."

Cissy held the old catalog up to the little shaft of light sneaking through the half-moon window and examined the black-and-white pictures of humidors.

"Cissy, you best answer me, gal."

Cissy slapped the catalog aside. "I hear you, Daddy. I'll be out when I'm . . . done."

Scuffling noises and mutters let her know her family was returning to the house. She blew out a breath and leaned against the wall. It stunk in there, and the air felt dead and hot, but she didn't want to leave. Tears stung her eyes and she sniffed hard. No way was she a real Hardin. No real mama and daddy would heap all the blame for everything on one of their own.

"I gotta be a foundling, left in the woods or maybe on the doorstep." She whispered in case one of the littler girls had stayed in the yard and might overhear. "They took me in 'cause Mama'd lost some babies, figured maybe I could take one of 'em's place. But then they had other babies an' they didn't really wanna keep me. But they did just so I could help with chores."

She pinched her nose shut and let her imagination roll, picking up pieces of the stories she'd heard Rebekah read to the little girls. "Betcha my real mama and daddy were rich, but some ol' ugly man—maybe even a troll—stole me from them to get money, an' then he lost me somehow. That's how Mama an' Daddy found me. Betcha my real parents are still huntin' me, mournin' me, wishing I—"

"Cissy!"

She sat up so fast the catalog fell on her foot. She yelped and grabbed her toes.

Fingers curled over the bottom edge of the moon cutout and yanked at the door. "Ain't you done in there yet?"

Cissy unlatched the door and gave it a shove. Jessie scuttled backward so fast she almost fell on her rump. Cissy wished she'd fallen flat. Would serve her right for standing outside and listening in. She scowled as she vacated the outhouse even though the cool, sweet-smelling air was so pretty it made her want to smile. "Thought Trudy needed to go."

Jessie pushed past Cissy, yanking up her skirt as she went. "She changed her mind."

Cissy rolled her eyes. Of course she had.

"Mama says come in. Time to eat."

"You mean she's gonna feed me?"

Jessie, perched on the outhouse seat, crunched up her face. "Why wouldn't she?"

Cissy sighed. "What're you doin', sittin' out here with the door open so anybody can see?"

Jessie shrugged. "Nobody but you out here. An' it stinks too bad with the door closed. You were in here forever. How'd you stand it so long?"

How'd she stand living on this patch of ground in a tiny, ramshackle house with so many others for so long? "Did it 'cause I had to." Cissy slapped the door closed, ignoring Jessie's howl of protest, and headed for the house. She muttered, "But I don't have to no more."

She was fifteen already. Some girls, even Mama, got married at fifteen. Fifteen was the same as being grown-up. Grown-up meant she didn't have to do anything she didn't want to do. Not anymore. And she wouldn't, either.

## Seven

*Rebekah*

Rebekah and Mama sat on Rebekah's bed and organized her belongings in neat stacks. Daddy's voice, telling the younger girls a story Granddaddy'd told him when he was a boy, drifted from the front room. Seemed only yesterday Rebekah sat at Daddy's knee and listened to the family tales. She battled tears—tears of sadness at leaving her family home and tears of joy for the blessing her salary would be. She traced the delicate embroidery on a calico chemise with her finger and sniffed hard.

Mama placed her hand over Rebekah's. "Here now. None o' that."

Rebekah looked up. "None of what?"

"Sorrowin'." Mama's lips formed a grim line. "Growin' up an' movin' on—it's part of life. S'posed to be a happy time. So no sorrowin', you hear?"

A sad smile tugged at Rebekah's lips. "Then how come you're frowning?"

"'Cause I'm better at givin' advice than I am at takin' it." Mama shook her head, regret flickering in her eyes. "I was awful hard on Cissy this afternoon. When she got home from school an' I told her how you'd be movin' to the estate, how I'd be needin' her more than ever to step up an' help, she got testy with me. So when she was pesterin' me, wantin' to talk in the middle of makin' supper, I lost patience. More'n usual, 'cause I was sorrowin' over lettin' you go."

Rebekah wished she could tell Mama an apology would set things to right again, but Cissy held grudges better than anyone else in the family. It would likely take days for the girl to let go of her resentment. And by then she'd find some other reason to stick her nose in the air and let out little huffs of aggravation. When would Cissy grow up and stop being so selfish?

Mama picked up the stack of dresses and laid them gently in the bottom of the musty, warped trunk Daddy'd brought up from the cellar. "Reckon I'll take her aside before bedtime, ask her what it was she wanted. She an' Andy, they're my quick-tempered ones. Natured like their Granny Hardin. She was a feisty one, always snipin' about this or that. They got her reddish hair and blue-green eyes, too. But Andy got over things a mite faster than Cissy ever has." When Mama spoke of Andy, her voice became gruffer, like scraping out the words pained her throat.

Rebekah said, "Cissy'll grow up by and by. Don't worry, Mama."

Mama offered a weary smile. "You sound like your daddy, tellin' me not to worry. Next you'll tell me to leave Cissy in God's hands 'stead o' tryin' to fix her on my own."

A knot of agony filled Rebekah's throat. How could Mama trust God to take care of Cissy when He'd let such harm befall Andy? She slipped the last of her clothes into the trunk and closed the lid. "Guess that's everything. Sure am glad we've still got that little pull wagon in the barn. It'll come in handy for toting my things to the estate. I won't have to bother Daddy to do it for me."

Mama stood and pulled Rebekah into a rare hug. "You ain't never been a bother, gal. Always a blessin'. An' you still are, takin' this job so you can help the family." She planted a quick kiss on Rebekah's cheek and stepped away. "Gonna send the li'l ones in now. They've got school in the mornin' an' need their sleep. You sleep good, too. Big d-day tomorrow for you."

The tears swimming in her mother's eyes nearly broke Rebekah's heart. "Mama, I—"

Mama hurried out of the room. Moments later the girls swarmed in with Cissy scuffing in last. They all scrambled into their nightgowns, the littlest ones yawning and the bigger ones giggling and chatting. Then they scrambled beneath the covers and turned expectant looks on Rebekah.

"Come pray, Bek," Trudy said.

A lump filled her throat. Her last night to sing a lullaby and say bedtime prayers with her sisters. Rebekah pressed her hands to her fluttering heart, wanting to prolong the moment. She moved between the beds shared by the youngest girls. She looked down first at Della and Jessie, both getting so big and leaving little-girlhood behind, then shifted her gaze to Tabitha, Trudy, and Little Nellie all crowded together.

She forced a smile. "Just think, Trudy and Nellie. Tomorrow night Della will sleep with Cissy, Tabitha can crawl in with Jessie, and you two will have a bed to yourselves. Won't that be nice?"

Tabitha's face puckered. "Where you gonna be?"

Rebekah eased onto the edge of the bed. There wasn't much room, given its trio of occupants. "Remember? Daddy told you I'll be working at the cave estates."

"But you'll come home at night, won'tcha?"

Pain stabbed. She shook her head, smoothing Tabitha's hair from her cherubic face. "No, honey. I'll be staying at the cave in my own little cabin."

From the bed on the other side of the room, Cissy's snort blasted.

Rebekah kept her gaze fixed on Tabitha. "But I'll see you on Sundays in service."

Trudy sat up. "Who's gonna tuck our covers down an' say prayers with us?"

Rebekah sent a glance over her shoulder at Cissy. She lay with her arms folded tightly over her chest, her face set in a scowl. She'd be no help. Rebekah eased Trudy onto her pillow and began singing the Highland lullaby Mama had sung to her when she was small. " 'Hush, hush, time to be sleeping; hush, hush, dreams come a-creeping—' "

Trudy bounced up again. "Bek, who's gonna sing an'—"

Tabitha sat up. "I don't wanna sleep with Jessie. I wanna—"

Little Nellie started to wail.

Della and Jessie left their beds and curled their arms around Rebekah, both sniffling.

Cissy blew out a huff heavy enough to close the shutters.

Rebekah opened her arms wide and all five girls tried to fit into her embrace. She held them as best she could. "Hush now, you hear? You don't need me to tuck you in and say prayers with you. You're all big enough to pull up your own covers and say your own prayers. Come on, now, all of you. Get back in your beds."

Slowly they disentangled themselves and stretched out on the straw-filled mattresses.

Rebekah stood between the beds. "Cover up."

They gripped the coarse cotton sheets and mended quilts and drew them beneath their chins. When they were settled, Rebekah turned to Della. "Will you sing?"

Della crinkled her nose for a moment, her cheeks splashing with pink, but she warbled out the familiar lullaby.

Rebekah rewarded her sister with a smile, then sent a firm glance over all five faces. "All right now, say your prayers."

Trudy's brown eyes widened. "All at once?"

It would take half an hour if they all took turns. Rebekah nodded. "God's ears can hear a hundred voices all at the same time, so He'll make out your prayers just fine. Go ahead."

They closed their eyes, folded their hands beneath their chins, and broke into a rumble of voices. Rebekah caught "God bless Mama an' Daddy" and "God bless Bek" and "God bless the chickens." She battled laughter and tears at the same time. Finally a chorus of "amens" rang.

Della angled her face toward Cissy. "Ain't you gonna pray, too?"

Cissy scowled. "That's baby stuff."

Della started to protest, but Rebekah put her hand on her sister's shoulder and shook her head. "Sleep now." She waited until her sisters all closed their eyes. Then she moved to the windows and fastened the shutters against the night air. She tiptoed to the little stand in the corner and extinguished the lamp. The room plunged into darkness, but she didn't need to see to find her way to the bed.

When she slid beneath the covers, a rush of too many emotions to define attacked. She blinked and grazed Cissy's arm with her fingers. "Cissy, I'm—"

Cissy rolled over with her face to the wall. "It's late. You gotta get up an' outta here early. Go to sleep, Bek."

Her sister was right. Morning would come soon, and she needed her rest. So she pushed aside the apology for heaping so much responsibility on her sister, closed her eyes, and willed herself to sleep.

*Tolly*

Tolly rounded the corner to the cave's opening, a coil of rope slung across his chest, a filled canteen bouncing against his hip, and a lantern hanging from his gloved hand. On the dew-covered, grassy knoll across from the jagged black maw, Rebekah Hardin sat on a sad-looking trunk that filled the bed of a child's coaster wagon. From all appearances the trunk and the wagon should have been tossed on a junk heap years before.

"Mornin', Reb. You's out an' about mighty early."

She leaped up. She gave a tug on the waistband of her britches before sticking her hand out to him. "Didn't I say I'd be waiting?"

"Yep, an' here you is." He respected people who kept their word. He let go of her hand and looked her up and down. She wore the same beat-up hat as the last time he'd seen her, a white shirt buttoned to the neck, and baggy tan trousers with the hems rolled up. He held back a whistle. She was here, as promised, but she looked as sorry a sight as the trunk and wagon. "You got a jacket? It be downright cold inside the cave."

"Uh-huh." She lifted the lid of the trunk and removed a brown jacket with mismatched plaid patches on the elbows. The thing looked big enough to swallow her whole. She shrugged it on and then yanked on the waist of her pants again.

Tolly frowned. "You got some suspenders or a belt in that trunk?"

She shook her head. One strand of wavy brown hair escaped the hat and straggled down her cheek. She reached to tuck it in again, and her trousers slipped. With a grimace she grabbed the waist and held tightly.

Tolly snorted. "Girl, you can't be holdin' on to yo' pants when we's movin' through the tunnels. Take that jacket off."

While she removed her jacket, he pulled out his pocketknife and sawed a three-foot length from the rope. It hurt him to cut into that rope, but he carried it for emergencies. Keeping her britches on her was a sure and certain emergency. He shoved the piece into her hands. "All right. Tie yo'self up."

The cut end frayed and made stringing it through the belt loops a challenge, but she got it done without a murmur of complaint. Then she tied a knot. Not the best knot he'd ever seen. It'd likely work itself loose midway through the tour. But he wouldn't retie it for her. Wouldn't be seemly even if she was dressed up like a scarecrow.

"Ready now?"

She nodded.

"No, you ain't. Put yo' jacket on."

She did.

"Got gloves?"

She rustled in the trunk and found some old cloth ones that had sure seen better days.

"Good. Put 'em on." He waited while she tugged on the raggedy things, then barked, "What about chalk, some watuh, an' a lantern or candles?"

Her brown eyes grew round as acorns. "Um . . . no, sir. I don't have any of those."

He scowled even though he'd known she wouldn't come prepared. How would she know? But if he was hard on her today, she'd always remember. "Lucky for you I do. You don't nevuh—an' I mean nevuh—go in the cave without bein' prepared." He patted the items. "All o' this is life-savin' equipment, Reb. We's accountable for them who go in the cave wit' us. We gotta have what we need to keep 'em safe. Don't you nevuh come down here again 'less you got rope, watuh, an' at least a pocketful o' candles an' lucifers wit' you."

"Rope, water, and candles. Or a lantern. And matches. Yes, sir."

"An' you don't nevuh go in all by yo'self. Only wit' me or one o' the othuh guides. You hear?"

She nodded, blinking fast, and he knew she was thinking about her brother.

He cleared his throat and gave her arm a clumsy pat. "Good." He dug a match from his shirt pocket and lit the wick on his lantern. He settled the globe in place, held the lantern out in front of him, and fixed her with a serious look. "Now, you stick wit' me. We's goin' in."

The girl's face went pale. Sweat beaded all along her upper lip. Her eyes grew round and fear filled. For a moment Tolly thought she might turn tail and run. But she sucked in a big breath and nodded. "Yes, sir."

She followed him like a brave soldier, but he felt her breath on the back of his neck. Short, panting breaths that told him she was as scared as a rabbit facing a fox. But she matched him step for step as they eased down the gaping, uneven tunnel that led to the cave. The sun's light and warmth faded away. Cool, pungent air surrounded them. A smile grew without effort behind his thick beard.

Tolly pulled in a slow, deep breath, letting his nostrils flare as he took in the cave's perfume. If he could, he'd live down here instead of coming and going. Down here it didn't matter if a man's skin was black, if he was born to former slaves, if he'd never gone to a real school. The cave accepted all, embraced all, challenged all. Moving through the dark passageways made him feel close to his pappy, his grandpappy, and mostly to the One who'd created the tunnels, caverns, and flowing rivers.

He didn't say a word as he led Rebekah along the familiar underground path. He talked to the tour groups. Them who took the tours expected him to tell everything he knew about the cave, and he knew plenty, so he talked plenty. And he jested. Answered their questions—even the ones he thought foolish. But today he wanted Rebekah Hardin to focus on the cave, not on him.

The lantern's glow skimmed the walls and formed a halo on the ridged ground. A shadow from the solid bottom filled the center of the halo. If a person watched the shadow instead of the halo, he would trip every time. Tolly hadn't tripped in years, but he heard Rebekah stumble a time or two. He held his tongue. Better to let her learn by experience.

By the time they left the long entry tunnel and entered a side shaft dubbed the Church by a slave named Stephen Bishop before Tolly was even born, she'd quit tripping and was moving as smoothly as a cave spider. He couldn't resist flashing a grin over his shoulder. Her expression drew him to a halt.

She stopped, too. "Is everything all right?"

To his surprise, tears gathered, and he had to blink to clear them. How long had it been since he'd gotten to see the wonder of Mammoth Cave reflected in someone's eyes? Oh, the tourists, they exclaimed about the long passages, the eyeless creatures swimming in the underground rivers, or the trunk-like formations left behind after years of mineral-rich water dripping down. They jabbered with glee when he let them scorch their names on the ceiling with a candle's flame or paused to watch a cave spider catch a cricket in its web. But so many of them didn't take the time to look—to really look—at the glory of the cave. Their excitement was for themselves. A selfish excitement.

But in Rebekah Hardin's eyes, he saw something different. Something deeper. He couldn't resist turning her question back on her. "What you say? Ever'thing all right?"

She turned a slow circle, her gaze drifting from the ceiling to the floor and then back to him. "Yes. Everything's fine."

If he'd had any uneasiness about hiring her, it faded clear away in that moment. Girl or not, she'd make a fine tour guide. He just knew it.

## EIGHT

*Mid-May*
*Devlin*

Devlin shifted his homburg to the back of his head and sent a slow look from one end of the Mammoth Cave Hotel to the other. Mother would turn up her nose at the row of adjoined, painted-white clapboard structures with their shutterless windows and simple boardwalks. But a fancy hotel would be out of place in these woodsy surroundings. He liked the rustic appearance of the two- and three-story mismatched sections.

He grabbed the handle of his suitcase and followed the other guests who'd vacated the trio of stagecoaches. He smacked at his suit as he moved along the dirt pathway. The open windows of the outdated conveyances had allowed in a cloud of road dust that covered each of the passengers from head to toe. He hoped the hotel had a laundry service and hot baths. He might not be as finicky as Mother when it came to cleanliness, but neither did he care for the grit sticking to his sweat-moistened skin.

Devlin listened to the excited chatter of the other new arrivals while he waited his turn at the check-in desk. A smile tugged at his cheek. He wished Father were here to witness the eager throng. It seemed the rumors concerning the cave's popularity were not exaggerated. The yard teemed with people, some clustered near an open wagon, waving tickets. Others filled the benches lined up along the buildings' fronts. Still more meandered over the grassy yard. So many people . . . and all of them handing over their coins for the privilege of entering the cave. Devlin's scalp tingled as he envisioned the government's coffers growing, thanks to the acquisition of the cave.

"Next!"

Devlin stepped forward and placed his valise at his feet. Since the check-in desk was in an airy pass-through between buildings rather than indoors, he didn't bother to remove his hat. "Devlin Bale. I have a long-term reservation."

The clerk searched a large notebook, sliding his finger along a row of penned names. His face lit. "Ah, here you are—Mr. Bale from the University of Kentucky." He aimed a smile at Devlin. "Our cartographer, yes?"

He was technically the college's cartographer, but he nodded. "That's correct."

The man gestured to the guest register and the ready pen and ink pot. "Please sign in, sir. We're delighted to have you with us. Mr. Janin left a letter for you." He removed a sealed envelope from a little basket on the corner of the counter and gave it to Devlin. "He also instructed me to give you one of our cottages. You're a goodly walk from the dining room but close to the tour wagon pickup post. I trust you'll be satisfied with your lodgings."

Devlin slipped the envelope into his pocket, dipped the pen, and signed the register with a flourish. "I'm sure I will be. Although I intend to spend more time in the cave than out of it."

The clerk laughed heartily. "I suppose you'll need to if you plan to record all the explored passages." He leaned across the desk and lowered his voice. "The guides say the tunnels stretch for miles under the ground. A fellow could get lost down there and never come out again."

Devlin frowned. "Are you trying to scare me?"

He straightened so abruptly that his hair, slicked back with oil, bounced. "No, sir. You do what you need to with Mr. Janin's blessing. But as for me? I'm staying aboveground." He pressed a key into Devlin's hand, leaned sideways to peer past him, and barked, "Next!"

Devlin gripped his valise and moved out of the way of a family with several boisterous children. He checked the leather tag on the key. The number two was stamped in gilt. He wove his way between other guests across the yard to a stretch of single-story connected cabins at the west edge of the property. He stepped up on the covered boardwalk and inserted his key into the lock on the second door. The lock clicked, and he entered what would be his home for the next several months.

Heavy shadows hid the space. He plopped his valise on the end of the bed, tossed his homburg next to it, then moved to the windows flanking the door. With a flick of his wrists, he whisked open the curtains. Light flowed in. He released a low chuckle. Had the clerk called this a cottage? In one glance Devlin decided the term *cottage* was far too grand. *Cabin*—or maybe *hovel*—seemed more apt when compared with his previous experience of hotel stays.

Log walls bearing a coat of whitewash enclosed a space perhaps twelve feet square, half the size of his room at home. A rock fireplace filled the center of one wall. Devlin doubted he'd make use of it. The May weather was exceedingly mild. Besides the fireplace, the cottage contained a bed draped with a striped coverlet, a small stand with a raised panel door, a tall bureau, a washstand holding a china pitcher and bowl, and a stuffed chair. The absence of a desk troubled him. Where would he do his drawing? And where would he store his surveying and mapping equipment when the boxes arrived on the next supply wagon?

A door and another window hidden behind slatted shutters divided the back wall. He crossed the plank floor, turning sideways to ease between the bed and the bureau, and folded the shutters flat against the log walls. His gaze met a rolling, grass-covered expanse leading to a thick cluster of aspens, pines, and oaks. A shimmering ribbon of blue captured his attention, and he rose on tiptoe to better see the winding stream. With a little grunt, he pushed the lower window upward and rested his elbows on the sash. A sweet breeze poured over him, and the melody of rustling leaves and trickling water reached his ears. Devlin sucked in a satisfied breath. He smiled. Ah yes, this would do nicely.

Leaving the window open, he sank down in the chair and retrieved the letter the clerk had given him. He opened the envelope, angled the pages to the sunlight streaming through the window, and read the missive typed onto a sheet of Mammoth Cave stationery.

Dear Mr. Bale,

 Welcome to the Mammoth Cave Estate. I am delighted you've chosen to chart the cave's extraordinary tunneling as your senior project for the prestigious University of Kentucky. This letter is meant not only to welcome you but also to offer you necessary information.

I have assigned our finest, most knowledgeable guide to accompany you on your excursions into the cave. His name is Tolliver Sandford, but you may address him as Tolly. I assure you he will give you his full attention, will take you to every known nook and cranny of the Mammoth Cave system, and will guarantee your safety during the explorations. Tolly resides in the first of the staff cabins north of the dining room. Any of our employees can direct you to his cabin as needed.

During your stay please feel free to make use of our dining facility. Breakfast is served each morning from six until nine, a satisfying buffet is available every midday from eleven until one, and we offer the finest dining each evening from five until nine.

I also invite you to utilize our laundry services. Please leave whatever items require laundering beside your door. Our competent cleaning staff will carry it to the laundry room, ascertain it is handled promptly and respectfully, and return it to you the following dawn.

Hot water is delivered to the cottages every morning at six o'clock. If an earlier or later time better meets your schedule, please leave a note at the desk with any of the clerks. Your preference will be accommodated. Given your status as a long-term guest, you may make use of our bathing room once a week. Please reserve a day and time at the front desk.

I sincerely hope this letter has proved valuable to you. If you have further questions or requirements, please do not hesitate to inquire of any of the staff members. They are all at your service and will do their utmost to make your stay as comfortable and enjoyable as possible.

Your faithful servant,

Mr. Albert Covington Janin, trustee for the Mammoth Cave Estate

Devlin propped the letter on the bureau top for easy reference and then transferred his clothing from his valise to the bureau drawers. He arranged his shaving items and toiletries around the pitcher and bowl on the washstand. He started to move the washstand, which lurked next to the front door, to the corner to give himself a little more floor space. But whoever brought the hot water probably preferred it remain near the door for easy access. Last he placed his wind-up clock on the table beside the bed. He rolled the empty valise and propped it in the corner, behind the chair.

As he turned, he realized his accommodations lacked something besides a desk or worktable. Where was the toilet? He scanned the room, and he noticed the little door on the bedside stand. He cringed. Surely not . . . Holding his breath, Devlin eased the door open. He blew out the breath and let his shoulders sag. He hadn't made use of a chamber pot since he was a boy still in knee pants. The thought of using one for several weeks held no appeal.

Mr. Janin's letter instructed him to ask if he needed something, so he would inquire about toilets or, at the very least, an outhouse. If neither was available, he supposed he would be able to make do with the chamber pot. Father's candidacy was worth a little suffering. Although Mother would say being forced to use a chamber pot was hardly a little suffering.

He snapped the door closed, sealing away the offensive porcelain pot, and snagged his homburg from the foot of the bed. The lunch buffet was open and his stomach rumbled with emptiness. He'd locate the dining room, enjoy a hearty meal, and then spend the afternoon exploring.

Eagerness propelled him out the door. As he stepped from the boardwalk, the crunch of wagon wheels and the chatter of voices caught his attention. He paused and watched a wagon pulled by four horses approach. A black man with a full white beard and a sheeny top hat perched at an angle over his white hair held the reins. A young white man, smooth faced with a thick jacket bunched up under his chin, sat on the edge of the seat beside him. The bed overflowed with well-dressed, flush-faced, smiling men and women who were most likely returning from a tour. He'd try to sit near them at lunch and listen in on their reflections about their cave excursion.

The man drew the horses to a stop, then angled himself sideways in the seat and aimed a bright smile at those in the back. "Here you be again, folks. I surely thank you for yo' attention durin' the tour. If you di'n't get enough feastin' on the sights o' our Mammoth Cave, then you jus' go ahead an' sign up again. I'll be sure the spiders an' crickets an' bats are all ready to greet you anothuh time."

Laughter rolled. The younger of the pair on the seat hopped down, trotted to the rear of the wagon, and began assisting the women and children to the ground. Before leaving the wagon, the men shifted to the front of the bed and shook the driver's hand, exchanging a few words and, if Devlin wasn't mistaken, pressing money into his palm. The driver bowed his head in thanks and joshed with the gentlemen, his smile never wavering. Devlin couldn't stifle a chuckle. The cheerful black man had every person in the wagon treating him like a long-lost uncle.

The last man climbed down from the bed. A child ran up to grab his hand. Then the child raised his other hand in a wild wave and called, "Bye! Thank you!"

"You's welcome, li'l man. You come see ol' Tolly again now, y'hear?"

Tolly . . . Devlin gave a start. He jerked his gaze to the driver. This must be the guide Mr. Janin had assigned him. Devlin hadn't anticipated being shown through the cave by an elderly black man who sported an Abe Lincoln hat. Not that he doubted Janin's glowing praise of Tolliver Sandford. The tourists' response to the guide spoke volumes about his joviality and ability.

Tolly gestured the younger man to the front of the wagon and stretched out his hand. "Here ya go, Reb. Yo' share o' the tips."

The one named Reb drew back. "No, sir. I didn't guide anybody. I just followed along. You keep it."

Tolly's forehead crunched. He bounced his hand. "Now listen here, Reb, I's downright tired o' arguin' wit' you. You's a 'ficial estate workuh now. I don't want nobody sayin' Tolly cheats his 'sistant. Take this. Twenty-five percent o' what they done gib me is s'posed to go to you."

Devlin sent a glance over the assistant's clothes. He'd never seen such a ragtag getup. Reb could use the money to buy a new pair of trousers, a decent hat, or a jacket that fit. He found himself willing Reb to take the money.

But he backed away from the wagon, shaking his head. "Huh-uh. My daddy taught me not to take something I didn't earn."

"Now, Reb—"

Another dust-stirring step in reverse brought Reb almost to the board-walk. "You're the guide. You earn the tips. I don't want any of it. Not unless I've honestly earned it."

Tolly stood. The wagon creaked, and the horses pranced in place, nickering. He planted his feet wide and glowered at the youth. "Reb, you gonna be this ornery fo'evuh? 'Cause if you is, I just might hafta find me a new 'sistant. You's tryin' my patience, fo' sure."

Reb took one more backward step. The heel of his scuffed boot connected with the edge of the boardwalk. Devlin ducked out of the way as the man flailed his arms and then landed hard on his backside. His feet flew up, his head collided with the wooden walkway, and the battered hat popped free. Long, tangled waves of dark-brown hair spilled across the toes of Devlin's shoes.

He stared down in horror. This was no smooth-faced youth but a lovely young woman. And he'd been ungentlemanly enough to let her fall right at his feet. While he stared down at her, abashed and rueful, she looked up from her ungainly position and locked gazes with him. Her stunned expression changed to irritation.

Her brown eyes snapping, she stretched one hand toward him. "Well? Are you just going to stand there with your mouth hanging open, mister, or are you going to help me up?"

## NINE

*Rebekah*

Tolly bounded to her side, coins flying in every direction, and gripped her hand between his. "Lawsy, Reb, is you all right?"

Truthfully, her head throbbed and her tailbone ached. But she'd never admit it. Not with the handsome gentleman with soft-looking curls the color of spun honey peeking from beneath the brim of his hat and eyes bluer than Daddy's gazing down at her. She struggled to sit, but the bulky jacket and the stabbing pain in her back hindered her. "I'm fine. Just get me up before anybody else sees me here like a turtle on its back."

The gentleman bent down and gripped the shoulders of her jacket, lifting, while Tolly pulled her hand, and within seconds Rebekah stood on wobbly legs. She touched the knot forming on the back of her head and grimaced. Great-Granddaddy's hat hadn't provided much of a cushion.

"You sure you's all right?" Tolly looked as worried as a mother hen. "Mebbe I oughta take you to the estate doc, getcha some analgesic powduhs."

Rebekah glanced at the guest, who hadn't budged from his spot near her left elbow. She wanted those analgesic powders, but she didn't want to seem like a crybaby to Tolly. Or to the handsome stranger. So she tossed her head, making her hair flow over her shoulders, and forced a dry laugh. "Nothing damaged but my pride." She angled a look at the guest. "You can move on now. The performance is over."

"Reb!" Tolly gawked at her.

Rebekah couldn't recall ever being so snide with someone. Especially someone she didn't even know. But this man's steady perusal was making her skin crawl. Or, more accurately, her flesh tingle. The reaction frightened her more than the unexpected tumble had.

A grin twitched at the corners of the man's lips, bringing a dimple into play on one smooth-shaven cheek. He stepped past Rebekah and held his hand to Tolly. "I believe I should introduce myself since you and I will be spending quite a bit of time together. I'm Devlin Bale from the University of Kentucky."

Rebekah retrieved her hat and jammed it onto her head while Tolly gave Mr. Bale's hand a thorough pump. "Yessuh, yessuh, Mistuh Janin tol' me awhile back you'd be comin' an' that I was to take good care o' you when you got here. Glad to make yo' acquaintance, Mistuh Bale."

"Call me Devlin, please."

"All right, I will. An' you call me Tolly, same as ever'body else does."

"Thank you, Tolly."

Rebekah stood to the side and rubbed the base of her spine with both palms. She was probably going to be black and blue back there.

Tolly began gathering up his scattered coins. "'Course, Mistuh Janin, he done said you likely wouldn't be arrivin' 'til summuhtime. So I had end o' May or beginnin' o' June in my head to watch fo' you. But maybe the city colleges don't go as long as the schools in these here parts?"

Mr. Bale chuckled, a low rumble that sent butterflies dancing through Rebekah's stomach. "My professors allowed me early dismissal to begin my project. I apologize if my untimely arrival causes you any inconvenience."

Tolly pocketed the last of the coins and stepped back onto the boardwalk, grinning. "No, suh, no inconvenience at all. I'll jus' let the othuh guides know they gots to pick up my tours 'til you finish yo' business. Me an' Reb"—he gestured her forward—"we'll take good care o' you, Devlin."

Devlin turned his smile on Rebekah. Everything inside of her went fluttery. That bump on the head was affecting her more than she'd first realized. He removed his hat, bringing his thick, curly hair into full view. "Reb . . . Is that short for 'Rebel'?"

Rebekah's face flamed. She ducked her head.

Tolly laughed, slapping his knee. "You's a card, Devlin, that be fo' sure.

Rebel jus' might fit my 'sistant, seein' how she's decked out like a man an' bound to be stubborn headed. But no, this here is Rebekah Hardin. She only just hired on, finishin' up her first full month. She's done a right fine job, too, keepin' ever'body movin' along, even if she is jus' a slip of a girl."

Tolly's praise made her cheeks burn even hotter. She inched away from the men. "Tolly, I'm going to my cabin. I need to put my hair up again." She must look a sight with her stringy locks straggling down from Great-Granddaddy's hat.

"Getcha some lunch, too, an' then meet me back here at one thuhty fo' the two o'clock tour." He pointed at her with his thick, blunt-tipped finger. "An' aftuh that you catch some rest. Don't want you ovuhdoin' aftuh that thump you took on the noggin."

"Yes, sir." She limped in the direction of the staff cabins.

Behind her, Devlin Bale's smooth voice called, "It was good to meet you, Miss Rebel. I look forward to working with you."

Another flock of butterflies broke free and flittered through her chest. Her back and head throbbed with every clop of her boots against the ground, but Rebekah broke into a trot anyway. Devlin Bale was too handsome, too sure of himself, and too rich for the likes of a squatter's granddaughter, and she needed some time alone to remind herself of those facts.

## Devlin

Why had he poked fun at her name and laughed at her? Any fool—and Devlin had never been called a fool—could see she was hurting by the way she pressed her hand to her back and moved stiffly. He'd behaved worse than a grammar school boy who strove to gain attention from a girl by punching her on the arm or stealing her hair ribbon. The next time he saw Rebel—Rebekah—Hardin, he'd make a sincere apology and hope she accepted it.

He turned from observing Miss Hardin's departure and caught Tolly Sandford scowling at him. Distrust glimmered in the man's dark eyes.

Devlin cleared his throat. "I, er, was on my way to the dining room. I suppose I should hurry on before they close the buffet."

"Reckon so." He folded his arms over his thick chest. "Just so y'know, none of us on staff take our meals wit' the guests."

"So . . ."

"So don't be lookin' to eat wit' Reb."

Devlin feigned surprise. "Why would I look to eat with Miss Re—Miss Hardin?"

Tolly raised one eyebrow.

Devlin straightened his shoulders and adopted the authoritative pose his father used in front of his classroom. "When will you be ready to accompany me to the cave? If you need a day or two to make arrangements, I'm not averse to waiting."

The man scratched his cheek. "Well, this bein' Friday an' tomorruh Satuhday, an' the day aftuh that Sunday, when nobody goes to the cave, mebbe we should plan to start our workin' togethuh on Monday. That be agreeable to you, Devlin?"

By Monday his equipment would be here, and he'd be able to enjoy a couple of days exploring the grounds surrounding the estate. He smiled, relieved the man had regained his friendly demeanor. "Perfectly agreeable."

"Good, good. I'll settle things wit' the othuh guides this evenin', an' Monday mornin' we'll git started with yo' mappin'. Mistuh Janin tol' me you'd likely take up the whole summuh, so sooner we git to it, the bettuh fo' you." He shrugged, grimacing. "Gonna hafta be mindful o' the othuh tours, though—can't be interferin' wit' the pleasure o' the payin' guests. Mistuh Janin, he be real firm wit' me about that. So we need to stay outta the way o' groups comin' through or set out afore the tours start an' then go in again in the early evenin' when the tours be done fo' the day." He squinted one eye. "You opposed to risin' early, Devlin?"

"How early?"

"First tour goes in at nine o'clock. So to beat 'em in an' out I'd say . . . mebbe . . . seven'd be good."

He'd have time to eat breakfast before entering the cave. He nodded. "Seven sounds fine."

"All right. You see that buildin' right there?" Tolly pointed to a nearby two-story structure with a railed observation platform on the flat roof. "Me 'n' Reb'll meet ya at the no'theast cornuh at seven Monday mornin'. You evuh been in a cave befo'?"

Devlin shook his head.

"It's somethin', I'll tell ya that. Mysterious. Mesmerizin'."

Excitement quivered through Devlin's limbs. Tolly's statement combined with everything he'd read about the underground world made him itch to catch the next tour and witness every detail for himself.

Tolly sent a look up and down Devlin's length. "Them clothes o' yours are mighty fine fo' goin' to dinnuh an' such, but you's gonna need traipsin' clothes—like what Reb an' me is wearin'—fo' down unduh the ground. You got traipsin' clothes?"

Devlin held back a groan. Why hadn't he thought about bringing something other than suits? Neither he nor Father had considered that the inside of the cave would be dirty. But his letter from the cave's trustee had indicated laundry services were available. He'd choose his oldest suit and make it his "traipsing outfit." He nodded.

Tolly continued to stare at him with one eye squinted. "Sturdy walkin' boots? Warm jacket? Gloves? An' a hat other'n one meant for a dandy?"

Devlin's scalp prickled. He happened to like his homburg.

"Not tryin' to aggravate ya, Devlin. I'd be no sort o' guide if I di'n't tell you how to be prepared."

His irritation melted. He should appreciate the older man's straightforwardness. "Thank you for the warning. Is there a place to purchase clothing on the estate?"

"Hunt's sto'. That's where most o' us git our supplies an' such."

"Are guests allowed to shop there?"

"Don't reckon the sto' owner'd refuse yo' money."

Devlin nodded. "Very well. I'll acquire a heavy jacket, gloves, and a suitable hat before Monday's excursion."

Tolly's face broke into a smile, his teeth a slash of white between his full pink lips. "Good, good. Now you go fetch yo'self some o' that buffet food. Me an' Reb'll see you first thing Monday mornin'."

## Cissy

Cissy pinched the crust from her cheese-on-brown-bread sandwich and threw the pieces into the bushes for the birds. Mama'd have a fit if she knew Cissy was wasting food, but the dry crust stuck in her throat. She glanced at the open magazine draped across her knees, and her mouth watered for tiny cucumber sandwiches cut into pretty shapes and served on a china plate all painted with roses, like the ones the ladies in the serial illustration were enjoying.

Pansy ambled over and plopped down next to the log Cissy used as a seat. "Ain't you finished readin' that thing yet? My mama's been pesterin' me to bring it home again."

She wasn't finished, but maybe she shouldn't read *Vogue* anymore. The articles and pictures only stirred her dissatisfaction. Cissy slapped the magazine shut and handed it to her friend. She took a nibble from her sandwich and gazed across the school ground. The same kids she'd known her whole life sat in little circles, eating biscuits or sandwiches or cornbread wedges from battered tin pails. They all laughed and talked, happy and content. Cissy's stomach soured. She didn't belong here.

She rested her chin in her hand and sighed. "Pansy, you ever notice how I look?"

Pansy stuck a pickle slice in her mouth and giggled. "Kinda hard not to notice, since you an' me been sittin' together every day of school since we was little."

Cissy scowled. "That's not what I mean. Look at my sisters." She waited until Pansy shifted her gaze toward Della, Jessie, and Tabitha, who sat jabbering with a passel of other girls. "Do I look like them?"

Pansy stared for several minutes across the ground, then turned to Cissy and shrugged. "You all wear calico dresses. You all have braids."

Cissy held back a huff. Sometimes Pansy didn't have any more sense than a goose. "I'm not meanin' our clothes or how we wear our hair. Don'tcha see? They have brown eyes an' brown hair. Look at me." Pansy stared intently into Cissy's face. "Do I look like them?"

"Nope."

Cissy sat back, smug. "Didn't think so."

"What does it matter?"

This time Cissy let the huff come out. "Matters a lot, Pansy Blair. 'Cause I'm for certain sure I'm not a Hardin."

Pansy crinkled her nose. "Cissy, sometimes you talk nonsense."

"It ain't nonsense." She dropped the uneaten sandwich in her pail, slipped from the log, and settled close to Pansy with her legs crisscrossed. "I been thinkin' on it a lot. My mama an' daddy just don't seem to take a shine to me. Not like they do to the others. An' I don't look like any of the rest of 'em."

Pansy gaped at Cissy. "What're you sayin'?"

"I'm sayin' I think my mama an' daddy aren't really my mama an' daddy. I think they took me in instead o' birthin' me. An' I think they wish they hadn't done it." Every day since Bek had moved to the cave estate, all Cissy'd heard from her folks was how she couldn't do anything right. Her sisters fussed at her, too, wanting her to sing or pray or play like Bek.

Hurt welled up inside of her. As mad as she got at her sisters and her folks, the idea that they didn't really want her stung more than she wanted to admit. "I'm leavin', Pansy. Goin' off on my own, someplace where I'll be wanted an' . . . an' loved." Her chest ached. "Really, truly loved."

Pansy pushed the copy of *Vogue* and her lunch pail aside and threw her arms around Cissy. "I don't want you to go, Cissy. You're my best friend in the whole world."

Cissy hugged Pansy, then pulled away. She sniffled and rubbed her hand under her nose. "You're my best friend, too. That's why I told you." Then she glared at the freckle-faced girl. "But don't you tell a soul, Pansy Blair, you hear me? If my daddy gets wind I plan to set out, he'll lock me in the cellar."

Pansy's green eyes widened. "He'd do that?"

"To keep me around to tend to chores, he sure would." A bald lie. But Pansy believed it. And the threat should keep her from spilling the secret to anybody else.

"When're you settin' out?"

"Dunno yet. Gotta set my hands on some money first. But soon."

Tears flooded Pansy's eyes. "I'm gonna miss you."

"I'll miss you, too." Cissy leaned sideways and bumped her shoulder against Pansy's. "But I gotta do it. I can't stay. Not with people who don't really want me around."

Pansy slipped her arm around Cissy's waist. "Will you write to me? Let me know where you settle?"

Cissy rolled her eyes. "If I do, my folks'll find out where I am an' might come after me. I gotta keep my whereabouts a secret, Pansy."

Tears slipped down Pansy's cheeks. "I don't think I can stand you goin' away an' never knowin' where you went. Please write to me? I won't tell nobody where you are. I promise."

Cissy gritted her teeth together for a minute, thinking. "Oh, all right. Soon as I'm settled, I'll send you a picture postcard. I won't write nothin' on it, though. You can look at the picture an' figure out where I am, but if there ain't no words, nobody will have to know it came from me."

Pansy threw her arms around Cissy and squeezed. "Thank you, Cissy."

She wriggled. "You're welcome, but let go. People are gawkin'."

Pansy giggled and released her hold. "Sorry."

Cissy smiled at her friend. "It's all right. Nice to know somebody'll miss me."

More tears spilled past Pansy's freckles. "Oh, I will, Cissy. I'll miss you 'til my dyin' day. Won't nobody ever be as special to me as you are."

For a moment Cissy considered changing her mind and staying put. She hated to break Pansy's heart.

"Maybe we should exchange keepsakes. Just so we remember each other."

Cissy frowned. "Whaddya mean?"

"Well . . ." Pansy tapped her chin. "My mama hides a little paper box in her underwear drawer. Inside it she's got a lock of hair tied with a ribbon that came from her first beau. She said she gave him a lock of her hair, too, and they swore to keep it forever so they'd never forget each other."

Cissy couldn't imagine timid Mrs. Blair ever having a beau besides Mr. Blair. "Your daddy don't mind that she keeps it?"

Pansy hunched her shoulders. She glanced quickly right and left and then whispered, "He don't know it's there."

Cissy drew back.

Pansy nodded, her expression knowing. "I ain't never told a soul. It's a secret between you an' me, all right?"

Seemed like lots of people had secrets. And keeping Pansy's secret was a good way to make sure Pansy kept her secret. "I won't tell nobody."

"If you're gonna go away, we should exchange something. Something that'll remind us of our friendship an' how special we are to each other."

"I don't wanna cut off any of my hair, Pansy."

Pansy laughed and smoothed her hand over her wavy blond locks. "Neither do I."

The teacher stepped out on the platform and pulled the rope for the bell. The girls picked up their lunch tins, looped arms, and ambled toward the schoolhouse.

"I'm gonna think on it," Pansy said, "an' you think, too." She squeezed Cissy's arm against her ribs. "Don't you go until we've exchanged our keepsakes, all right?"

Cissy couldn't go until she'd sneaked some money from the tin in the cupboard, and that could take a while. "All right."

# TEN

*Rebekah*

Rebekah held the torch high and to the right, away from her head and away from any of the tourists who moved in a throng in front of her, their gazes roving the rock walls. Analgesic powders dispensed by the estate physician—how nice to have a doctor at her beck and call—had eased the pain in her head and back, but her shoulder ached from the weight of the folded wad of flaming birch bark tied around the pine pitch. She traded arms and angled the ball of fire to the left.

From back here she couldn't see Tolly, but his voice echoed against the tight walls and low ceiling. "See them ripples on the wall there? They's as smooth an' shiny as silk, don'tcha think? Years an' years of watuh runnin' down the rock an' leavin' minerals behind is what done it. Yessuh, the good Lawd don't leave no bit o' His creation, not even the parts clear down deep in the earth, untouched by beauty."

She listened close. If his words dropped so low she couldn't hear him, she knew to hurry the visitors. After a month of following the same course two times a day, she could guide people out without his help, if need be, but she didn't want to lose Tolly. He hadn't needed to warn her about going into the cave alone.

Remembering how Andy went in by himself and got carried out, draped over Tolly's arms, was enough to make her stay close at all times. She wouldn't put Mama and Daddy through the heartache of another Hardin child lost in the cave.

Somewhere in the middle of the group, Devlin Bale was also listening. She hadn't expected to see him on the Friday afternoon tour since he'd only just arrived, but apparently he was eager to see the cave. Was he as fascinated by the winding tunnels, the mineral formations, the odd sightless creatures as she had been the first time Tolly brought her into the tunnels? She hoped so. She didn't know why she wanted him to appreciate and marvel at the cave's majesty, but she wanted him to see it the way she did so badly it created an ache in the center of her chest as real as the ache in her shoulder.

She squinted against the glaring torch and watched the guests' bobbing heads. If somebody fell behind or started to wander off, she needed to be ready. She longed to examine the cave walls where people from years past—maybe even Andy—had left marks behind, but duty beckoned. When she, Tolly, and the college student who intended to draft a new map of the caves came in on their own, she'd be able to explore more deeply. For now, she needed to pay attention to the guests.

The group rounded the bend leading to Gothic Avenue, and Rebekah quickly switched hands.

Tolly's throaty commentary drifted from up ahead. "Any of y'all thinkin' o' gettin' hitched? How 'bout you two ovuh there? You look to be a likely pair." Laughter rolled through the group, and Rebekah couldn't help smiling. Tolly gave the same spiel every time, and she could imagine him pointing out a fellow and gal from the crowd to tease.

The tourists formed a loose half circle around the trio of dripstone columns that the cave owners had dubbed the Bridal Altar. Rebekah positioned herself at the center in the rear and peeked between shoulders to Tolly, who stood in front of the columns, his white beard and white teeth shining in the light from his lantern.

"Not today, huh? Well, when you're ready, this is a right purty spot to say yo' nuptials. Betcha none o' yo' friends can say they married up a hunnert an' fifty feet unduh the ground, now can they?"

While Tolly explained how the columns formed when stalactites and stalagmites met in the middle—"Kinda like a bride an' groom comin' togethuh as one"—Rebekah skimmed her gaze back and forth across the crowd. A movement caught her eye. Someone was separating himself from the group. She automatically took a step in the direction of the person. The torch's glow fell over Devlin Bale. Her pulse leaped when his gaze met hers, and a smile curved his lips.

He eased his way to her side and leaned in. "The torch is quivering, Miss Hardin." His whisper teased her ear as his warm breath touched her cheek. "Would you like me to hold it for a while?"

If he'd melt into the crowd, her hands would stop quivering. So would her middle. She shook her head and changed hands. "It's my job."

"I know, but I'm willing to help. I imagine it seems especially heavy after the fall you took this morning."

He was right, but she wouldn't hand off that torch, no matter how much her shoulders complained. She couldn't give Tolly a reason to think she wasn't strong enough to be an assistant. She needed the money from this job.

"I'm fine."

He gave a nod and then turned his attention to the front of the group, where Tolly lifted his hand in invitation. "All right, folks, we's headin' to Giant's Coffin now. But don't none o' y'all ask me ta lift the lid an' letcha peek inside. I got no hankerin' to disturb a sleepin' giant, no sirree, an' if you got such a inklin', well, I'd say you're more'n a little tetched." Laughter blasted as the crowd surged forward.

Devlin stayed at the back of group, just ahead of Rebekah, and she spent the remainder of the tour forcing herself to pay attention to the group as a whole rather than focusing on the delightful curls touching the collar of his suit or the fine expanse of his shoulders.

When the tour came to an end and everyone followed the passage out of the cave, Rebekah blinked rapidly against the sunlight filtering through the trees. Birdsong seemed extra loud after the cave's silence. Even after a full month of coming from the dark underground into the light, the change took her by surprise. She plunged the flickering torch into a bucket of water at the mouth of the cave and trailed the jabbering tourists to the transport wagon that was hitched to a rail at the edge of the forest.

The warm, humid air made perspiration break out over her form. She wished she could take off her jacket and gloves, but Tolly always left his on, and she was inclined to follow his example. Devlin, however, shrugged out of his jacket and draped it over his arm. Some of the tourists moved slowly, their shoulders slumped, proving the two-hour trek over uneven pathways had taxed them. But Devlin moved alongside her in an effortless gait. When Tolly had told her they'd be escorting a college student, she expected someone lazy and even out of shape from sitting at a desk. It pleased her to have been wrong.

At the wagon Rebekah lowered the hatch and set out the little stool for people to climb in more easily. She gave women her hand and allowed men to push off from her shoulder. Devlin stepped up last, but instead of climbing aboard he rounded the wagon and stopped next to the high seat where Tolly sat, reins in hand.

"Is it all right if I walk back?"

Tolly scratched his chin. "Makes no nevuhmind to me, but it's a fair stretch. 'Specially aftuh walkin' so long inside the cave. You sure you don't wanna ride?"

"I'm sure." Devlin reached up to Tolly, and the pair shook hands. "I'll see you Monday morning, Tolly." He strode off into the trees.

Rebekah stared after him, uneasiness tiptoeing up her spine.

Tolly angled a grin at her. "Reb? You comin'?"

Her face flaming, Rebekah hooked the hatch into place and trotted to the front. She settled herself next to Tolly. "Are you sure he should walk back to the hotel? Especially through the woods?"

He flicked the reins. "Why you worryin'?"

She hugged herself, a chill creeping across her flesh despite the mugginess. "He's from the city. He won't know what to do if he encounters a bear."

Tolly chuckled. "Oh, now, Reb, he be a college boy. I figure a college boy's gotta have enough sense to stay away from bears." He gave her a little nudge with his elbow, a teasing bump, and then began a back-and-forth exchange with the guests, leaving her to stew in silence the rest of the way to the hotel.

Rebekah stayed beside the wagon until all the guests departed. Then she turned to go to her cabin. Her head was starting to hurt again, and she wanted to lie down.

"Reb, you hold up there."

She paused.

Tolly strode to her side, lifted her hand, and pressed several coins into her palm. "I ain't gonna argue wit' you no more 'bout these tips. What you do is impo'tant, keepin' ever'body togethuh, an' this's my way o' sayin' thanks fo' doin' a good job fo' me." He curled her fingers around the cool disks. "So you put this in yo' pocket an' give it to yo' daddy. Or buy yo'self somethin'. Mebbe a Sunday-go-to-meetin' hat. One that's got flowuhs on it. Make yo'self up purty."

Heat stirred in her chest and climbed upward.

"Gonna be a while befo' we start gettin' tips again, what with us spendin' all our time with that cartographuh. So enjoy this money, y'hear?" He gazed at her as sternly as Daddy ever had.

With a headache stealing her gumption, she didn't have the energy to argue. Rebekah slipped her hand free of his grasp and pushed it into her pocket, her fist still balled around the coins. "All right. Thank you."

"You's welcome. Now, I's wantin' you to take tomorruh off an' jus' rest up, give yo' head a chance to lose its achin'. Gonna be out early come Monday an' ever' day thereaftuh 'til them maps get drawed." Whistling, he took off toward the main building.

Rebekah passed through the narrow gap between the row of guest cottages and the observation building, then headed north across the open grassy area where guests often played badminton, croquet, or a strange game called lacrosse. Only the roofs of the staff cabins showed, the buildings nestled side by side behind a knoll. She crested the rise and released a sigh. Downhill from there. She was eager to take that rest Tolly had advised.

Halfway down the hill she realized someone was sitting on the little stoop outside her front door. She slowed for a moment, squinting until she recognized Cissy. Then she broke into a smile and trotted the remaining distance, ignoring the persistent pounding in the back of her head. Cissy stood, swinging the basket Rebekah had always used to carry mushrooms.

Rebekah grabbed her sister in a hug. "Hi!"

Cissy pulled back and looked Rebekah up and down. "Why're you dressed that way? You look awful. An' you smell like you've been rolling in mold."

Rebekah stifled a snort. "Well, I think you look and smell just fine." She glanced at the basket. "Have you been gathering mushrooms?"

"Mama said I had to. Said the cook depended on 'em." She pulled a few coins from her apron pocket and frowned at them. "Seems like a lot of work, pickin' 'em, cleanin' 'em, an' cartin' 'em over here, for no more'n what he pays."

Rebekah peeked into Cissy's hand. A quarter, a dime, and a nickel glinted in the sun. "Let's make it look like more then." She fished the money Tolly had given her from her pocket and added it to the coins in Cissy's hand.

Her sister quickly counted the coins, and her eyes widened. "A dollar an' fifteen cents? Where'd you get so much?"

Rebekah hadn't realized the amount. Tolly must be half-rich from tips. She stared longingly at the quarters and dimes. She could've picked out a new shirt and gloves at the company store and had a few cents to spare. But she wouldn't take it back. "It's my tip money for taking people through the cave."

Cissy continued to gawk at the money. "I wish I could take people on tours."

Rebekah laughed. "You'd have to dress like a man, and you'd come out smelling like you rolled in mold. I don't think you'd like it much."

Cissy wrinkled her nose. She dropped the coins in her apron pocket. The fabric sagged from the weight. "Maybe not. But I'd sure like takin' in that money."

The gleam in Cissy's eyes troubled Rebekah. She took her sister's hand and squeezed it. "There's more important things in life than money, Cissy. You can't buy love, and you can't buy happiness." Their family never had money in the bank, but she wouldn't trade Mama, Daddy, and her sisters for any amount of money.

Cissy shrugged and stepped away. She hung the basket over her wrist and blew out a breath. "Guess now that I've seen you I'll head on back. There's always chores waitin'. Mama said to ask if you was comin' for Sunday dinner."

"Yes. I'm coming for service, too, so save me a seat, all right?"

Her sister rolled her eyes. "Like the chapel's so full you hafta worry about not gettin' a seat."

Rebekah forced a smile. "I meant by you, Cissy." Loneliness spiraled through her, and she dared to open a bit of herself to her sister, hoping she might soften. "I miss seeing you every day, even miss your cold feet on the other side of my bed at night. I'm grateful for the job and for my own little place to live, but it sure is quiet here. I'll be glad when the tourist time is over and I can come home again."

Cissy stared at Rebekah as if she'd sprouted chin whiskers. "You're plumb crazy. You got your own cabin, no pesky little sisters yankin' at you, no daddy barkin' orders or mama tellin' you to hurry up an' get to your chores. You're makin' all this money. Why would you wanna come back?"

Now Rebekah gawked at Cissy. She'd long sensed a restiveness in her sister, but the cynicism and resentment stole her ability to speak.

Cissy released a huff and tossed her head, making her thick, straight reddish-brown braids bounce against her bodice. "I gotta get home. Bye, Bek. I'll tell Mama to set a plate for you at the table Sunday."

Rebekah sank down on the stoop and watched until Cissy disappeared into the trees. *Why would you wanna come back?* The question taunted her. She'd sent Andy away and lost him forever. Now she'd gone away and it seemed Cissy was trying to lose herself. Rebekah's chin quivered and a half prayer, half accusation slipped from her lips.

"God, I'm supposed to be helping my family. Why does it seem like I'm hurting them instead?"

# ELEVEN

*Cissy*

She carried a whole dollar and fifty-five cents in her pocket. The wonder of it made her giddy. Each time she took a step, the weight of the coins pressed her thigh and sent a thrill clear up to her scalp. If only that money was all hers. Why, there was likely enough to buy a ticket that would take her from Cave City all the way to Louisville.

She'd never been to Louisville, but the teacher said it was a big city — big enough for factories and dress shops and all the other things Cissy wanted to explore. If she could get to Louisville, she'd find herself a job. Maybe in a sweets shop. She'd like sampling all the candies and other goodies. If itty-bitty Good Spring had a sweets shop, she'd be tempted to visit it right then and there and buy something really special just to find out how it felt.

She had to see the money again before Daddy took it away from her. Just off the trail, a little stream with several large rocks at its edge beckoned her to have a seat. She perched on the largest, flattest rock and withdrew the coins one by one. She laid them on the rock's smooth surface. Fingers of sunlight sneaked through the trees and danced on the glittering coins. A laugh built in her throat, and she let it out. She felt as rich as a queen sitting there with the coins spread out beside her.

"Maybe I should leave right now." She touched each quarter, dime, and nickel by turn, her thoughts rolling. "Betcha I could hitch a ride to a train station and ride the Cumberland all the way to Louisville. Or even Nashville, Tennessee." Pansy'd ridden the Cumberland to Nashville once to visit her mama's aunt, and she bragged about it for months. Cissy'd like the chance to brag about riding the Cumberland.

Her body twitched with eagerness to catch that train, and she started to jump up and go. But as she opened her apron pocket, she realized what she was wearing. She couldn't board a train in this faded dress and patched apron. People would turn up their noses. Besides, she and Pansy hadn't exchanged their keepsakes yet. Did she want Pansy, the only person who really cared about her, to forget her? No, she couldn't go yet. She settled back on the rock with a sigh.

While a breeze brushed her cheeks and the creek sang its merry song, Cissy closed her eyes and drifted away in a daydream. When she took the train to Louisville, she'd hire on to work in a sweets shop where the air smelled like taffy and fudge and gingerbread. She'd use her first wages to buy herself the prettiest dress in town. Then she'd wear it to work. When handsome boys brought in their girls, and when the girls weren't looking, she would flutter her eyelashes at the boys and tantalize them away from their girls. She'd flirt only with the ones who had lots of coins to spend. Before long one of them would fall in love with her, and he'd take her to his fine house, and she'd live there forever just as happy as a lark.

"Hello, miss."

She jerked. Two coins slid off into the thick moss and feather-like ferns growing along the base of the rocks. With a gasp of alarm she knelt and began pushing aside the ferns. A shadow fell over the spot where she was searching, and she looked up with a scowl. "Hey! Why don'tcha—"

The most handsome, best-dressed fellow she'd ever seen stopped next to the rock and gazed down at her. Cissy gulped and forgot what she planned to say.

He bent down on one knee beside her. The same way heroes in the magazine serials did when they offered their intended a ring. She sucked in a breath and held it, not sure if he was real or she was still caught up in dreaming.

"I'm sorry I frightened you."

His voice was real. She liked the sound of it, and even more the way he looked at her—really looked at her, with eyes so deep blue she never wanted to turn away. "I-it's all right. No harm done." The lost coins didn't even matter anymore.

He slipped off his hat and placed it on his knee, still looking her straight in the eyes. "Were you asleep?"

She might never sleep again. How could any dream, no matter how wonderful, compare to having a handsome stranger in a three-piece suit, a little dimple winking in his cheek and hair the color of sand curling up over his ears, fix his blue-blue eyes on her?

"How much did you lose?"

She blinked twice. "Huh?"

He finally shifted his gaze from her, tipping his head toward the coins. "Your money. You had it all counted, didn't you?"

Fire attacked her cheeks. The money! She hunched over the rock and began plucking up the coins. Her fingers shook, and a ten-cent piece slid into the ferns. "Oh!"

"Here now." The gentleman took hold of her elbow and gave a little tug.

She jerked free and tried to wriggle between him and the rock. "Leave that be."

He stopped with his hand halfway to the rock. "Let me help you."

"You sure you ain't gonna help yourself to my money?" It wasn't really her money, but he didn't have to know that.

His forehead pinched like she'd hauled off and kicked him in the shin. "Of course not. But the way you're trembling, you could lose even more. See what's left, and let's determine how much has been lost."

She stared at him for a few seconds, uncertainty holding her captive. But those blue eyes of his won her over. No man with such pretty eyes could be dishonest. "All right." Aware of him watching, she lifted the coins one at a time and kept a careful count, determined not to make a mistake. "Twenty-five, fifty, sixty, seventy, seventy-five, eighty-five, ninety-five, a dollar, dollar twenty-five, dollar thirty-five."

"You're very good at ciphering."

Warmth flowed through her. She ducked her head and giggled. "Thank you."

"How much did you have to start with?"

Cissy chewed her lip. "A dollar fifty-five." That meant she'd dropped a dime and two nickels. Daddy'd likely take that amount out of her hide when she admitted what she'd done. And she'd have to admit it because Bek would be there on Sunday, and sure as Mama made jelly out of crab apples every fall, Bek would brag about her tip money. Cissy blinked back tears.

"Well, here." The man stood and pushed his suit coat aside to reach into his trouser pocket. He offered her a silver quarter.

She gaped up at him. "Y-you're just gonna gimme that?"

"If I hadn't startled you, those coins would still be on the rock."

"But . . . but . . ." She couldn't imagine having so much money a person could just give it away without a thought. He must be rich.

"Since the loss of the coins is my fault, allow me to replace them." He cupped her hand and slid the coin, warm from being in his pocket, onto her palm. "There. Now all is well."

Cissy stared at her fist, her mind racing. She'd lost only twenty cents, but he'd given her twenty-five. That meant she could keep five cents of the mushroom money, and nobody would ever know. Maybe she could come back here tomorrow and find the dime and nickels, and then she'd have a whole twenty-five cents that was all her own.

Warm fingers caught the underside of her chin and lifted her face. She looked up at his smile, and her heart started such a *thump-thump* she feared she would faint dead away.

"Have I restored your happiness, little one?"

Could a person melt from a tender gaze? Slowly Cissy nodded, her breath caught in her throat.

"Good." His fingers slipped away and he moved toward the path. "I'll leave you to your musings. Enjoy the rest of your day."

Her breath whooshed out. She dug in her pocket for a nickel and slipped it into her shoe. Then she grabbed up the basket, and with her apron pinched tightly in her fist so no coins would bounce out, she raced for home.

## Devlin

Pattering footsteps enticed Devlin to peek over his shoulder. The girl who'd
been absorbed in dreamland beside the creek raced up the pathway as fleet as a
deer. He smiled. Wasn't she a cute little thing? He recalled her big searching
eyes and winsome expression. Never having had younger siblings, he enjoyed
playing big brother now and then. His brief encounter with the hills girl re-
freshed him more than a drink from a cold mountain stream.

He made his way toward the hotel, comparing the two encounters he'd
had with young ladies that day. Rebekah Hardin had demanded his help when
she'd fallen, and the little hills girl had demanded him to leave her alone. When
offered money Miss Hardin refused, but the girl beside the stream, once she
recovered from her shock, eagerly pocketed his coin. He believed if he'd held
out a dollar coin, she would have taken it. An interesting contrast.

Not that it mattered. Girls, to his way of thinking, were confusing creatures, innately tuned to wreak havoc on the hearts of men. Mother continually
tried to push the daughters of associates and friends at him, but he hadn't suc-
cumbed to a female's charm yet. And he wondered if he ever would.

He snagged an unfurling leaf from a sumac and twirled it between his
fingers as he continued along the winding pathway. If he pursued cartography
as he intended, he would spend a great deal of time traveling. A wife might
enjoy accompanying him for a while. Until children began to arrive. Then
she'd want to nest. And she'd want him in the nest with her.

Father had given up his wandering ways when Mother entered her confine-
ment with Devlin. Then, after he was born, Father began teaching at a private
boys' school and eventually at the college. Sometimes, when a train whistle cut
through the air, Devlin caught his father gazing out the window with a faraway
look in his eyes, and he experienced a twinge of guilt for having been responsible for nailing Horatio Bale's feet to the floor.

But if Father secured the position as senator, he'd travel again. Now that
Devlin was grown and capable of caring for himself, Mother could go with
him. A whole new chapter in their lives waited to be written, and this massive
cave and its lovely surrounding area would provide the paper and ink.

He stepped from the woods onto the grassy stretch behind the hotel. Dusk was near, the sky changing to pale yellow with smudges of pink. Devlin ambled past a pair of teenage boys who tossed a ball back and forth and a circle of little girls playing ring-around-the-rosey. On the observation deck, several couples watched the sunset or the children at play. The men curled their arms around the women's waists or the women held the men's elbows. Each pose spoke of companionship, possessiveness, and affection. Oddly, jealousy pinched.

He shifted his attention to the boardwalk and followed it to the dining room, determined to set aside the peculiar emotion. But it swept over him again when he entered the room and discovered more couples and families sitting at the linen-draped tables.

The host approached Devlin with a smile. "Are you ready for dinner, sir?"

For reasons he didn't understand, his appetite had fled, but he knew he should eat. By morning he'd be ravenous. He nodded.

"Follow me." He led Devlin to a table in the corner and gave him a paper menu. "The waiter will be with you soon. May I bring you something to drink? A bottle of wine or a pot of tea?"

"Tea, please."

The man scurried off. Devlin tried to read the menu—it contained some marvelous choices—but loneliness pressed on him, inviting him to examine those who sat in pairs or groups.

The waiter set a steaming pot and a cup and saucer on the table. "Have you made a selection, sir?"

Devlin laid the menu aside. "What do you recommend?"

"The pork loin with cherry sauce and steamed greens seasoned with onion, mushrooms, and slivered almonds has been very popular this evening."

Even though he'd never been particularly fond of pork, he said, "That sounds fine."

The waiter picked up the menu and turned to leave.

"By the way . . ."

The waiter turned back.

"If you need to seat someone else with me, please feel free to do so."

The man smiled and flipped his hand. "That won't be necessary, sir. The early diners have come and gone. We're rarely crowded at this time of night."

The reply disappointed him. He didn't look forward to an entire summer of dining alone. "Well, just in case, I'm willing to share."

The waiter smiled again and then hurried off.

Devlin poured tea into his cup and lifted the aromatic liquid to his mouth. He sipped, letting his gaze rove across the room. He hadn't expected to see so many children at the cave already. School was still in session. But he supposed families had come for a weekend outing, something to entertain the youngsters now that spring and pleasant weather had arrived. The weekdays would probably be less busy, which hopefully meant more time in the cave. He didn't mind taking the summer to complete his drawings, but he wouldn't complain if he finished early and ended up with a few free weeks to engage in his own activities before his final year of college began.

A family with six children, two older boys and four girls ranging in age from perhaps five or six years to eleven or twelve, entered the dining room. The host escorted them to a long table, which accommodated six diners, and began transferring chairs from another table. The husband scowled, shaking his head. He spoke to the host in hushed tones, but Devlin didn't need to hear to know the man was complaining about being forced to scrunch together.

The waiter hurried over and whispered something in the host's ear, gesturing toward Devlin. The host held his finger to the unhappy gentleman and then marched across the room to Devlin.

"Sir, Harry said you were willing to share your table. Is this correct?"

"Yes." At that moment the youngest girl of the family began stomping her feet and pounding the air with her fists. Devlin hoped the host wouldn't ask to put her with him.

"Both of our longest tables are in use, and none of the tables available comfortably accommodate eight chairs. May I have the McGowen boys join you?"

Devlin sent a quick look at the family. The two boys stood beside the table and angled their gazes away from the little tantrum thrower. Devlin sensed their embarrassment from the distance of twenty paces. "Of course."

"Thank you very much, sir." The host bustled off again.

Moments later Harry escorted two dark-haired youths to Devlin's table. "Mr. Bale, please meet Thaddeus and Trevor McGowen. Thaddeus and Trevor, this is Devlin Bale, who is here as part of his senior project at the University of Kentucky." The pair nodded politely. The waiter turned to Devlin again. "Thaddeus will be a student at the university next year, and Trevor hopes to follow in three years when he's finished his rudimentary studies."

Devlin held out his hand, and both boys gave him a firm shake before seating themselves, Thaddeus at Devlin's left elbow and Trevor across the table. Harry promised to bring each of the boys water and then darted back to their parents' table.

Thaddeus grinned. "Do you feel like an open book?"

Devlin raised one eyebrow, uncertain.

He jabbed his thumb toward the waiter. "Harry knows everything. I think he listens at all the tables and saves the information so he can gossip with the other guests."

Devlin laughed. Harry had been able to provide more than names as an introduction. "Maybe we should guard our conversation then, hmm?"

Both boys grinned.

Devlin took a sip of his tea. "Is this your first time at Mammoth Cave?"

Trevor snorted. "Our father has brought us here the third weekend of May since 1895. It's a family tradition."

Devlin hid a smile. Trevor's pimply face and overgrown knuckles gave mute testimony to his age. Ah, the gawky teenage years. Devlin remembered them well. "What's wrong with traditions?"

"Nothing when they don't mean sharing a cottage with your bratty little sisters."

Thaddeus bumped his brother on the arm. "It's not that bad. During the day we do what we want to, away from Father and Mother and the girls. And it's only one weekend a year."

Trevor huffed. "And you're leaving home next fall, so you'll never have to do this again. Next year I'll be stuck here alone with Daisy, Penelope, Lulu, and—"

A piercing screech rent the air.

Mr. McGowen plucked the youngest girl from her chair and scurried out of the dining room with her bucking in his arms.

"Sadie," the two chorused.

Trevor propped his chin in his cupped hands. "A fate worse than death."

Thaddeus and Devlin both laughed.

Devlin asked, "What parts of the cave have you explored?"

The three of them spent a lively hour visiting. Despite the years separating them in age, Devlin enjoyed talking with Thaddeus and Trevor, and before they parted, he promised to meet with them Sunday afternoon and show them his waywiser and other cartography equipment. He left the dining room with a lighter step than he'd used going in, bolstered by the time of conversation. But when he rounded the corner toward the cottages and encountered a young couple sauntering along the boardwalk hand in hand, their moon-eyed gazes pinned on each other's faces, the jealousy he'd experienced earlier returned in a rush.

He sidestepped around them and closed himself in his cabin, away from any other couples, away from families, away from nosy staff members. If his attitude didn't improve tremendously in the next few days, it would be a very long, lonely summer.

Without invitation an image of Rebekah Hardin flashed in his memory. Hadn't Tolly said they'd spend hours of each day in the cave? Rebekah, as the guide's assistant, would be there, too. He smiled. Maybe not so lonely after all.

# TWELVE

## Rebekah

After donning men's baggy britches and shirts for six days in a row, wearing a full-skirted, snug-bodiced dress seemed foreign. But Mama would have fallen over in a dead faint if Rebekah entered the Good Spring Chapel attired in anything but a dress, so she tugged at the rounded neckline to give her throat a little space. She'd be in her comfortable clothes again tomorrow.

"So remember, good brothers an' sisters in the Lawd," the preacher thundered from his spot behind the tall pulpit, "we must avoid engagin' in drunkenness."

How could they forget? He'd already told them three times before this reminder. Beside her on the oak bench, Cissy fidgeted. Rebekah battled the urge to wriggle, too. Preacher Haynes tended to repeat his points—Daddy called it "beating a dead horse"—until it took great effort not to yawn or start woolgathering.

She glanced to the far end of the bench where Daddy sat next to Mama. She caught him peeking at his old, faithful timepiece. She hid a smile. Daddy was ready for the service to end, too. He caught her looking, and he gave her a weary look that made her want to giggle. But nobody giggled in church. Except for the littlest kids, and they were promptly shushed or hauled to the outhouse for correction. She wouldn't set a bad example. She turned to the front and managed to at least give the pretense of attention until the closing hymn.

They mingled in the churchyard for a few minutes, catching up with friends and neighbors, and then Mama grabbed Daddy's arm. "Let's head for home, Festus. These children need fed."

"Yes, Nell." Daddy scooped up Little Nellie and settled her on his hip, then turned a smile on the other girls. "You heard your mama. Let's go."

They moved in a swarm out of the churchyard and onto the winding road. Sunshine and shadows painted the dirt road with splashes of yellow and gray. Daddy, with Little Nellie toying with his ear and Mama at his side, walked down the middle of the road, his strides wide and sure. Trudy and Tabitha darted back and forth in front of Mama and Daddy, hopping from sunspot to sunspot. Their giggles competed with Della's and Jessie's endless chatter. The pair gently swung their hands between them as they moseyed behind their parents.

Rebekah automatically fell to the back of the group. When she realized what she was doing, she chuckled. For years she'd led her sisters, but after one month of going last, it now seemed the natural thing to do. Her dress felt unnatural. Being in the lead seemed wrong. How could such a short time make so many changes?

Cissy scuffed along just ahead of Rebekah, stirring dust with her toes as she went. With everyone else in pairs, she seemed lonely, and Rebekah's sympathy rose.

She trotted up beside her, then slung her arm across her sister's shoulders. "Would you like to pick mushrooms this afternoon? I could take them to the cook for you when I go back to the estate."

Cissy scowled. "You think I can't do it good enough?"

"Of course not."

"Then why're you tryin' to do it for me?"

Sharp words formed on Rebekah's tongue, but she held them back. She wouldn't engage in an argument with Cissy. Not when they would have only a short time together. And especially not on Sunday. Sunday should be a day of peace and rest.

"I thought maybe you wouldn't want to come all the way to the estate. It's a long walk."

"Not that long. Besides, it gets me away from home an' Mama fussin' at me an' the little girls pullin' at me for a little while. It's the one chore your leavin' got pushed on me that I actually like."

Cissy's retort pierced Rebekah, but she forced a smile and gave her sister's shoulders a little squeeze. "Then you keep doing it. And when you bring the mushrooms to Mr. Cooper, stop by my cabin and say hello. It'll help me not feel so alone."

Cissy sighed and shrugged away Rebekah's arm. "Don't know how you can be alone with all those people stayin' at the hotel. You get to have all the fun." She darted past the others and jogged around the bend leading to their lane.

The smell of roasted meat drifted all the way from the house to the road. Rebekah's mouth watered, and she hurried her steps to join Mama and Daddy.

"What're you cooking, Mama?"

"Your daddy bought a leg of lamb from the Ritters."

They purchased such delicacies only for birthdays and holidays. Had she forgotten a special occasion?

While she pressed her memory, Daddy set Little Nellie on the ground. Swinging the little girl's hand, he grinned at Rebekah. "Your mama's quite the temptress. She brought the fire down to coals an' put that leg in the roastin' pan last night. I almost went out an' had me a snack at midnight, it smelled so good."

"The last of our taters an' carrots from last year's garden are in the roaster, too." Mama looked happier than Rebekah could remember in ages. "We'll have us a fine Sunday dinner today thanks to you."

Rebekah touched her bodice and raised her eyebrows. "Me?"

Mama stopped at the base of the steps. "We couldn't have bought the leg o' lamb without that money you sent with Cissy." She waved her hands at the girls, who chased each other around in the yard. "C'mon now, you gals, an' get in here. That lamb's been slow-roastin' all night. Much longer an' it'll be tough as boot leather. Cost a whole fifty cents. We don't wanna waste it."

Laughing and jostling, the girls clambered into the house. Daddy followed them, calling directions to wash up and settle down.

Mama looped arms with Rebekah and took the steps slowly. "Probably won't be nothin' like the fine meals you've been eatin' at the estate all week, but I hope it'll please you."

They needed to get inside and put dinner on the table, but Rebekah pulled her mother into an embrace. "Mama, no matter what you fix, it always pleases me. I'm glad the extra money pleases you. I know you weren't sure about me taking a job at the cave."

Mama sniffed and pulled away. "Always hard for a mother to say good-bye to her children. But it's the way of things, children growin' up an' movin' on. Pretty soon it'll be Cissy." She opened her mouth as if she planned to say something more, but then she turned away and hurried inside.

Rebekah followed. The table was already set, the girls and Daddy in their places.

Little Nellie looked up and patted the empty spot next to her on the bench. "Sit by me, Bek."

"Lemme help Mama first."

"No, no." Mama shooed her to the bench. "Today you're a guest. Cissy'n Della'll help me. C'mon, gals, get up from there an' make yourselves useful."

Even though the lamb, potatoes, and carrots were delicious, Rebekah fought tears the entire meal. She'd stayed so busy she didn't realize how much she missed her family until she was with them again. Regret also nibbled at her. She'd been stubborn about not taking those tips from Tolly, but thinking about how much money she'd turned away and the things Mama and Daddy could have bought filled her with self-recrimination. She'd do better about considering her family's needs first from now on.

When they finished eating, Trudy dragged Little Nellie to their bedroom for naps. Tabitha and Jessie cleared the table, and Della and Cissy washed the dishes. Mama settled in her rocking chair with the Bible draped across her lap and read aloud while the girls worked. Rebekah wandered around the room, guilty for not helping but grateful the younger girls were capable of handling the chores. She didn't have to worry about Mama being left short handed with her working away from home.

Daddy emerged from his and Mama's bedroom in his everyday overalls. He quirked his finger at Rebekah. "Come with me, gal. Got somethin' to show you."

She trailed him out the back door and into the yard. "What is it, Daddy?"

"Just wait an' see."

He led her along the path through the woods. Already the barberries were filling in along the edges of the leaf-strewn pathway. She pointed out a thick cluster of yellow trout lilies blooming beneath the pines. Since they'd eaten the last of their potatoes at noon, Daddy could dig up the roots. When boiled and mashed, they made a fine substitute for potatoes, and Mama served them up regularly while they waited for the garden to sprout. But Daddy picked only a handful of the bell-shaped flowers, gave them to Rebekah, and continued on, apparently not thinking about their stomachs.

All at once Rebekah knew where he was taking her. She added a dozen stems of larkspur to her bouquet as she and Daddy continued onward to the family burial plot.

For a moment Daddy stood at the edge of the simple fence built of sticks and string, hands in his pockets, face solemn. Then he took the flowers from her and stepped over the fence. He knelt at his mama's grave and laid a few of the flowers next to her wooden cross. "Been stoppin' for a bit every day on my way back from the field, clearin' out the dead leaves an' pullin' up the wild grasses." He shifted and put a single larkspur stem on each of the other graves except Andy's. "Things get a mite disheveled when somebody don't come around. I wanted it all cleaned up an' pretty before I brought Andy's headstone out here."

Rebekah lifted her skirt and joined Daddy inside the enclosure. She crouched and swept a few dead leaves away from the row of little crosses where the babies who never drew a breath lay covered with sod. "It looks fine, Daddy."

He smiled briefly, arranging the remaining flowers in a fan at the base of Andy's cross. "When Cissy came home with that money the other day, it got me to thinkin' about something. I wanted to hear your thoughts on it, too."

Her heart started to pound. Daddy wanted her advice? He was the one who told her what to do. Did he think her time at the estate had made her wiser? Being asked to share her thoughts made her feel both grown up and scared at the same time. "About what?"

"About doin' more than putting a headstone on Andy's grave." Daddy's expression turned serious. He sat on his bottom, drew up his knees, and circled his legs with his arms. He looked young and uncertain, and Rebekah came close to putting her hand on his knee to assure him. "I've always wanted an iron fence around this plot. One with a gate that can latch, like a real cemetery."

He glanced across the crosses. A sigh heaved from his chest. "Your mama wants a headstone for Andy, an' that'll be the first thing I get when the money's all saved up, but wouldn't it be nice if each o' these graves had a stone marker? Already the markers for your great-granddaddy and great-grandmama 've fallen away. Can't say for sure where they lie in this plot now. So I'm thinkin' I'd like to put somethin' that'll still be here a hundred years from now so your grandchildren an' great-grandchildren can come an' see the names of their ancestors. Can know the stock they came from."

Daddy met her gaze. "I don't have much to leave to you an' your sisters. Some stories passed down from the old country, a little patch of land, and this." He gestured to the circle of graves. "But if I can put stone markers here, then my gals'll always remember the ones who come before 'em."

Rebekah blinked back tears. Daddy'd never spoken so brokenly, so openly to her. Protectiveness washed over her. He wanted her and Cissy and all the others to remember not only Granddaddy and Great-Granddaddy but him. He'd be laid out here someday, too, and he wanted it to be a nice place for him to rest. She wanted it, too.

"I think it's a fine idea, Daddy. All the money I make from the cave and the money Cissy gets from selling mushrooms can be our cemetery money, all right?"

"You sure you don't mind? You're all grown up now, Rebekah. You promised to get Andy's marker, but after that you could be settin' that money aside for yourself. Maybe to take yourself to the city an' — "

"No, Daddy." She wouldn't leave her family. She'd stolen Andy from them. She owed them. Besides that, her whole life Daddy had taken care of her. All he'd ever asked in return was for her to obey and serve the Lord. She couldn't recall one time he'd been selfish and demanded something for himself. If her earnings could give him the satisfaction of leaving something of value behind, then she'd gladly hand over every penny. She didn't need anything more than to see him happy.

"I want you to have the money. For the cemetery."

He stretched his hand toward her and squeezed her knee. "Thank you, gal." His voice turned husky, and he sniffed. "Means a lot to me."

She gripped his hand. "It'll mean a lot to me, too, to bring my children here someday, open up the gate and invite them in, and let them meet their ancestors."

Daddy smiled. He rose and pulled her up with him. "Since that's settled, let's get on to the house. Mama'll want some time with you before you go back to the estate." They stepped out of the plot and turned toward the path. Then Daddy paused, his fingers tightening on her hand.

"Don't say anything to your mama about our plans here. Just in case something happens an' we don't get to put up the headstone for Andy or all the other things. If she gets her heart set on it an' it doesn't happen, it'll only disappoint her. An' your mama's suffered enough disappointments already, comin' here with me an' not seein' her family again, losin' Andy an' our other babies. If it happens, it'll be a nice surprise, all right?"

Rebekah nodded. In her mind's eye she saw it already—the crisp black iron fence with little arrows pointing to the sky, the gray headstones with carved flowers or birds or praying hands and the names stamped deep. It would be a glorious surprise. She leaned against Daddy's bibbed-overall front and sighed. "It'll happen, Daddy. Wait and see."

# THIRTEEN

*Cissy*

As soon as the dishes were clean, dry, and back on the shelves, Cissy interrupted Mama's reading. "Can I take a trek in the woods?"

Della clasped her hands beneath her chin. "Can I go, too, Mama?"

Cissy grunted. "Not with me, you can't."

Mama aimed her frown straight at Cissy. "Now, it wouldn't hurt you any for Della to go along."

Yes, it would. She'd spent all day Saturday choring and hadn't been able to go to the rock by the creek. She wanted to search out those coins hiding in the ferns, and she didn't want Della tagging along. "I wanna go by myself."

Mama shook her head. "Gal, sometimes I wonder what mischief you're up to, always wantin' to go sneakin' off on your own."

Cissy's face blazed. She folded her arms over her chest and clamped her lips tight.

Mama set her Bible aside and rose. She crossed to Cissy and smoothed her hand over Cissy's hair. The touch was gentle, loving, and it sent Cissy's tummy twirling. "Then again, I recollect wantin' time to myself for thinkin' an' dreamin' when I was on the brink of womanhood. Hard to think o' you bein' there already, but I suppose you are."

Cissy held her breath, daring to hope.

"Go ahead."

Her breath escaped on a happy sigh.

"But watch the sun. Be back in time to help with supper."

"I will, Mama. Bye!" She darted out the door and set her course for the stream. The nickel in her shoe bit into her heel with every step, but it didn't bother her. She ran as quickly as the uneven, crooked break carved through the trees allowed, pushing aside scraggly branches and leaping over water-carved dips in the path. She arrived at the stream breathless but eager. She went directly to the flat rock, dropped to her knees in the moss, and began separating the ferns with her fingers.

After several minutes of careful searching, a tiny glint of silver rewarded her. A nickel! She pinched it up and held it to the sun, laughing with delight.

"Whatcha got?"

Cissy spun around, half expecting to find the handsome man who'd come upon her Friday afternoon. But Della stood near the path in a slash of shade, grinning.

Cissy jumped up, hiding her hand in her skirt. "What're you doin' here? Mama said I could be alone."

Della's brown eyes glimmered. "She said you could be alone, but she didn't say you had to be alone." She sauntered forward a few steps, swinging her arms against her skirt and making the rose calico fabric sway. "You found somethin'. I saw you. What'd you find?"

Cissy balled her hand tight. "Nothin' that concerns you. Go on, Della. Go . . . pick wildflowers. Or go pick your nose. I don't care. But get outta here."

Della circled around to the other side of the rock and sat, stretching out her legs and crossing her ankles. "Only Little Nellie picks her nose anymore. An' I don't feel like gatherin' wildflowers. I wanna stay with you."

"Why? To pester me?"

"No, 'cause I'm tired of always bein' with the little girls." She poked out her skinny chest. "Gonna be thirteen soon. I'm not a little girl anymore."

Cissy slid her hand into the pocket in the seam of her skirt and dropped the nickel inside. Then she sat on the opposite side of the rock and placed her feet over the spot where she'd found the coin. "You ain't gonna be thirteen 'til next October."

"Still, I don't play with rag dolls like Jessie does with the little ones. An' I'm almost as tall as you already." She gave Cissy a pleading look. "Can't I stay? I won't pester you. I promise."

Her being here was pestering enough. Cissy wanted to find those coins before the afternoon got away and they had to go home again. "Look, Della, if you're not a little girl anymore, like you say, then you ought to understand what Mama meant about needin' to be alone to think an' dream." She patted the warm rock. "This is my thinkin' an' dreamin' spot. Go find your own."

Della wrinkled her nose. "I don't wanna be all by myself."

Cissy sighed. "But I do."

Della puckered her lips and stared at Cissy for several seconds. Then she blew out a dramatic huff like the ones Cissy let out a half-dozen times a day. She bounced up. "All right, I'll go an' leave you be. But you know somethin', Cissy?" She balled her hands on her hips. "I think Mama's right about you bein' up to somethin', always wantin' everybody to stay away from you." She flounced off with her nose in the air.

Cissy sat stiff as a poker, watching the spot in the trees where Della'd slipped away, listening for rustling sounds that meant she was coming back. She watched and listened for what seemed like hours. And finally when her backside ached from sitting so tense and still, she relaxed and slipped to her knees beside the rock again.

She'd find those coins, she'd hide them in her shoe, and then she'd never come back to this rock again.

### Tolly

Tolly fastened the straps on Reb's backpack and stepped aside. Her knees buckled and she wobbled. If she went over backward and refused to get up again, he wouldn't blame her. He bent down and peeked into her face. Sweats dots were popping out all over her pale face even though the morning air was plenty cool.

He shook his head and started to remove the pack. "That's gonna be too much fo' you to tote."

"No." She grunted and leaned forward some, balancing the weight. "I'm fine."

"You ain't fine, Reb. You's almost foldin' up unduh that thing."

She shot him a stern look. "I'll earn my keep."

Tolly swallowed a laugh. Stubborn-headed girl. Or maybe she just had gumption. "All right then. That'll be yours." He plucked the pack free and hefted it into the bed of the pony cart next to the second pack loaded with extra torches, matches, and tools. The canvas pack, along with his ready coil of rope, canteens, and pickax, would make a goodly burden. But he could handle it.

He gave the pack a solid smack with his gloved palm. "We got all we need to spend the day down unduh the ground. Soon as Devlin gits here"—he squinted at the sun peeking up over the horizon—"we's goin' in."

Reb adjusted her hat. She'd stopped shoving all her hair up under the hat and let it hang down in a braid tied off with a bit of string. The thick plait of deepest brown always seemed to wind up draping across her left collarbone. She grabbed the end of the braid and flipped it over her shoulder. "Did you tell him to be ready by seven?"

"'Course I did. An' I 'spect a college fella oughta know how to tell time."

"Maybe he overslept. Do you want me to knock on his door?"

No way Tolly'd send her to a man's door. "It's just now creepin' up on seven. We can be patient a mite longer."

"Will he have a pack, too?"

"Reckon he will."

"We're already toting a lot of stuff." Reb worried her lip between her teeth and gazed at the pile of plunder. "Could we have the mule pull the cart into the cave? You tell the tour groups men used wagons in the cave during the war for independence."

Tolly propped his elbow on the edge of the cart. "True enough mules an' wagons was put to work back in the 1770s an' '80s. Even durin' the War between the States. Fact is, my pappy was one o' those who guided a wagon in an' out. So I s'pose we could do that, too, if we was keepin' to the tour passageways an' bigger sections. But Devlin, he say he wants to map the whole cave. So we's gonna be goin' through places too skinny fo' a wagon to pass." He chuckled. "Truth be, you an' me might have trouble goin' through wearin' our packs. If we hafta leave 'em behind now an' then, guess we'll do it."

"Leave them behind? Our candles and things?" Her eyes grew big.

Tolly laughed and clapped her on the shoulder. "Not our candles, Reb. I don't go nowhere without some way o' seein' what's ahead. No mattuh how small the passage, I find a way fo' my candles an' rope an' chalk an' watuh to go wit' me. Mappin' is mighty impo'tant, but bein' safe is the most impo'tant. You remember that, Reb."

"I will, Tolly."

"I'll remember it, too." Devlin moved up alongside the cart. He held a leather satchel and pushed a strange one-wheeled something or other ahead of him.

Tolly smiled at the college boy. "There you is. Reb here was worryin' you'd changed yo' mind 'bout goin' in this mo'nin'."

"No, sir. I'm ready."

Tolly took a gander at Devlin from his head to his toes. If it wasn't for the familiar face showing underneath the brim of his wide-brimmed beaver hat, he wouldn't have recognized him at all. "Hoo-ee, boy, you sure enough found yo'self some traipsin' clothes. Reckon you done bought out the comp'ny sto'."

Devlin grinned. "I only bought what you told me to, but you're right that everything on me is new."

Tolly ambled close and bent over to examine the big wheel with a round clocklike dial attached to it. "What you got there? Some kind o' newfangled velocipede?"

Reb inched close and looked at the contraption, too. Or maybe she was sneaking a peek at Devlin. If Tolly didn't miss his guess, sparks could fly between the two young people. He'd keep a close eye. Devlin seemed a nice enough fellow, but Reb was a mighty pretty girl even in her manly getup and, Tolly was certain sure, plumb ignorant when it came to handling attention from men. Over his years at the estate, he'd seen romances between guests and staff flare up and then die out just as quick. He wouldn't want Reb taken in by a city dandy who planned to stick around only long enough to complete a project.

Devlin ran his hand over the glass-covered face of the dial. "This is a way-wiser. It's used to measure distances. It will let me accurately determine the length of each passage in the cave."

Tolly scratched his cheek. "Awful fancy. An' big. Might have some trouble pushin' it through in some places."

The college boy grinned and bobbed the satchel. "Then I'll use my retractable tape measure. It can stretch up to a hundred feet, and it's no bigger around than a caterpillar."

Tolly whistled through his teeth. "They's makin' some mighty fine inventions these days."

"I also have a compass, a sextant to measure angles, and my journal and pencils."

Now he was just showing off. And he might be speaking a foreign language for all the sense he made. Tolly shook his head. "I reckon you know what you're doin'. But we've stood around yakkin' long enough. Mo'nin's gettin' away. Let's go."

He slipped his fingers under the mule's chin strap and sent a glance over his shoulder. "If you two wants to ride, climb in. Ol' Bitsy here won't mind."

Devlin held his hand to Reb. "May I assist you?"

She took hold so quick Tolly would've missed it if he'd blinked. Her cheeks bloomed as pink as the morning sky. He frowned, never looking away while Devlin handed his waywiser to Reb, laid his satchel next to the packs, and then climbed in. The little cart groaned, rocking on its pair of wooden wheels.

Tolly barked, "Sit across from Reb, not next to her." Both Reb and Devlin sent him curious looks. "It'll balance the weight."

Devlin nodded and sat on the opposite edge of the cart from Reb. The wooden box righted itself and stopped creaking.

Tolly took a firm grip on the chin strap. "Ready?"

"Ready," they said at the same time and then grinned at each other like they didn't have an ounce of sense between the two of them.

Tolly harrumphed. "C'mon, Bitsy, let's go." He clicked his tongue on the roof of his mouth. The mule jerked forward, bouncing the cart. Reb let out a little gasp, Devlin chuckled, and Reb answered it with a sheepish giggle.

Tolly shook his head. "Sit still back there. This ain't no carnival ride."

They both laughed.

He guided Bitsy up the road, sending looks over his shoulder every few seconds so they'd know they were being watched. Here he'd thought these were two were full grown, but it appeared he was spending his summer with a couple of silly youngsters. Well, he'd be on his toes. He'd keep the candles lit, make them think about the job at hand, and stay between them as much as he could. Wouldn't nobody end up hurt—in body or heart—while Tolly was in charge.

# FOURTEEN

## *Devlin*

For the second time since his arrival at the estate, Devlin followed Tolly from sunlit fresh breezes through a dirt tunnel into dark stillness. The first time, as part of a crowd of two dozen people, the jaunt had seemed a light-hearted adventure. Tame. Easy. But this time, with the waywiser rolling and the weight of his satchel pulling on his shoulder, with Tolly and Rebekah each burdened by large packs, with Tolly's solemn statement— *"Mappin' is almighty impo'tant, but bein' safe is the most impo'tant"*—ringing in his memory, the excursion had a completely different feel. One that he couldn't quite define but that left him battling uneasiness.

The opening was cavernous, wide enough for three wagons to travel side by side. Tolly's torch painted a misshapen circle on the floor. Devlin aimed his toes for the edge of the glowing circle. A ceiling stretched high above, and walls stood proud on both sides, but the torch didn't reach them, making Devlin feel as though they moved across a bridge suspended in the middle of nothingness. Dizziness gripped him.

He squinted into the shadows, determined to set aside the odd sensations tormenting his mind. On their right, pale yellow light skimmed the tops of hollowed logs lying end to end. Devlin frowned, trying to recall what Tolly had told the tour group about those logs. Something about saltpeter, if he remembered correctly.

"Tolly?" His voice echoed through the space, intrusive. He winced.

"Whatcha needin', Devlin?" Tolly didn't slow his stride. How could he move so confidently when every part of Devlin battled apprehension?

"What purpose do these logs serve?"

Tolly stopped and swung his torch toward the logs, bringing the closest one fully into view. "These here? Well, don't s'pose they serve any purpose these days othuh'n a reminduh, but they was used to bring watuh into the cave. The men minin' out the saltpetuh for bullets an' such, they needed watuh."

So he'd remembered correctly. He inched closer to the logs, careful not to change the course of the waywiser enough to distort his measurement, and squinted along the layout of logs. "How many are there?"

"Don't rightly know I've counted. But they stretch the whole length o' the cave's entry tunnel—a good quarter mile or more."

Devlin shook his head. "Amazing . . ."

"Sure is." Pride colored the black man's voice. He started forward, and Devlin and Rebekah followed. "A passel o' slaves turned them trees into a watuhway by chiselin' an' careful scorchin'. An' all by hand! Yessuh, if it wasn't for them hard-workin' slaves an' the saltpetuh they brung outta this here cave, our whole country might still be livin' unduh England's rule."

Devlin was certain he'd misunderstood. "This was built during the war with England?"

Tolly stopped again and turned to face Devlin. "Durin' the scuffle o' 1812, England shut down importin' goods, includin' powduh for makin' bullets. They figured, an' they figured rightly, they could squash us real quick if they took away our means o' fightin'. But that English king didn't figure on this nation's detuhmination. They found anothuh way to load their rifles an' stand up to the redcoats."

While he spoke, Tolly's voice turned rich, husky, filled with wonder. Mesmerized, Devlin listened as much to his tone as to his words.

"The saltpetuh comin' from deep inside this cave let our fightin' men defend theyselves an' defeat England. Yessuh, you's lookin' at history, boy."

Devlin sent his gaze up and down the pipeline. He couldn't see its length, but he could imagine it. His flesh tingled. This was the kind of information Father needed to share with the governor. A part of the nation's history didn't belong in the hands of a private owner—it belonged to the entire country. He reached for his satchel to remove his paper and pencil.

Tolly aimed the torch forward and set off. "Let's get movin'."

Rebekah fell in behind him, and Devlin stayed close. "I wish I could measure the length of the waterway."

Tolly's droll chuckle rumbled. "I wish you could, too, boy, 'cause it'd be interestin' to know. But wouldn't do much good. Not these days."

"Why not?"

"Back when folks started comin' into the cave for a paid look-around, the ones who owned the grounds tore up parts o' the pipeline an' dragged the logs to the big cavern, the one named the Rotunda. Then they burned 'em in a bonfire so's guests could take a good look at the size o' the space." The man shook his head, and even from his position behind him, Devlin sensed Tolly's remorse. "What was they thinkin', burnin' up a piece of history? Piece o' my history, seein' as how my kin was part o' them who built the pipes an' brought out the saltpetuh."

The man's voice turned melancholy, emotional. Devlin understood. Slaves, caught in bondage, helped secure their owners' freedom from English reign. The incongruity created a sense of sadness in the center of his soul.

He trotted past Rebekah and moved alongside Tolly. "It's hard to fathom that these logs are still here, intact, after more than a hundred years."

Tolly stopped and sent a wry grin at Devlin. "You's not thinkin' clear, college boy. Feel the air down here."

Devlin sucked in a slow breath and sampled the air. "It's cool. And dry."

Tolly nodded, his expression knowing. "Most anything'll stay preserved in the cave. Logs. Remains."

"Remains?"

"Animal or human remains."

Rebekah's face went white in the torchlight.

Tolly grimaced. "Sorry, Reb. I shouldn't 've said that in front o' you, considerin'."

A look of understanding passed between the two, piquing Devlin's curiosity. Considering what? Before he could question them, Tolly spoke again, much more matter-of-factly.

"Explorers 've come across all kinds o' things, includin' mummified carcasses from way back when."

Devlin swallowed. "We won't encounter any such findings, will we?"

Tolly blasted a laugh that bounced for several seconds before fading. "Now, since I'm only takin' you to the already-explored parts, I reckon we don't hafta worry none 'bout that." He glanced at Rebekah, who stood white faced and unsmiling. He grimaced. "'Nough talk about mummies an' such. You got a lot o' measurin' to do. Let's go."

By midmorning, Devlin had followed Tolly all along the paid tour route and past an area called Pineapple Bush, named by Stephen Bishop, the first person to map the cave. At the foot of each passageway, they stopped and held the torch over Devlin's journal so he could record the numbers from the way-wiser's meter as well as any information that Father might find of interest from Tolly's seemingly fathomless knowledge. The brightness of the torch against the blackness of the surroundings made spots dance in front of Devlin's eyes and distorted the pencil strokes against the paper. He hoped when he returned aboveground the markings would make sense.

They passed Pineapple Bush and meandered through a half-mile-long snake-like tunnel to a dead end. Tolly pulled off his pack and then sank down next to it. He pushed the end of the torch into the dirt and patted the spot beside him. "Sit. Rest. We'll have us a drink an' eat a little bit o' the victuals Coopuh packed fo' us."

Rebekah remained upright. "I thought we had to get out of the way of the tours."

Tolly held his hands wide, smiling. His white teeth nearly glowed against the dark backdrop. "This ain't a through path, so no tours come this way. So we can sit an' rest while they's moseyin' on the circle path an' goin' out again."

"Is there a tour going now?"

Tolly nodded. "Sure is."

She angled her head, appearing to listen. "I don't hear them."

"Ain't gonna from where we are. We're all shut off. Sit yo'self down now, Reb."

Devlin leaned the waywiser against the wall and reached for her pack. "Here. Let me help you." He lifted the canvas pack from her back, and he nearly dropped it. He gaped at her. "This thing must weigh forty pounds! How did you manage to cart it so far?"

She rotated her shoulders, wincing. "How far?"

He considered his notes, adding the numbers he'd taken from the way-wiser. "More than four miles."

"That's not so far."

Devlin shook his head. Perhaps four miles wasn't so far in distance, but the trek had been sometimes uphill, sometimes downhill, winding, twisting, ever challenging, with uncertainty—at least in his mind—lurking beyond each step. He wouldn't have thought less of her if she'd complained, but her staunch words despite her obvious weariness increased his admiration for her.

Every girl he knew from back home would be wilted and whining, but not Rebekah Hardin. These hills girls were tough, it seemed. He'd never been attracted to a girl who behaved even remotely tomboyish, but he liked Rebekah. He liked her a lot—more than he suspected Mother would approve. "Not so far, hmm? Well, it wasn't any short jaunt, either, so do as Tolly said and rest a bit. You've earned it."

She lowered herself to the dirt floor and folded her legs to the side. Resting her hands in her lap, she tipped her head back and released a delicate, airy sigh. "It does feel good to sit."

Tolly handed her a canteen and a cloth-wrapped lump. "Gonna rest here about half an hour. That'll give the tour group time to clear out befo' we go any fu'thuh."

Devlin sat within the torch's reach and accepted a canteen and another of the packages from Tolly's pack. He peeled back the cloth napkin and found a wedge of moist-looking cake. He pinched off a piece and carried it to his mouth. Cinnamon and nutmeg exploded on his tongue, and he couldn't hold back a murmur of pleasure.

Tolly grinned at him. "Applesauce cake. I special requested it when I knew we'd be down unduh fo' meals an' all." He patted the pack. "Mo' cake in here. An' sandwiches, an' boiled eggs, an' corn pone wit' honey, an' fried chicken, an'—"

Devlin held up his hand. "That's enough food to last a week. Are you sure you intend to lead me back to sunlight by evening?"

"The sun might be close to restin' by the time we come up." Tolly bit off a chunk of cake and washed it down with a swig from his canteen. "But if you wanna get out some early, you jus' tell me. I'm watchin' my timepiece."

Devlin hoped to have a few evening hours to transfer his notes to something more readable. "If we're out by dinnertime, that should suffice."

"Well then . . ." The torch began to flicker. Tolly opened Rebekah's pack and removed a fresh one. He touched the head to the dying torch and flames flared upward. Devlin instinctively drew back, squinting, but he got a good look at the smooth, rust-colored rock walls for a few seconds before the light shrank to a soft circle again.

Tolly rolled the head of the old torch against the ground until it was completely extinguished. He stood and rubbed the soles of his worn boots over the charred marks until they disappeared. Then he swished his palms together, sat, and continued as if he hadn't been interrupted.

"We prob'ly oughtn't go in more'n another mile or two today. Make sure we have plenty o' time to weave our way out befo' it gets too late." He took another bite and then spoke around it. "But fo' now, enjoy yo' treat. Enjoy yo' rest."

They fell into silence, only the rustle of Tolly's bag as he dug for another piece of cake and the squeak of the canteen lids intruding. Devlin stared into the torch's flame, watching the ball of yellow and white dance at the end of the dowel. Slowly he became aware of a strange, almost hollow echo. A sound yet not a sound. Confusion filled him, and he blurted, "What is that?"

Tolly raised his eyebrows. "What's what?"

"That . . . sound."

Rebekah looked right and then left, frowning. "I don't hear anything."

"That's just it." Devlin searched for words to describe what his ears—or was it his imagination?—heard. "I don't hear it, yet I do."

Rebekah stared at him as if he'd lost his mind. And maybe he had if he was hearing, or not hearing, things that weren't there. He turned to Tolly. "There's a hum I . . . I think."

A smile broke across the black man's face. Moisture glimmered in his dark eyes. Then he chuckled softly, nodding so hard he crushed his thick beard against the buttoned collar of his jacket. "You's tapped into it, boy."

Devlin exchanged a look with Rebekah. She appeared as puzzled as he felt. "This cave . . ."

Devlin jerked his attention to Tolly. The man's intense, serious gaze caused his pulse to double its tempo. Or maybe the cave itself was affecting him.

"It's a livin' thing, always changin'. While it changes, sometimes it sings. My pappy believed the cave took on a bit o' the spirit o' ever' person who entered its depths an' marveled at its wonduhs, an' those little pieces o' thousands o' spirits joined togethuh in a song."

The warmth of his jacket surrounded him, but Devlin shivered.

"I've heard the music o' the cave fo' so many years, it's become part o' me. Don't hardly notice it anymore." Tolly blinked fast. "But now you's hearin' it. It's a special thing, Devlin Bale, to become part o' Mammoth Cave."

Devlin didn't feel special. Apprehension spoiled the flavor of the cinnamon on his tongue. He rose, his limbs turning clumsy. "Is it time for us to move on?"

Tolly stood, too, but Rebekah remained seated, her quizzical gaze pinned on the older man. Tolly chortled, sending a smirk in Rebekah's direction. "You gonna stay here the rest o' the day, Reb, an' wait fo' us to cross paths wit' you on the way out?"

She shoved the last bite of cake into her mouth and pushed to her feet. She swallowed, wiped the back of her hand across her mouth, and aimed a tart look at Tolly. "You aren't going to leave me behind."

Tolly burst out laughing, destroying the odd web that had been wrapping itself around Devlin. Relieved, Devlin joined in, and even Rebekah offered a sheepish grin.

Rebekah and Tolly hefted their totes into place while Devlin slipped the satchel's strap over his shoulder. He took hold of the waywiser's handle and waited while Tolly plucked the torch from its spot. Then he fell in line behind Tolly and Rebekah.

# FIFTEEN

*Rebekah*

Rebekah shielded her eyes with one hand and crossed the thick grass to the pony cart waiting beneath a trio of pines where Tolly had left it that morning. Shadows fell from west to east, letting her know a whole day had passed while she followed Tolly through dark tunnels with Devlin Bale's warm breath stirring the fine hairs on the nape of her neck. Inside the cave, with no shadows to give a hint of the passing hours, time seemed to stand still. She fought a sense of confusion as she passed through fingers of waning sunlight.

Tolly strode to the mule and cupped Bitsy's hairy chin in his palm. "Hey, there, ol' girl. You ready to get outta them traces? We'll getcha to the stable an' let you loose." He turned to Rebekah. "Leave yo' pack wit' me, Reb. I'll fill it wit' supplies befo' we meet up again tomorruh mo'nin'."

She shrugged out of the pack and flopped it into the cart's bed. With the release of the weight, she experienced the strange sensation of floating. Gripping the edge of the cart, she waited for the feeling to pass, then removed her jacket and tossed it on top of the pack. She rubbed her shoulders and sighed.

Devlin lifted his belongings into the cart, grinning. "I wager you're relieved to shed that pack."

"I won't wager, but I will agree."

"Maybe tomorrow you should carry the food instead of the supplies."

The sympathy in his eyes sent a prickle of awareness down her spine. "With the amount of food Tolly packs, I doubt it'd make much difference."

Tolly chuckled. "Don't be complainin' none about the 'mount o' food. Not when you ate as much as eithuh o' us men today."

Heat attacked Rebekah's face.

"And only fair of her to do so, considering her hard work." Devlin beamed at her. "Truly, Miss Hardin, I couldn't help but notice how tirelessly you traversed the treacherous tunnels. You were an inspiration to me, keeping me moving when my legs felt too weak to continue."

The heat flowed into her chest. She couldn't decide if he was making fun of her or complimenting her. She scuttled to the opposite side of the cart. "Following Tolly wasn't any worse than following my daddy's work mule in our tobacco field."

"But I hope to smell some bettuh than an ol' work mule."

Tolly's dry comment earned a laugh from Devlin, and to Rebekah's relief he turned his attention to the older black man. "I have a lot of drawing to do this evening, Tolly. Can we return to the hotel now?"

"Sure thing. But I's ridin' with you'uns this trip. My feet're achin'."

The three of them clambered into the cart and Tolly flicked the reins. Bitsy let out a braying complaint. Tolly flicked them again, harder, but the mule still refused to move.

Tolly snorted and started to rise. "Oh, all right, you fool cuss, I'll—"

Devlin hopped out, making the cart bounce. "You two ride. I'll walk."

Tolly opened his mouth as if to argue, but Devlin put up one hand. "No, you two carried much more weight through the cave today than I did. It only makes sense that I should be the one to walk." He picked up his satchel and slung it over his shoulder. "I would appreciate it, however, if you would deliver my waywiser to my room. I'm staying in cottage two."

Tolly touched the brim of his battered top hat. "I surely will, Devlin. You have a good walk now. See you back at the meetin' spot tomorruh mo'nin' at seven." This time when he flicked the reins, Bitsy lurched to action.

Rebekah let her feet dangle out the back of the cart as Tolly guided Bitsy up the road to the cave estate. How could Devlin, who hailed from the city, have the energy to walk after the miles they'd covered? More than once, city fellows had come up to the door of her family's cabin seeking permission to hunt or fish on Daddy's land. Daddy, as kind and loving as he was with Mama and his girls, always seemed distrusting and even a little disdainful of those men. She'd once overheard him tell Mama, "Can't abide a dandy. Slick haired an' big bellied with soft hands, like they never done a lick o' work."

When she'd seen Devlin for the first time, she'd branded him a dandy in her mind. His fine suit, smug grin, and hands absent of dirt beneath the fingernails all painted the picture of a city dude. But he hadn't looked like one today in his work trousers and jacket. And he hadn't acted like one, either, keeping up pace for pace all through the cave and then choosing to hike the half mile to the hotel. Would Daddy approve of Devlin, or would he show disdain?

Tolly brought Bitsy to a stop in front of the row of cottages. He angled a look over his shoulder. "If you ain't too tired to move, would you take down Devlin's wheel-rolluh there an' set it by his door?"

Rebekah gaped at the man. "You're not going to put it inside?"

"How can I? I don't got a key to get in."

Rebekah carefully lifted the waywiser to the ground. She touched the round glass face, chewing her lip. "This thing looks expensive. Somebody might come along and take it. I don't think we should leave it outside. Not without someone keeping guard over it."

Tolly scowled. "I ain't stayin' here until he gets back. I gotta take care o' Bitsy an' then go see Coopuh, get fixed up with victuals for tomorruh. Gotta make up anothuh passel o' torches. Hopin' to get some sleepin' in, too, befo' tomorruh comes."

Rebekah grabbed her jacket and stepped away from the cart. "Then I'll stay."

He glared at her for several seconds, his lips set so tightly his mustache and beard meshed together. With his eyes still squinted, he pointed at her. "Mind all you do is guard that wheel. Don't you be goin' inside his cottage no mattuh if he ask."

Rebekah jolted. "Tolly!"

"All I's sayin' is he's a good-lookin' fella an' he's noticed you're a fine-lookin' gal."

Rebekah started fanning herself with the jacket.

"So you jus' mind yo'self, y'hear?"

A young couple meandered up the boardwalk, their curious gazes drifting in her direction. Rebekah scurried close to the cart and lowered her voice. "Tolly, my mama and daddy taught me right from wrong. I wouldn't ever go into a man's cottage. Not unless we were wed by a preacher in a church."

His stern expression faded. He patted her arm. "I's sorry if I sounded harsh. But when I hired you on, I made a promise to keep watch ovuh you, keep you safe. I wouldn't be doin' my job if I di'n't warn you 'bout men an' their wicked ways."

Rebekah's heart rolled in her chest. "Do you think Dev—Mr. Bale is wicked?"

"I think all men can be wicked when temptation snags 'em." Tolly's dark eyes glittered. "An' you, Miss Reb Hardin, would be mighty temptin' to any fella."

She ducked her head, embarrassed yet flattered. Mama and Daddy and Cal Adwell had all told her she was pretty, but somehow it meant more coming from somebody who didn't love her or want to court her. "Thanks, Tolly."

"So jus' mind yo'self an' be careful." His stern tone returned. He snapped the reins on Bitsy's back, and the cart rattled away.

Rebekah rolled the waywiser to the wooden walkway, placed it next to the door marked with a two, then leaned against the rough log wall to wait for Devlin. Within a few minutes, hardly a wait at all, he ambled along the row of cottages from the far end, whistling as he came.

He lifted a hand in greeting. "Reb!" He trotted the final distance and stopped near her, resting his palm on the wall and planting one toe against the boardwalk. He grinned at her. "Do you mind if I call you Reb? After hearing Tolly use the name all day, it seems natural."

Rebekah scooted a few inches away from him. "No, it's all right." She gestured to the waywiser. "I stayed and kept watch so nobody would take it." She hoped he understood she hadn't hung around to see him. Although Devlin Bale with blue eyes shining, perspiration moistening his curls, and a musky scent clinging to him made her stomach tremble in an odd but welcome way.

"Thank you. I appreciate it." He shifted his pose to withdraw a key from his pocket. "I'll put it inside where it'll be safe, and then would you like to walk to the dining room with me?"

"Um . . ."

He grimaced. "Oh. I suppose they wouldn't welcome me the way I look."

"I think you look just fine."

His eyebrows shot high.

She clapped her hands to her warm cheeks. Why had she said such a thing out loud? She'd spoken the truth, but only a brazen girl would tell a man he looked fine. "I mean, I don't think they'd keep you from coming in. But . . . but I can't go in with you."

He opened the door and rolled the waywiser inside, never shifting his gaze from her face. "Why not?"

"It's a workday. Staff members aren't allowed to eat with guests in the hotel dining room on workdays. We have our own room where we take our meals."

"Oh. Well." He blew out a breath. "I'm not keen on dining alone. Not when everyone else in the room has someone with whom to share the meal. I suppose I'll see if one of the dining room workers will deliver a sandwich to my cottage. Then I can work while I eat." He made a face. "That is, if I can find a workspace."

She'd never peeked into the cabins or any of the hotel rooms, but she couldn't imagine them being anything but nice, given the appearance of the rest of the property. It didn't seem as though the owners had spared any expense when building the hotel. Maybe Devlin was being particular, the way some of the other guests she'd encountered behaved. "Can't you use the table in your cottage?"

"There isn't a table. Or a desk. Only a bureau, which stands as high as my chest."

That would be high, given his height. "Oh."

"I suppose I could work at one of the tables in the dining room, but that would invite gawkers. I prefer to work without an audience."

She tapped her lips, thinking. "There's a table in my cabin that's not being used for anything. Except holding a pot of flowers." She didn't eat at it, write at it, or even sit at it. She wouldn't miss it if it were gone. "Maybe a couple of the porters could put it in your room."

Warmth glistened in his blue eyes. "That's very kind of you, Miss Reb, but would you believe me if I told you there isn't a place in this cottage for even the smallest table? The furnishings are very nice, and the view out the back window is enough to satisfy the most critical soul, but if they brought in a table, they would have to take out the bed. And I believe I'll have need of sleep during my stay."

He angled his head, his brows puckering. "If I'm to stay up-to-date with my project, I need to work on the map each evening. Do you suppose I could—" He shook his head, grimacing. "No, I shouldn't ask."

Curiosity got the better of her. "Ask what?"

He rested his shoulder against the wall, folded his arms, and set his face in a pleading look that reminded her of Little Nellie hoping for a striped stick of candy from the general store. "If you have no need for the table in your cabin, and if you wouldn't consider me an intrusion, do you suppose I could set out my paper and drawing materials there and make use of it?"

Allow Devlin Bale into her cabin every evening? Temptation tugged hard. If she said yes, would he think her forward? More important, would Mama, Daddy, or Tolly disapprove? She wished one of them was nearby so she could ask.

"I'd be certain to finish at a decent time and never enter your cabin without permission."

She stood mute, worrying her jacket in her hands. Tolly's comment about men's wickedness rolled in the back of her mind, competing with the gentle beseeching in Devlin's eyes. Blue eyes, like Daddy's. She bit her lip.

He sighed and pushed off from the wall. "Never mind. I can see you're uneasy with the idea."

"No, it isn't that. I just think I—"

"It's all right, Reb. I wouldn't want a stranger spending hours in my personal quarters, either. It was presumptuous of me to ask. I'll simply lay the paper out on the bed and—"

She snorted. "You can't put paper on a bed and then draw on it. The mattress is too soft. Your pencil will go straight through."

He smiled. "Actually, I draw with a pen and ink. But your statement about it piercing the page is accurate." He shrugged. "I suppose that leaves me working in the dining room."

She imagined him being interrupted by other diners, having to pick everything up and transport it back and forth between his cottage and the dining hall each day. Would she want to work under such conditions? She shook her head.

"Use the table in my cabin."

His face lit. "Are you sure you don't mind?"

She didn't mind, but Tolly probably would. She shook her finger, warning herself as fervently as she warned him. "We'll always keep the door open so anybody can look in and see that you're working. And I'll stay far away from the table"—as far as the size of the cabin would allow—"so you can work without being distracted."

Devlin released a huge sigh, his smile wide. "Reb Hardin, you're my hero."

Warmth exploded in her face. She waved her hand. "As a worker here at the hotel, it's my beholden duty to be sure the guests have what they need. I'm just doing my job."

Amusement twinkled in his eyes. He opened the door to his cottage. "Let me gather up my drawing materials and I'll follow you to your cabin now, all right?"

"All right."

He let the door slap into the frame behind him. She leaned her head against the wall and closed her eyes. *I'm just doing my job,* she'd said. She cringed. She hoped Tolly accepted that excuse.

## Sixteen

*Rebekah*

As she'd feared, Tolly had plenty to say about her and Devlin being in her cabin together even with the door open. When he spotted Devlin trailing her to the staff cabins, he pulled her aside and said, "Takes a whole lifetime to build a reputation, an' it can be all tumbled over with jus' one foolish choice." But after she explained her reason for opening her cabin to Devlin, Tolly offered a compromise both she and Devlin accepted. So they established a routine that gave him time to work on his map, protected Rebekah from supposition by other staff members, and set Tolly's concerns to rest.

While Devlin made use of the table in Rebekah's cabin, she accompanied Tolly to the kitchen to gather supplies—or "victuals," as he called them—and then sat on the stoop of his cabin with him, crafting torches for the next day's hours in the cave. Each evening he reminded her he was only trying to guard her good name, and she told him she thought he was overprotective. He always laughed and finished the conversation with a wry "I know, I know, Reb, you'd rathuh be wit' a handsome young fella than wit' an ol' white-haired man like me. But that's too bad. You's stuck wit' me."

On Friday evening as she and Tolly settled in to work on the torches, a drizzle began to fall. Tolly scowled at the sky. "God, couldn't You wait 'til we was done wit' these torches? They won't work if the bark gets wet." The drizzle changed to fat raindrops. He sighed. "C'mon, Reb, gathuh up our things. Gonna hafta go inside an' work."

She filled her arms. "In your cabin?"

"No. Folks'd be jus' as wonderin' about you an' me in there alone as they would wit' you an' Devlin all alone. We'll go to yo' cabin. Least then there's a chaperone—me fo' the two o' you, and him fo' the two o' us."

Rebekah didn't quite follow his thinking, but she trotted across the patch of grass between their two cabins and darted inside. Tolly followed close behind.

Devlin looked up from the table, pen in one hand and a strange metal instrument in the other. "Is everything all right?"

"Sorry to bothuh you, but it's startin' to rain."

Devlin looked out the window. Surprise registered on his face. "I was so intent on my map, I didn't even notice. I'll get out of here." He started to roll the map.

"No, now, no need fo' that. Me an' Reb'll stay out o' yo' way an' let you work." Tolly placed the pail of pitch and bundle of green wood staves on the floor near the door and aimed a curious look at the table. "But since we already interrupted, would you mind lettin' us take a peek at that map? Been wonderin' how it's comin' along."

Rebekah turned a hopeful look on Devlin. She, too, had wanted to see the drawing, but she hadn't touched the rolled paper, no matter how much it beckoned her.

Devlin smiled and held out his hand in invitation. "Come on over." He flattened the large sheet against the table and pulled the lamp closer. Tolly stepped up beside Devlin's right shoulder, and she scurried to his left. They both leaned in.

Devlin sat back with his arms crossed over his chest, his gaze roving from Tolly to Rebekah and then back to the map. "What do you think of it?"

Tolly scratched his cheek. "Hmm, to be truthful, I ain't sure."

A wry grin lifted the corner of Devlin's lips. "What do you mean?"

Tolly chuckled. "What is it?"

Devlin's jaw dropped. He spun his astonished look on her. "Reb? You can see what it is, can't you?"

She pulled in her lower lip and bit down on it. If she told him what she thought—that the drawing resembled a gathering of earthworms—she would hurt his feelings. "I, um . . ."

"You two . . ." Devlin huffed and then burst out laughing. "In five days I spent forty hours underground and then another ten trying to re-create an accurate scale of the twenty miles we covered, and all you can say is 'What is it' and 'um'?"

Rebekah squinted at the lines, trying to make sense of them. "I'm sorry."

Tolly shrugged. "Reckon a fella needs to be a cartographuh to read a map. I's just a guide."

Devlin chuckled and set his pen aside. "I suppose I shall be grateful that my professors are less critical than the two of you. I might stand a chance of getting a passing grade on this project."

Tolly plopped into the second chair and turned a puzzled look on Devlin. "Why you gotta draw a map o' the cave anyways? Seems to me there's already one been given ovuh to the district's clerk."

Devlin shifted sideways in the chair, looping his arm over its back. Rebekah perched on the edge of the bed and observed the play of the lantern light on his chiseled face. They spent so many hours in the dark and then kept apart by Tolly, she'd almost forgotten how handsome he was. Almost.

"The map registered with the District of Kentucky was drawn in the 1840s by an uneducated slave."

Tolly's white eyebrows formed a sharp V. "Somethin' wrong wit' that?"

"No, not for the time. And given that the map was drawn entirely by memory, without any of the tools we have today, it's an amazing accomplishment." Devlin gestured as he spoke. His hand movements appeared graceful yet masculine, mesmerizing her. "But without a key to determine lengths and widths of the tunnels, one can't get an accurate picture of the majesty of the cave by looking at Bishop's drawing. Don't you think Mammoth Cave deserves a true depiction?"

Rebekah nodded even though neither of the men were looking her direction.

Tolly's gaze drifted back to the paper on the table. "I don't gotta tell you how I feel about the cave. Been goin' inside o' it since I was big enough to stay up on my own two feet, trailin' aftuh my pappy, who spent his life trailin' aftuh his pappy."

He placed his hand over his chest and looked intently into Devlin's face. "That cave, it's become a part o' me jus' like it was a part o' my pappy an' grandpappy. Whatevuh you do wit' this drawin', I want you to honor the spirit o' the cave. Like you says jus' a bit ago, show its majesty." He flapped his hand at the page. "By the time you's done, is there gonna be all the unduhground rivers an' the diff'rent levels an' the places where the walls are like ripplin' cloth showin' on the map?"

"That's my intention."

For long seconds Tolly stared at the lines, his forehead bunched tight. Then he sighed and leaned away. "You gots a long way to go 'til then."

Devlin laughed. "But I'll get there. With your help. And Reb's." He swung his smile in her direction, and immediately her face heated. "I can't do it without the two of you."

Tolly harrumphed. "Well, fo' now, me an' Reb need to get the to'ches ready fo' goin' in tomorruh." He stood and reached for the pile of materials.

Devlin jolted. "Tomorrow's Saturday."

"That's right." Tolly sent him a wry look. "Satuhday follows Friday."

Devlin shook his head. "I didn't plan to go into the cave tomorrow. I planned to . . . explore elsewhere."

"Where?"

"Oh, around."

Rebekah's scalp tingled. Why did he seem so secretive?

Tolly must have wondered the same thing because he scowled. "You mappin' somethin' besides the cave?"

Devlin's left shoulder rose and fell in an odd half shrug. "No."

"But you ain't wantin' to go in tomorruh, that what you's sayin'?"

Devlin picked up his pen and fiddled with it. "If you aren't opposed to spending a day away from the cave, then yes, that's what I'm saying." He dropped the pen and faced Tolly. "I'd like to spend the morning working on my map. I still have several tunnels to add. And then, in the afternoon, I'd like to borrow a horse from the stable and ride through the hills surrounding the cave estates. Would you two"—he shifted his gaze to include Rebekah— "accompany me?"

Tolly shook his head. "I don't like to ride horses. If I'm gonna ride, it'll be on a wagon seat. But wagons won't go through 'cept on the roads, an' if I'm unduhstandin' you rightly, you's wantin' to go off the roads."

"Yes, I am." Devlin shifted in the chair, jerking his attention from Tolly to Rebekah, the movement reminding her of a chicken looking out for foxes. "I'm curious about the people who live near the cave. I'd like to see their homes, determine their livelihoods, perhaps visit with some of them concerning their satisfaction or dissatisfaction with their lives here."

Rebekah didn't know much about cartography, but his request didn't seem related to drawing maps. "Is this part of your project?"

"Yes." A strange, faraway look entered Devlin's eyes. "Yes, it is."

Over the past days, his steady presence in the cave, his willingness to offer his hand when they stepped over deep crevices or climbed steep pathways, his ready words of appreciation had built her trust in him. But at that moment, something in his expression bothered her. She wasn't entirely sure he was telling the truth, and she didn't want him traipsing around the countryside on his own. Partly because a person who was unfamiliar with the area could find himself lost, and partly because she wanted somebody keeping watch over him.

She said, "I don't mind riding horses. I've been riding our family's mule since I was little."

Delight broke across his features. "Are you offering to guide me tomorrow?"

Rebekah turned to Tolly. She wouldn't go if her boss said no. After all, she was supposed to work on Saturdays. Even if they didn't go to the cave, he might have things for her to do at the estate. "Tolly?"

He stared at her for several seconds with his brow puckered and his lips pooched out. He spun on Devlin. "I been watchin' you all week. 'Specially wit' Reb."

Red streaks climbed Devlin's cheeks.

She shifted uneasily on the corner of the bed.

"An' you been nothin' but gentlemanly. That's the only reason I'd even think about lettin' her go off fo' the aftuhnoon wit' you."

Devlin cleared his throat. "Thank you."

"Since you's wantin' to draw in the mo'nin', Reb an' me'll work on the torches tomorruh instead o' tonight. Then, Reb, you pack what you need fo' stayin' at yo' folks' place. First spot you an' Devlin go to tomorruh when you set out is yo' house. If yo' daddy say it be all right fo' you to take Devlin on a look aroun' the countryside, then I won't get in the way. But it's goin' be his decision, not mine. Y'hear?"

Rebekah nodded.

Tolly shifted to Devlin. "Only a mile to Reb's house from the cave. Her family's one o' the closest o' them who live 'round here. Won't take but a five-minute ride on a good horse to reach her place. I'll be takin' note o' what time you two set out, an' I'll be checkin' wit' her daddy on what time you two get to her place. If there's any shenanuhgans along the way, I'll be figurin' it out, an' I promise to teach you some mannuhs if you do anythin' to sully this girl's name. Are you hearin' me clear, Devlin Bale?"

After listening to a threatening speech, would Devlin take his business away from Mammoth Cave? Would he turn Tolly in to the cave's directors for over-stepping his position? Tolly only wanted to protect her, but he'd just moved onto dangerous ground. Some white people didn't take kindly to being given orders by those with dark-colored skin. Rebekah bit her lip and held her breath, waiting for Devlin's response.

Devlin stood, moving so slowly it seemed his joints had gone rusty while sitting in the chair. He took one step toward Tolly, then planted his feet wide. "Tolly . . ." He extended his hand. "I give you my word I won't do anything to sully Reb's name."

Tolly stared hard into Devlin's face, as if trying to see all the way to his soul. When he reached out and grasped Devlin's hand, Rebekah nearly col-lapsed with relief.

"All right, boy, I's trustin' you wit' her."

The two shook hands, and then Devlin returned to the table and orga-nized his tools.

Tolly stood near, hands in his pockets and chin high. "But like I say, if her daddy tells her no, you's on yo' own tomorruh. An' it's only fair to warn you some folks in these parts are plumb skittish 'round stranguhs. You might get hollered at. Somebody might throw a rock at you. Somebody else jus' might point a rifle barrel at you. So think twice befo' ridin' up on somebody's property 'less there's someone along who can introduce you." He chuckled, proving he'd set aside his sternness. "I'd hate to see yo' new clothes get a hole poked clear through. 'Specially with you inside 'em."

Devlin grinned. "Thank you, Tolly. I appreciate the advice."

"Advice is free," the black man said, his grin wide. He looked out the window. "Rain's stopped. Reckon you can go on back to yo' cottage now, Devlin, an' I can take these torch things to my cabin, let Reb have a little time to herself. Haven't had much o' that since Devlin come along, have you, Reb?"

Tolly was right. She'd spent every minute of wakefulness either in the cave with both men or under Tolly's watchful gaze. Having an hour to herself should be a treat. So why didn't excitement fill her? She shrugged.

Tolly shook his head, as if disgusted with her. "Come on now, Devlin, let's clear out. Them papers an' things'll still be here in the mo'nin'." He gave Devlin a clap on the back that sent him out the door. Tolly scooped up the staves, bark, and pail of pitch. "Be seein' you in the mo'nin', Reb. You an' me can work aftuh breakfast, all right?"

She followed the men to the door. "That sounds fine, Tolly. Good night."

Tolly crossed the short expanse to his cabin, and Rebekah remained on her stoop, watching Devlin stride across the ground toward the hotel. The farther he went, the more loneliness pricked. She sighed.

The gruff sound of a throat being cleared intruded. Rebekah glanced at Tolly, who stood outside his door watching her.

Her face flamed. "Good night, Tolly." She hurried inside and closed the door.

# SEVENTEEN

*Devlin*

Devlin swung himself into the saddle of a sorrel mare named, of all things, Marey. The horse snorted and he patted her sleek neck.

The stable hand gave Devlin the reins. "Here you go, Mr. Bale. Enjoy your ride."

"Thank you. I'm sure I will." He turned to Rebekah, who sat straight spined and at ease on a spotted gelding the hand had called Jinx, and his heart caught.

She wore a dress this afternoon, a calico frock lacking even one embellishment of lace, a stark contrast to his belted jacket with its carved wood buttons and his sporty jodhpurs, his standard riding suit. He'd settled a gray wool ivy cap over his hair, but her dark hair was uncovered, giving him a full view of her long, thick braid. How could she be so simply attired and still steal his breath? He hoped he'd be able to keep his eyes on the trail. Miss Rebekah Hardin was an arresting sight.

"Are you ready?" She curled her reins around her hand and leaned forward slightly in her sidesaddle, as if preparing to race.

He grinned. "Yes, but take it easy on me, will you? I'm not as experienced at riding as you are."

She wrinkled her nose—an adorable gesture. "Riding I've done, but I'm not so sure about this saddle."

Her full skirt spread out like a curtain across the horse's side, but he glanced at what little he could see of the saddle. "Isn't it fastened correctly?" He lifted his hand to beckon assistance.

"I don't know. I've never used a saddle before."

Devlin froze with his hand in the air and gawked at her.

"And this thing's pretty peculiar."

The stable hand hurried over. "Did you need something, sir?"

"N-no, my apologies." He waited until the young man trotted off. Then he leaned toward Rebekah and forced a question past his raspy throat. "You . . . you've never sat a saddle before?"

She shook her head, making her braid swing across her spine.

"Then how do you ride?"

She shrugged. "Bareback."

And likely astride. An earthy picture flooded Devlin's mind, and he straightened abruptly. Marey pawed the ground and snorted in protest. He absently patted the horse's neck and forced the images from his head. "Well, er, do you suppose you'll manage to remain seated as we ride?" He didn't want her falling off.

"I'll be fine, but we better take it slow."

Devlin couldn't prevent a smile from growing. "But not too slow, or Tolly will suspect we were up to shenanigans."

A rosy blush stole over her cheeks. She aimed her face to the opening in the corral and chirped to the horse. Jinx obediently moved forward, and Devlin encouraged Marey to follow.

He stayed behind, allowing Rebekah to lead the way from the hotel grounds to the road. Trees lined both sides of the dirt road, and the overhead sun lit the pathway with burnished gold. He couldn't have requested a more perfect spring day for a ride through the country. He'd intended to examine the area so he could share his findings with Father, but instead he became enraptured with Rebekah Hardin, with her braid bouncing lightly against her narrow back and the graceful way she held herself in the unfamiliar saddle.

Had he ever been so intrigued by a woman before? Although he could list a half-dozen girls who'd briefly captured his interest when he was younger, none of his boyhood infatuations compared to the affection and admiration expanding his chest as he gazed at this hills girl's plainly dressed form. What would she look like in city clothes and with her hair done up in a poufy roll? He tried hard to envision it, but instead images of her trekking across the grass in her trousers intruded. Maybe Rebekah wasn't meant for city finery. The idea didn't settle well.

One of the hotel wagons lumbered toward them, its bed filled with jabbering guests apparently returning from a tour. Rebekah angled her gaze to watch as the wagon rolled past. Devlin enjoyed the brief view of her profile, her cheeks rounding with her smile, and then she faced forward again. If her father refused to allow her to accompany him for the afternoon, he wouldn't get to enjoy her smile again until Monday.

"Get up there, Marey." He bounced his heels against the horse's flanks and brought her alongside Rebekah's horse. Close enough that he could reach out and stroke Jinx's neck. But if he reached out, it would be to take Rebekah's hand instead.

She didn't turn her head, but her eyes darted in his direction, and a slight grin lifted the corners of her lips. With the sun shimmering on her dark hair and bringing out the gold flecks in her brown eyes, she was almost too pretty to be real.

Devlin swallowed. "Tell me about your family."

She sent a startled look in his direction, as if she'd expected him to say something else. But then she laughed, the sound airy and carefree. "Are you worrying about what Daddy will say when I ask to take you around to the neighbors?"

"Dreading a refusal, perhaps, but not worrying. No, I'm curious. Tolly told me you're working at the cave to help your family. That's very noble of you."

Her brow pinched. "Not noble. Something I have to do."

"They're forcing you?"

She frowned at him. "No. My daddy let me choose."

"Then why—"

"Never mind about that." She lifted her chin slightly and aimed her gaze forward. "You asked about my family. There's me, of course, and Daddy and Mama—Festus and Nell Hardin. Then there's Cissy, Della, Jessie, Tabitha, Trudy, and Little Nellie. I'm the oldest."

Strangely, no joy lit her face as she listed her family members. He whistled through his teeth. "That's quite a list. And all girls?"

She offered a stiff nod.

Her distant behavior troubled him. He affected a lighthearted tone in the hopes of chasing away her stiltedness. "I can't imagine being part of such a large family. At my house, it's my parents and me."

"All by yourself all the time?" She didn't look at him, but her lips formed a slight sympathetic pout. "How . . . lonely."

He'd never considered it so when he was a boy basking in his parents' full attention, but in that moment he rued his solitary childhood. "Will I meet all your family today?"

"I imagine so. And it'll be soon, because this is my lane." She tugged Jinx's reins, and Marey automatically trailed the other horse up a narrow, curving, rutted trail with thick aspens, pines, and scrubby oaks crowding in on both sides. The trail opened into a grassy clearing enclosed by a rugged fence formed of split timber. A log house with a full front porch, tin roof, and open shutters waited at the top of a low rise.

Rebekah drew Jinx to a stop next to the fence and slid down. She looped the reins over the top rail, removed the small sack from the saddle horn, and then ducked under the horse's neck. She offered Devlin a shy smile. "This's it. Come on in."

*Rebekah*

It seemed strange to have Devlin follow her across a sunlit yard instead of through dark cave tunnels, yet she liked having him so near. Her heart thudded beneath the bodice of her dress. What would Daddy and Mama think of him? His strange clothes—she'd never seen men's britches shaped like a pair of chicken drumsticks—might make them raise their eyebrows. But Tolly had called him a gentleman, and she agreed. Hopefully her folks would look past what he wore to his insides.

Because Rebekah liked his insides a lot. Probably more than she should.

She called for her mama as she stepped through the open door, but the cabin was empty. She tossed her sack of clothes for her overnight stay on the table and quirked her finger at Devlin. "They must all be outside. This way."

The back door also stood open, and as she approached it she heard Mama chiding Trudy to mind where she aimed the hoe's blade. Rebekah stepped into the backyard and spotted her mother and the three youngest girls in their large garden plot. Daddy and the older ones were nowhere in sight.

"Mama!"

Her mother was kneeling, working the dirt the way she worked bread dough. Her face lifted, surprise in her eyes. "Rebekah? That you, gal?"

Little Nellie came running, arms outstretched, but she stopped when Devlin stepped from the cabin. She changed directions and darted behind Mama, peeking out with her thumb in her mouth. Tabitha and Trudy paused in chopping at the dirt clods and stared, too, their mouths hanging open.

Rebekah cringed. Devlin probably thought they'd never seen a stranger before. But then, how many strangers came around? Especially strangers wearing squashed-flat caps, funny-shaped pants, and black shiny boots that went all the way up to their knees. To Little Nellie, he probably looked like a character from one of the fairy-tale books she read at nighttime.

She gestured Devlin forward and tried to pretend she brought people home every week to visit the family. "Mama, I'd like you to meet Devlin Bale from the University of Kentucky. He's a cartographer, and he's spending the summer at the estate to make a new map of the cave. Mr. Bale, this is my mama, Nell Hardin."

Mama stood, wiping her hands on her apron, and stepped out of the garden. Her bare feet were filthy, her skirt smudged from the rich soil. Hair straggled across her cheek, and when she pushed it aside she left a smear of dirt behind. If she knew how bedraggled she looked, she'd probably try to hide like Little Nellie. But she nodded politely. "Hello, Mr. Bale."

"Call me Devlin." He bounced his smile from Mama to the little girls. "And who are you?"

Tabitha bounded forward like an eager puppy. "I'm Tabitha. That there's Trudy, an' that one with her face in Mama's skirt is Little Nellie. She's the baby." She crinkled her nose, looking Devlin up and down. "How come your britches—"

Rebekah slung her arm around Tabitha's shoulders and pulled her sister tight to her side. "Tabby, why don't you and Trudy get back to the garden? See if you can get a whole row chopped and ready for seeds by the time we're done talking."

"All right." Tabitha grabbed Trudy by the hand and darted off. Little Nellie peeled herself away from Mama and toddled after them.

Rebekah blew out an airy breath of relief and faced Mama. "Mr. Bale wants to meet the folks who live around the cave, but since he isn't familiar with the back roads, he needs someone to take him. Would it be all right if I . . . escorted him?"

Mama fiddled with her apron, turning the skirt into a wad and then flapping it. "Just you two?"

Rebekah nodded.

Mama slowly shook her head. "That ain't wise, gal." She jerked her gaze to Devlin. "No offense. Got nothin' to do with you. We wouldn't let Rebekah traipse off into the hills by herself with any fella, not even Cal Adwell, an' we've known him his whole life. It ain't . . . seemly."

Devlin locked his hands behind his back and gave a nod. "I understand."

Rebekah didn't dare look at him. If she saw regret—or worse, indifference—she'd dissolve on the spot.

Mama turned to Rebekah again. "But if he's wantin' to meet folks 'round here, take him to the field an' let him meet your daddy. Della an' Jessie're there, too."

"Not Cissy?"

"Cissy left just a bit ago, takin' a basket o' mushrooms to the cook at the estate. She's gonna finish the housework when she gets back." Mama began reversing slowly, still worrying the apron. "Nice to meetcha, young man." She hurried to the garden.

Rebekah pointed to the break in the trees between the outhouse and the chicken house. "The field's this way. That is, if you still want to meet my daddy." After the skittish way Mama acted—and why had she mentioned Cal Adwell?—she wouldn't blame Devlin if he climbed up on Marey's back and took off.

"Of course I would."

"You sure?"

"Absolutely." His smile warmed her more than the bright sun.

She quirked her finger. "Follow me."

The path to the meadow that Great-Granddaddy had turned under to plant tobacco seventy-five years earlier had never seemed shorter. After Devlin and Daddy met, she'd have to send Devlin off by himself. So she took her time, pointing out wildflowers and a squirrel den and the creek that provided her family's water supply. Not once did Devlin make fun or act bored, which made it even harder to think about cutting short her time with him.

They moved from the woods to the open. On the far side of the field, Daddy followed their mule, plow in hand, carving furrows in the winter-packed earth. Della and Jessie trailed behind him, picking up rocks and tossing them on the growing pile near the trees. They all had their backs to the trail's opening, so Rebekah waited until Daddy turned the mule in their direction before waving her hand over her head.

Daddy hollered out, "Whoa there." He draped the reins over the plow handle and trotted across the uneven ground toward Rebekah, his smile bright. Della and Jessie scampered behind him, calling, "Bek! Bek!"

As hard as it had been to leave her family, these homecoming moments made it all worthwhile. She darted forward and met Daddy in a hug.

"What you doin' here, gal? Thought you worked on Saturdays."

"I do, generally, but Tolly told me I could take today for something special."

"What's that?"

"Taking one of the cave guests around to meet folks." Rebekah caught Daddy's hand and led him toward Devlin, who waited in the shade at the edge of the field. Jessie and Della came along. She gave Daddy the same introduction she'd given Mama and then watched her father shake hands with the college boy. Her heart pounded in hopeful beats. She wouldn't explore why it was so important, but she wanted Daddy to like Devlin. And Devlin to like Daddy.

"It's very nice to meet you, sir." Devlin used his customary polite speech, his blue-eyed gaze pinned on Daddy's face. "You and your wife have a very neat, well-kept farm."

Daddy aimed a steady look at Devlin. "It was my daddy's before me, an' his daddy's before him, so I guess you could say I take pride in it."

The girls pulled at Rebekah's sleeve, and she ushered them forward. "Mr. Bale, these are my sisters Della and Jessie."

He nodded at them and said hello. Both girls giggled instead of replying. Daddy raised his eyebrows at them, and they ducked their heads and pinched their lips tight.

Daddy folded his arms over his overall bib and set his boots wide. "So you're makin' the rounds to the hills folks, is that it?"

"Yes, sir." Devlin imitated Daddy's stance.

"What for?"

The two men were the same height, but Daddy's shoulders were broader, his arms thicker. Even more so as he puffed up like a grizzly bear. Daddy only acted bear-like when fellows came "sniffing," as Mama put it, and it worked for keeping would-be suitors from taking advantage of any of his gals. Most boys cowered beneath Daddy's glower, but Devlin didn't appear intimidated. He seemed respectful but at ease, which pleased Rebekah.

"Curiosity, I suppose—discovering how people make a living, what they do for entertainment. I grew up in the city. Country life intrigues me."

Daddy slid his hands into his pockets. "Reckon if I came to the city, I'd be curious about the same kinds o' things. Who all've you met so far?"

Rebekah stepped forward. "Just you and Mama. Tolly thought it would be better if Devlin had an escort with him—someone everybody knew—so folks wouldn't take a shot at him when he came on their property. I know everybody, and I could introduce him around, but Tolly wanted me to get permission to escort Mr. Bale. So we came here first."

Daddy rubbed his chin with his fingers, staring at Rebekah.

"Mama already said it isn't a good idea for him and . . . and me to go up in the hills. All by ourselves." Daddy's unsmiling perusal was making her stomach tremble. What was he thinking? "So I brought him out to meet you." She wished she could add, "Do you like him, Daddy? Huh, do you?"

"Your mama's right. Folks might get ideas if they seen you an' him goin' from place to place together." Daddy brushed his knuckles along her cheek, his familiar means of softening a denial. This time it didn't help at all. "But I s'pose it wouldn't be indecent if you had somebody else with you, too. A . . . what's it called? Somebody who sticks close to a young couple an' makes sure everybody behaves."

"A chaperone?" Devlin suggested.

"Yep, that's it." He grinned at Rebekah. "Maybe . . . one o' your blabbety little sisters."

She swallowed a happy chortle. Daddy approved of Devlin or he wouldn't have made such a suggestion. "Can you spare one of the girls?"

"Won't take no helpin' hands away from your mama. But I don't need both gals pickin' up rocks behind me. Della or Jessie could go." He swung his narrow-eyed gaze on Devlin. "'Course, if you got some opposition to havin' one of 'em taggin' along, you can always just go on by yourself."

# EIGHTEEN

*Cissy*

Cissy left the kitchen with an empty basket on her arm, forty-five cents tied up in a handkerchief in her pocket, and a nickel pilfered from the mushroom money in her shoe. How much did Daddy have in the money tin now? Bek had brought home one half month's pay, and tomorrow she'd have more. Was the amount getting high enough that Daddy might not notice if she sneaked a dollar or two out?

Her stomach went all trembly as she thought about taking money that didn't belong to her. The preacher gave some thundering sermons about stealing. But how else would she get enough? The piddly amount she got from selling mushrooms wouldn't get her far. Only one more week and school would let out. Then she'd be stuck working with Daddy in the field or with Mama in the garden. Every day, all day, getting sweaty and bug bit and rashy from weeds. If only she could catch a train right now and go far, far away.

She took her time leaving the hotel grounds, stopping to watch some boys use what looked like butterfly nets to toss a ball back and forth. It seemed a silly game, but by their hoots of laughter they were having fun. Neither of them paid her any mind, though, so she moved on.

More shouts and laughter and a donkey's bray carried from behind the barn. Curious about what kind of game would include a donkey, Cissy hurried in that direction. She rounded the corner to the small enclosed corral, and she gasped in indignation. Three boys who looked to be around Jessie's age had climbed up on the fence and were jabbing a little burro with sticks. The animal darted in circles in the small space, braying and bucking, but a rope strung from its neck to a post kept it from escaping. Their taunts and laughter pierced Cissy.

She tossed the basket aside and charged over, fury roaring through her. She grabbed the first boy by the tail of his jacket and yanked so hard he lost his footing and fell onto his backside.

He shouted, "Hey!" The other two boys jerked their heads toward Cissy. One of them jumped down, and the other shifted to sit on the top rail and gawk at her.

More angry than she could remember ever being, she grabbed the stick from the boy on the ground and held it like a sword. The burro continued its complaint, forcing her to holler to be heard over its frantic cries. "You think it's funny to get poked at? How 'bout I poke you an' see how you like it, huh?" She jabbed the end of the stick at the boy at her feet, and he rolled away, then came up spluttering near the fence, his jacket and pants coated with bits of grass.

Cissy aimed the stick at the other two, giving the air a sharp jab for every shrill word leaving her throat. "What's the matter with you, pickin' on a poor beast that can't defend itself? A bunch o' bullies, that's what you are. Somebody oughta teach you a lesson."

The middle of the boys aimed his stick in Cissy's direction and sneered. "And I suppose you believe you're the one to do it, hmm? Well, I'm game. See if you can best me, you crazy girl."

Cissy growled low in her throat and bent her knees slightly, her body tense. "I'll best you, you—"

"What in tarnation is going on here?" A male voice exploded from behind Cissy.

The boys took off running, tossing their sticks aside as they went.

Cissy dropped her stick, too. She dashed forward, slipped between rails into the corral, and curled her arms around the burro's neck. "There now, you're all right. They're gone. Ain't gonna hurt you no more, I promise." The animal rolled its eyes, stamped its feet, and shifted nervously. But she kept stroking its neck and ears, speaking low and soft, and eventually it calmed, trembling only a bit within her hold. She smiled, triumphant. "See there? You're just fine."

"But you're in a peck of trouble, young lady."

Cissy whirled toward a tall man who leaned his elbows on the fence. The upper half of his face was shaded by the brim of his bowler hat, so she couldn't see his eyes, but his mouth was set in a frown beneath a thick gray mustache.

She frowned back at him. "I don't know what for. I didn't do nothin'. Them boys was tormentin' this beast, pokin' at him with sticks." She rubbed the burro's velvety nose, trying not to smile when it snuffled against her palm. "Nobody else was around to chase 'em off, so I did it."

The man's mustache twitched. He looked her up and down. "You're not a guest at the hotel, are you?"

Her face went hot. From his tone, he already knew the answer, and he thought the less of her for it. "No, I ain't."

"What are you doing on the hotel grounds?"

"Deliverin' mushrooms."

"Excuse me?"

The burro tried to stick its nose in Cissy's apron pocket. She giggled and shifted aside, curling her hands beneath its fuzzy chin and pulling upward. "Here now, stop that." Scratching the animal's lumpy jaw with both hands, she gave the man a sidelong look. "My family grows mushrooms, an' Mr. Cooper—that's the cook—"

He snorted. "I know who Mr. Cooper is."

She rolled her eyes. "You gonna let me talk or not? Mr. Cooper buys 'em. I had just finished deliverin' mushrooms when I heard a ruckus over here an' came to see what it was. That's when I spotted them boys bein' mean to this poor critter." She got mad all over again thinking about it. She wrapped her arms around the burro's neck and rubbed her cheek against its prickly hide. The animal smelled awful, but she didn't care. No creature deserved to be mistreated, no matter how smelly or unattractive it was.

"Come on out of there, young lady."

Cissy gave the burro a kiss between its eyes and then climbed out the same way she'd gone in. She stood before the gentleman, squinting against the sun and scowling. "You can ask Mr. Cooper. He'll tell you Cissy brings him mushrooms."

"So your name is Cissy?"

"That's right. Cissy Hardin."

He pushed his jacket lapels aside, giving her a good look at his striped vest. He slid his hands into his trouser pockets and drew in a breath that made his vest fill out. "Do you live around here, Cissy Hardin?"

"'Bout a mile west o' here."

"With whom?"

Why'd he care? "My folks an' my sisters."

"You have a way with animals."

She shrugged. "Always've had critters on our place. Pigs, goats, chickens, a mule . . ." Her throat went tight. "An' we don't treat any of 'em bad. My daddy says God entrusted the animals to our care an' it's our beholden duty to see to them properly. That burro there?" She pointed at the animal with its drooping head and sloped back and ratty tail. "Whoever owns him oughta be ashamed."

"Why?"

She gawked at the man. "Ain't you got eyes, mister? He needs brushin' an' a good wash. He's all tied up, so he can hardly move. The sun's beatin' down on him, an' he don't have water close by to drink." She huffed, crossing her arms tightly over her chest. "Those boys were plumb cruel to be pickin' at him like they did, but whoever owns him's just as bad, leavin' him stuck where he can't drink or even lie down."

Very slowly the man pulled his right hand free and placed it over his chest. "Miss Hardin, my name is Judson Temperance, and I'm the, er, proud owner of that sorry-looking beast."

Cissy wished the ground would open up and swallow her. "Oh."

He popped his hat off and held it against his thigh. Now that she could see his whole face, she noticed his eyes were almost as gray as his mustache. And they were twinkling. So he wasn't mad. The realization restored her courage. And her indignation.

She tipped up her chin and met his gaze. "If you're gonna own a burro, Mr. Temperance, you oughta take better care of it." She marched over to her basket and scooped it up. "So see that you do." She started for the road.

"Wait a moment, Miss Hardin."

She stopped and glared at him over her shoulder. "What?"

He laughed. "I believe you're even more prickly than the burro."

She wasn't sure how to respond to a comment like that. So she stayed in place with her lips clamped tight and waited for him to amble up beside her.

He fanned himself with his hat. "Miss Hardin, I purchased the burro from a farmer near Bowling Green two weeks ago and brought him here to be used as a prop for photographs."

Cissy squinted. "Photographs?"

"Yes." He touched her shoulder and guided her to the shade of a large cottonwood. "I've been hired to take souvenir images of guests for the hotel over the spring and summer seasons. I thought it would be clever to include a burro, allow the guests to sit on its back or hold its reins for a photograph." He grimaced. "Unfortunately, the animal is most disagreeable. Yesterday it bit two guests and bounced around so exuberantly that another guest fell off its back before I could take the picture."

Cissy covered her mouth with her fingers, but her giggle sneaked out.

He scowled at her. "It's hardly amusing. Someone could have been hurt."

"Maybe he don't want to have his picture taken. Burros have feelin's, too."

"It's not his choice." Mr. Temperance frowned at the animal. "I canceled all of today's scheduled photographs to give him time to adjust to his new surroundings. But if he doesn't settle down and start behaving himself, I intend to sell him to a glue factory and purchase something more docile."

She gasped. "You can't sell him to a glue factory!"

"I certainly can, and I will. Unless . . ." He turned a sly smile on Cissy. "He seemed very well behaved for you. Would you come to the estate tomorrow afternoon? I'd like you to serve as the donkey's trainer, so to speak, and convince him to pose for the photographs. If he cooperates, then I won't need to replace him."

She scratched her cheek. Her hand smelled like the burro. He really needed a bath. "You're wantin' me to make him stand still while somebody's sittin' on his back?"

"Long enough for me to take the photograph, that's right. Are you interested?"

She squinted up at him. "Is this a payin' job?"

"Only if you're successful in controlling him."

Then it'd be a paying job. She swung the basket, plans whirling in her mind. "The thing is, Mr. Temperance, I go to church with my folks on Sunday, an' I'll prob'ly be wearin' my best dress when I come over here. I can't be standin' next to a smelly burro in my best dress. So before I can say yes, I gotta know if you plan to clean him up some before tomorrow."

The man's lips twitched. "I can arrange for him to receive a thorough scrubbing."

"An' brushin'? He's got burrs in his tail an' his mane. He'll be a good bit happier if all them're combed out, an' I won't hafta worry about gettin' stuck, either."

He raised one eyebrow. "Anything else?"

She chewed the inside of her cheek, gathering courage. "How much do folks pay you to have their picture took?"

"Twenty-five cents."

"How much o' that you gonna give me?"

"Two cents."

She frowned. "That ain't much."

"You won't be doing much. Simply holding the reins."

"An' keepin' him from buckin', boltin', or bitin'. Ain't that worth more'n two cents?"

He sighed. "Very well. Three cents." His forehead furrowing, he pointed at her. "But that's my final offer, and it applies only if you control the animal so I can take a suitable photograph."

Cissy grinned and stuck out her hand. "You got a deal."

Mr. Temperance shook her hand. "Be at the corral no later than one thirty tomorrow. I intend to open the photograph booth at two."

She pulled loose. "I'll be here. Make sure the burro's clean an' lookin' pretty."

He pursed his lips.

"I gotta get now. See you tomorrow." She scampered a few feet away, then remembered something. She turned back. "Mr. Temperance, what's the burro's name?"

"As far as I know, he doesn't have one."

That wasn't right. Every critter should have a name. "He does now. We'll call him Beauregard. Beau for short." She waved at the photographer, then flapped her hand at Beauregard. "Bye, Beau! See you tomorrow!" She lit out for home as if her feet had wings.

# Nineteen

## Rebekah

Rebekah coiled a strand of Trudy's damp hair around her finger and then tied it with a piece of rag. In the morning the little girl would have lovely curls for church. Rebekah reached for another rag.

Cissy flopped onto her tummy next to Rebekah. The entire bed bounced, and the strips of muslin danced out of reach. Cissy propped her chin in her hands and grinned. "It's kinda like havin' a party with you sleepin' over, Bek."

Rebekah stifled the complaint rising on her tongue. Cissy had been in an exceptionally good mood all evening. She shouldn't spoil it by scolding. So she smiled at her sister and gathered the rag strips in a pile beside her knee again.

"Had my party all day." Jessie sat cross legged on the next bed with her nightgown scrunched up over her knees, examining the pink lines marking her calves. "Didn't even mind gettin' all scratched up when Bek took that horse o' hers between prickly shrubs. I wish I could go ridin' with Bek an' Mr. Bale every Saturday."

Della nudged her. "Quit your braggin', Jess. The rest of us had to work. We didn't get to go gallivantin' through the hills with Bek's good-lookin' fella."

Jessie flopped backward, her limbs thrown out in all directions, and sighed. "He is mighty handsome. An' nice, too." She sat up. "Is he your beau, Bek?"

Rebekah's heart lurched. Her throat went tight. She wished she could say yes. Her day with Devlin had been so pleasurable, so enlightening. Seeing how easily he talked to people—all people, even the ones who were standoffish or a little grumpy—increased her admiration for him. Watching him tease with Jessie, always kind and patient, gave Rebekah a peek at what kind of father he would be. She was supposed to introduce him to the folks nearby, but instead he'd introduced himself to her in a whole different way.

She tied off the last of Trudy's pin curls, gave the little girl a gentle push from the bed, and finally answered Jessie. "No. He's not my beau."

"Think he might be someday?"

Rebekah turned firm. With Jessie and with herself. "He'll be going back to Lexington when he finishes the map of the cave. So it'd be a waste of time for me to think about being sparked by Dev—Mr. Bale."

Jessie sighed, her expression dreamy. "I liked him. A lot better'n any o' the fellas 'round here."

Cissy shook her head. "Jessie, you ain't old enough to be thinkin' about fellas. Besides, you ain't seen handsome 'til you seen—" She bolted off the bed and tossed the covers aside. "If we don't all stop yammerin', Daddy's gonna come in here an' threaten to wear us all out."

The younger girls muttered, but they climbed under their covers and nestled against their pillows. In unison, they recited their bedtime prayers, and then Della said, "Turn out the light, Bek."

She turned the key on the lamp, and shadows shrouded the room.

Cissy wriggled onto her side facing Rebekah and tapped her shoulder. "Bek?"

Caught up in remembering bits and pieces of her day, she didn't want to be disturbed.

"Rebekah?" Cissy still whispered, but her tone changed from calm to insistent.

Rebekah sighed. "We're supposed to go to sleep, Cissy."

"I know but . . ." Her warm breath touched Rebekah's cheek, as light as the fingers resting on her shoulder. "Are you keepin' some of the money you make at the cave?"

"No. I'm giving it all to Daddy." Only one more week and she'd get her first full pay envelope. Daddy'd already shown her the little sack where he intended to set aside every penny of her pay for their legacy.

"Don't you wanna keep any of it?"

Not until the cemetery was done. And that would be a while. "No."

Cissy sighed. "You reckon Daddy'll expect me to give over everything Mr. Temperance pays me tomorrow? I was kinda hopin' to keep some. Use it for . . . myself."

Rebekah had been plenty surprised when Daddy gave permission for Cissy to work at the cave on a Sunday afternoon. Sunday was resting day—always had been. But maybe Daddy decided Cissy was getting old enough to make some decisions for herself. She hoped Cissy would make wise choices. She loved her sister, but she worried about her penchant toward foolhardiness.

She whispered, "Ask Daddy in the morning. With my money coming in and the money from the mushrooms, he probably won't mind you keeping some of it."

"How much do you think? Half? Maybe more?"

"I don't know, Cissy. Now stop talking and go to sleep before we bother the little girls."

Cissy huffed and rolled to her back. She lay quiet for so long Rebekah thought she'd drifted off to sleep. But then her soft voice tiptoed through the darkness again. "If I can't keep enough money for a ticket, I'll buy me a new dress. An' that'll be my ticket."

Rebekah jerked toward Cissy. "What's that mean?"

Her sister didn't answer.

Afraid of waking the others, Rebekah settled against the pillow and closed her eyes. But sleep evaded her for many hours.

## Cissy

Before taking the burro from the stable, Cissy caught hold of his jaw and made him look at her. "All right, Beau, you listen up now. If you don't wanna be turned into a pot o' glue, you're gonna need to be good today. Good as you smell." Whoever'd bathed him used a rose-scented soap. The burro smelled good enough to go courting. "So you just stand real still by me, let them rich people climb up on your back long enough for Mr. Temperance to take their picture, an' don't make a single little fuss. We'll both fare well."

Beau bobbed his head and tapped one shoe against the ground.

Cissy laughed. "That's a good boy." She pulled the traces. "C'mon now. Let's go."

Mr. Temperance smiled as she guided Beau to the spot on the lawn where he'd set up a screen painted to look like a barn front. Hay lay all over the ground, and a barrel and little length of picket fence sat in front of the screen. She wanted to ask why he didn't take the pictures in front of the real barn, but she decided not to pester him too much about his business. He might change his mind about letting her stay.

She positioned Beau in the center of the hay. The burro lowered his head to take a bite, but she gave the traces a little pull. "Huh-uh. None o' that. I told you, you gotta stand still an' be nice."

Mr. Temperance chuckled and came out from behind the three-legged stand holding up his camera. "I'm glad to see you're taking control of our cantankerous creature."

Cissy patted the pocket in the seam of her skirt. "I brought two cut-up apples from our cellar to treat 'im when he does good."

"Very wise. Do you find his appearance pleasing?"

She nodded. "He looks real good. Not a burr to be found, an' he smells even better than me. Like a whole bouquet of roses. I just used lye soap in my bath."

The man laughed long and hard. Her hackles rose. She bit the insides of her cheeks to stay quiet. She'd told Beau to behave, so she needed to set a good example by not telling the photographer to stop poking fun at her, but it wasn't easy.

Still chortling, Mr. Temperance crossed to a wooden box beneath a nearby cottonwood and removed a straw hat. He plunked it on Cissy's head, then stood back and gave her a head-to-toe look. He nodded. "Perfect. With your homespun dress, braids, and that hat, you could easily pass for a little stable hand."

Cissy seethed. He thought her nicest dress, the one Mama'd sewn from store-bought green muslin and touched up with hand-tatted lace, looked like something a person wore to work in a barn? She grabbed the brim of the hat, ready to throw it at him and storm off.

He looked beyond her, and his face lit. He waved. "Come on over, folks! We're ready for you." He aimed a warning look at Cissy and lowered his voice. "Keep a grip on ol' Beauregard now. I've got a dozen people signed up for photographs, and that means three dollars coming in." He hurried behind the camera.

She quickly added it in her head. If he made three dollars, then thirty-six cents would be hers. She leaned close and whispered in one of Beau's pointed ears, "Be good, you hear me?"

Just as she'd asked him to, Beau stood meekly next to Cissy and didn't even bray when people climbed onto his back. To reward him, she sneaked him little pieces of apple in between Mr. Temperance's use of the camera. As the hours wore on, she wondered how Beau managed to stay in one spot. Her feet hurt and she wanted to wiggle. But time and again she stood as still as a statue, holding on to Beau's reins and smiling for the camera.

At six o'clock Mr. Temperance folded up the camera's stand and laid it gently in the grass. Then he crossed to her and tapped the top of her straw hat. "Well done, Miss Hardin. Old Beauregard was as good as gold today. You transformed an irascible beast into a purring pussycat." He reached to scratch Beau's ears, but the burro shied away and snapped at his hand. He leaped back and scowled at the animal. "Then again, maybe you haven't."

Cissy slipped her arm over Beau's neck. "Remember what you promised, Mr. Temperance. You said if he behaved today, you wouldn't sell him to the glue factory."

"He isn't going to do me an ounce of good if the only time he behaves is in your presence."

Cissy's mind started whirling. Quick as a striking snake, she blurted, "Then I guess you're gonna hafta to hire me on for good."

The man shook his head, his lips puckering up. "You're still in school. You couldn't be here every day even if I wanted to hire you."

"But school's almost out for the summer. Just one more week an' I could be at your beck an' call." Cissy had to convince him to take her on as his assistant. If she made thirty-six cents every day, she could put almost four dollars in her pocket every week. That was more than Bek made. By the end of summer, if she stuck around and if Daddy let her keep half her pay, the way he'd told her at breakfast, she'd have enough money for new clothes and tickets for the stage-coach and train, and enough left over to get her set up in her new town.

She clasped her hands under her chin. "Please, Mr. Temperance? You said yourself Beau's as good as gold when I'm around. Keep me around, an' you can keep bringin' in money."

"I could bring in just as much or more by selling him and purchasing a more reliable animal. One I can control without any help."

She didn't think that was true. The glue factory didn't pay top dollar, but a farmer would ask plenty for a gentle burro. Before Cissy could voice her argu-ment, a man holding hands with a little girl about the same size as Little Nellie approached.

Mr. Temperance turned to the guest with a smile. "Yes, sir? How may I help you?"

"My little girl would like to pet the pony. May we . . ."

A pony? Cissy snorted. These city folks didn't know much.

"Of course, sir." Mr. Temperance held his hand toward Cissy.

She swallowed a smile and placed the reins in his hand. "There you go. Bye now."

Beauregard curled his lips and brayed.

The little girl grabbed her father around the leg.

The photographer shoved the reins at Cissy.

As soon as she took them, Beau bowed his head. Cissy flashed a saucy grin at the burro's owner and then quirked her fingers at the child. "C'mon on over. He's as nice as can be. Wanna pet his nose?" She ignored Mr. Temperance's sharp gasp and crouched down. The child scurried over and stood close to Cissy. She curled her arm around the little girl's waist. "His nose is so soft. Soft as your silk dress. He likes it when people rub his nose real gentle."

The child slowly raised her hand and placed her palm on Beau's nose. He snuffled and the girl laughed. "He's funny!"

Cissy laughed, too, because Mr. Temperance's face had gone all red. "Yep, he sure is. Funniest burro in the whole county, I reckon."

The little girl wriggled away from Cissy and ran to her father. "I wanna ride the horsy."

The man pulled his wallet from his jacket and opened it. "How much for my daughter to have a ride?"

Cissy stood. "Beauregard isn't a ridin' pony, mister. But your little girl can have her picture taken sittin' right on him. I'll stay close an' make sure nothin' happens to her." She looked expectantly at Mr. Temperance.

He cleared his throat and reached for his camera. "Yes, of course, sir. If you'd like a souvenir photograph, I'll get my camera set up." He glowered at Cissy, but she only smiled and swung the little girl's hand.

"Thank you. I believe she would enjoy having a photograph to carry home with her. How much?"

Cissy said, "Fifty cents."

The gentleman handed over a fifty-cent piece without even blinking.

Cissy lifted the little girl onto Beau's back and put her straw hat on the child's head.

She giggled and waved at her father. "Look at me, Daddy!"

He beamed as brightly as if his daughter had just won the Kentucky Derby.

Cissy gripped the reins with one hand and used her other hand to keep the child steady. "You gotta hold real still until you hear a pop, but don't be scared. The camera won't hurt you none."

"She's had her portrait done many times," the father said. "Haven't you, Ruby?"

The little girl nodded so hard she almost lost Cissy's hat.

Jealousy struck Cissy with force. Until today, she'd never had her picture made. Nobody in her family had.

Mr. Temperance peeked out from behind the camera. "Well, let's make this photograph the best one ever. Look right here, smile, and . . ." He pressed the bulb.

A soft *pop* reached Cissy's ears. She held her position for a few more seconds before catching the child under the arms and lifting her down. "There you go. Have your daddy come see Mr. Temperance tomorrow to pick up your picture." She repeated what she'd heard the photographer tell the other customers all day.

The gentleman frowned. "My family is departing the estate on the late stage this evening, so you'll need to send the photograph through the post."

While Mr. Temperance and the gentleman exchanged information, Cissy retrieved her hat and put it in the crate. Then she carried the crate to the barn with Beau slogging along on her heels. She settled him in a stall and told one of the stable workers to give the little burro water, oats, and a brushing. The young man scurried into action, and Cissy couldn't help puffing up. Nobody'd ever followed her directions so fast before. She liked being important.

When she returned to the false barn front, Mr. Temperance was standing next to his camera with his hands on his hips, scowling. "You think you're pretty slick, don't you?"

Cissy feigned innocence.

"Don't give me that look. You know exactly what I'm talking about. Doubling my price and taking over with that spoiled little girl. You think I can't do this job without you."

She grinned. "I didn't do too bad, did I?"

He smirked. "You did very well. But you already know that." He sat on the barrel and pinched his chin. "As much as I hate to admit it, you and that ill-behaved burro make a good team."

Cissy's pulse doubled as hope filled her. "So . . . you gonna let me keep workin' for you?"

He squinted at her for long seconds. Then he sighed. "Until school lets out for the season, it will be quiet here during the week, so there would be no sense in you coming around. But if your parents give their approval, I'd like you to come next weekend both Saturday and Sunday. And then, when the summer break begins, every day until school starts again."

Cissy let out a whoop of joy.

He burst out laughing. "Now, you haven't gained permission from your parents yet, so don't start celebrating until then."

"Oh, they'll let me. Just wait an' see."

"If you're half as convincing with them as you've been with me, I have no doubt." He caught her hand and turned it palm up. "Here you go. Today's pay."

She gazed down at the coin, astounded. He'd given her the fifty-cent piece. "But . . . But . . ."

"Call it a bonus."

She slipped the coin into her shoe, wiggled her toes, and then grinned at the photographer.

He winked. He slapped his knees and stood. "I have work to do—photographs to print. I'll hope to see you next Saturday, Miss Cissy."

"No need to hope. You'll see me for sure. Bye now!" She dashed around the barn, smiling so big her cheeks hurt, and plowed straight into somebody. She bounced backward and landed hard on her bottom. The air left her lungs, and her head spun.

Someone knelt beside her and took her arm. "Please forgive me. I didn't see you. Are you all right?"

Gasping, she forced her bleary eyes to focus. And when they did, she gave a start. The person who'd knocked her down was the same man who'd plagued her thoughts and dreams since the day he found her counting money at the stream. She wheezed, "It's you."

# TWENTY

## Devlin

Devlin gripped the girl by the upper arms and helped her to her feet. "Are you all right? We collided pretty hard."

She touched her forehead and grimaced. "That hurt."

He fingered his chin and chuckled. "I agree. I think your head dislocated my jaw." She blinked at him, her round green-blue eyes appearing a bit glassy. Maybe the bump had done more damage than he'd realized. He reached for her arm.

She skittered backward, her movements clumsy. "I gotta go home, mister. Gotta talk to my daddy." She spun and took off.

Devlin, watching after her, shook his head. He'd never seen a flightier child. He hoped she made it home without any further mishaps. He continued on to the barn, fingering his sore chin and situating the sextant he'd slipped under his jacket before setting it more securely in the waistband of his trousers. She'd jammed the bronze instrument against his ribs. If they both didn't sport bruises by morning, he'd be surprised.

He located the stable manager, Alvis Vance, in a small room in the far corner of the barn, sitting in a rickety chair tipped back on two legs and sipping from a thick ceramic mug. He looked so relaxed Devlin hated to disturb him, but he couldn't take a horse without permission.

"Excuse me?"

The man thumped the chair on all four legs and slapped the mug onto the nearby desk. "Yes, sir. Mr. Bale, ain't it? What can I do for ya?"

"I wondered if I might borrow Marey for a few hours this evening." She'd proven herself a gentle, cooperative beast during yesterday's long excursion with

Rebekah and her little sister. The ride wouldn't be as enjoyable alone, but he needed to do some private exploration today.

Alvis frowned. "I could have Junior or Elton saddle her for you, but to be truthful, Mr. Bale, I don't think it's wise to go off this late in the day. Sun sets mighty early in the hills an', well . . . it just ain't wise."

The remembrance of something Rebekah had said yesterday writhed within him, and he knew he wouldn't be able to rest until he'd satisfied his curiosity. "I took careful note of the roads yesterday. I'm confident I won't become lost."

The man's frown didn't fade. "You bein' a map drawer an' all, I'm not denyin' you've got some know-how the average stranger in these parts don't, but when dark falls a person can lose his bearings right fast. An' dark is when the critters start prowlin'. I'd be shirkin' my duties if I sent you off at this time o' day without givin' you a firm warnin'."

They were wasting time arguing. He wished he'd come earlier in the afternoon and written the letter to Mother and Father during the evening hours instead.

"Tell you what." Alvis perched on the edge of his creaky desk and folded his beefy arms over the straining buttons of his dirty shirt. "I'll send Junior Berry with you. He grew up not two miles from Mammoth Cave, an' he knows these hills inside an' out. He could bring you back here safe even if you put a blindfold on him."

Devlin chuckled. "I wouldn't test him in that manner."

Finally Alvis smiled. "You wait here. I'll fetch Junior, an' you an' him can be on your way real quick."

Devlin's definition of "real quick" and Alvis Vance's were quite different. By the time Devlin and Junior set off—Devlin on Marey and Junior riding a plodding, gray-muzzled horse named, ignominiously, Lightning—the shadows lay long across the ground and a sliver of moon glowed against the pale sky. When Devlin told Junior where he wanted to go, the younger man offered a silent nod and nudged Lightning into motion. Devlin urged Marey to follow.

Junior balanced a rifle, the barrel pointing skyward, on his thigh and led them through trees and up a rise. Devlin ducked away from branches, unwilling to receive a second smack on the face that evening. The farther into the woods they rode, the cooler the air became and the deeper the shadows. Devlin's frame involuntarily shuddered. Maybe Alvis had been right about choosing this time of day for a ride.

"Purty sure the cave you was talkin' about is right close in here." Junior's voice took on an eerie quality drifting from the cool gloaming. "I'll show you the openin', but ain't no way I'm takin' you in it. Not without a lantern."

Devlin didn't necessarily want to go in, but he needed to judge its entrance in relation to the tunnels he'd thus far explored in Mammoth Cave. "That's fine. Thank you."

Still pointing the rifle skyward, Junior brought Lightning to a stop and slid down from the horse's back. "Come on over here."

Devlin swung to the ground and, keeping a tight grip on Marey's reins, followed Junior through a very narrow gap in the trees. A small, sloping patch of thickly grassed ground, deeply shadowed, waited on the other side of the gap. A crooked opening with rocks and brush at its base appeared black against the hillside.

Junior pointed. "There it is."

Devlin moved directly to the crevice and then removed his sextant from beneath his jacket. Generally used by sea captains, it had proved useful in providing information about general locations on land, as well. He located the North Star through the peephole, adjusted the plumb line, tightened it to preserve its position, and then returned the instrument to his waistband. He turned to find Junior gaping at him.

Devlin smiled and patted the bump beneath his jacket. "If my measurement proves accurate, I won't need your help finding the cave next time."

The youth closed his mouth and shook his head. "That's about the strangest thing I ever seen somebody do. You sure you ain't a bootlegger lookin' for a likely place to put a still?"

Devlin burst out laughing. He would remember to share Junior's comment with Father. "I'm very sure."

"So you all done?"

Devlin squelched his amusement and nodded.

Junior gave a lithe leap onto Lightning's back. "Let's get back then. Time for bears an' cougars to start prowlin'."

Devlin didn't need a second prompting. Back in his cottage he returned the sextant to its wood carrying case and then used the case as a lap desk to add to the letter he'd begun earlier.

> *I recorded the location of a small cave in the hills roughly three-quarters of a mile north of Mammoth Cave. According to locals—namely, Rebekah and Jessie—there are dozens of small caves in the hills.*

Excitement stirred within him. He placed the pen's nib on the paper again.

> *If each of them is somehow linked to Mammoth Cave, the possibilities for exploration are endless; the possibilities for furthering the tourism of this estate are infinite.*

Dollar signs danced in front of his eyes. He closed the letter, sealed it inside an envelope, and set it aside for posting in the morning. He hoped the summer weeks would provide adequate time to discover every potential benefit of securing Mammoth Cave and the surrounding acreage for the fine state of Kentucky.

Devlin ducked low and eased sideways through the most narrow, winding, low-ceilinged passage he'd traversed since his first day in the cave. Rebekah, candle in hand, followed him. She and Tolly had deposited their torches, as well as their packs and his waywiser, nearly a quarter of a mile back in a small igloo-shaped cavern. The candle's dancing flame did little to provide guidance, and he'd bumped his head on outcroppings twice so far.

Bumps didn't bother him, though. At least not much. His greater concern was unwittingly encountering a bat or a spider. Given his inability to escape, trapped within such close quarters, he'd be at the creature's mercy.

Somewhere ahead Tolly waited with Devlin's tape-measure case in hand. When Devlin caught up to him—assuming he didn't get wedged in somewhere and spend the rest of his life trapped in a crevice in Mammoth Cave—he'd mark the one hundred feet in his book and then hold the end of the metal ribbon and let Tolly move ahead again, releasing the ribbon until it reached its full length.

They'd repeated the process nearly a dozen times in the past hours, progressing at a snail's pace. Devlin's stomach growled, and his impatience to be finished with the tunnel grew. When would it end?

"Ouch!" Rebekah cried out sharply and then darkness descended like a curtain falling.

Devlin froze in place, his heart thudding into his chest. "What happened?"

"The candle burned my thumb. I dropped it."

"Well, light another one," he snapped. The darkness, the tightness, the inability to discern where he was raised a wave of panic.

"Give me a minute. It's hard to reach in my pocket when I can hardly bend my arm." Her words held a bite, too.

He counted the seconds, waiting with his jaw clamped so hard his teeth ached, expecting a bat to swoop in and tangle in his hair any minute. He heard the strike of flint, and light flared behind his shoulder. Startled, he bounced his temple against the close rock wall. He winced.

A soft glow flowed over his shoulder. "I'm sorry it took me so long. Are you all right?"

He wasn't. His head throbbed. His shoulders ached. His stomach was full of knots. But he said, "I'm fine. Are you ready to move on?"

"Yes. Go ahead."

Devlin swallowed against his dry throat—what he wouldn't give for a sip of water—and forced himself forward a few inches.

Tolly's voice carried from somewhere ahead. "Hold up. I'm comin' yo' way."

Rebekah called, "Is something wrong, Tolly?"

"Jus' at the end, an' it's plenty tight. Dunno why I di'n't think of it befo', but there ain't no need fo' you to come all the way to the end, too." He sounded as if he spoke from the inside of a barrel.

Devlin frowned. "What about the measurement, Tolly?"

"Pulled the tape as far as seventy-two feet. Write that down, Devlin, an' stay put."

Rebekah thrust the candle forward, and Devlin wriggled until he connected the stub of pencil with his notebook. He checked the list of numbers and determined they'd gone 1,472 feet into a tunnel Stephen Bishop hadn't included on his map. Despite the morning's tension, he couldn't stop a smile from growing. What an accomplishment.

Scuffling sounds sifted through the tunnel, and then a timid flicker of light let them know Tolly was near. His smile gleamed in his candle's light as he squeezed next to Devlin. "Dunno 'bout you, but I's ready to get outta this pinchin' spot an' have some san'wiches. I worked up a powerful hunguh wigglin' my way through here." He pressed the measuring tape into Devlin's hand.

"That sounds good to me, too." By twisting himself like a contortionist, Devlin managed to slip the tape into his jacket pocket and reverse his direction. He found himself nose to nose with Rebekah and her candle. The tiny flame ignited the gold flecks in her brown eyes. For the first time since they entered this sliver of a passageway, he didn't rue the small space.

Tolly cleared his throat. "Um, you two wanna get movin'? Gonna take a while to get back out, an' my belly's grumblin'."

Rebekah laughed softly, her expulsion of breath making the candle flame dance. "Devlin, would you take the candle, please?"

He worked his arm upward and tightly pinched the length of beeswax. Her hand slipped away, and she squirmed sideways, giggling, until she faced the opposite direction. Devlin leaned back as far as he could to prevent scorching her braid.

"Well, boy, you got that candle now. Prob'ly gonna hafta keep it until we get to a spot big enough to stretch yo' arm full out. Reb, can you see good enough to go?"

"I can't see a thing in front of me, Tolly, but with the walls so tight, I can't possibly go off course. Follow me."

Devlin gripped a handful of Rebekah's jacket and held the candle as high as possible. Slowly they inched their way back up the tunnel, the scuff of their clothes against the walls and the hollow thuds of their boots creating an inharmonious melody. Devlin strained to capture the music of the cave, but it remained elusive. Maybe it couldn't reach so deep into the crevices. He missed its presence.

The candle burned down and they stopped to light a new one. This time Rebekah kept it, and Devlin focused on the little glow of light beyond her shoulder and hat, choosing to see it as a beacon rather than a mere flicker. At last they emerged into the domed cavern where the waywiser and packs awaited them.

Devlin staggered to the center of the area and stretched, extending his arms straight up and arching his back. He groaned as his muscles released. When he lowered his arms, lightheadedness attacked, and he grabbed the wall to support himself. His palm descended inches above the waywiser.

He stared at the wheeled instrument, confusion striking hard. He'd leaned the waywiser against the wall beside the crevice's opening before going in. So what was it doing opposite the crevice? And why was it showing a distance of twelve feet instead of being on zero, the way he'd reset it after reaching the dome?

He turned a slow circle, frowning through the shadows. Rebekah stood near Tolly, candle held aloft, while Tolly bent over the packs. The man was muttering, and Rebekah's lips were set in a grim line.

Devlin joined them. "What's the matter?"

She turned a worried look on him. "Some of our torches are missing."

"Four of 'em." Tolly rummaged through the second pack. "An' somebody's done took off wit' my extra canteen, half our san'wiches, an' the applesauce cake Coopuh baked up special jus' fo' me." He rose slowly, his dark eyes searching the space.

Devlin looked from the pair of guides to the packs and then to the waywiser. Chills broke out across every inch of his flesh. "Do you suppose one of the tour groups came through and helped themselves to your supplies?"

Tolly snorted. "None o' the daily paid tours take these passages. Too hard to get through. An' too dangerous. We's gone way deepuh than any tour group 'cept the all-day-long explorin' ones that don't start 'til midsummuh. Even then, the people'd be with a pair o' our guides, an' they'd have they own supplies. No need for none o' them to bother things left by anothuh guide. No, suh, this ain't the work of no guide, I can tell you that."

"Who do you suppose was here, Tolly?" Rebekah sounded as unnerved as Devlin felt.

"I dunno. Mr. Janin'll have a fit when he finds out somebody 'sides us's been this far in." Tolly's black face glistened in the flickering candlelight. "Whoevuh it be, no good's comin' of them bein' here, that's fo' sure."

# Twenty-One

## Tolly

Tolly wadded the empty napkin and threw it into his gaping pack. That sandwich had tasted awful good, and he wanted another one, except there wasn't another one. He hoped their thief enjoyed the ham-and-cheese-on-rye-bread sandwiches.

He glanced at the two young people sitting on the other side of the candle. Both Devlin and Rebekah held empty napkins in their laps, so they were done, too. "Now that we got our bellies filled"—as best they could with only a sandwich apiece—"we'd best be skedaddlin' outta here. We can't be stayin' in the cave the rest o' the day like we'd planned."

Devlin frowned. "I don't mind skipping our afternoon snack."

Tolly shook his head. "Gots nothin' to do wit' not havin' a snack. Gotta have enough torches to get ourselves back out. Whoever pilfuhed Reb's pack left us only three. We go in any fu'thuh, we ain't gonna be able to see to get out. 'Cept with candles, an' them's s'posed to be for 'mergencies, not all-the-time usin'."

Besides, he needed to talk to the estate trustee. The sooner he did it, the better. He buckled the strap on his pack, slung it on his back, and scooped up his coil of rope. "Reb, get one o' those torches lit an' then we'll go on out to daylight."

Tolly raised the flaming torch and set off with Devlin and Rebekah trailing him. He didn't talk as he went. Too many worries nibbled at him. Reb and Devlin stayed quiet, too, and he sensed their unease. Tolly gritted his teeth, stifling a growl. First rule of being a good guide, his pappy'd told him, was keeping his charges safe. The second was easing their fears. He wasn't being a good guide today.

The rock corridor widened, space for two good-sized men to walk side by side. So Tolly stopped and waited for Devlin to ease up beside him. Pasting on a big smile, he said brightly, "How'd yo' travelin' through the hills on Satuhday go? You get to meet lotsa folks?"

Surprise showed on the college boy's face for a moment. But then he nodded. "Yes, I did. The country around here is beautiful. I understand why folks want to live in the hills. But . . ." He shot a puzzled look over his shoulder at Rebekah. "I noticed something."

"What's 'at?"

"The people have their own unique dialect."

Tolly scratched his cheek. "They's own what?"

Devlin chuckled softly. "Dialect—manner of speaking. But Reb's doesn't quite match." He sent another quick look behind him. "Why is it, Reb, that you don't speak like your family and those who live around you?"

Tolly was interested in the answer, too. Youngsters in these parts went to the same school, same churches. The black folks in the area had one way of speaking, the white hills folks another. But Devlin was right—Reb spoke different from them all.

"I speak English, same as my family."

Devlin shook his head. "You speak English, but not the same. Your English is more . . . refined. As if you were raised in an educated family."

Rebekah's snort carried plainly to Tolly's ears. He whistled and nudged Devlin with his elbow. "Careful there, boy. I think you might be gettin' her danduh up."

Devlin made a face. "I didn't intend to insult you. Or your family. *Educated* and *intelligent* aren't necessarily synonymous. But after spending the afternoon with you and your sister, the differences in your speech became quite evident. Why do you have a more pronounced speech pattern, Reb? Have you done some traveling, perhaps attended school outside of the hills?"

They trudged onward, the torchlight bouncing off the walls and painting a circle for them to follow. After several seconds of silence, Reb finally sighed.

"I've never been farther from home than I am now at the estate. But . . . I used to read."

Tolly's chest clenched. Reading was a touchy subject for folks of his color. Having been born into slavery, he didn't get the chance for schooling until after the war. But even then, the school open to black children didn't have the same books and such as the white children's schools. And the teacher didn't seem to think the dark-faced children sitting on the benches had sense enough to learn. What he picked up in the way of education mostly came from watching and doing and studying on his own.

But he could read some. And he could write his full name instead of making a mark. His pappy'd been right proud of him for learning to spell out his full name—Tolliver Moses Sandford. But he'd never in his fifty-four years of life read a book from its beginning to its end. Not even his grandpappy's Bible. Someday he sure hoped to.

Devlin's eyebrows shot up. "There's a library around here?"

"No. But a woman started coming around with a book wagon nine or ten years ago. She rides through twice a month, and folks borrow whatever they want and then give it back when she returns. I've borrowed dozens of books from her."

Why hadn't the woman ever come to the estate? He'd have borrowed a book or two.

Devlin said, "Who is your favorite author, Reb?"

"I'm particularly fond of Hawthorne and Dumas, and my sisters like me to read Alcott's works to them at bedtime."

The two of them chatted about *The Count of Monte Cristo,* talk beyond Tolly's understanding, but he stayed quiet and let them jabber on. They didn't sound scared or worried anymore, and with them talking to each other, he could give some thought to who might have come along and poked around in their packs.

During the summer months families with youngsters old enough to be running around on their own but not grown up enough to develop good sense yet spent weeks at the estate. And every summer they'd had to watch to make sure none of them sneaked into parts of the cave not open to guests. It was still early—school still going—so he didn't think he could blame the theft of the torches and food on visiting school-age boys. But maybe some local youths, too old for school but not staying busy in their daddies' fields, had come in without invitation. Maybe a thief or some other kind of criminal was using the caverns as a hiding spot from the law. The cave's entrance was unblocked all day even though the guides came and went for only three different tours. Somebody could go in easy enough.

The passage narrowed, and Tolly moved into the lead again. The tire on the waywiser *squeak-squeaked* along behind him, and Devlin and Reb started talking about some poor woman who'd been forced to wear a red letter on her dress so everybody would know she'd sinned. As aggravated as Tolly was with whoever'd come along and taken those turnovers—his mouth watered just thinking about the moist cake spiced with cinnamon—he wouldn't publicly shame the thief. He'd give him a good talking-to, though, about being foolish.

He might not have been educated in a schoolhouse, but he knew this cave inside and out. His pappy'd pounded into him the importance of never going in alone, of always taking emergency gear, of marking his way and counting his steps and always—always—watching where he put his feet. Children looking for adventure didn't have safety in their heads. That's how come they ran into trouble, like Reb's brother had done. Finding one boy dead in the cave was too many for Tolly's heart. He couldn't take it if somebody else came up lost and dead in his cave.

The passage curved gently, bringing them to the final leg of the Grand Crossing. Up ahead the Corkscrew waited—a taxing climb to Broadway, the large tunnel that led to the outside. He'd light a new torch when they reached the Corkscrew, make sure they had good light for the climb, and as soon as they made it back to the hotel, he'd tell the trustee it was time to post guards outside the entrance day and night. The man claimed he appreciated Tolly's knowledge of the cave, but he didn't always act like he appreciated getting advice from a white-bearded black man. And he didn't always take the advice, either.

Well, if Mr. Janin didn't see fit to follow Tolly's suggestion, then he would put the guides on a watch-keeping schedule himself. Maybe, if he was real lucky, one of them would catch his thief coming out of the cave and he'd be able to give the reckless person a dose of sense.

## Rebekah

Rebekah's hands trembled as she battled hickory bark into a tight bundle around the ball of pitch at the end of the river-cane handle. She sat on her stoop alone. Tolly had gone to the main building to talk to the cave's trustee. With him gone and Devlin at work at the table in her cabin, it seemed as if she and Devlin sat side by side.

She listened to the *scritch-scritch* of his pen on the paper, the occasional creak of the chair as he shifted positions, the soft clearing of his throat. How could such insignificant noises affect her so deeply? It was as though her entire being was connected to him somehow. A disconcerting feeling. And she needed to break the spell.

Without conscious thought she began singing one of the ballads Mama used to sing at night as the fire began to die in the hearth. "'It was in and about the Martinmas time, when the green leaves were a-falling, that Sir John Graeme, in the West Country, fell in love with Barbara Allen . . .'" She held back, not singing so loudly she would attract the attention of the other guides who'd left their doors open to invite in the evening breeze but loudly enough to cover the sounds proving Devlin's presence.

On she sang from verse to verse, almost mindlessly, while continuing to fashion the torches. The gentle breeze teased her hair. She pushed the waving strands behind her ears, never missing a beat of the ballad. She reached the final verse and finished as breathily as if she'd been running a footrace. "'Since my love died for me today, I'll die for him tomorrow.'"

"It's a lovely song, but the words are somewhat depressing, don't you think?"

She jolted. The torch slipped from her hands and bounced on the grass, the bark coming loose. She shot a look over her shoulder. Devlin leaned against the doorjamb, his arms crossed negligently over his chest and one toe planted against the floor. Oh, what a pose of relaxation and confidence he painted.

Heat attacked her face. She reached for the torch. "I suppose most of the ballads the hills folks sing are sad stories set to music."

"Are they all so haunting in melody?"

She wasn't sure what he meant by "haunting." She rolled the bark tightly and didn't answer.

His sigh drifted on the breeze. "I'm sorry I disturbed you. I'll return to work. Feel free to sing another ballad, Miss Reb. I find your voice very pleasing."

The scuff of footsteps followed by the squeak of the chair legs told her he'd settled himself at the table again. She swallowed the odd lump of longing his kind words had stirred and searched her mind for another ballad. She chose one Daddy liked to sing, "The Wayfaring Stranger." "'I'm just a poor wayfaring stranger, traveling through this world of woe . . . '"

The final stanza, which spoke of going home to see one's Savior, tugged at Rebekah's heart in a sweet way even though it referenced death. Heaven, the true home for each of God's followers, waited at the end of her life's journey. Grandpappy, Grandmama, all the little babies who'd gone straight from Mama's belly to Jesus's arms, and Andy were already there. She wasn't in any hurry to join them, but it gave her a lift to know she'd be with them again someday.

"Very nice, Miss Reb." Devlin's warm voice carried from inside the cabin, sending a spiral of pleasure around her frame.

She hugged herself, smiling, and then a worrisome thought attacked. She sat up straight and tried to peer through the doorway. "Devlin?"

"Yes?"

"Will you go to heaven when you die?"

Silence fell inside the cabin for long seconds. Then a soft chuckle rolled. "What kind of question is that?"

An important one. He'd leave at the end of the summer, and she might not ever see him again. Except in the land of glory. She planted her palms on the stoop to hold herself in place. "I want to know. Are you heaven bound?"

The chair legs screeched. His feet thudded on the floor. He stepped into the doorframe, a scowl marring his brow. "Are you asking me seriously?"

She nodded, her entire body tense.

His scowl remained intact. He pushed his hands into his trouser pockets and tucked his elbows tight. "I hope so. The thought of going to . . . the other place . . . holds no delight. I'm a good person. I follow the laws penned by men, and I don't believe I break any of the commandments written in the Bible." His stiff pose melted, and relief crept across his features. "So, yes, I suppose you could say I'm heaven bound."

Tears stung Rebekah's eyes. Preacher Haynes's voice echoed in her memory. *"Hell's depths'll be filled with good folks who never took the time to meet Jesus."* Slowly she shook her head, partly in response to Devlin's statement and partly in unwillingness to accept the truth of what his answer indicated. Unless something changed in his heart, she wouldn't see him again after this summer. And that thought pained her worse than anything ever had.

# TWENTY-TWO

*Rebekah*

Rebekah bolted upright, sending the unfinished torch rolling across the ground. "Devlin, you—"

"Reb!" Tolly jogged toward them, his face glistening with perspiration in the early-evening sunlight. "Go tell all the guides to meet in my cabin. We gots somethin' impo'tant to talk about."

Rebekah wrung her hands. She had something important to talk to Devlin about. "But, Tolly, I—"

"Get 'em now, Reb. An' hurry. Gotta get this settled befo' the sun sets."

She felt the same way, but she couldn't argue with her boss. She sighed. "Yes, sir."

Devlin went back inside, and she made her way along the row of cabins, knocking on doorjambs and directing everyone to meet with Tolly. Within a few minutes, they'd all crowded into his cabin and found places to sit.

Rebekah perched on the corner of Tolly's bed next to a burly guide named Luther and listened while Tolly explained the day's theft. "Mr. Janin, he already has men hired to guard the cave's openin', but they ain't scheduled to start work fo' anothuh couple weeks. So even though he agrees we best start early an' keep the openin' to the cave secure from trespassuhs, he say he might not be able to bring them fellas in befo' the summer season. An' it ain't likely somebody's gonna wanna take on a job that only lasts a week. So I tol' him we guides would take turns until his fellas could get here."

Complaining mumbles rolled through the room.

Tolly raised his pink palms. "I know, I know, means we's gonna be losin' some sleep. But trust me when I say we'll lose less sleep keepin' watch than we will if somebody gets lost in there an' ends up dyin'."

More murmurs circulated, these offering agreement.

Tolly smiled. "I figure we can do this one o' two ways. Each o' us takes a few hours ever' day, or we can go ever' othuh day coverin' longuh hours. I's gonna let y'all choose."

Rebekah didn't care, so she sat in silence. While the men established a daily schedule, she planned how she would address the topic of knowing for sure where a person would spend eternity. Her heart felt weighted by Devlin's uncertainty. How could folks live day to day not knowing for sure their souls were secure? His frown and uncertain comment—"I hope so"—haunted her. She twitched with eagerness to leave this meeting and talk to Devlin.

"Reb, you gonna be all right takin' the early-mo'nin' shift?"

She jerked. "What?"

Tolly scowled at her. "Ain't you listenin'?"

All eight guides were looking at her. She hunched her shoulders, wishing she could shrink. "I . . . I'm sorry. I guess I wasn't."

Tolly huffed. "Well, listen up now. The men don't want you sittin' out at the openin' alone in the dark. So they's willing to take the nighttime hours an' give you the ones aftuh the sun comes up an' befo' the tours start. Is you agreeable?"

She flashed a grateful smile across the sea of faces. "Yes, and thank you."

Tolly shook his head, his lips pursed in a tight line.

She lowered her head.

He addressed the others, his tone brisk. "All right then, Crit, you head on out there now. Argil'll relieve you at midnight. Belvy, take ovuh at three, an' then Reb'll come take yo' place at six. Reb, you stay put there 'til Luthuh brings the first tour group at nine."

"All right, Tolly." Then she gave a start. "But wait. I can't be at the opening from six to nine. We take Devlin in at seven."

Tolly's face pinched into a grimace. He gestured to the others, and they filed out. As soon as they were gone, Tolly guided Rebekah onto his stoop and stood with his hands in his pockets. "Listen, Reb, next few days, I'm plannin' on purty much campin' in the cave. Gonna be goin' in too deep to come back out ever' evenin'. Just wouldn't be right fo' you, bein' female, to stay nights in there wit' the two o' us men. So I'm gonna have you pair up wit' Crit, an' I'm takin' Lee in wit' me an' Devlin."

Her heart sank. "But, Tolly, I—"

"Now, you'll be jus' fine wit' Crit. He knows that cave as good as I do, an' I'd trust him wit' my own daughter if I had one. So no worryin'. I tol' Crit he could count on you." He squinted one eye at her. "I di'n't tell 'im wrong, now did I?"

She swallowed a protest. "No, sir."

"That's what I thought." Tolly patted her shoulder and then gave her a little nudge toward the pile of torch materials lying in the grass next to her stoop. "Now, I already put Coopuh on packin' up a goodly portion o' victuals, an' we's also gonna need a whole passel o' torches. So c'mon, let's get busy."

Rebekah shot Tolly a hopeful look. "Is it all right if I talk to Devlin while we work?"

An uneasy glimmer entered his eyes. "You's gonna miss gettin' to see him ever' day, ain'tcha?"

More heat flooded her face. She wished she could deny Tolly's statement, but she couldn't. Not without telling a bald lie. But Tolly didn't know everything. "He and I were talking about something important when you came along and interrupted. I want to finish the conversation."

Tolly glanced through her doorway. Regret—or was it relief?—pursed his face. "Well, I's sorry, Reb, but that talk's gonna hafta wait fo' anothuh day. Devlin's already gone on to his place."

## Devlin

Rebekah's sweet yet poignant melodies played through Devlin's memory as he readied himself for bed. It was early yet for sleep, but according to Tolly they would have a more taxing day tomorrow than any thus far and then they would sleep in the cave. He speculated tomorrow night would be a restless, wakeful one, so extra sleep tonight would benefit him. If he could manage to fall asleep.

Most of the guests had departed on yesterday's evening stagecoaches, including the young couple who'd spent the weekend in the cottage next to his. Their constant chatter and laughter had filtered even through the solid log wall, intruding upon his privacy. Tonight, however, the silence seemed cloying, and he missed the sounds that proved how much they enjoyed each other's company.

Loneliness panged. A surprising emotion. He couldn't honestly recall ever experiencing loneliness, even though he'd spent a good portion of his childhood alone. But lying there in his bed with fading evening light slanting through his window, he pondered the strange emptiness holding him captive, such a contrast to the full, blissful feelings he'd experienced while listening to Rebekah sing from her spot on the cabin's stoop.

A smile pulled at the corners of his mouth in response to his reflections. She was a woman of surprises. Somehow, even attired in men's clothing, she possessed a graceful femininity. She carried a heavy tote mile after mile over uneven terrain and offered not even the slightest complaint. She spent her days toiling to earn a wage but not for her own uses. Instead, she worked to benefit her family, which spoke so clearly of her unselfish character.

The hollow ache in his chest magnified. Was he truly lying here in his shadowy room pining for a young woman from the hill country? Mother would be appalled. Generally the thought of his parents' displeasure would send him scurrying in a different direction, but his desire to spend time with Rebekah didn't diminish. Not even a smidgeon.

He blew out a noisy breath, punched the pillow twice, and rolled to his side. He closed his eyes, determined to set aside thoughts of Rebekah and indulge in a deep, restful sleep. A snippet of the last song Rebekah had crooned whispered through his mind.

*"I'm going home no more to roam . . ."*

The words taunted him, but he didn't understand why. And the confusion held sleep at bay for hours.

*Cissy*

Cissy herded Della, Jessie, Tabitha, and Trudy out the door and up the road. Her heart beat a happy patter. Only one more week of school and then she'd be free of studies and books and clumsy boys who took glory in teasing. The summer stretched out in front of her like the open arms of a handsome gentleman, beckoning her to step into the embrace and experience bliss.

She fell behind the others, enjoying a few moments of solitude while birds chirped in the trees and squirrels chased each other through patches of shade. She couldn't remember the last time she'd felt so happy. So carefree. And all because Daddy and Mama had told her she could take the job at the cave with Mr. Temperance.

She'd always hated working. Hated doing her schoolwork. Hated doing her chores. Hated looking after her little sisters. But the idea of working for Mr. Temperance made her want to dance and sing. She giggled and spun a little circle, swinging her lunch pail so high it almost tipped out her sandwich and dried apples.

"Cissy Hardin, you're actin' plumb loco this mornin'. What's got into you?"

Cissy grinned at Pansy, who ambled up beside her. "Happiness, Pansy, that's what got into me. Pure, sweetly flowin' happiness."

Pansy scuffed up road dust with her bare feet. "Glad you're so all-fired happy, seein' as how you're gonna be leavin' me without a best friend here before long."

Pansy'd moped off and on ever since Cissy told her she planned to go live in the city, but she wouldn't let her friend's doldrums drag her into despair. Not today. "Well, guess what? I ain't gonna leave right away after all. Gonna stay around all summer instead."

Pansy's face lit. "Truly, Cissy?"

"That's right. I got me a job at the cave estate. Gonna be workin' there every afternoon for a man who takes photographs."

"Whatcha doin' for him? Cleanin' up?"

Cissy explained about Beau, enjoying Pansy's laughter when she talked about the burro trying to bite at Mr. Temperance's hand but taking little pieces of apples from her without the tiniest nip. "Guests line up to sit on Beau's back an' have their photograph made. An' you know what Mr. Temperance's payin' me? Three whole cents."

"A day?"

"No, silly, three cents for every picture."

Pansy squealed. "Cissy, you're gonna be rich!"

Cissy made a face. "I hafta give Daddy half of it. But even so, I'll be puttin' enough in my pocket to get me all the way to Nashville, Tennessee." She tossed her head, making her braids bounce. "If that's where I decide I wanna go."

Pansy shook her head, wonder blooming over her round face. "You could go just about anywhere in the world, I reckon." Then she grabbed Cissy's hand and made her stop. "But before you go, remember you gotta give me a keepsake. You been thinkin' on it?"

Cissy nodded. "But I ain't come up with anything yet. How about you?"

Pansy slipped her arm through Cissy's and tugged her forward. "I got somethin'. Somethin' real special."

"What?"

Pansy grinned. "I ain't gonna tell you yet. Not 'til you settle on your keepsake. Then it'll be a surprise."

Up ahead, Della turned around and waved her arm. "Hurry up, Cissy! Bell's gonna ring soon."

"I'm comin', I'm comin'." She and Pansy ran the rest of the way and slid onto their bench together.

The teacher called the roll and then started handing out assignments. Cissy listened with only half an ear. Who cared about long division or the latest addition to the Bill of Rights? She was going to be rich, and rich people didn't have to know anything.

# Twenty-Three

## Devlin

Time spent with Lee paled in comparison to time with Rebekah. Devlin appreciated the man's knowledge, strength, and diligence. The guide even buried their bodily waste without so much as a wrinkled nose. But he didn't talk about books, he didn't sing ballads, and he didn't have a long dark braid swinging gently against his spine to distract Devlin when the shadows of the cave tried to overwhelm him.

Tolly kept up a stream of chatter, though, and he knew the best places to stop for breaks. On their second day under the ground, Tolly allowed a twenty-minute rest at the cave's underground flower garden found along a tunnel called Cleveland Avenue. Devlin would never forget the beauty of the gypsum formations. He held a lantern aloft to better examine the delicate swirls and tiny crystal petals.

"Yessuh, hard to 'magine that minerals left behind from drippin' watuh could make somethin' so beautiful." Tolly's voice carried the same wonder that filled Devlin's mind. "The Almighty Creatuh, He sure did some good work down here."

Devlin shot Tolly a curious frown. "Almighty Creator? Do you mean God?"

"'Course I mean God. He made the earth an' ever'thing in it. So don't it go to reason He planned this, too? An' you know what else, Devlin? He knowed we'd be here on this very day an' time, a-lookin' at 'em an' marvelin' at the wonduh o' His creation."

A strange feeling—of discomfort or desire?—tiptoed through Devlin's center. Unable to discern its source, he moved the lantern closer and put his attention fully on the intriguing formations. The soft flow of light made the crystals shimmer, and Devlin extended his fingers toward one.

Tolly's hand smacked. "Nuh-uh, no touchin'. Got some firm rules about that."

Lee stepped forward, his movements timid, as if he feared Tolly might bat at him next. "Back when the tours started, guides'd let folks fill their pockets with as many crystals as they could hold."

Tolly shook his head, regret carving furrows in his forehead. "Foolsome people done ravaged the cave. Who knows what this'd all look like if those folks wouldn't have bothuhed nothin'? From here on out, we's gonna let God keep on creatin', an' we ain't gonna mess it up."

Lee bent close to the wall, sucking in a breath. "Tolly . . ."

"What?"

"Look." He angled the lantern close to a low-growing section. One of the largest crystal formations showed a clean break at the base.

Tolly frowned. "Mebbe a bat flew too close, knocked it off."

Lee swept the lantern slowly along the floor. "Then why ain't it lyin' here somewhere? A bat wouldn't carry it off." The man turned a worried look on Tolly. "Look at the size. Gotta be as big around as my thumb. If it was still here, we'd find it."

Chills broke over Devlin's frame. He whispered, "We aren't the only ones in the cave, are we?"

Tolly snorted, but Devlin suspected he was faking his disdain. "Now, we ain't seen proof o' somebody else bein' in here, have we? No burnt patches from campfires. No food scraps lyin' around." He glanced at Lee, and Devlin was sure he glimpsed a warning in his frown. "That crystal could've broke off weeks ago an' been carted off by some little cave creature that mistook it for somethin' good to eat. Plumb silly to think there's somebody lurkin' in these passages." He waved his arm. "C'mon, we've lollygagged here long enough. Let's get to measurin'."

Devlin followed, but he couldn't shake the uneasy feeling that somewhere, someone hid behind boulders or outcroppings and observed their progress. The edginess still lingered when Tolly dropped his pack in the open area he called

Call's Rotunda and announced, "We'll set up camp here, get ourselves a good night's rest. In the mo'nin' we can measure the three tunnels leadin' off o' the rotunda, an' when that's done, we'll make our way out to daylight fo' a day or two, let Devlin get caught up on his drawin' befo' comin' in again."

Lee plopped down next to his pack, apparently ready for rest, but Devlin placed his waywiser next to the wall and then picked up a lantern. He circled the space, peeking behind tumbles of rocks and into crevices large enough for a man to hide.

Tolly chuckled. "You searchin' fo' an outhouse, Devlin? I done tol' you when we started out, gotta think o' these rocks like trees in a forest an' just go behind."

Devlin wouldn't go behind anything until he was satisfied someone wasn't already there, crouched and waiting. His perusal turned up nothing more than shadows and a few nearly translucent, long-legged spiders that gave him the shivers as much as a masked bandit might. He quickly rejoined the other two men in the center of the room.

Tolly had opened his pack and spread sandwiches, fruit, and cookies on a square of linen. "Help yo'self. Bread's gettin' a little dry on these san'wiches, but they'll still fill yo' stomach."

Devlin crouched beside the makeshift table, but he didn't reach for a sandwich. "How can you be sure the person who rifled your pack isn't still in these tunnels?"

Tolly took a generous bite from a sandwich and shrugged. "I's sure, 'cause there ain't no way fo' somebody to stay holed up in here fo' days on end without supplies an' such. An' if they was stealin' from my pack, they di'n't have no supplies o' their own. So they had to 've skedaddled outta here already."

"How do you know they didn't gather supplies and come back?"

Tolly chuckled. "Devlin, you's bound an' detuhmined to borrow worry, ain't you? I got ever' confidence the guides're keepin' watch ovuh the openin'. They ain't gonna let nobody come in 'less they's part of a tour group."

"But—"

He pointed at Devlin with his sandwich. "Ain't you learned the scriptures 'bout not givin' way to worry? The God who looks aftuh the birds an' flowuhs is surely gonna look aftuh His children. Ain't nothin' gonna befall us that He don't see comin'."

Slowly Devlin settled himself with his legs crossed and his hands on his knees. Of course he'd attended church services with his parents, and he'd heard ministers preach on the futility of worry. He was fairly certain he'd read the scriptures Tolly referenced. But the niggling apprehension lingered. "Still, something could befall us that *we* didn't see coming. It troubles me to think someone could be lurking about and might sneak up on us while we're sleeping and take our remaining torches or lantern fluid."

The thought of being trapped in the dark sent prickles of fear through him. He shivered despite his heavy jacket and gloves. "Maybe we should set up camp someplace less . . . open. Couldn't we bed down in a tunnel that has a dead end?"

Tolly shook his head, his expression firm in the glow of the lantern. "You don't never stay fo' hours on end in a place wit' only one way out. What if the earth was to shake an' rocks to come down? Then you'd be trapped. Nossuh, we's stayin' right here. We'll lay ourselves in a circle wit' our supplies in the middle. Somebody'll hafta step ovuh one o' us to git to the torches an' things." He waggled his white eyebrows. "Somebody goes to steppin' ovuh you, Devlin, you jus' let out a holluh. Me an' Lee'll tackle him to the ground."

Lee grinned as if savoring the idea.

Devlin clamped his lips tight. Tolly's attempt to make light of his fears aggravated him more than assured him.

Tolly tapped Devlin's knee with the toe of his boot. "'Nough o' that frettin' now, boy. Lemme tell you what my mammy taught me to think on when I's feelin' scairt o' somethin'. Comes from the Bible, book called Fuhst Petuh, an' says to cast all our cares on Him, 'cause He cares fo' us." Tolly smiled, a serene glimmer entering his dark eyes. "Yessuh, the God Almighty, He knows where we is, an' He can see even through the dark. So hand off yo' worries to Him, Devlin, 'stead o' stewin' on 'em. You'll rest a lot easier when we put out the lantern fo' sleep."

Tolly and Lee began planning the route they'd take out of the cave when they'd finished sleeping. Devlin picked up an oatmeal cookie and nibbled its edges. He worked his way slowly to the center and finished it with one bite. Then he ate a second one. But the presence of the hearty cookies didn't dispel even an ounce of the worry settling in his belly.

### Rebekah

Fear tried to grab Rebekah as she made her way through the early-morning shadows to the mouth of Mammoth Cave. The sky in the east was casting off its dark gray and easing into a soft pink, but no fingers of sunlight stretched over the trees, and the chill air nipped at her exposed ears.

She tugged Great-Granddaddy's hat down more snugly and crisscrossed her arms over her jacket front. When would the estate trustee finally put the hired guards to work monitoring the opening? All the guides were fussing about the added duty. With Tolly away, she feared they might decide to ignore the schedule he'd given them. She was tempted herself. Even though she carried a shotgun, creeping through the predawn gloom by herself left her edgy. She'd rather stay in her cabin until the sun made its appearance.

A twig snapped somewhere in the trees, and she froze in place, her pulse scampering into double beats. Moments later, a shadowy figure emerged from the trees. Rebekah released a yelp of alarm and swung the shotgun barrel in the direction of the gray shape. "Who's there?"

"Rebekah Hardin, put that thing down before you hurt somebody."

She nearly collapsed with relief. She lowered the gun and glared when Calvin Adwell stepped completely onto the road. "Cal, what are you doing sneaking around out here?"

He grinned, the slash of his teeth ominous in the dim light. "I reckon I could ask you the same thing." His gaze roved up and down her frame. "Took me a minute to figure out it was you. Why're you wearin' your daddy's duds?"

She set her feet in motion again, chagrined when he ambled alongside her. "These aren't my daddy's clothes. They're mine. And I'm wearing them because I'm working as a guide here at the cave. Dresses aren't exactly suited to taking groups of people through the tunnels."

Cal threw back his head and laughed. "You must be joshin' me! I heard tell you'd took up workin' for the estate, but I figured as a maid or a washerwoman. You're really guidin' folks in an' out?"

She glared at him, stung more than she wanted to admit by his condescension. "Yes, I am, and as well as any man, I might add."

He held up his hands as if surrendering. "All right, all right, no need to get testy. Just hard for me to think o' my favorite gal doin' anything like a man, you bein' so sweet an' womanly."

Hadn't she made it clear to Cal she wasn't his gal? And she never would be. Feelings didn't ignite when he came around. At least, not the kind she pined for. Her heart seemed to save those feelings for somebody she could never have. "Cal, you didn't answer me. What are you doing on the estate property this early in the day?"

"Word's out they're hirin' guards. I wanted to get in before anybody else, let the big boss know I'm available."

"I thought you were putting in your own crop." At least that's what he'd told her when he asked to court her. He claimed he'd be able to provide for her since his daddy'd given him a section of ground.

Cal made a face. "Aw, diggin' in the dirt ain't for me, Rebekah. I got higher ambitions."

More than likely he thought guarding would be less laborious than farming. But she wouldn't offend him by saying so. They were childhood friends, after all, and their families were neighbors. She stopped and touched his coat sleeve. "I hate to tell you, but enough guards have already been hired. They'll start when the summer season begins."

"Oh." He scratched his chin, the scrape of his nails loud against his coarse whiskers. "Well, what about other jobs? Maybe I could do some guidin', huh?"

"No. Those positions are filled, too."

For a moment he stared down at her, his forehead puckered and his lips pulled to the side in a strange grimace. "You thinkin' on quittin' anytime soon?"

She shook her head.

He snorted. "Maybe you oughta. Gal like you, gettin' up in years, prob'ly should be huntin' a husband 'stead o' spendin' her days dressed up like some ol' scarecrow an' traipsin' in an' out o' caves."

Had she really wanted to spare his feelings? Anger rolled through her chest, and she opened her mouth to let it spill out.

"Who's out there?"

Apparently the guide watching from three to six had heard them talking. Rebekah called, "It's just me, Belvy, and a man from Good Spring."

Belvy melted from the shadows, his gun drawn. "Next time holluh out, Reb. I near shot fuhst an' questioned latuh."

Cal curled his upper lip. "You'd 've been in a heap o' trouble if you'd taken a shot at me."

Rebekah aimed a scowl at Cal. Why was he being so difficult? Belvy was only doing his job. Cal was the trespasser.

Belvy barely glanced at Cal. "Reb, you ready to take ovuh?"

"Yes." The pink spread higher, giving her a better look at Cal's glower and Belvy's relaxed grin. "Did you have a quiet night?"

"Been quiet as sleepin' doves since I got on. Not so much as a raccoon tried to sneak in."

Cal bounced a frown over both of them. "I thought you said guards weren't goin' on duty until the summer season started."

Rebekah sighed. "They're not. But until then, we guides are taking turns keeping trespassers from entering the cave. And it's my turn to guard, so goodbye, Cal."

He didn't budge.

Belvy leaned closer to Rebekah. "Want me to stay 'round fo' a bit, Reb? I don' min'."

Cal's scowl deepened.

She appreciated Belvy's concern, but it wasn't necessary. Cal talked big, but he'd never hurt anybody. Especially her. "I'll be fine, thank you. Go get some rest."

"Hmm, well, all right, Reb. See you at dinnuhtime." He sauntered up the road, occasionally sending frowns over his shoulder.

Cal scowled after him. "You're keepin' some strange company these days, Rebekah."

She made her way to a large rock near the cave's yawning entrance and sat. She rested the shotgun across her knees. "Go home, Cal."

"So you're really guarding this place every mornin' at six all by yourself?"

She patted the shotgun. "I'm not alone."

He coughed out a laugh. "You're somethin' else, Rebekah. If you hear of any jobs at the estate, would you send word?"

"Sure, Cal. Bye now."

He gazed at her for a few tense, silent seconds. Then finally he strode up the road, muttering.

# Twenty-Four

*Devlin*

Sunlight, brighter than a hundred Edison light bulbs, attacked Devlin's eyes as he climbed the final slope to exit the cave. He grimaced and lifted his satchel to shield his face. Tolly and Lee blinked, too, their eyes squinted to slits. For a moment, Devlin gazed at the two men, puzzled. They'd been in and out of the cave hundreds of times, emerged from the darkness into the light hundreds of times, and still the light affected them. He didn't know why he'd expected them to be impervious to the sudden onslaught of light, but their response to the brightness startled him.

One of the other guides, Marshel, ambled over and offered to take the waywiser. "Stay there in the shadows fo' a little bit, Mistuh Bale, an' let yo' eyes adjust. It'll go easier on ya if you don' fo'ce it too quick."

Devlin decided to take the man's advice. He released the handle on the instrument and inched to the deeply shadowed area just inside the cave's opening. He kept his gaze low, his eyelids barely open, and slowly lengthened the time between blinks until he could bear to hold his eyes open without cringing.

Marshel stood not far away, grinning at him. "Bettuh?"

Devlin managed a small smile. "Better. Thank you. What time is it?"

Belvy pulled his timepiece from his pocket and held it out to Devlin. The dial showed fifteen minutes past four. Late afternoon. For reasons beyond his understanding, he felt as if he'd lost days in the cave.

"Want I should put yo' machine in the wagon? Tolly an' Lee got ever'thing else packed up an' ready while you was restin' yo' eyes."

Devlin gave a start. How helpless he must appear to the other men. He'd tossed and turned with worry during their sleeping time, and now he cowered in the shadows instead of helping load the wagon. He strode from the shade and took hold of the waywiser, determined not to give them further reason to question his manliness.

"I'm fine now, Marshel." He forced a smile, pretending the sun wasn't stabbing his eyes. "Thank you."

"I'll mosey on ovuh to the wagon wit' you anyway. Wanna talk some to Tolly."

The two of them crossed the uneven ground to the waiting wagon. Lee waited in the back amid the packs and rumpled bedding. Devlin loaded the waywiser and then climbed in with Lee, listening to Tolly and Marshel's conversation.

Tolly stuck his hand out to Marshel. "Ever'thing go all right while I was deep inside?"

"Jus' fine, although some o' the men been complainin' about the extra duty. I kep' tellin' 'em, only a couple mo' days an' summuh season'll be here." Marshel chuckled. "Sometimes they's worse'n little chillun."

Tolly didn't laugh. "They di'n't shirk their duties though?"

"Oh, nossuh. All came an' guarded jus' like you set up. An' di'n't nobody sneak in. Although you might wanna talk to Belvy 'bout some fella who was botherin' Miss Reb fuhst thing this mo'nin'."

Protectiveness washed through Devlin. He leaned toward the two men, determined to hear the rest.

"She say she all right, but Belvy, he wanted you to know 'bout it anyways."

"Thanks, Marshel. I'll ask 'im." Tolly pulled himself onto the wagon seat, released the brake, and sent a smile into the back. "You ready to go, Devlin? Reckon you's wantin' a hot bath an' a good dinnuh."

He'd take a bath before bedtime, and he'd enjoy a sit-down dinner in the dining room, but first he wanted to get a few lines drawn on his map while the memory of the cave was still fresh in his mind. And of course, since his drawing materials were in Rebekah's cabin, he'd get to see her, too. His chest went tight with the thought. He'd missed her. More than he'd expected.

Tolly drove the wagon to Devlin's cottage first. Devlin braced himself before leaping out. "I'd like to put my waywiser inside, but then could you take me to Reb's cabin?"

Tolly's lips formed a firm line. "How come?"

"My map-making tools are there."

"Yep, they is. An' so's . . ."

Devlin grabbed the waywiser and rolled it to the cottage. With it secure he heaved himself into the wagon bed and barked, "I'm ready."

The rumble of the wagon's wheels buried Tolly's mutters. Minutes later the wagon rattled to a stop in front of the row of staff cabins. Tolly turned backward. "Lee, put the beddin' an' packs in yo' cabin fo' now. I'll fetch 'em latuh. Aftuh you've rested up a bit, go to the kitchen an' tell Coopuh we's back an' we's gonna need mo' victuals come Monday. Tell 'im I sure did like them oatmeal cookies if he'd be inclined to bake up a goodly batch."

Devlin, half in and half out of the wagon, shot Tolly a startled frown. "Did you say Monday?"

"Yessuh."

"How long will we stay in this time?"

"Mebbe . . . Monday 'til Thu'sday." Tolly fiddled with the buttons on his jacket. "Then you can be drawin' Fridays an' Satuhdays, rest up good on Sundays, an' we'll head back in fo' anothuh deep trek the nex' Monday mo'nin' 'til we gets the whole cave covuhed. 'Less you's thinkin' you wanna do all the explorin' at once an' all the drawin' at the end."

He'd never admit that his first thought about being under the ground four days of the week was it didn't allow nearly enough time with Rebekah. It also cut short his exploration of the area aboveground, something else he shouldn't mention. "No, your plan sounds fine, Tolly. I . . . I'll get busy transferring these measurements to the page."

"Fine, fine. Now hop on outta there so's I can git my work done."

Devlin slid to the ground, groaning a bit as a muscle in his back complained. He didn't look forward to more nights on the hard cave floor. He held his satchel flat against his ribs and stepped up to Rebekah's door, which stood open, telling him very clearly she was inside. He gave the doorjamb a series of taps with his knuckles.

"Come on in, Tolly." Her cheerful voice carried from somewhere in the cabin.

Devlin cleared his throat. "Um, it's not Tolly, Reb. It's me." He paused. "Devlin."

Then there she was, thick braid falling sweetly over her left shoulder, smile lighting her face. "Devlin!" Instead of ushering him in, she joined him on the stoop. "How was the exploration? Did you cover as many miles as you'd hoped?"

He stood for a moment and simply enjoyed her presence, her welcome, her enthusiasm. She'd greeted him the way Mother greeted Father when he returned at the end of a day's work, with smiles and questions about his day, interest glowing in her eyes. Even though they stood on a humble stoop instead of in a decorated vestibule, even though he wore a wrinkled, dust-smudged jacket and trousers instead of a crisp suit and her frame was hidden beneath men's overalls and a plaid shirt instead of enhanced by a lacy day dress, the image of his parents' greeting at the close of a day tangled with his current situation, and he automatically did what he'd seen his father do hundreds of times. He leaned down and deposited a kiss on her pink-flushed cheek.

She immediately clapped her hand over the spot and stared at him with wide brown eyes.

He jolted upright, more stunned than she appeared. "Reb, I . . . I . . ." He swallowed. Would she stop staring at him as if he'd impaled her with a sword? "P-please forgive me. I didn't mean to offend you."

Her rosy lips parted. A soft gurgle left her throat. She closed her mouth, swallowed, then slowly lowered her hand. "Devlin, I—"

"I hate you!"

Both Devlin and Rebekah jerked their attention to the grass. The girl Devlin had encountered near the stream in the woods and then again beside the barn threw a woven basket on the ground and glared at them, red faced, her hands balled into fists.

Rebekah gave a lithe leap from the stoop and hurried over to the girl, reaching for her. "Cissy . . ."

Cissy—hadn't Rebekah said she had a sister named Cissy?—darted back a step. "What're you doin' kissin' him?"

"I didn't kiss him," Rebekah said.

"She didn't kiss me," Devlin said at the same time.

Cissy shot her glare from Rebekah to Devlin. "I saw you two kissin'."

He crossed quickly to the pair. The fury pulsating from the younger girl was enough to melt steel. "We weren't kissing. Yes, I gave Rebekah a little peck on the cheek. A hello after having been away for several days." He wished he'd chosen a better time for such a personal greeting. Rebekah's face still hadn't faded from its bold pink, and her sister seemed ready to combust. "It hardly warrants such an adverse reaction."

Her blue-green eyes widened. "But I— You— Oh!" She snatched up the basket and whirled away.

Rebekah started after her. "Cissy!"

Devlin caught her elbow and pulled her back. "Let her go, Reb."

She begged him with her eyes. "But she's hurting. I hurt her somehow."

"You didn't do anything wrong. You have no reason to apologize." Would she believe him?

Suddenly her gaze narrowed. "Do you know my sister?"

He would never have guessed the two were related. Cissy held no resemblance to the other Hardin girls, and her changeable behavior also set her apart. "She and I have met."

Rebekah aimed her puzzled gaze after her sister's retreating form. "I wonder why she never said anything."

"Our meetings were never formal, Reb. I doubt she even knows my name." He led her back to the stoop. "I'm sure once the shock of what she saw dissipates, her anger will fade and she'll be fine. As for what she saw . . ." He gazed into her velvety-brown eyes and couldn't resist giving the end of her braid a little tug. "I'm sorry if I frightened you with that hello kiss. It simply seemed like the natural thing to do."

She lifted her hand and touched her fingertips to the spot on her cheek where his lips descended. "It seemed very unnatural to me. You've never greeted me that way before."

If he had his way, he'd greet her in that manner every time they'd been apart whether for days or minutes. But he'd aim better next time. Her full, rose-tinted lips seemed a much more delightful place to connect. He pushed aside the whimsical—or was it whimsical?—thought and forced a serious bearing. "I hadn't faced the prospect of never seeing you again before now. Have you been into the depths of Mammoth Cave? It's like entering the belly of a bear. No, a whale. No, a monstrous mythical beast that breathes fire." He shuddered. "I feel fortunate to have emerged unscathed."

Her lips curved upward. "You're teasing. It couldn't have been that bad."

"If it were, would I be forgiven for kissing you?"

"Yes. I suppose."

"Then believe me when I say it was that bad."

Her smile faded. "Have you changed your mind then about completing a map of the cave?"

During his three days in the darkness, he'd questioned his intentions, pondered whether he wanted to witness the cave in its entirety. But quitting meant failing his senior project. It meant disappointing his father. And it meant never seeing Miss Rebekah Hardin again.

He shook his head. "No. I'll finish."

She smiled. "Good."

But in order to complete the map and hopefully have some time during the days aboveground to do some more exploring for other openings, he'd need to put his hands to work instead of standing in the late-afternoon sunshine with Reb. Such a pity.

He slid his hands into his pockets. "I honestly didn't come to give you a kiss of greeting. I came to add some tunnels to the map. May I take over the table in your cabin?"

A pretty blush stole over her cheeks. "I was folding my laundry before you knocked. Will you give me a moment or two to put everything away? Then I'll leave you to your work."

"Of course."

She scurried inside, and he waited, pacing back and forth, for her return. Only a few minutes later she emerged and said, "You can go in now."

He stepped onto the stoop and paused next to her. She looked up at him, both expectation and consternation in her expression. He couldn't decide which to reward. Then she stepped aside, putting too much space between them for him to reach her even if he wanted to. "I'd like to spend at least a couple of hours this evening, if you don't mind."

"Take as long as you'd like. I can busy myself elsewhere."

"Thank you." He took one step toward the door, but then he paused and fixed her with a steady gaze. "Reb, Belvy said someone was bothering you at the cave entrance. Do you think it was the person who came in and helped himself to our torches and food?"

Once again her face flooded with color. She shook her head hard.

Such an intense reaction. Devlin's curiosity instantly roused. "How can you be sure?"

"Because I know the person well. I grew up with him."

Curiosity departed and a different emotion swooped in. "Oh?"

"Yes. His family owns the land behind ours."

The Adwells, if he remembered correctly.

"Cal and I went to school together."

Devlin frowned, folding his arms over his chest. "And why was he at the cave's opening so early this morning?"

"He was looking for a job." Her fine brows came together. "How do you know about Cal's visit?"

He cocked his eyebrows and glowered at her. "That doesn't matter. What matters is whether he intimidated you in some way."

"Intimidated?"

Devlin nodded emphatically. "Belvy was certainly concerned, and so was Tolly. If this man . . . this Cal, as you call him . . . gave you any reason for fear or apprehension, I shall—"

Rebekah's brown eyes flew wide, her lips parted, and a soft laugh spilled out. "Why, Devlin Bale, you're jealous!"

# Twenty-Five

*Rebekah*

I am not."

His firm statement didn't convince her. Rebekah laughed again. "If you could see your face . . . You're the picture of the indignant suitor."

To her surprise he threw his hands wide. "Very well. You want the truth? Yes, I am jealous. I happen to like you, Rebekah Hardin, and the thought that some other man has been in your life since girlhood, is familiar enough to steal moments of your time in the early hours of the morning without causing you distress, and is viewed so fondly that you want to defend him makes me want to punch him in the nose."

He wanted to punch Cal? "But you don't even know Calvin Adwell."

"I know enough to dislike him."

She wanted to laugh again, but she couldn't. His declaration that he liked her, that he was jealous of Cal, set her heart aflutter. But how could she let herself fall in love with a man who was here only for the summer? A man who belonged to a world far away from her beloved hills? She was treading on dangerous ground, and she needed to choose another pathway quickly.

"Devlin, there's no reason for you to be jealous."

His face lit with hope. "Because you don't have true fondness for this Adwell fellow?"

"Because . . ." The words resisted release. But one of them needed to be sensible. And since he'd kissed her without a moment's warning, clearly he wasn't going to be the sensible one. Regret formed a fierce ache in the center of her heart. She sent up a silent prayer for strength. "Because we don't have the kind of . . . relationship . . . that warrants jealousy."

He took a step back. "Oh."

She'd hurt him, which made her pain even worse. She blinked back tears and held her hands to him. "I like you, Devlin. But we can't be more than friends. You and I, we're too . . . different." Would he understand?

"Different." The single word demanded explanation.

"Yes." She fidgeted before him, wishing he wouldn't appear so stricken. "You're from the city. I'm not. You're educated. I'm . . . not." He had to know these things. Why didn't he stop her so she didn't have to list her shortcomings one by one? "Your family is wealthy. Mine doesn't have much more than a cabin and little plot of ground to call our own. You see? We're . . . different."

He stood still as a statue, his blue eyes pinned on hers for several seconds. Then he gave an abrupt nod. "I see."

She wheezed out a breath. "Good."

"I won't kiss you again."

She wouldn't say "good" to that declaration.

"But I would still like for you to accompany me to more of the surrounding areas, continue to introduce me to people."

"I'd like that. Because there's something important I need to tell you." She'd prayed every day during their separation for the chance to tell him how he could be sure he'd go to heaven when he died.

"Well, that important talk will have to come another time. I have work to complete."

She wanted him to be more relaxed when she approached the subject of heaven. She offered a meek nod. "All right."

"And I hope you'll allow me the further use of the table in your cabin since I don't have another place to work."

Did he have to sound so stilted? "You're welcome to work here as often as you need to. And I hope . . ." She swallowed. She wished the warmth would return to his eyes. They seemed so icy, so unlike the Devlin she'd gotten to know in the past weeks. ". . . we can discuss Hawthorne. And Dickens."

His lips formed a grim line. "Of course. Anytime you like. Now if you'll excuse me, I need to get busy on my map." He turned and strode into the cabin. And he slammed the door closed behind him.

## Cissy

Cissy ran until her lungs ached. Then, panting, she leaned against a tree and closed her eyes, waiting for the deep pain in her chest to ease. Her breathing slowed, but the pain remained. Cissy hugged the tree, battling tears. How could she? How could Bek let the man Cissy'd decided was going to be her beau kiss her? She'd never felt so betrayed and ashamed and angry all at once.

She should go home and give Daddy the fifty-five cents she'd earned from selling the mushrooms. She should help Mama put supper on the table. But she didn't want to go home. She wanted to talk to somebody. Somebody who would feel sorry for her and tell her Bek was wrong to steal her beau. If she tried to talk to Mama and Daddy, they'd tell her she was too young to be thinking about beaus and would stick up for Bek the way they always did. But Pansy would be on her side.

She popped her eyes open. Evening shadows were starting to fall. Dark would come behind the shadows. If she took the shortcut through the trees, there'd be time to see Pansy before full dark came on. She'd probably arrive there at suppertime, but Pansy's mama wouldn't mind. She'd welcome Cissy to their table, and afterward she'd tell the girls to go on to the swing hanging from the big oak in the backyard and talk. That's when Cissy would spill her heart to her dearest friend and receive the sympathy she badly needed.

She wove her way through the trees, using the basket to slap at hanging tree branches. She startled a hoot owl and two rabbits, but she didn't care. What did wild critters matter when her future happiness had been shattered? She pressed onward until she broke through to the small clearing where the Blairs' cabin waited.

Smoke rose from the rock chimney, flavoring the air with a homey aroma. She hoped they were having something besides black-eyed peas. After seeing her handsome stranger kiss her traitorous sister, she couldn't possibly eat black-eyed peas.

Cissy pattered up on the porch and banged her fist on the door. Moments later it opened, and Mrs. Blair stood in the doorway.

"Why, Cissy Hardin. What're you doin' out here this time o' the evenin'?"

"May I come in, ma'am? I need to talk to Pansy."

"Well, honey, Pansy ain't here."

Cissy frowned. "But I need her."

Mrs. Blair's mouth pinched into a pout. "I'm sorry, but she's gone over to the Constant place for supper."

Cissy's mouth fell open. "How come?"

The pout changed to smugness. "Burrel invited her."

Cissy gawked at the woman. "Burrel Constant asked Pansy to supper?"

"He sure did. Ain't that somethin'?"

It was something, all right. Something awful. Burrel Constant was too scrawny and too clumsy, and his feet and nose were too big for the rest of him. Cissy wouldn't choose Burrel for a beau. And she didn't want Pansy to choose him, either. "Why'd you let her go?"

Mrs. Blair blinked, drawing back. "Because she wanted to go, and because I didn't have any reason to tell her she couldn't." Now she frowned. "Maybe you better hurry on home, honey. Dusk'll come on soon, an' you shouldn't be wanderin' in the woods after dusk. Ain't safe for you."

Cissy didn't move.

Mrs. Blair swished her hand. "Go on now. You can talk to Pansy in school tomorrow—give you somethin' special to talk about on your last day o' school for the season. I'm sure she'll be happy to tell you all about her supper with Burrel." She closed the door in Cissy's face.

She stayed put for a few more seconds. Her body felt like the strings on Mama's mop after they'd given the floor a good scrubbing. She wasn't sure her legs would hold her up if she tried to move. But she couldn't stay on the Blairs' porch all night. Daddy was waiting for the money in her pocket. Mama would want help with the little girls. She needed to go.

With a heavy sigh she turned and trudged down the steps. She moved along the cleared pathway to the road, her hurt increasing with every plod of her foot against the trail. How could she have gone from happy to sad so quickly? She'd gone by Bek's cabin to show her sister the pictures of the pleated shirtwaist and ruffled skirt she'd torn out of the Sears, Roebuck catalog. She planned to order the outfit as soon as she had money. She'd wanted to ask Bek if the outfit would make her look more grown up so she could impress her handsome stranger.

But then she'd found her stranger kissing Bek.

If that wasn't bad enough, Pansy was taking supper with Burrel Constant. Cissy wasn't stupid. She knew what it meant. She'd seen other gals and fellows pair up at school over the years. And once they paired up, they didn't pay attention to anybody else. She might as well say good-bye to Pansy as her best friend.

The hurt faded and a hot anger replaced it. How dare Pansy take a beau without talking to Cissy first? She wanted to tell her so-called friend exactly what she thought of her. And she wanted to do it now, not tomorrow. Daddy'd probably give her what for when she got home late, but she didn't care. She hadn't been able to tell Bek what she wanted to. She'd have her say with Pansy. She turned away from home and followed the road to the Constant cabin.

Lights glowed behind the windows—glass windows, slid up in the frame to let in the evening breeze. Talk and laughter escaped the opening, and Cissy came close to picking up a rock and throwing it right through one of those glass squares. She ducked into some bushes beside the path. Swatting at bugs and shifting her feet, she waited for what seemed like hours until the door opened and Burrel and Pansy stepped out on the porch.

Burrel's mama called, "Bye now, Pansy. You come back anytime, you hear?"

Cissy gritted her teeth when Pansy tittered and answered, "Thank you, ma'am. I'll come as often as Burrel invites me."

She stayed in the bushes, watching Pansy take hold of Burrel's skinny elbow. His egg-sized Adam's apple bobbed in his too-long neck. Then he guided her down the steps and across the yard.

When they were close, she jumped out. "Pansy!"

Pansy shrieked and dove behind Burrel.

"Don't you hide from me. Come out here."

Pansy peeked out. "C-Cissy? Is that you?"

"Yes, an' you an' me're gonna have a talk."

Pansy took a hesitant step from behind Burrel, who gawked at Cissy like he'd never seen her before. Pansy smoothed her hair, tipping her chin high. "What about?"

"About you—an' him." She jammed her finger at Burrel.

Pansy grabbed hold of his elbow again, fluttering her eyelashes. "What about him?"

Burrel grinned and puffed out his scrawny chest.

Cissy rolled her eyes. "What're you doin' over here anyway? I came by your place 'cause I needed to talk to you. I couldn't believe it when—"

Pansy wasn't listening. She was too busy making eyes at Burrel.

Cissy growled. She grabbed her friend's arm and yanked her away from the boy.

"Ow! Cissy, let go."

She pinched harder. "No. You ain't listenin' to me."

Pansy wriggled free. Rubbing her arm, she pranced back over to Burrel. "I don't know what's put a bee in your bonnet, but you're actin' like a spoiled brat. Burrel invited me to supper an' said he'd walk me home afterward."

"I'll walk you home." She didn't want to bellow at Pansy anymore. She wanted to tell somebody what Bek had done. She wanted to tell her best friend how her sister had betrayed her.

"No." Pansy stuck her nose in the air. "Burrel's gonna walk me home. You go home, too, Cissy. Your mama's prob'ly wonderin' where you are by now." She curled her hands around Burrel's arm and aimed him for the road, flashing a saucy grin over her shoulder. "C'mon, Burrel. Cissy's just throwin' one o' her childish fits. I never pay her no mind when she takes on so."

Cissy gawked as Pansy and Burrel sauntered up the road, Burrel tripping over his own feet now and then and Pansy giggling and pressing her cheek to his arm. Cissy went hot, then cold, then hot again. When they were a good hundred yards away, she cupped her hands around her mouth and let loose. "Pansy Blair, you ain't my best friend anymore! If you want ol' Burrel Constant instead o' me, then you can have him! The two o' you oughta get along just fine, him with his empty head an' you with your fickle heart!"

The cabin door popped open. "Who is that out there bellerin'?"

Cissy answered Mr. Constant. "It's Cissy Hardin, an' I don't care if you tell the whole hollow what I said 'cause I meant every word!"

"Cissy, you best get on out o' here before I fetch your daddy."

She looked up the road one more time. Pansy and Burrel had rounded the bend. With a shriek of mingled fury and heartbreak, Cissy turned and barreled for home.

# Twenty-Six

*Rebekah*

Saturday morning Lee volunteered to go with Crit on the nine o'clock tour so Rebekah could take Devlin into the hills. He wanted to explore southwest of the Mammoth Cave grounds. She wasn't as familiar with folks who lived in the Joppa community, but most everyone within a twenty-mile circle at least knew her daddy's or granddaddy's name. So if somebody got nervous about her riding onto their property, she'd mention Festus or Chester Hardin, and that should be enough to set their fears at ease.

Since she wouldn't be trekking through a cave, she chose a dress from the wardrobe in the corner of her cabin. As she fastened the pea-sized buttons marching from her waist to her throat, she wondered if Devlin would comment on the pale-yellow dress scattered all over with orange flowers resembling coreopsis blooms. Cal Adwell favored this dress because he said it brought out the honey-colored strands in her dark hair. Maybe, if Devlin didn't seem taken with her appearance, she'd mention Cal's comment and see if it changed his mind.

Or maybe she wouldn't.

She tied her shoes and braided her hair, checked her small mirror, and then set out across the dewy grass for the barn. Her lungs battled pulling in a full breath—a sure sign of nervous excitement. No matter how many times she told herself he could only be a friend, no matter how many times she chided herself for the stuttered heartbeats, the thought of time with Devlin always affected her. She sent up a quick prayer for God to guard her heart, and a rush of guilt followed the petition. Because she'd waited too long to ask.

Devlin had stolen a piece of her heart, and she feared he would own it forever.

She entered the barn, a welcoming place with rich, earthy aromas that always brought to mind Granddaddy Hardin. One of the stable hands, Junior, paused in raking out a stall and raised his hand in greeting.

"Mornin', Reb. You wantin' to take another ride?"

"Yes. Would you prepare Jinx for an outing?"

"Sure thing. Gonna need Marey saddled, too, for Mr. Bale?"

She nodded, hoping the heat flooding her face was hidden by the barn's shadows. While Junior saddled the horses, she nibbled her lip. Before she could go off with Devlin, she needed an escort. She wished they could take Cissy. She needed to make amends with her sister. But Cissy was scheduled to work with the photographer in the afternoon, and Rebekah couldn't be sure they would return to the estates in time. So she'd have to choose a different sister.

Or someone else.

Or not go.

She shook her head, scowling. Of course she'd go. How many opportunities would she have to enjoy Devlin's company now that Tolly was taking Lee on their excursions instead of her? Besides, she still hadn't spoken with Devlin about the assurance of heaven. Surely the opportunity would present itself while they followed trails through the trees.

Junior led Jinx over and handed her the reins. "Here you go, Reb. Enjoy your ride."

"Thank you." She urged Jinx to a stable wall and used the rails to climb up in the saddle. "Junior, I need to run a quick errand. If Mr. Bale arrives before I get back, would you ask him to wait for me? I shouldn't be long."

"Sure. Ride safe, though, huh?" His freckled face reflected worry.

She grinned. "Jinx and I are good friends already. He'll take good care of me." She patted the gelding's dotted neck. "C'mon now, Jinx, let's go."

## Devlin

Instead of donning his riding suit, Devlin pulled on a pair of work trousers, a blue shirt, and the thick twill jacket he wore in the cave. The clothes smelled fresh and looked clean thanks to the laundress's attention, and even if the outfit was unconventional by Lexington standards, he might startle fewer folks than he had in his jodhpurs.

He slipped a notebook, pencil, penknife, and his sextant into his satchel. The sextant kept the satchel from lying smoothly along his side, but he'd survive. It was better than jamming the bulky measuring tool into his trouser's waistband. His ribs still showed faint bruises from the last time. And he wouldn't leave the brass instrument behind. Accurately recording the locations of caves surrounding the estate was critical.

As he followed the road to the barn, the rhythmic play of horse hooves met his ears. He turned at their approach, and his double-crossing heart gave a leap when he glimpsed Rebekah Hardin, wearing a dress of springtime yellow and orange, sitting prettily in the saddle. Despite his determination to separate himself emotionally from the girl, his lips curved into a smile of welcome in response to her sunny presence.

"Oh, good. I was afraid I'd make you wait for me."

Devlin drew back, puzzled by her strange greeting.

"I've been home and back already."

A pair of bright eyes peered over Rebekah's shoulder and a little hand lifted in a wave. "Hi, Mr. Bale."

He leaned sideways a bit to get a peek at the child clinging to Rebekah's waist. "Hello. Who's back there?"

"Tabitha."

Rebekah offered a sheepish grin. "We can't go out alone, and Daddy needed Jessie with him today. So Mama sent Tab instead."

Devlin couldn't stifle a chuckle. "So I'm spending the morning with Reb and Tab. With names like that you two could be a vaudeville team."

Tabitha's curious face popped up over Rebekah's other shoulder. "What's vaudeville?"

Before Devlin could form an answer suitable for an eight-year-old's understanding, Rebekah nudged her little sister lightly with her elbow. "Nothing that needs to concern you, Tabby. Hush now, you hear?"

The child hunkered down, disappearing from view.

"Junior has Marey saddled and ready to go. Do you want to fetch her and then meet us by the estate entrance?"

"That sounds fine." A few minutes of separation should help him get his tumbling emotions under control.

She tugged Jinx's reins, and the horse and its riders departed, dust stirring with every fall of the horse's hooves. He remained rooted in place, frowning, unable to pull his gaze away from Rebekah's slender form. Why, of all the girls in Kentucky, had this one so thoroughly stirred the embers of his heart to life?

Suddenly, unbidden, a comment Tolly had made at the cave's flower garden whooshed through Devlin's memory. *"He knowed we'd be here on this very day an' time . . ."* Troubling questions followed the remembrance. Had God known his pathway would cross Rebekah's? Had He planned for them to meet? Rebekah had wisely pointed out their differences, and even though he'd initially balked, he'd come to accept her statements as true. She knew they didn't belong together. He agreed. Shouldn't an all-wise, all-knowing God also recognize there was no point in allowing affection to kindle between them?

He gave himself a little jolt that put his feet into motion. Mooning over Rebekah Hardin was a waste of time, energy, and emotion. "Think about why you're here, Bale," he muttered as he strode briskly through the morning sunshine. "Finish the job. And then get yourself home before you lose any more of yourself."

### Rebekah

The morning eased away, the minutes slogging rather than racing, yet the time wasn't enough to satisfy. Her conflicting emotions left her edgy and out of sorts, the opposite of how she wanted to feel in Devlin's presence. And it helped not a bit that each time she glanced at him her heart rolled over in her chest.

Nearly an hour ago, Devlin had settled Tabitha in front of him because the little girl had trouble staying on the back of Rebekah's horse during uphill climbs. So now Tabby leaned trustingly into Devlin's form, his protective arm across her belly, her small hands curled over his forearm. The two of them seemed so natural together, so comfortable. The sight pained her in ways she couldn't understand.

She turned her attention to the trail leading to the Minyards' place. The Davises, Hogans, and McCauleys had answered Devlin's questions even if they seemed a little confused by his interest. For some reason he'd seemed dissatisfied by their responses, and she found herself hoping that whatever he discovered at the Minyards' would be more pleasing to him. Especially since they needed to return to the estate after this visit.

The Minyards' cabin door stood open wide, but no one was in the front yard. Devlin reined Marey to a stop at the edge of the yard, and Rebekah rode up to the sagging porch. "Mrs. Minyard? Anybody home?"

An older woman with sloped shoulders and lank gray hair hanging along her wrinkled cheeks appeared in the doorway. She wiped her hands on her faded apron and scowled at Rebekah. "Who's askin'?"

"Rebekah Hardin, ma'am. I'm Festus and Nell Hardin's daughter."

The woman's face lit with recognition. "Why, sure, I know your kin, gal. How's your mama farin'?"

They exchanged a few pleasantries, and then Rebekah gestured Devlin forward. A hint of uncertainty creased the woman's face. Rebekah launched quickly into her standard introduction. "Mrs. Minyard, this is Devlin Bale. He's a cartography student from the University of Kentucky, and he's spending his summer at Mammoth Cave. He'd like to ask you a few questions, if you don't mind."

Mrs. Minyard gazed at Devlin with distrust. "What's a college boy need from the likes o' me?"

He smiled, seemingly unperturbed by the woman's prickly query. He asked for the same information as at every other stop—the number of people residing on the property, the size of the landholding, how they made their living, and if any caves were on the property.

Mrs. Minyard answered the first three questions hesitantly, but at the final question she set her lips in a stern line and glared upward. "Why you need to know that?"

Devlin shrugged. The gesture seemed a bit too casual to be honest, setting Rebekah's senses on alert. He tapped his pencil point against his notebook. "Since I'm crafting a map of Mammoth Cave, I want to be certain to include any entrance points. If there is a cave on your property, I'd like the chance to take a look inside, find out if it connects with the large cave."

Mrs. Minyard marched to the warped front of the porch and balled her hands on her hips. "Just 'cause we butt up against the estate property don't mean the owner can lay claim to any part o' our holdin'. My husband's pappy fought off Injuns an' faced blight an' blizzards an' Lord knows what all else to carve us a livin' here. Nobody's gonna come along an' say this place ain't ours."

Rebekah touched Devlin's wrist. "Let's go."

He touched Marey's sides, shifting her far enough away from Jinx that Rebekah couldn't reach him. "So you do have a cave?"

The woman snorted out an angry breath. "You got cotton in your ears? Yes, we got a cave, but you ain't goin' in it." She looked at Rebekah. "Tell your mama I send her my best. An' now you take this college boy off my land." She stormed into her cabin and closed the door behind her. Moments later, the edge of the curtain on the one window lifted and she glared out.

Rebekah turned Jinx toward the road. "Come on, Devlin."

"Where?"

"Back to the estate."

"But I need to go to the Minyards' cave."

Hadn't he heard the woman? "Mrs. Minyard said no."

"She said I couldn't go in it. She didn't say I couldn't record the cave's location."

Rebekah shook her head. He was going to get himself shot. "She told us to leave. If we don't, she'll bring out a rifle. I assure you, she knows how to use it."

"Very well." With a sigh, he tugged Marey's reins, and the horse obediently changed direction. When they reached the road, Devlin sent a frown over his shoulder. "I've never encountered anyone so disagreeable. All I wanted to do was find the cave opening and chart its location in conjunction with the big cave. I meant no harm."

His disappointment pierced her. Rebekah offered him a sympathetic grin. "I know, but you have to understand how the people around here feel about their land. Folks in this area are hard working but poor. They have very little to call their own, so they do all they can to protect that little bit."

"But their protectiveness is ill placed. Consider what it could mean for them if their cave does connect with Mammoth Cave."

Rebekah squinted against the high sun. "What could it mean?"

"The difference between a hardscrabble existence and a comfortable one." Excitement tinged his voice and brightened his expression. "Think, Reb. Each part of the cave has its own unique markings and flavor. Tour groups relish the chance to explore every uniqueness. The Minyards could very well own a portion that would be of interest to visitors. If they allowed the estate to bring people onto their property to access the cave from a new entrance, they'd receive a portion of the revenue."

Rebekah couldn't consider the possibility from the Minyards' point of view, but she knew how her daddy would respond. "Having strangers cross their property, trampling their plants and intruding upon their privacy, wouldn't be worth any amount of money, Devlin."

He huffed. "That's ridiculous."

His attitude stung. She drew her horse to a stop, and he pulled back on Marey's reins, too. She met his obstinate gaze. "The folks around here will fight to protect what's theirs. They don't want money. They don't want recognition. They just want to live their lives quietly on the land their daddies and granddaddies bequeathed to them. The land is their . . ." Warmth flooded her chest, and she chose Daddy's word. "Legacy. Don't you see? A legacy is worth protecting."

"Sounds like a bunch of hillbilly hooey to me. What person with even an ounce of a brain wouldn't want to better himself? And you do that with money."

A huge lump of hurt filled Rebekah's throat. Devlin thought he was speaking about the Minyards, but in truth he was speaking about her.

## Twenty-Seven

*Cissy*

Cissy ran the curry brush over Beauregard's coarse hide. Mr. Temperance hadn't said she needed to take care of the burro, but she felt beholden to the little beast. If it wasn't for him choosing to like her, she wouldn't be earning a wage. A brushing every day was a good reward. Besides, with everybody in the world turning their backs on her, it was nice to have a friend, even if the friend was a slope-backed, gray-muzzled burro.

She moved around to the back corner of the stall and began gliding the brush through Beau's tail. It sure got tangled in short order, and she wanted it as smooth as silk for the photographs.

Two horses and riders entered the barn, and Cissy peeked over the top of the stall wall. Her hand stilled and her breath caught in her throat. Bek and Devlin! She ducked low and peeked between rails at the pair who'd trampled her heart.

Devlin swung down, then lifted Tabitha from the horse's neck, swooping her through the air. She squealed, and he laughed, and Bek smiled at them the way Mama smiled at Daddy when he bounced Little Nellie on his knee or gave Trudy a ride on his shoulders. Cissy's stomach trembled.

One of the stable workers hurried over and took the reins of Devlin's horse, but Bek held on to hers. Then Bek and Devlin stood close in the pathway of sunlight pouring through the big doorway and talked to each other. Their voices were too soft to reach her, but they both looked serious, as if whatever they were saying was the most important thing in the world.

Cissy's chest burned. She ground her teeth together until they ached. She shifted her attention to Tabitha, who'd started wandering the barn. Tabby stopped at each stall and looked in. Cissy held her breath, crouching behind Beauregard's bony rump, hoping Tabitha would go right on by. But her little sister's gaze found her, and her face lit up.

Cissy popped out from her hiding place, glowering her fiercest glare, and jammed her finger against her lips before Tabby could call her name.

Tabitha backed up a step, her eyes wide.

Cissy grated in a harsh whisper, "Don't you tell I'm here, Tab, or else."

Tabitha scurried over to Bek and grabbed on to her skirts. "Let's go home, Bek."

Bek looked down and sighed. "All right, Tabby, we'll go." She made as if to climb into the saddle, but her skirt got in the way.

"Here, let me help."

Cissy seethed when Devlin grabbed Bek's waist and gave her a boost. Then he caught hold of Tabitha and lifted her up behind. Cissy hugged herself, battling a wave of longing. How would it feel to have his strong hands take hold of her that way?

Devlin and Bek left the barn, and Cissy slowly rose to her full height. Her whole person ached and her chest heaved as mightily as if she'd just finished a fight. But then again, maybe she had. She'd battled the urge to charge out and tell them both how awful they were. She'd carried a fire-hot anger inside of her for two days, and she didn't think it would ever leave her.

"Cissy, where are you? I've got folks waiting."

Mr. Temperance's impatient call pulled her from her thoughts. She slapped the curry brush onto a shelf and grabbed the reins on Beau's bridle. "I'm comin'."

The first person in line was an old lady. It took Cissy three tries to boost her onto Beau's back, and she got a good view of the woman's ruffled drawers and petticoat during the process. Not a pretty sight even though the lace was snowy white and delicately woven. She figured she earned twice her promised three cents on that one. Next came twin boys who jumped up on Beau so quickly the poor burro brayed in protest. Cissy calmed him with a bit of carrot from the hotel's kitchen, and Mr. Temperance sent her a smile of thanks.

The line grew longer as the afternoon wore on. The sun beat down, too, and the waiting folks gathered in the shade of the cottonwood behind the camera. Cissy wished she could stand in the shade. Sweat tickled her temples, and the bodice of her dress stuck to her sticky flesh. Between photographs, she used the straw hat Mr. Temperance had given her to fan herself.

She fanned Beau some, too. The animal looked droopy, stirring Cissy's worry. She intended to ask if they could start setting up the painted barn screen in the shade the next day. June, July, and August would be hotter than May. Poor old Beau might collapse from the heat, and then Mr. Temperance would for sure sell him to the glue factory.

"Next!" Mr. Temperance bellowed.

A young man stepped free of the crowd. Tall and slender with a narrow face, straight nose, and green eyes, he was every bit as handsome as Devlin. And he was staring straight at her.

Her face went hot. And not because of the sun.

He stopped in front of her and smiled. A fetching smile. One that could melt butter. "Hello."

"H-howdy." She couldn't resist sweeping her gaze from the polished toes of his black boots to the little brim of his black-and-white plaid cap. He couldn't be much older than her, but he dressed like a gentleman. Ladies in the magazine serials swooned at the sight of handsome men, and for a moment Cissy thought she might be in one of those stories. She swallowed. "You need help climbin' on ol' Beau?"

He shook his head, his eyes never shifting from hers. "I don't want my photograph with the donkey. I want it with you." Quick as a wink, he moved beside her and sneaked his arm around her waist. A few people in the crowd snickered.

Mr. Temperance angled himself away from the camera, frowning. "What are you doing?"

The young man shrugged. "Posing."

"But . . ."

"I want my picture taken with this pretty little lady."

He called her a lady. Cissy snatched off her hat and fanned her face. More snickers rolled. She slapped the hat against her thigh and froze in place.

Mr. Temperance shook his head. "It's your two bits." He moved behind the camera. "All right now. Hold still, smile, and . . ." A muffled pop sounded.

The boy didn't move. "Take a second one."

Mr. Temperance followed his directions.

After the second pop, he finally stepped away from Cissy. But only a few inches. He slipped his little cap to the back of his head, letting free a thick shock of red-gold hair, and grinned at her. "What's your name?"

"Cissy."

"I'm Nicholas Philip Ross, but you can call me Nick."

She licked her dry lips. "It's nice to meetcha, N-Nick."

He tipped toward her, lowering his voice to a whisper. "That second photograph is for you. Just doesn't seem fair that you have your picture taken again and again and don't get to keep one for yourself. So now you'll have one."

And he'd be in it, too. Her heart fluttered. "Th-thank you."

"Next!" Mr. Temperance bellowed the command.

Nick scuttled backward, his grin holding her captive. He tipped his cap. "See you around, Cissy." He turned and trotted off.

Cissy gawked after him. Someone tapped her shoulder. She gave a jolt. A sour-faced woman and a little girl holding a lollipop stood beside her. "Whatcha want?"

More snickers rolled from the crowd, and Mr. Temperance's eyes rolled skyward. "Cissy . . ."

She gulped. "I mean, who's goin' on Beau? You"—she looked from the woman to the child—"or her?"

The woman stuck her nose in the air. The sun brought out a dozen hairs growing from her chin. "My granddaughter, of course."

Cissy scurried around and lifted the little girl onto Beau. The child waved the lollipop until it caught in Beau's short mane. When she pulled it loose, it looked as hairy as the grandmother's chin. The child wailed, but Cissy smiled, and Mr. Temperance shot the picture. The woman snatched her granddaughter from Beau's back and stormed off, the little girl still crying.

The crowd thinned as late afternoon arrived. The final person stepped up for a photograph, a man so tall his toes touched the ground on both sides when he straddled Beau. Cissy thought he looked ridiculous, but she held the reins and forced her stiff lips into one more smile.

Mr. Temperance accepted a quarter from the guest, pocketed it, and then turned a weary smile on Cissy. "That's it. Twenty-two photos in all! A good day, hmm? But let's get things put away before somebody else comes along."

She tossed her straw hat into the box next to the camera. "Want me to clean up the hay an' such?"

He shooed her. "No. Take care of the burro. I'll see to everything else."

As soon as she put Beau in his stall, she'd find a drink of water, maybe even stick her feet in the watering trough before she put on her shoes again and headed home. She grabbed the burro's reins and gave a little tug. "C'mon, Beau. Quittin' time."

She scuffed around the corner of the barn, enjoying the brush of soft grass on her bare soles. And then she stopped so quickly Beau's nose nudged her hindquarters. Because there stood Nick, leaning on the barn doorway.

"Hello again, Cissy."

She pushed her trembling legs into carrying her forward. "Hello." She glanced around. "What're you doin' here?"

"Waiting for you." He straightened and took the reins from her hand. "You look exhausted. May I help you take care of your donkey?"

"He ain't—" She made a face. Nick talked so fine and proper. She ought to try to. "He isn't a donkey. He's a burro. An' he's not even mine. He belongs to Mr. Temperance, the photographer. But I kinda take care of 'im. 'Cause he likes me."

Nick grinned. "I can see why."

She hunched her shoulders and giggled. She couldn't help it. His words made her insides feel all tickly. She pointed. "Beau's stall is over there." She led him across the hay and then rested her arms on the top rail of the stall wall.

He led Beau into the narrow stall and removed his bridle. He gave Beau's forehead a scratch, winking at Cissy while he did it. "There you go, my good fellow." He draped the bridle over a peg on the wall and put his hands on his hips. "What's next? Should I feed and water him?"

"No. Stable hands'll do that."

"So you're not a stable hand?"

The tickle under her skin became a prickle. "Do I look like a stable hand?"

"Not like any I've ever seen. But if you were, I'd trade places with Beau just like that." He snapped his fingers.

Her prickliness scooted far away. She smiled. "You're pretty funny."

"And you're pretty, so we make a good team, don't you think?"

She gaped at him. Was she awake or dreaming?

He stepped from the stall. She eased off the rail and faced him, staying quiet. If she was dreaming, she didn't want to wake up. He hooked his fingertips in the patch pockets of his suit jacket and quirked his lips into a half grin. "What are you thinking?"

"Are you real?"

He laughed, showing her his straight white teeth. Normally she didn't like being laughed at, but Nick's laugh sounded like a melody, prettier than birdsong or Mama's ballads or even the creek splashing over rocks. She could listen to it all day long. She smiled while his laughter echoed from the barn rafters.

Finally he grinned at her again. "I assure you, Miss Cissy, I am very real. Is there anything else you'd like to know?"

She nodded eagerly. "How old are you?"

"Seventeen." Two years older than her.

"Where do you live?"

"My family resides in Nashville."

Tingles attacked. She hugged herself. "How long'll you be at the estate?"

He looped his elbow over the top rail and angled his head. "My parents have rented side-by-side cottages—numbers nineteen and twenty, in case you're interested—for all of June and midway into July. So that means I will be at the estate for a little over six weeks."

Six weeks! The men and women in the serials fell in love in two weeks. Sometimes two days. She'd have lots of time to win Nick's heart. That is . . . She drew in a breath and asked the most important question. "Are you rich?"

He treated her to another dose of his laughter. "As Midas."

She didn't know who he meant, but he hadn't said no. That was good enough. She smiled and swung her arms, stirring her skirt with her palms. "You wanna know anything about me?"

"Only everything."

She loved his answer. With a giggle, she caught his hand and drew him to a short bench tucked at the far wall of the barn. "Come over here an' ask me anything you want." She perched on the bench and folded her hands in her lap.

He sat next to her—close, but not too close—and stretched out his legs. He crossed his ankles, folded his arms over the buttons of his coat, and rested his head against the barn wall. He acted like he meant to stay for a good long while, and that suited Cissy fine. "Tell me, Cissy, how old are you?"

Should she fib? No, because it would be too hard to remember what she'd said. "Fifteen. And a half."

A grin pulled at the corners of his mouth. "Where do you live?"

He was turning her questions back on her. He hoped he wouldn't ask if she was rich, because she might have to lie after all. "West o' here about a mile."

"So you don't live on the estate?"

Did he sound disappointed? She shook her head slowly, hoping her answer wouldn't upset him. "But I'm here every day, helpin' Mr. Temperance. That's the photographer. I'm his assistant."

"How many hours do you work each day?"

"One o'clock to five o'clock Mondays through Saturdays an' two o'clock to five o'clock on Sundays. Plus a little time before an' after to help him set up an' take down his props."

His eyebrows rose. "Every afternoon, huh? Are you ever here on the grounds when you aren't working? Say . . . early morning? Or late evening?"

She delivered mushrooms anytime. "Sometimes." Her heart gave a hopeful thump. "Why do you ask?"

Nick held up his finger and shook it back and forth. "Huh-uh, Miss Cissy, I'm asking the questions now."

She giggled and dipped her head, peeking at him out of the corner of her eye.

He grinned. "You're off work now, right?"

She nodded.

"So what are you doing next?"

She chewed her lip. She was supposed to go home. Mama would need her help with supper. Then with getting their tub filled for everybody's baths— Mama wanted them all clean and smelling good for the church service. Then with getting the little girls tucked into bed.

She held her hands outward. "Nothin'. You got somethin' in mind?"

He laughed again, and this time Cissy joined in.

# TWENTY-EIGHT

*Devlin*

Sunday morning Devlin dressed in his best suit, borrowed a Bible from the small bookshelf in the hotel lobby, asked Junior to saddle Marey, and then set off for the Joppa Missionary Baptist Church. After spending Saturday afternoon stewing over the Minyard woman refusing to let him visit the cave on her property, he decided she told him no only because she didn't know him. Once she knew him and trusted him, surely she'd change her mind. And what better place than church to get to know and trust someone?

He tugged the tight celluloid collar. He sure hoped the Minyards were churchgoers. It seemed everyone else in the valley attended. Folks in wagons, on horseback—sometimes two and three riders per beast—and on foot traveled the dusty, winding road. Devlin fell in with the lot, nodding, smiling, acting as if he made this trek every week. The ones to whom Reb had introduced him nodded and offered weak smiles in return. Their hesitant acceptance gave him hope.

The church waited just ahead, a whitewashed clapboard structure standing sentry over a graveyard. Wagons crowded along the road in front of, behind, and on the far side of the church, but none parked near the headstones. Out of respect or in deference to some strange superstition? He probably shouldn't ask. Those who came on horseback were looping their horses' reins over wagon wheels or in bushes. Since Devlin didn't know who owned the wagons, he chose to tie Marey's reins to some scraggly looking shrubs at the far edge of the church grounds.

Two doors faced the road, but only the one on the right stood open, so he trailed others up the wooden steps into the sanctuary. A row of hooks high on the west wall already held a half-dozen hats. Devlin wanted to shuck his jacket—the windows were all closed tight, and it was already stuffy in the small room—but none of the other men wearing jackets removed theirs. So he slipped into the center of the last pew, where the open door allowed in a bit of a breeze.

He glanced around, hoping his face didn't reflect his dreary thoughts. He'd never seen a sadder place of worship. The church was clean, not a speck of dust or smudge anywhere, but where were the stained-glass windows, the tapestries, the murals? Plain painted walls, a painted rather than carpeted floor, simple pews lacking cushions or decorative embellishments, unlit lanterns hanging on wires from the ceiling, and a planked dais holding a simple wood podium offered nothing of beauty on which to feast his eyes.

Directly in his line of vision, the dented black pipe of a potbelly stove stretched to the ceiling. He scooted a bit to the right so he'd have a clear view of the podium. Then he shifted again to better see around the heads of people filling the benches. By the time a black-suited man stepped onto the dais, every pew, including the one he'd chosen, was full. And the stuffiness was nearly unbearable.

"Good mornin'," the man on the dais said. His strong, deep voice rumbled like thunder.

"Good mornin', Brother Neville," those seated in the pews replied with equal enthusiasm.

Brother Neville unfastened his celluloid collar. "Brother Coats an' Brother Gentry, would you open the windows for us please an' let some o' our good fresh air come through? The ladies are already fannin', an' the singin' hasn't yet commenced."

A light rumble of laughter rolled through the room, and Devlin smiled. The minister at the church in Lexington was never so informal, but Devlin liked the country preacher's relaxed approach.

"Shall we stand an' sing?" Brother Neville held his arms wide, his smile spreading from ear to ear. The entire congregation from youngest to oldest rose. Without warning and without piano or organ accompaniment, the preacher blasted, "Blessed assurance, Jesus is mine! O what a foretaste o' glory divine!"

Voices joined him, rousing in their rendition. The coursing breeze stirred feathers on women's hats, ruffled bows on little girls' hair, and lifted long strands of hair combed across men's domes, but no one seemed to mind. Devlin didn't know the words, and he couldn't locate a hymnal, so he couldn't sing, but he could listen and enjoy.

When they sang the chorus for the third time, Devlin hesitantly added his voice to theirs. "This is my story, this is my song, praising my Savior all the day long."

"Oh, such a glorious sound, a choir o' God's children praisin' His name. Must sound like angels singin' to our Maker's ears." Brother Neville patted the air. "Sit, sit, an' let's lift up the Lord's name through readin' of the Holy Scriptures."

He flopped open the huge black Bible on the podium. "Readin' from Second Samuel, the twenty-second chapter, 'And David spake unto the LORD the words of this song in the day that the LORD had delivered him out of the hand of all his enemies, and out of the hand of Saul: And he said, The LORD is my rock, and my fortress, and my deliverer; The God of my rock; in him will I trust . . . '"

All around him people were riffling pages in worn Bibles. The preacher's deep voice filled the room as he continued reading. He was halfway through the chapter before Devlin located the passage in his borrowed Bible. He scanned the verses until he caught up.

"'For thou art my lamp, O LORD: and the LORD will lighten my darkness.'" The preacher looked up and bounced a knowing grin across the parishioners. "Any of you ever been trapped in a place o' darkness?"

People nodded, Devlin included. Memories from his days in the cave swept in.

"Most people don't enjoy bein' in the dark. Well, unless they happen to be those who are tryin' to hide their deeds—then they want to embrace the shadows. But I can't say I'm lookin' at any people like that this mornin', amen?"

A chorus of "amens" rose.

The preacher nodded. "Yessir, folks with pure hearts, folks who try to do good—they find the darkness frightenin' an' unwelcome. So they don't knowingly enter a dark place unprepared. They take along a lantern or a candle."

Or a torch, like Tolly.

"An' they battle back that darkness with light. Even the tiniest candle can hold back a whole roomful of darkness, amen?"

"Amen," the people repeated.

The preacher stepped from behind the podium and paced the small dais, his feet thudding so hard the echo pounded in Devlin's chest. "Let me tell you, my brothers an' sisters, there's a different kind o' darkness than the kind that exists in cellars or closets or in the woods in the dead o' night. There's a darkness that lives in the center of men's souls. An' that darkness is the separation between man an' his Maker. Amen?"

Heartier "amens" rang.

He raised one fist in the air, his voice increasing in power. "The darkness of a man's soul can be lit by only one thing an' that thing is the person o' Jesus Christ! The Lord, brothers an' sisters, is the Lamp that casts a light on the wickedness of men's souls. He is the Lamp that frightens the devil an' his minions back to the depths of hades."

"Amen! Amen!" The cries rose all across the sanctuary.

Devlin shivered.

"He is the Lamp that delivers lost souls unto the Light of eternal glory!" He leaped behind the podium again and flicked pages so quickly they became the blur of a hummingbird's wings. "John, chapter eight, verse twelve, 'Then spake Jesus again unto them, saying, I am the light of the world: he that followeth me shall not walk in darkness, but shall have the light of life.' Did you hear me? The light of life!"

By the time he finished the verse, he was shouting. The windows rattled with the force of his voice, and Devlin's pulse pounded in his temple like beats on a bass drum. "If you're lost in darkness this mornin', dear brothers an' sisters, there is only one way to bring yourself into the light. By trustin' in the holy name o' Jesus. By askin' Him to forgive you of your sins."

Once again he took up pacing, his footfalls echoing along with the pound of his thundered words. "All the dark stains that turn your soul as black as pitch will wash away in the precious blood o' Jesus. Then light—light like you've never experienced before—will shine bright on you an' in you an' through you, amen?"

Devlin gave a start as the loudest "amens" yet rang. Apparently none of them had ever stepped from the darkness of Mammoth Cave into the sunlight. Sometimes the light hurt.

"Are you trapped in darkness today? Then you come. Come to the Light while we sing. Stand! Stand an' sing!"

The congregation rose, the benches creaking and floorboards groaning.

Throwing his head back and opening his mouth wide, the preacher bellowed, "At the cross, at the cross where I first saw the light, and the burden of my heart rolled away . . ."

Devlin eased his way out of the pew. He sent a quick look toward the front of the church, where a smattering of people had gathered and the preacher stood in their midst, eyes closed and mouth moving but no longer singing. Something deep within him gave a tug in the preacher's direction, but the open door behind him was closer.

He headed into the churchyard and sucked in a deep breath of air that held the crisp tang of rain.

*"Are you trapped in darkness today?"*

The preacher's words pulled at him, urging him to return to the little place of worship and discover the Light. He looked skyward and shivered. Clouds, dark and billowing, rolled across the sky.

*"Are you trapped in darkness today?"*

He'd be caught in a dark storm if he didn't hurry back to his lodgings. He pushed aside the persistent tug, loosed Marey's reins, climbed into the saddle, and dug in his heels. "Hurry now, girl. Let's get out of here."

## Rebekah

Thunder rolled in the distance as the congregation of the Good Spring Chapel sang their end-of-service hymn. Little Nellie grabbed Rebekah's hand and looked up with wide, fear-filled eyes. Rebekah lifted her to her hip and finished singing with her sister's weight—a welcome weight—in her arms.

Her heart still ached from her last conversation with Devlin. She knew they were different in many important ways. She'd already convinced herself it was foolish to pine over him. So why did his insistence that people around the estate should be willing to give up portions of their landholdings for the sake of money bother her so much?

When they'd parted Saturday, when his hands spanned her waist and his strong arms lifted her onto Jinx's back, she'd wanted to cry. They had argued, hadn't reached an agreement, and still he'd been the perfect gentleman. How could he be obstinate and so admirable at the same time? Her heart wouldn't survive working at the estate all summer when it meant encountering him week after week. Should she tell Daddy she wanted to quit and come home? But if she did, how would they pay for the cemetery?

It was all her fault they needed a headstone for Andy. She couldn't quit.

She shifted Little Nellie to her other hip, shifting her thoughts at the same time. With their new schedule of him spending days at a time in the cave, she wouldn't see him every day. She'd be fine. Just fine.

The hymn ended, and the preacher offered a closing prayer. Then he dismissed them, teasing, "Try to stay dry out there. Sounds like a gullywasher is sweepin' in from the other side o' the hills."

Rebekah set Little Nellie down and held her hand as they trailed her family up the crowded aisle toward the church doors. Someone bumped her from behind, and she glanced over her shoulder. Cal Adwell stood so close she saw her own reflection in his blue eyes.

"Hey, Rebekah, wonderin' if I could take you back to the estate this afternoon when you're done visitin' with your family. Got somethin' important I need to tell you."

"What is it?"

A secretive smile played on the corners of his mouth. "Nuh-uh. Ain't gonna say 'til I getcha alone."

If she rode with him, it would save her a long walk. "I suppose that would be all right."

He bounced on the balls of his feet, as eager as a runner waiting for the starting pistol. "What time?"

They stepped from the church. Daddy waited at the base of the steps, his gaze aimed skyward. Rebekah scurried to him and touched his sleeve. "Daddy, Cal said he'll drive me to the estate after we have lunch. What time should I tell him to pick me up?"

Daddy shot a quick look at Cal and then settled his worried frown on her. "Gal, if you can eat somethin' at the estate, I'd say it'd be best to hurry on to there now. That's a terrible storm buildin'. Can't say when it'll hit, but when it does it's gonna be hard to get through on these ol' roads."

She'd looked forward to time with her family, but she wouldn't argue with Daddy. He was one of the best storm predictors in the whole hollow. With regret weighting her chest, she turned to Cal. "Is it all right with you if we go now?"

His grin broadened. "Sure enough. Fact is, I got a little jinglin' money in my pocket. Enough, I reckon, to buy you dinner at the hotel dinin' room if you've a mind to give it a try."

Cissy darted close. "What about me, Daddy? Can I ride with Cal, too? I can pay for my own lunch with the money I made yesterday, an' I gotta meet Mr. Temperance at one thirty to get the picture-takin' screen an' Beau ready."

Daddy's lips formed a grim line. "No, Cissy."

"But—"

"Gal, that photographer ain't gonna be takin' photos today. Not with this wind pickin' up an' rain comin' in. Besides, after how late you've got home the last two nights, I'm not sure I'm ever gonna send you back to the estate."

"Daddy!"

He shook his head, his expression stern, and turned his attention to Rebekah and Cal. "Go on, you two, an' don't dally."

Cal gripped Rebekah's elbow and propelled her across the yard. Church folks aimed knowing looks at them as they passed by, and Rebekah wanted to tell them she was only accepting a ride, not a proposal to marry. When they reached his wagon, he caught hold of her around the middle. His fingers dug into the underside of her ribs, and she winced.

"Cal, let me cli—"

He boosted her with such force he nearly flung her into the seat.

"Never mind . . ." Cradling her rib cage with one arm, she inched to the opposite side of the springed bench.

Still grinning, he clambered up beside her and took hold of the traces. "Ready?" Without waiting for her reply, he slapped the reins onto the horse's back, and the startled animal shot forward.

She hadn't settled herself yet, and she yelped as she caught her balance. She gripped the seat with both hands and tried not to notice how many folks stared at them as Cal's wagon rolled out of the churchyard. She wished she'd told him she wanted to walk. She might be soaked to the skin by the time she reached the estate, but she wouldn't be bruised, and half of Good Spring wouldn't be speculating about whether she and Cal were courting.

They didn't talk as they rolled through an uncommonly dark midday. Cal's face held its silly grin the entire distance, though, and by the time they reached the hotel, Rebekah's appetite had fled along with her good humor.

"Cal, could you take me to my cabin instead? I'm really not hungry, and it would be a waste of money to buy me a meal."

He lowered his brows. "I'm hungry, though. We can still go in. I'll talk to you while I eat."

She gaped at him. He really expected her to sit there and watch him eat? Devlin would never behave so ungraciously. She closed her eyes for a moment, silently praying for patience. Why couldn't Cal be gallant and gentlemanly, the kind of man who made her heart sing? He was good looking in a rugged sort of way, and he came from a decent family. If one examined a romance from a logical angle, Cal was a likely choice for her life's mate. But when she was with him, all she wanted to do was get away, and no logic could erase that truth.

She opened her eyes and sighed. "I've changed my mind. I'll eat something."

"Good." He leaped to the ground and reached for her, but she clambered down the other side and met him at the front of the wagon. He held out his hand, but she pretended not to see and walked ahead of him up the boardwalk to the dining room entry.

The savory aromas drifting from the room and the sight of dozens of diners obviously enjoying their meals renewed her appetite. Until she realized how everyone was dressed. All the men wore suits with ribbon ties or bright-colored ascots creating a splash of color against their crisp white shirts. The women's dresses of pastel linen bore tucks and gathers and miles of lace. Embarrassment struck hard, and her cheeks blazed. How dowdy she and Cal must appear in their homespun clothes, Cal even absent a jacket.

She turned to urge Cal out the door, but the dining room host, a slender, energetic man named Eugene, hurried over. Rebekah couldn't ignore his bright smile.

"Reb! Good to see you." His gaze zipped to Cal. "Are you and the gentleman together?"

She fingered her muslin skirt, wishing she could melt into the stained and polished floorboards. "Y-yes. This is a friend of mine, Calvin Adwell. Do you have an open table?" She prayed he'd say no so they could leave.

"Of course. We can always squeeze in two."

She stifled a groan. Wasn't God listening?

"Especially when someone is treating one of our hard-working staff members." He picked up two menus from a cloth-draped table near the entry and waggled his fingers. "Follow me, Reb and Mr. Adwell."

He led them through the center of the dining room. Her face blazed so hot she wondered if steam rose from her hair. She kept her head down and focused on the toes of her scuffed shoes appearing and disappearing beneath the hem of her dress so she wouldn't know if some of the guests turned up their noses at her.

They stopped at the far edge of the room. A gentleman sat alone at a square table facing the windows. Eugene touched the man's shoulder. "I found some people to share your table, so you'll have some company after all." He gestured Rebekah and Cal forward. "Please meet Miss Rebekah Hardin, one of the employees here at Mammoth Cave, and her friend Mr. Adwell."

The gentleman stood and turned, his blue-eyed gaze landing directly on Rebekah. His lips curved into a wry grin. "Thank you, Eugene, but Miss Hardin and I have already met."

Rebekah's stomach tightened into a knot. She forced a wobbly smile. "H-hello, Devlin."

# Twenty-Nine

*Devlin*

Devlin sat in silence while Rebekah and the overgrown country boy she'd brought with her ordered breaded trout, wilted greens, and wild rice. He took note of her trembling hands, the slight waver in her voice. But he couldn't determine the source of her nervousness—was it him, her clumsy dining companion, or the well-to-do people surrounding them?

When the waiter left, Devlin rested one elbow on the edge of the table and settled his gaze on Rebekah's pink-stained face. "I didn't think staff members ate in the dining room."

She spread her napkin over her lap. "We don't. I mean, not on our workdays. But this is Sunday, so . . ."

"So you brought a friend to enjoy Mr. Cooper's good cooking."

She turned her face to the window and didn't answer.

Devlin gave Cal Adwell a slow perusal. This was the man who Belvy claimed pestered Reb, the one she said had grown up on the land behind hers. She said she knew him, but she hadn't called him a friend. And yet here they were together. A knot formed in his throat, and he forced a sharp "ahem" to clear it.

The man jumped.

"Sorry," Devlin said, but he didn't mean it. It tickled him that such an insignificant sound caused such a start. He tapped his foot, wishing someone would say something. Anything. Conversations rose from every other table in the room—children jabbering, parents scolding, lovers whispering. He felt as alone as he had before Rebekah and her pal Cal joined him.

He cleared his throat again and dropped his hand to the tabletop with a light smack. Both Reb and Cal looked at him. "So what brings the two of you here this fine sunless noon?" *Are you trapped in darkness today?* He pushed the inner voice aside.

Cal flicked a solemn look at Reb and then shrugged.

She sighed and faced the table. "Cal and I were at church together, and he offered to give me a ride to the hotel since Daddy predicted rain."

Just as she said the word *rain,* fat drops dotted the window.

Devlin grinned. "It appears he was correct."

A slight smile lifted the corners of Rebekah's lips. "Cal also wanted to talk to me about something, so we decided to have lunch together so he could . . . talk."

Which meant Devlin was creating a barrier. He ought to feel guilty about it, but he didn't. He swung his grin on the big-boned, blond-haired man who sat scowling from the other side of the table. "Please don't allow me to interfere with your intentions. I'm happy to watch the raindrops race one another down the window. I won't pay you a bit of attention." He held up his hand as if making an oath. "I promise."

Cal's scowl deepened.

Rebekah ducked her head. "I'm sure Cal would rather wait until we're alone."

The man hadn't said a word to Reb or Devlin. If he hadn't ordered his dinner, Devlin wouldn't know whether or not he was capable of speech. Now a cunning look entered Cal's eyes, and he slowly shifted to Reb. "If you don't mind this fella listenin' in, I'll tell you what I wanted you to know. Y'see, I—"

The waiter arrived carrying a large round tray with three dinner plates. Two held whole trout complete with eyes and tails, and the third, Devlin's, contained a very tame-looking serving of lamb chops. He deftly transferred the plates from the tray to the table and then cast a smile over them. "Do you have need of anything else?"

Cal licked his lips. "Can I have some ketchup?"

Rebekah coughed into her hand, and Devlin nearly choked, swallowing a laugh.

The waiter seemed to freeze for a moment, but then he nodded. "Yes, sir. I'll bring some right away."

"Thanks." Cal looked happier than he had since they sat down.

The waiter scurried off, the tray tucked under his arm.

Rebekah raised her eyebrows, her expression innocent. "Who would like to say grace?"

Devlin wasn't surprised by her question. She and Tolly had bowed their heads over the meager picnic items they carried into the cave. Since she'd indicated she and Cal attended church together, he expected Cal to volunteer. But the big man clamped his mouth closed and didn't look up from his plate.

Devlin's father offered long-winded prayers when guests visited on holidays. He supposed he could emulate and shorten one to satisfy Reb. Someone needed to before their food grew cold. "I will."

The other two bowed their heads and closed their eyes. Devlin followed their example and started. "Dear Father in heaven . . ." Reb's question about whether he'd be going to heaven someday intruded in his thoughts. "Th-thank You for this food. I ask You to bless it, the hands that prepared it, and those with whom I share this meal today. Amen."

He looked up and caught a glimmer of approval in Reb's eyes. Warmth spread through him, and he smiled as he picked up his fork and knife. "So, Cal, before the waiter came, you were about to tell Reb . . . ekah something. Would you like to continue now?"

"Oh!" Cal plunked his fork back onto the table and turned a serious look on Reb. "See, my grandpa Tilly, Ma's pa—"

"Your ketchup, sir." The waiter slid a small porcelain saucer filled with thick red paste next to Cal's elbow and darted away, as if unwilling to discover what Cal intended to do with the condiment.

Cal spooned globs of the ketchup on the trout, the rice, and even the greens. "My grandpa Tilly, Ma's pa who lives over in Rhoda, has been farin' poorly for a couple years already."

Reb nodded sadly. "Yes, my parents and I have prayed for him."

Devlin cut away a bit of lamb, dipped it in the creamy herbed mashed potatoes, and carried it to his mouth, pretending not to listen, but Reb's genuine sympathy made it hard for him to swallow.

"Lots o' folks have. But he ain't gettin' any better." Cal shoved a huge portion of greens dripping with ketchup in his mouth and spoke around them. "He needs somebody to look after him. So come July, Ma an' Pa intend to pack up an' move to Rhoda."

Reb paused in flaking the meat from the trout's bones. "For good?"

Cal nodded and took a bite of rice. A few grains dropped from the fork, bounced off his shirt front, and disappeared somewhere below the tabletop. "Ma'll inherit Grandpa's house an' all his household belongin's, an' she told Pa they won't have need for two houses, so Pa's handin' me the family cabin an' land. All twenty-two acres'll be mine."

He paused long enough to break off the trout's crispy tail and pop it into his mouth. "It won't be long, an' I'll have a whole lot more to offer than I did the last time I asked to court you. I figure once your daddy knows what all I'm inheritin', he won't have no reason for opposition."

A tiny smear of ketchup decorated his upper lip, giving his grin a lopsided appearance. "So, Rebekah, get ready for sparkin', 'cause I'm gonna be your beau."

The lamb turned to sawdust in Devlin's mouth. He set aside his fork and dabbed his lips with the napkin. He forced a smile. "Perhaps it would be best if you had this conversation in private." He dropped the napkin on the table and started to rise.

Rebekah held her hand out to him. "No, Devlin, don't go."

The genuine begging in her eyes stilled his movements.

"Y-you haven't finished your meal."

He wasn't sure he'd be able to take another bite. The ketchup swimming in Cal's plate combined with the unpleasant images of the clumsy hills man's hands circling Rebekah's slender form turned his stomach.

"And you might want to ask Cal about the cave on his father's land."

Cal shot her a sharp look. "My land. It's my land, Rebekah."

She gave a meek nod. "Of course." She turned her pleading look on Devlin again. "So . . . stay. All right?"

She knew how to capture his attention. Devlin eased into the seat and draped his napkin across his knee again. He took up his fork and knife. "Tell me about your cave, Cal."

The man shrugged. "Just a cave. Lots o' folks in these parts have holes on their property. Rebekah's pa's place has one, too, although the one at my place is—"

"There's a cave on your family's property?" Devlin gawked at Rebekah. At her slight nod he clapped his fork onto the table. "Why didn't you ever tell me?"

Her fine eyebrows tipped together. "You didn't ask."

He covered his eyes with his hand and groaned. Her family's property was so close to the cave estate. What if hers proved to be a new entrance point?

"It's just a small one, Devlin. A single cavern, actually more like a dome, where we grow mushrooms. I can't imagine it would interest you."

He opened his eyes and met her puzzled gaze. "No tunnels leading farther into the earth?"

"No."

Disappointment eased in, followed by a wave of relief he didn't understand.

Cal stabbed a chunk of trout. "Mine's deeper. Crack opens to a tunnel, an' the tunnel leads to a cavern. The cavern sprouts in three diff'rent directions. Used to go explorin' there until Andy died. Then my ma had a conniption fit if I even talked about goin' inside."

Devlin frowned. The man wasn't making sense. "Who's Andy?"

Cal bobbed his head in Rebekah's direction. "Her brother."

Rebekah's face drained of color. She stared at her plate, blinking rapidly.

Devlin's heart turned over. "He died?"

She nodded.

Cal said, "Been more'n two years ago now. Long time o' not goin' inside my cave."

Devlin couldn't take his eyes away from Rebekah's sorrowful pose. She'd never mentioned a brother. Two years ago Cal had said, but her pain must still be raw. A silvery tear slipped down her face, reminding him of the raindrops sliding across the glass window. He reached across the table and touched her hand. "What happened to Andy?"

Her throat convulsed. She sucked in her lips. Another tear rolled.

Cal went on eating, seemingly unaware of his friend's distress. "Fool boy got himself lost in Mammoth Cave."

Rebekah jerked to her feet. She sent a frantic glance across both of them and choked out, "P-please excuse me." She darted from the table.

Cal gawked after her. "Rebekah? You ain't done eatin'." But he didn't rise and follow her.

So Devlin did. She wove her way between tables, murmuring "excuse me" to other diners as she went, moving surprisingly fast for someone hindered by a full skirt and probably half blinded by tears. She was out the door before he made his way out of the dining room, but he found her the moment he stepped out on the boardwalk.

She huddled against the wall with her hands covering her face. Rain, carried by the breeze, fell at a slant and dotted the bottom half of her skirt. The pale pink fabric slowly darkened to the color of cooked salmon. His chest pinched. He wasn't her beau. He wasn't even sure he was her friend anymore after their heated disagreement. But he couldn't leave her alone in such distress.

He took hold of her shoulders and pulled her into his embrace. She continued to hide her face with her hands, but she leaned into his frame. Her body shuddered with silent sobs. Devlin rubbed his hands up and down her shoulder blades. "Go ahead and cry. It'll wash some of your pain away."

"It'll never go away. Not until I—"

He waited, but she didn't finish her sentence. "Here now." Gently he set her aside and pressed his handkerchief into her hand. Rain splatted against his back and speckled her clothes. Tears stained her face. She swiped at her cheeks, but new moisture spilled from her eyes, dampening them again. Her chin quivered.

Devlin wished he knew how to help. He'd always been powerless against women's tears, and not having experienced the loss of a sibling, he couldn't honestly say he understood her pain. But his heart ached for her.

He brushed his thumb over her cheek. "You told me about your sisters. Why didn't you ever tell me about your brother?"

She gulped, her gaze dropping to the handkerchief she worried in her fingers. "We . . . my family . . . we don't talk about him. It's too hard for Mama. And thinking about him only"—she swallowed—"hurts."

The backs of Devlin's pant legs were getting soaked. He shifted to lean against the wall beside her, bringing himself more securely beneath the sheltering eave. "When my grandfather died, the whole family gathered, and we took turns telling our favorite memories of him." A smile of fond remembrance tugged at his cheek. "I was only twelve, but I recall how good it felt to talk about him, to share how important he'd been to all of us. It eased the pain of losing him."

Devlin licked his lips and lowered his voice to a rasping whisper. "It might help ease your pain to talk about your brother instead of hiding him away in the corner of your heart."

She jerked her gaze to his. Her eyes snapped, no longer swimming with tears. "Did you kill your grandfather?"

Devlin drew back. "Of course not."

"Then your loss isn't the same as mine. I'm not only grieving. I'm guilty. And guilty is even harder to bear." She jammed the handkerchief into his palm, whirled, and clattered up the boardwalk and around the corner.

Reeling from her unexpected vehemence, he couldn't make himself go after her.

Footsteps scuffed up behind him. "She gone?"

Devlin turned his worried scowl on Cal. "Yes. She's very upset."

Cal sighed. "I know. But she left half her dinner in there. Waste of a dollar an' ten cents."

Devlin's jaw dropped. He'd never encountered a more callous individual. "I hardly think the cost is as important as Reb's—" Should he say *grief* or *guilt*? He wished he understood what she'd meant. He fully faced Cal. "You said Andy got lost in the cave. Was Rebekah with him?"

Cal shrugged. "No. He was in there by himself. Why?"

If she'd accompanied him, become separated somehow, and he'd died, then her guilt would make sense. He shook his head. "It doesn't matter. Will you go talk to her?"

"Why? Won't change the fact that Andy's dead an' he ain't comin' back. 'Bout time she accepted it." Cal shoved his hands into his pockets and hunched his shoulders, squinting at the gray sky. "Don't look like this rain's gonna let up. I might as well head on home." He sighed, his breath carrying the scent of fish and ketchup, a nauseating combination. "Wish I'd brung a jacket or hat. Don't much like getting wet from head to toe. But there ain't no other way of it." He angled a glance at Devlin. "If you wanna see the cave I told you about, come on out to my place sometime." A calculating gleam entered his eyes. "Might wanna put it on your map."

# THIRTY

*Cissy*

Cissy paced the narrow space between beds in her sleeping room. She grit-ted her teeth so hard her jaw ached. Daddy'd sent her in after their lunch as a punishment. Most times she wanted the room to herself—wanted privacy for dreaming or thinking or just being. But she also wanted to make the choice to be alone, not have it forced on her. How humiliating to be banished to soli-tude. Daddy was downright cruel sometimes.

The rain fell and fell and fell, pattering against the roof and the closed shutters. When would it ever stop? Daddy was right about Mr. Temperance not being able to take photographs today. Who'd want to stand outside and get all wet? Even if the people didn't mind a soaking, Mr. Temperance wouldn't risk ruining his camera. He babied that Seneca City View camera like it was a living creature. As much as he liked her, if she and the camera fell in the river, he'd go after the camera instead of her, and that was a fact.

She plopped onto the edge of the bed and hugged herself, bouncing her heels against the floor. Seventeen people had signed up to sit on Beau today and pay their quarter for a photograph, but she didn't worry about them. Mr. Tem-perance would find a way to fit them in during the week. She'd get her money by and by. But she'd never be able to make up the lost time with Nick.

She growled and jabbed her fists in the air. He'd go to the barn just like he promised at five o'clock, but she wouldn't be there. Because Daddy wouldn't let her.

*Pop-pop-pop* exploded from the front room, and a cheer rang out. Cissy whirled toward the sound, her mouth watering. Mama was making pop-corn. Cissy loved popcorn, all crisp and snowy. She liked it best in a glass with milk poured over it. They were probably fixing the treat just to torment her.

Daddy's chuckle rumbled. "Here now, settle down. Mama'll serve up that popcorn when it's ready. Lemme get this fairy-tales book open. Seems like we read 'Rapunzel' already, so we're ready for 'The Three Little Men in the Wood.'"

"Are there three little men in the woods behind our house, Daddy?"

He laughed, and Cissy held back a snort. Trudy didn't understand what *tale* meant. If Cissy wasn't in disgrace, she'd be able to tell her little sister that a tale was a made-up story. She pictured them out there, gathered around the fire, munching popcorn and listening to the story written by the Brothers Grimm. She growled. Wasn't fair how they—

An idea swooped in, setting her heart to pounding.

Daddy'd told her to stay in her room, and he'd told the little girls to stay out. For the whole day. That meant she had hours stretching in front of her when not a one of them would pay her any mind. She could probably go all the way to Alaska and back without anybody noticing. But she didn't want to go to Alaska. She only wanted to go the Mammoth Cave estate.

She squeaked the door open a crack and peeked out. Sure enough, they were all gathered on the rug watching Mama shimmy the covered pot back and forth over the flaming logs. Daddy held the open book on one knee and Little Nellie on the other. For a moment her heart caught. They all looked so happy together. Something deep inside of her wanted to sit with them, feel the fire's warmth, smell the popcorn, and hear Daddy's voice saying all the pretty words from the fairy-tales book. Would they maybe look up and say, "Come on, Cissy"?

She waited, watching, listening, holding her breath, but no one looked toward the bedroom door. No one called out her name. She clicked the latch and turned toward the pair of closed shutters above her bed. She'd slipped out the window before. Never in the rain, though. Raindrops would come in and wet the pillows and quilt. When Della lay down, she'd probably complain, and then Mama and Daddy would ask how the bed got wet, and Cissy'd be in trouble all over again.

Her heart *bump-bumped,* thinking about stirring their wrath. She'd suffered through two bad scoldings already for staying out past dark. Did she want to hear another one? Then she thought about Nick's smile, how good it felt to rest her cheek against his chest, the way he talked to her like she was all grown up and not a kid to be bossed around.

She had to see him. She had to see him today.

Cissy scampered up on the bed, cringing when the springs twanged, and peeled back the shutters. Raindrops spattered her face, but she scrunched her eyes to slits and clambered out the window. She hit the soggy ground heels first. Her feet went out from under her, and she fell flat on her bottom. The cold and wet soaked clear through to her skin, but she stayed still for a moment, listening for somebody to come see what she was up to. Nobody came, so she scrambled to her feet and took off through the trees.

### Rebekah

Rebekah couldn't remember the last time she'd cried so hard. Harder even than the day they laid Andy in the ground. She must have shed as many tears as raindrops already, and just as the rain continued to fall, so did her tears.

Some of the tears were for Andy, some for Mama, some for herself, and a few even for Devlin because he'd tried to help her and had failed. They poured down her cheeks in rivulets until her skin felt raw, her head ached, and she was too exhausted to hold herself erect.

She curled up on her bed and pulled the quilt around her. The cabin was dark and held a chill, but the quilt's embrace offered a touch of comfort, just as Devlin's arms had. She covered her sore eyes with her arm and willed the deep pain inside to ease. Only that morning Preacher Haynes had declared God forgave the most heinous of sins. Losing her temper with her brother and shooing him off to a place where he couldn't find his way out was worse than heinous. Could God forgive even that?

A tap at the door brought her upright. Still clutching the quilt like a shield, she said, "Who is it?"

"Tolly, Reb. Need to talk to you 'bout tomorruh's tours."

Groaning, Rebekah rolled from the bed and padded across the floor. She cracked the door just enough to peek through with one eye. "What about it?"

"I'd rathuh talk to you inside. It's plumb mis'rable out here."

Rain ran in little streams from his hat, and his hands were buried in his jacket pockets. Even his white beard dripped water. She couldn't leave him on the uncovered stoop. She moved back, opening the door at the same time. "Come on in."

The sound and smell of rain washed into the cabin. He stamped his boots before stepping over the threshold. He stayed just inside the door where anybody passing by could see. "Gonna cancel all o' tomorruh's tours. Road's gonna be a slick, muddy mess, an' folks won't wanna—" His thick eyebrows descended. He leaned forward, squinting at her. "You sick?"

Hugging the quilt more tightly around her frame, she shook her head. "No, sir."

"But yo' face is all red, yo' eyes is full o' watuh, an' you's bundled up like an Injun on a wintuh night. If you ain't sick, then what's the mattuh?"

She offered a weak shrug and sat in one of the chairs by the table. She slipped one hand free of the blanket and toyed with the corner of Devlin's neatly written notes lying out where he'd left them. "I guess I'm having a sad day, Tolly."

The man grabbed a chair and settled it with its legs butting against the raised threshold. He eased into the seat, his gaze never wavering from hers. "Seems on a day like this a gal should be singin' an' dancin'."

She searched her memory, but she couldn't find anything of importance. "What's so special about today?"

"I run into Cal Adwell when he was drivin' off 'bout a hour ago. He tol' me to expect to see him comin' around 'cause you two is fixin' to start courtin'."

"Oh, Tolly . . ." She slunk low.

"Was that s'posed to be a secret?"

"Not a secret. A misunderstanding. Cal wants to court me, but I don't want to be courted. Not by him."

Tolly's lips pursed, his whiskers splaying. "S'pose you's still thinkin' Devlin'd make a good catch, is that it?"

"Tolly!" She jerked straight up and glanced out the window, but no one was out. She sank back in relief. "Don't say such a thing."

" 'Cause it ain't how you feel?"

She wouldn't lie. "Because it isn't possible."

He nodded adamantly. "You's right 'bout that. Oh, now, Devlin's a good man an' all. Reckon he'll make a real fine catch fo' some city gal. But if you an' he was to match up, one o' you would hafta make a awful lot o' changes. I don't reckon he'd be willin' to give up his city life, an' you's a gal o' the hills. You'd wither up an' die in the city. No, you'd be bettuh off lettin' Cal Adwell call on you. You an' him—you's two o' the same kind."

Tolly wasn't making her feel any better. She pressed her chin to her shoulder and muttered, "I don't want to be courted by Cal Adwell."

"There some reason why not?" Tolly's tone held an edge. "Did you fib when you tol' me he didn't do nothin' to you on the road the othuh mo'nin'? Did he—"

Rebekah shook her head. "He hasn't done anything to me." He hadn't done anything for her, either, except brag about how he would inherit his parents' land soon. Realization bloomed. "I think the only reason he wants to court me is so I can do the farming for him. Cal is lazy, and he doesn't have even a portion of Devlin's compassion."

Anger struck with force. She jolted to her feet and flung the quilt aside. "Cal talked about Andy as if it didn't even matter that he was gone. When I couldn't hold back my t-tears"—she gulped, tears flooding her eyes again— "he didn't try to comfort me. He just went on eating his trout and ketchup."

Tolly made a horrible face. "Trout an' ketchup?"

"The food was more important to him than my feelings. But Devlin left his plate behind and came after me. Devlin dried my tears. Devlin held me." A sweet tingle tiptoed up her spine, soft as the fall of raindrops on the roof. She sank into the chair and gazed into Tolly's dark, shimmering eyes. "I know now it's folly to think about being courted by Devlin. It might be the most foolish notion in the whole world. But I can't help thinking about it. He . . . he moves me, Tolly."

Tolly blinked, his eyes fixed on her face. "You thinkin' you's in love wit' him?"

"I don't know. But I feel more deeply for him than anyone ever before." She hung her head. "If this is love, I'm not sure why poets write about it. It isn't nearly as beautiful as it is painful and confusing."

"Mebbe 'cause you's feelin' it fo' the wrong puhson."

She frowned. Shrugged. "Maybe."

Tolly stayed quiet for a few seconds, working his lips back and forth. Then he leaned forward and rested his elbows on his knees. "I's thinkin' it's a good thing you's stayin' abovegroun' while he's goin' in the cave. Time apart'll give you time to get yo' feelin's straightened out again."

Rebekah nodded sadly.

"Bettuh yet, since we ain't runnin' tours tomorruh, mebbe you should go home, talk to yo' mammy 'bout Cal an' Devlin an' which o' the two makes mo' sense fo' you. Reckon she could advise you bettuh than this ol' man who ain't nevuh done no courtin'."

Awareness jolted her. "If there aren't any tours tomorrow, will the guides still be paid? I—I need every penny of what I'm earning."

Tolly straightened. "Ain't yo' fault the rain's comin' down. You's drawin' a salary, Reb. You's goin' get ever' bit o' yo' twelve dollahs at the end o' the month."

She blew out a breath, her spine collapsing again.

He shook his head, chuckling. "I think you's needin' a rest, gal. Yo' mind's so cluttuhed up you cain't think straight."

She managed to corral her thoughts well enough to form another question. "How many months will I be able to work here, Tolly?"

He scratched his cheek. "If you don't choose courtin' ovuh earnin' a wage, the tours'll go 'til end o' Septembuh, middle o' Octobuh. Depends on how quick the cold sweeps in."

A sigh heaved from her lungs. "Oh, good." In six months she'd earn over seventy dollars. "I'll be able to buy Andy's headstone for sure."

Tolly put up his hands, frowning. "I thought you was buyin' a stone fo' yo' sick mama. Ain't that what you tol' me when you come lookin' fo' a job?"

She nodded. "It is for Mama. She wants a headstone for Andy so badly it's making her sick inside." Tears welled, stinging her eyes. "She can't set aside her mourning until his grave has a marker that will last. That's why I'm working here. To buy a stone for Andy. And to help Daddy put a fence around our cemetery. He called it his legacy."

"If it's his legacy, how come you's the one earnin' the money fo' it?"

What would Tolly say if she told him the truth? She pushed the words past her dry throat. "Because I sent Andy off to the cave. I was mad at him. I was trying to read, and he wouldn't leave me alone, so I told him to get lost. And he did."

"You tol' him to go get hisself lost in the cave?"

Agony writhed through her. "I didn't mean for him to. But he did. And he . . . he never came back home." She swallowed, another wave of sadness rolling through her. "I've never taken one single book from the library wagon for my own pleasure since then, either."

For long, silent seconds Tolly gazed at her without speaking. Then he rose, unfolding his joints so slowly he resembled a flower opening its petals. "So you's sacrificin' yo'self to appease yo' guilt?"

She gulped. "I . . . I . . ."

He slid his hands into his pockets and drew in a breath that expanded his chest. "I know lots about appeasement. Hired you on here to appease my guilt ovuh leavin' yo' family short one son. Been keepin' a close watch on you out o' a sense o' appeasement, fearful o' owin' yet anothuh debt to yo' folks."

Conflicting emotions roared through Rebekah's chest—appreciation for his concern, amazement that he, too, carried guilt over Andy's death, and embarrassment that he'd hired her not because he found her worthy of the task but because he'd discovered a way to pay a debt. A debt he didn't owe. "Tolly, you—"

"Lemme ask ya somethin', Reb. Wouldja have took this job if you didn't feel guilty 'bout yo' brothuh dyin' in the cave? Wouldja have spent yo' hours some othuh way if Andy was still livin'?"

She chewed her lip, unwilling to explore how things would be different if Andy were alive.

"Befo' you give up makin' a future o' yo' own, give some good thought to what you's doin'. Sacrifice is a hon'rable thing unless it's done fo' the wrong reasons." He turned to the doorway and his face lit. "Why, lookee there. The rain done stopped while we was talkin'. Clouds're clearin'. Oughta have sunshine tomorruh. That's good. That's real good." He bobbed a grin in her direction and ambled out the door.

Rebekah crossed to the threshold and peered out at the gray, water-soaked landscape. It would take more than one day of sunshine to dry up the effects of the rainstorm. And it would take more than one day of sunshine to chase away the dark blot of guilt binding her spirit.

She gulped back a sob and whispered, "Andy can't ever come back. Will a headstone really make things better?"

# THIRTY-ONE

*Cissy*

The rain finally stopped but not before she'd gotten as wet as if she'd taken a dip in the creek. Cissy huddled in the stall with Beau, shivering and waiting for Nick. He'd promised, so she knew he'd be there. She hoped she'd be dry by the time he came. Otherwise he might be so put off by her soggy appearance he'd never want to set eyes on her again.

She curled on the clean hay, knees drawn up and arms folded over her ribs. The smell of hay and moist earth filled her nose—a sweet smell. Beau munched from his feedbox, the *crunch-crunch* as steady as the tick of a clock pendulum. As she listened to it, Cissy's eyelids grew heavy, heavy, and slid closed. When a warm palm cupped her jaw, she gave a shriek and scrambled to escape.

Nick sat on his haunches in front of her and laughed.

This time she didn't much like the sound of his laughter. Her pulse still pounding, she plastered herself to the stall wall and glared at him. "You like to scared me outta ten years' growth. Why'd you sneak up on me that way?"

He stretched to his feet, still grinning. "I didn't sneak. And I said your name twice before I touched you. You were deeply asleep."

She rubbed her eyes and yawned. "What time is it?"

"Almost six."

"Six?" She bolted to her feet and plunked her fists on her hips. "You were s'posed to meet me at five. I was gonna head for home by six."

Nick's grin faded to a frown. He scratched Beau's ears. "I had to finish my chess game with my father. He and I play every Sunday afternoon."

If she didn't make it back by dark and the little girls told Mama and Daddy she was missing, she'd get a whipping for sure this time. She scowled and tossed her braids over her shoulders. "Ain't you a little old to be playing games with your daddy?"

He took a step out of the stall. "Look, Cissy, if all you're going to do is grumble, I'll return to my cabin and—"

She flew at him and grabbed his arm. "No. Don't go. I'm sorry." She put on her best begging face. "I'm always a little cranky when I first wake up."

He raised one eyebrow. "A little?"

She tittered. He was teasing now. "Well, maybe more'n a little. It's just that I got all wet comin' over here—"

His gaze roved from her head to her bare toes and up again.

"—an' then I waited so long for you that I fell asleep." She hugged herself. "I was lonely. An' sad. An' it all came out wrong."

A slow smile grew on his cheek. "All right, Cissy. I forgive you."

She beamed at him.

He chuckled, looking her up and down again. "And you really are a mess." He began plucking little bits of hay from her hair while she slapped at the wrinkles in her damp dress. "I planned to introduce you to my parents today, but—"

"Your parents?" If he wanted to show her off to his folks, he must really like her.

"Yes, but I think it's best to wait until you aren't so disheveled." He shook his head. "The next time you decide to take an afternoon nap, I hope you choose some place other than a burro's stall. You look a sight and smell awful."

"Nick!" She slapped his chest. "That ain't nice."

"Well, you ain't smellin' nice."

He grinned. She grinned. They both laughed.

Then he blew out a rueful breath. "My parents expect me for dinner at six thirty, so I can't stay."

"Aw, but, Nick . . ."

He touched her chin with his knuckles. "You should head home, anyway. Get yourself out of those wet clothes and warm up. I wouldn't want you to come down with a cold."

Her heart expanded. He was so thoughtful.

"My brother and I are going to hike with a few other fellows tomorrow morning, but our afternoon tour has been canceled because of the rain. I'll have the whole afternoon free if you want to meet at the end of your shift."

She nodded eagerly. "Sure. Right here?"

"Right here." He pointed to the spot of ground between them.

She giggled. From now on, every time she stepped over that patch of ground, she'd think of Nick. "All right. See you tomorrow." She tipped her head, fluttering her eyelashes. "An' Tuesday? An' Wednesday? An'—"

"Thursday, Friday, and Saturday." He grinned, winked, and ambled out of the barn in his easy, confident gait.

Cissy released a little squeal of happiness. "He wants to see me every day, Beau!" She smacked a kiss between the burro's eyes and then ran the whole mile home.

When she reached the house, light still sneaked between the cracks of the shutters on the windows of the main room, but the bedroom windows were black. Either nobody was in the room or Daddy'd already put the little girls to bed. Her heart pounding, she crept up to the house. When she stood beneath the window, she heard her folks and sisters singing "Swing Low, Sweet Chariot." She smiled. The bedroom was empty.

Using an upside-down barrel as a step, she managed to boost herself up high enough to grab the window ledge. Then she pulled herself in and fell onto her bed. The springs twanged something awful, but her family was singing loud enough to cover claps of thunder. Nobody came to investigate.

She breathed a sigh of relief and scrambled out of her dress. She wadded it up and shoved it under the bed, then felt her way to the bureau for a nightgown. On tiptoe, she returned to the bed and reached to turn down the covers. Her fingers encountered damp fabric. She huffed. As she'd feared, rain had come through the open window and dampened both pillows and the edge of the quilt. She chewed her thumbnail for a minute, thinking. Then she turned the pillows over and flipped the quilt the opposite way. Now Della wouldn't notice. Giggling at her cleverness, she started to climb into bed.

But she remembered her muddy feet. She shouldn't muck up the sheets. Cringing, she pawed under the bed until she found her discarded dress. She used it to clean the worst of the mud. As she picked out the hardening clumps from between her toes, she remembered Nick picking hay from her hair. She'd better give it a good brushing.

While her family sang "Am I a Soldier of the Cross?" Cissy whacked the hairbrush through her straight tresses. By the end of the second verse, she'd removed every tangle and, hopefully, every tiny evidence of hay. She returned the brush to the bureau top and turned for the bed, but a need struck. She should've visited the outhouse before she came in.

Holding her breath, she eased the bedroom door open. She waited until Mama caught her eye. Then she clamped her knees tight and mouthed, *I gotta go.* Mama nodded, so Cissy scurried across the floor and out the back door while Daddy and the children kept singing. The sliver of moon seemed to smile in the blue-gray sky, and she paused long enough to smile back. That old moon would keep secret where she'd been today.

She finished her business, then held her gown high and crossed the yard in a dozen leaps. As she entered the house, Daddy was praying, so she stopped and bowed her head.

"Give us a good night o' rest, our dear an' lovin' Father, an' wake us in the mornin' ready to do Your biddin'. Strip us of any desire to be displeasin' in Your sight."

Cissy gulped. She sneaked a look at her father. Heat attacked her face when she realized he was looking at her.

His eyes snapped closed. "These things I pray in Jesus's name. Amen."

"Amen," the little girls echoed.

"Bed now," Mama said. "Sleep good, gals."

"Sleep good, Mama. 'Night, Daddy."

Cissy stayed put until all the little girls said their good nights, kissed Mama and Daddy, and scampered into the bedroom. Then she started to follow.

"Cissy?"

Her heart skipped a beat. She sent an uneasy look in Daddy's direction. "Yes, sir?"

"Tomorrow's a new day. A new start. Slate's wiped clean."

She nodded.

"Sleep good now, you hear?"

"Yes, sir." She darted into the bedroom and closed the door. Safe, she leaned against the thick planks and stared in wonder at the gaping window. She'd got by with it. She'd sneaked out, stolen a few minutes with Nick, and made it back without anybody knowing. The relief melted her bones. She slid down the wall and sat there, smiling.

"Cissy, what're you doin'?" Tabitha put her hand on her hip and gave Cissy a saucy look.

Cissy kicked at her. Not hard, just enough to make her jump away. "Never you mind. Get ready for bed now, all o' you. Summer's here. Chores'll be waitin' in the mornin'."

She snuggled into the bed and rolled to her side with her face to the wall. She smiled. Summer was here, all right, but there was more than chores waiting for her. Nick was waiting.

The next day at lunchtime after a morning in the field, Daddy told Cissy she could keep working for Mr. Temperance. "But one more time of comin' in after dark an' that job'll be done. I won't have you worryin' your mama again. You understand me, gal?"

Cissy promised, inwardly grinning. Daddy forgot that with summer the days stretched longer. If she could stay out until the edge of dark, she'd have at least two hours with Nick every day after she finished posing with Beau. She told Nick as much when he came to the barn Monday.

"That's wonderful, Cissy. It'll be the best part of my day."

Her heart pat-patted so fast she marveled that it stayed in her chest. They sat in the barn and talked the hours away, and right before they parted, Nick gave her the photograph of him with his arm around her.

Looking at the image of them standing so close made her all fluttery inside. Her flutters got worse when he whispered, "Keep it in a safe place, a secret place." She tucked it in her bodice right over her heart.

Tuesday they went walking in the hills behind the estate. When the path was wide enough for them to walk side by side, Nick held her hand. The rest of the time he led, glancing back every few seconds as if making sure she was still behind him, still doing all right. She felt secure, cherished, special with him. And even more special when, at the end of their walk, he gave her a green agate he'd dug from the ground on an excursion with his brother and told her to think of his eyes when she looked at the stone.

On Wednesday he borrowed some fishing poles from one of the guides and asked her to take him to the best fishing hole in the hollow. She led him straight to the creek where she'd first met Devlin Bale. They sat together on the flat rock and dropped their lines in the water. She didn't catch a single solitary fish, but she caught him making sheep's eyes more than once, and that day chased every thought of her "stranger beau" from her memory.

She had to wait nearly a half hour for him Thursday. She spent the time pacing, building up her temper, but when he finally arrived, he had a bouquet of purple rocket in his hand and a sweet smile on his face, and she forgave him even before he apologized for making her wait. She thought her heart would melt as he laid the slender stems of delicate lavender blossoms in the bend of her arm and said, "I found them growing along the stream by our rock. I think I picked every last one of them. I couldn't help myself. They're almost as beautiful as you are."

She gazed at him in wonder. "You think I'm beautiful?"

He laughed, but the laughter told her everything she wanted to know. They went back to the rock and soaked their feet in the frigid water. They talked—seemed they never ran out of words to say to each other. And they laughed—seemed every minute together was so joyful they couldn't hold it in. When dusk fell, he asked to kiss her good-bye. She tipped her cheek to him, and she nearly danced all the way home, her cheek tingling from the brush of his lips.

Friday after the last guest paid for the privilege of sitting on Beau, Mr. Temperance rolled up the barn scene, and Cissy scanned the grounds for a glimpse of Nick. The photographer sent her a sideways look and released a snort.

She frowned. "What was that for?"

"You're playing with fire."

She fiddled with Beau's reins and stuck her nose in the air. "I don't know what you mean."

He strode over, the rolled canvas bobbing on his shoulder. "Yes, you do, because you're not a stupid girl, no matter how you've been acting lately. But if you want to pretend ignorance, I'll explain it for you. I've spent years photographing people. Mostly rich people. And I've learned a thing or two. Rich people enjoy a diversion. They're willing to pay for it, too. But in the end that's all it is to them—a bit of entertainment."

Cissy scowled at the photographer. "What's wrong with entertainment? It's fun, ain't it?" She'd had more fun in the past few days than she could remember in all the years leading up to them.

"Fun, sure. But dangerous for the one who involves her heart in the game and expects things to last forever." A hint of worry showed in the pinch of his brow. "Listen, Cissy, the problem with an entertaining diversion is that eventually the person gets bored and moves on to . . . other means of amusement."

She curled her fingers tightly around Beau's reins. "So what you're tellin' me is Nick's just playin' with me for a while an' then he's gonna trade me off for something else."

Mr. Temperance nodded. "That's what I'm saying."

She stared at the patch of thick green grass between their feet, biting the end of her tongue to hold back angry words. Bits and snatches of her time with Nick paraded through her mind. The remembrances pushed away her anger. She curved her lips into a smile and faced him again. "I appreciate what you're sayin', Mr. Temperance. I know you're only tryin' to look out for me." Or was he looking out for himself, scared of losing the person who made Beau behave? "But you don't know nothin' about Nick an' me. We're real special to each other."

"Oh?" The photographer raised his eyebrows. "Has he introduced you to his family or asked to meet yours?"

She frowned. "N-no. But he wanted to take me to his folks one time. He just couldn't."

"Why not?"

"Ain't your business. All that matters is he wanted to."

Mr. Temperance dropped the screen in the grass. It bounced twice, and Beau pulled back on the reins. Cissy held tightly to keep the burro from escaping, and the photographer curled his hands over her shoulders, holding her in place. "Cissy, there will likely be other things Nick wants to do—things he'll try to see through. But I want you to promise me you'll use your head. You won't do anything you don't want to do."

She huffed a short laugh, remembering walking through the hills, bobbing a fishing line in the water, wading in the creek, teasing and laughing and talking. She touched the place on her dress covering the photograph. "I ain't doin' nothin' I don't wanna do."

"Then promise me you won't do anything a good girl shouldn't."

She didn't feel like laughing anymore. "Mr. Temperance, you're actin' like you're my daddy."

"I suppose I am." He squeezed her shoulders and stepped back. He scooped up the screen and settled a serious look on her. "I just don't want you to get hurt. I've lived a long time, and I've never seen a boy from a family like the Rosses do right by a girl like you."

She stuck out her bottom lip. "You mean a poor girl."

"I wish it wasn't so, but it is. The classes don't mix. At least not beyond entertainment. You can't change it. It's better not to get entangled with him."

"All right." Cissy shrugged and gave Beau's reins a pull. "C'mon, Beau."

She sensed Mr. Temperance's worried gaze following her. He meant well, giving her a warning based on what he'd seen in his travels, but his warning had come too late. She liked Nick. She wanted him. And she'd have him forever, no matter what it took.

# THIRTY-TWO

## Devlin

He should be sitting at the table in Reb's cabin, adding to his map, but after four days inside the cave and then a day closed up in the cabin, Devlin needed air and light. Someone else had taken Marey for the day, so he asked the stable hand to saddle Lightning instead. The old horse was plodding, but Devlin wasn't in a big hurry. He could take his time.

He followed the road leading to the Hardin cabin. The Adwell place was behind the Hardins', so he'd watch for a lane, a gap in the trees, or some other means of reaching Cal's property. If he missed it somehow, he'd ride up to the Hardins and ask them for directions. They were kind people. They'd help him.

Kind people . . . He'd met several kind people in the hollow. He'd met some who held strangers at bay, cooperative but watchful, and a few others who wanted nothing to do with anyone who wasn't related to them. Yet he'd brand the least friendly more defensive than unkind. Even so, he chafed at their treatment. No one liked to be rebuffed. But no matter what Reb said, he believed their attitudes would change if the person knocking on their door offered a stack of silver dollars. He'd never met anyone who disliked the sight of glittering coins.

His careful observation revealed no roadway prior to the familiar lane to the Hardins' cabin, so he turned Lightning and followed the winding dirt path to the opening of their yard. Mrs. Hardin was on her knees in front of the porch, busily digging in the soil. Two little girls played in the yard, their dark-brown braids bouncing on their shoulders and the sun shining on their happy faces. He smiled—such a homey picture they painted.

The girls stopped playing as Devlin drew near and stared at him with round eyes and O-shaped mouths. Then in unison they ran to their mother and tapped her shoulder. She turned, frowning, but the frown faded when her gaze fell on Devlin. She pushed to her feet, brushing the dirt from her skirt, and crossed the grass on bare feet.

"Good mornin', Mr. Bale."

The woman possessed a quiet gentility, but a deep sadness lurked in the depths of her brown eyes. Devlin believed he knew its source. "Good morning, Mrs. Hardin. Are you planting flowers?"

She glanced at the area where rich dark patches showed where she'd applied the trowel. "Transplantin' some shootin' star bulbs Festus dug up. I'm hoping they'll bloom for me next spring. Then I'll scatter some daisy an' sweet-pea seeds on top. If they take root, ought to give us some nice color as summer wears on." She shielded her eyes with her hand. "But I don't reckon you came to hear me blather on about flowers."

He chuckled, patting the horse's neck. "No, ma'am. And I promise not to bother you for long. I met Cal Adwell a few days ago. He invited me to come to his property and explore his cave. But I can't seem to locate his place. Would you please advise me?"

"Well, since you're already here, the easiest way to go is between our house an' barn to the path in the woods—the one Rebekah took you on to go see her daddy when you was here last." She gestured as she spoke, her movements graceful. "Follow it to our field, then you'll see another break off to your right. Stay on that path until it goes over the rise, an' you'll come out on the Adwell land."

"Thank you, ma'am."

She shrugged. "You're welcome. When you've finished explorin' you won't need to come out this way. There's a road leadin' to the Adwell place. But it runs north an' south 'stead o' east an' west, so you gotta turn off at the bend. That's likely why you missed it."

He tipped his hat and offered another smile. "I appreciate your help." He aimed his grin at the two little girls, who covered their mouths and giggled before scampering off in a wild game of tag.

Devlin tapped his heels and urged Lightning forward. He rode through the yard, waving at Jessie, who chopped at weeds in a large garden plot, past the barn with its leaning walls and shake roof to the pathway he and Reb had taken. Memories of that day teased him as he ducked beneath low-hanging branches now heavy with leaves. Odd how many memories he carried of Rebekah when he'd known her such a short time, and during the past two weeks they'd been apart more than together. Yet everywhere he looked—at a patch of wildflowers or a rabbit nibbling clover—something she said or did whispered through his mind. The woman was unforgettable.

He drew alongside the field where Mr. Hardin and two more Hardin daughters—Tabitha and another one whose name he couldn't recall—were at work. Devlin counted in his head and came up short one daughter. Shouldn't Cissy be working with her family? But maybe she'd been in the house. And that was probably best. She and he weren't exactly on the best terms.

As he rode slowly between the trees, he noticed an opening ahead on the left. He frowned. Mrs. Hardin had said the gap would be on the right. Had she misspoke? He slowed Lightning to a near crawl, prepared to turn in at the opening, and when he realized what waited off the path his heart lurched.

"Whoa, boy."

Lightning stopped, and Devlin swung to the ground. He wrapped the reins around a drooping branch and stepped over a ramshackle stick fence into the deeply shadowed cleared space between towering trees. Five large crosses and four tiny ones marked the loss of loved ones. He stood in the middle and let his gaze rove across the simple homemade wood crosses. None of the little crosses bore any markings, but names were carved crudely on the horizontal bars of the large ones—Fenway Hardin, Birch Hardin, Sallie Hardin, Chester Hardin, Luella Mae Hardin, and F. A. Hardin. On the last cross a second carving marched down the vertical bar. Only four letters.

A
N
D
Y

A knot filled his throat, and he stared a long time at Andy's cross.

He raised his face to the waving branches overhead, trying to get his bearings on where he now stood in conjunction to the estate. Would this portion of land be swallowed up if Father convinced the government to assume ownership of Mammoth Cave? His chest went tight. How many other family burial plots existed in this hollow? And how many of the departed souls found their way to heaven?

Devlin shook his head, shaking off the unease that had gripped him. These souls were long gone. Foolish to worry over them now. As for the graves, if the government took over the land, these burial plots would be treated respectfully. The government might even put up permanent markers in place of the wooden ones, make the plot a recognized part of the park. The people wouldn't be forgotten.

He moved carefully around the graves, his feet falling soundlessly on the thick carpet of decayed leaves and pine needles. He pulled himself into the saddle and gave Lightning's sides a nudge. "Come on now. We've got a cave to explore."

### Rebekah

After a night of little sleep, a malady she had suffered several times in the past week, Rebekah overslept and missed breakfast. She peeked in the kitchen mid-morning and asked for a piece of toast or some fruit to hold her over until lunch, but Mr. Cooper told her to sit at the work counter and he'd whip her up an omelet.

She wrinkled her nose at the funny word.

He laughed at her. "Hold your opinion until you've tasted it, hmm?"

She watched him beat three eggs with a little milk and fry the mixture into a flat patty. Then he placed a sprinkling of goat cheese, some chopped tomatoes, and—of all things—three stalks of a woody-looking vegetable called asparagus, which he'd sautéed in butter, on half of the egg patty and folded it over like a sandwich. With a huge grin on his face, he placed the plate in front of her and handed her a fork.

She'd never seen such a strange dish, and she carried the first bite to her mouth with no small amount of trepidation. But after the first taste she couldn't eat fast enough. From now on if she was lucky enough to eat in a restaurant where fine foods were served, when she saw a dish that included asparagus, she'd order it.

"Mr. Cooper," she said between bites, "you're not nearly as pretty as my mama, but you sure know what to do with eggs."

He winked at her and returned to his work.

Rebekah left the kitchen, her stomach achingly full and her mouth happy. She sighed as she scuffed across the lawn, staying along the edge so she wouldn't bother the groups of women sunning themselves on quilts or the children playing games. By now Devlin had probably taken over the table in her cabin. Which meant she should find somewhere else to go. But where? She'd explored every possibility before going to the kitchen in search of a snack.

Tolly didn't need her. Crit had taken Lee on the morning tour instead of her. Even the stable hands refused her offer to help rake out the stalls. She suspected they wanted privacy to talk about the twin girls named Daphne and Delphinia, who'd arrived on the morning stage. She grimaced when she thought about the pair in their matching white lace frocks shaped like inverted tulips, sweetly flowered straw hats, and white kidskin boots.

The twins were probably somewhere near Rebekah's age, but she wouldn't try to befriend them. They'd aimed snooty looks at her when she trudged by in her overalls, ungainly boots, and her great-granddaddy's floppy hat, but she didn't blame them. She knew she looked a sight. And why would she want to befriend guests anyway? "Here today, gone tomorruh"—that's what Tolly always said. He wanted the guests treated respectfully, but he always cautioned the guides not to get too friendly. It would only lead to heartbreak.

He was right, too. Especially when it came to Devlin. The days apart, rather than removing him from her thoughts, only made her miss him more. No matter how many times she prayed for God to erase all affection for the man from her heart, she awakened each morning still achingly in love with him. Even though he abandoned the table before she returned to the cabin, the ghost of his presence haunted her. Devlin was etched into her soul.

She approached the staff cabins, her steps slowing as her pulse increased. If he was at work, she would sit on the stoop. Not to bother him. Not even to talk to him. But to listen to the scratch of his pen on the paper, his occasional mutter, and the sounds of the chair creaking beneath his weight.

Then her spirits sagged. Her door was closed and no lamp burned on the table. So Devlin wasn't there after all. She gave herself a mental shake and forced her resistant legs to trot the remaining distance. If she didn't have to work until afternoon when she and Tolly planned to take a group on the shorter of the two tours, she could spend part of her day in women's clothing. Even if her dresses were nothing like the ones Daphne and Delphinia had worn, she'd feel much more ladylike once she changed.

She turned the lock on her door in case Devlin returned unexpectedly, closed the shutters, and opened her wardrobe. With the cabin encased in shadows, she couldn't see well enough to make a selection. Releasing a little huff, she crossed to the table and lit the lamp. She started to carry it to the other half of the cabin, but the glow spilled across the drawing on the table, and she found herself captivated by its intricate detail.

The first time she'd seen Devlin's map, she thought it looked like earthworms squirming together in the bottom of a bucket. But now the lines expanded toward the bottom right-hand corner of the large sheet of paper. She recognized the flow of the tunnels and caverns and domes of Mammoth Cave.

She slipped into the chair and traced with her finger the paths she had taken with Tolly and Devlin. Then she searched out the areas Tolly, Devlin, and Lee had explored without her. She'd known the cave was large, but she hadn't realized how monstrous. She shook her head, marveling. So many tunnels. No wonder Andy hadn't been able to—

She jolted to her feet so abruptly she bumped the table. The large sheet of paper went askew. A second drawing, much rougher and smaller in size, peeked out from beneath the larger one. She cringed. She shouldn't have disturbed his work. She started to put the drawings back the way she'd found them. But something in the second drawing caught her eye.

Frowning, she pulled it completely from beneath the cave map and held it up. Clearly the cave's tunnels were represented by the squiggles in the center, but what was the misshapen oval marked by a dotted line around the cave? And why did the letter $X$ appear in spots within the oval but outside of the cave's reach?

Rebekah lowered the paper to the table, her pulse thrumming and a sense of foreboding creeping over her. What was Devlin really doing here?

## Devlin

Shivers of excitement trembled across Devlin's frame. He held the lantern high and eased forward a few more feet. The walls were jagged in areas, the floor littered with rocks of various sizes. But just as Cal had said, the cave was deep. He estimated he'd traveled three hundred yards into the center passage branching away from the good-sized cavern, and he'd counted at least fifty yards from the entrance to the cavern itself. The tunnel was narrow, the ceiling low, but it was passable. Most encouraging to him, it followed a downhill pattern. If his instincts were correct, it could lead to a northernmost, lower-level area in the big cave.

"You all right in there?"

Cal had stayed in the cavern, unwilling to traverse the rocky tunnel. His voice bounced against the walls, creating an eerie echo. A few feet ahead of Devlin, some fist-sized rocks broke loose from their hold and slid down the wall in a rattling *whoosh*. A bat, apparently disturbed from his sleep, released the ceiling and flapped its way past Devlin's head. He shuddered. Time to leave.

He reversed his direction and eased back out, careful not to bump the walls and knock any other rocks or cave creatures loose. When he reentered the cavern, he drew in a big breath and let it out in a mighty rush.

Cal grinned at him. "Saw a bat come out. Did it smack you?"

He shook his head. "No, but the wind raised from his flapping parted my hair."

Cal laughed, the sound reverberating.

Devlin cringed. He hoped the man didn't bring the ceiling down. "Let's go outside, huh? I'd like to talk to you."

Cal led the way, swinging his arm with his lantern and creating ghostly shadows on the walls and ceiling. Devlin stepped into the light of noonday with another deep sigh of relief. He was glad he'd gone in—this particular cave was an amazing find—but he was equally happy to be out.

Cal extinguished his lantern and then stood grinning at Devlin. "Whatcha think o' my cave? Ain't as big as Mammoth Cave. Don't reckon any of 'em around here are. But still, it ain't just a little hole in the ground, now is it?"

Devlin turned down the wick on his lantern until the flame sputtered and died. He set the glass globe on the grass and then sank down next to it. "It's far from a mere hole in the ground, Cal." He considered sharing what he suspected about the center tunnel but decided it would be wiser to wait until he'd done more exploring to prove his theory before mentioning it to Cal.

He angled his head and squinted against the sun. "Have you ever gone all the way to the end of any of the passages?"

Cal plopped down next to Devlin and plucked a long piece of grass. He stuck the broken end in his mouth like a cigar. "Nah. I used to want to. Curiosity, you know." The grass blade bobbed up and down with his words. "Got pretty far into the one that feeds east, but the openin' got so tight I turned back."

"What about the one I entered—the center one leading south?"

"That'n? I'd get so far an' come upon bats. Must be hunnerds of 'em in that tunnel. Didn't much care to get my hair parted." Cal snickered. "My pa an' me thought about shooting a rifle into the tunnel, scarin' 'em all out, but Pa was fearful we'd bring down the ceilin'. So we never did it."

He shrugged and tossed the grass aside. "Then o' course Andy Hardin went an' got himself lost in Mammoth Cave an' three days later came out draped over Tolly Sandford's back, dead as dead, an' that was the end o' my cave explorin'. Not that I was afraid to go in, but no sense in gettin' my ma all worked up with worry."

Devlin nodded and pushed to his feet. "Thanks for letting me see it. I appreciate it."

"Sure thing. Anytime you feel like explorin', just come on along."

Devlin tapped his chin, thinking. "Would it be all right if I returned Sunday afternoon?" He'd bring his sextant, measuring tape, and notebook— things he would have brought today if he'd had any idea of the scope of the Adwell cave.

"Fine by me. Why not have lunch with my folks an' me? My ma's a mighty fine cook."

"Thank you for the kind invitation. I would enjoy that." A slight fabrication. He held no desire to spend hours of time in Cal's company. But if he must suffer a bit to gain access to the cave, he would do so.

"All right then. Sunday lunch an' then explorin'." He grinned. "You're welcome to the place."

Devlin made his way down the rise to Lightning, who drowsed beneath a cluster of aspens. Cal's parting comment— *"You're welcome to the place"*— echoed in Devlin's mind as much as if he'd shouted it in the cavern. He hoped his suppositions proved true. And if they did, he hoped Cal would release this property.

# THIRTY-THREE

*Cissy*

Shortly after noon Cissy entered the hotel kitchen, plunked her overflowing basket on the edge of the work counter, and let her breath out. She slumped on the counter. Felt good to rest. "Here you go, Mr. Cooper."

The cook grabbed the basket and pushed it at one of the kitchen workers. Two mushrooms rolled out and landed on the floor. He shot Cissy a wry look. "If you're going to wait so long between days to bring these in, you ought to get a bigger basket."

She rubbed her aching arms. They hurt so much she wanted to take them off. How would she carry a bigger basket the distance between her family's cave and the hotel? "Sorry. I been pretty busy lately, too busy for mushroom pickin'." Daydreaming about her life in Nashville with Nick ate up the hours.

He stirred a pot on the stove, making steam swirl. "I will warn you I had a visit from another local farmer who found a patch of morels in the woods behind his house. I turned him away because I've been buying your family's mushrooms for over a year now. But if I can't depend on you, I will spend my money elsewhere."

Cissy poked out her lower lip. "You'd really quit buyin' from us after a whole year just 'cause I didn't come in durin' one week? That don't seem right."

He folded his arms over the bib of his starched white apron and frowned at her. "I plan my menus a week in advance, Cissy. I chose recipes that included mushrooms for last week's dinners, and then I had to change plans at the last minute because the mushrooms weren't here. That's not right."

The kitchen worker bounded over with the empty basket. "Weighed fifteen and a half pounds."

Her jaw dropped open. Little wonder her arms hurt, carting that much up the hill. How heavy would it have been if she'd picked all the mushrooms instead of leaving some behind?

"Stir the sauce, Lyle."

While the young man took control of the wooden spoon, Mr. Cooper crossed to a little desk and pulled a tin box from the drawer. Cissy nibbled her lip and listened to the *clink-clink* of coins. That jingle had to be one of the prettiest sounds in the world. Almost as pretty as the sound of Nick's laugh.

The cook marched to Cissy and dropped several coins into her waiting hand. "Here you are—seventy-seven cents."

She curled her fingers around the cool, round disks and smiled. "Thank you."

Mr. Cooper didn't smile back. "I expect another basket of mushrooms on Monday."

Cissy scrunched her nose. Monday was washday, and she'd have to help Mama before she came to the estate for work. So she'd need to pick mushrooms Sunday evening. Which meant she wouldn't get her time with Nick. "You sure you can't wait until Tuesday?" Mama did the ironing by herself, so she could scoot out to the cave Tuesday morning and gather up the mushrooms for Mr. Cooper.

"Monday, Cissy. And if you don't bring them Monday, don't bother bringing them ever again. I'll find someone who's dependable." He turned his back on her and took the spoon from Lyle's hand.

Cissy stayed near the counter for a few moments, letting her lip hang in a pout, but when Mr. Cooper didn't even glance at her, she grabbed her basket and pranced out of the kitchen. She scuffed across the yard, swinging the basket with wide, angry swoops. What a grumpy man. And demanding, too. Acted like he owned her time, getting so pushy with her.

She angled her steps to avoid running into a tall shrub trimmed like an egg. Mr. Cooper was shaped that way, too, with a full chest and belly. In her mind's eye she saw the cook in place of the shrub. She balled one fist on her hip, cocked her head at a saucy angle, and told him exactly what she was thinking. "That's just fine an' dandy, Mr. Cooper, if you wanna buy morels from some ol' farmer. Heap sight harder to find morels than it is to get the nice white mushrooms from our cave, but if you wanna take the chance and if you're gonna be all crabby about it, I'll just save my mushrooms for somebody else."

Titters sounded behind her. She spun around. A pair of look-alike girls wearing fancy lace dresses and holding pink parasols over their heads were watching her. They put their fingers over their lips and giggled again.

Cissy's face went hot. "What're you laughin' at?"

The one on the right lowered her hand. "Were you speaking to the bush?"

"No."

The one on the left tittered some more. The pair exchanged snide looks.

Cissy gritted her teeth. "I was talkin' to myself. An' it's rude o' the two o' you to be listenin' in."

They broke into laughter and hurried away, their narrow skirts shortening their stride and making the satin ribbons trailing from their shoulders to the upward sweep of the lowest layer of lace flutter. Their dresses were just as pretty from the back as from the front.

Jealousy hit her so hard it stole her breath for a moment. The Sears, Roebuck catalog didn't carry dresses half as nice as the ones those two snobby gals wore. She'd never have anything so nice. She clenched her fists and growled.

"Cissy?"

She turned again, eager this time, expecting Nick and a dose of sympathy. But instead Devlin Bale sat in the saddle of a gray-muzzled horse. She wouldn't get sympathy from him. She scowled. "What do you want?"

He swung down from the saddle and crossed to her, pulling the old horse along with him. "A moment of your time if you have it to spare."

She was due at the stable at twelve thirty, but she figured she could give him a minute. Especially since the matching girls had stopped in a patch of shade and were watching Bek's beau show her attention. She swallowed a snicker. Now who was jealous?

She aimed a smile at Devlin. "I reckon so."

"Good. I wanted to apologize for offending you. I'm sure it was a shock witnessing me give your sister a kiss on the cheek. Kisses are meant to be private, and my impulsive action was inappropriate. Will you forgive me?"

She'd almost forgotten about catching him kissing Bek. She shrugged. "Sure. It don't matter if you wanna kiss Bek. I reckon that's what beaus do." Nick had kissed her cheek only once, but she looked forward to more kisses.

Devlin's eyebrows formed a V. "Cissy, you're mistaken. I'm not your sister's beau."

She laughed. "Sure you are. You must be. You kissed her."

He turned his face to the sky for a second and sighed. Then he settled his gaze on her again. He looked serious. And sad. "As I said a moment ago, it was an impulsive act. I shouldn't have done it because Reb—your sister—and I are only . . . acquaintances. That's all we can be."

Cissy's heart started thumping hard. She fingered the stiff shape of the photograph beneath her bodice. "You ain't makin' sense."

A strange, sorrowful smile formed on his face. "I care about your sister, but I can't be her beau. I'm here only for the summer. Then I'll be going to Lexington, back to my parents, back to school, back to . . . my life. And Reb will stay here with her family and her life. You see?"

She was beginning to see, and she didn't like the picture. Devlin's talk sounded too much like the warning Mr. Temperance had given her. She whacked the basket against her green-sprigged skirt and huffed. "I reckon what you're tellin' me is you won't be kissin' Bek no more, an' that's just fine. Now I gotta get to work."

"Cissy?"

She stopped again.

"Would you mind taking Lightning with you?" He offered her the reins. She was heading to the barn anyway. She caught hold.

"Thank you. Have a good afternoon." He strode off across the grass toward the staff cabins.

Cissy tugged Lightning's reins. "C'mon, boy."

Giggles erupted from the pair of girls. One of them said, "No wonder she's wearing nothing but a rag. She's a stable worker."

The second one added, "At least the horse has shoes."

Still laughing, they linked arms and sashayed up the boardwalk.

Cissy blinked back tears of hot anger. She wasn't wearing shoes. She never did after school let out, except on Sundays to service, because it saved the soles. But this muslin dress with its ivy vines climbing in all directions was one of the nicest she owned. And they'd called it a rag.

## Devlin

Since he'd spent the morning away from the estate, he'd need to work especially hard this afternoon on his drawings. On Monday Tolly intended to take him to the lower levels of the cave nearest the entrance. So next week he'd add a new layer to his map. An intimidating prospect, much more complicated to represent in lines on a page than to experience in person. But if he represented it well, his professors would be pleased, and Father would benefit. He wouldn't shy away from the challenge.

He broke into a trot as he neared the row of simple cabins where the guides lived. He aimed himself for Rebekah's cabin, eager to apply pen to page. But as he stepped onto the stoop, uneasiness replaced the zeal. The shutters to Rebekah's cabin were sealed against the midday sun. She always opened them before leaving for the day. Was she still in there? If so, why? Unpleasant pictures flooded his mind.

He raised his fist and pounded on the door. "Reb? Reb, are you in there?"

Before he'd even completed the question, the door swung wide, and she stood before him in a calico dress, her hair in its familiar braid, and her lips set in an unsmiling line. Even though she appeared far from happy to see him, relief nearly collapsed his frame. He placed his palm on the doorjamb and hung his head, breathing heavily.

"Thank goodness you're all right. When I saw the closed shutters, I thought—" How quickly worry had risen. How unexpectedly the instinct to rescue her had seized him. Would he ever set aside his useless infatuation for this woman? He shook his head, forcing a laugh. "Never mind what I thought." He straightened and assumed a businesslike bearing. "May I come in? I'd like to work on the map."

Wordlessly she stepped aside, allowing his passage. He crossed the threshold and paused. The lamp burned brightly on the far corner of the table, and his map and other drawings were rolled together on the opposite side. His pencils, pens, and box of drawing instruments lay next to the rolled papers.

He held his hand toward the neatly organized items. "Is this your way of letting me know I need to work elsewhere?"

She gazed at him for several silent seconds, still unsmiling, seeming to study him with uncertain brown eyes. "I rolled them up so I would stop looking at them. They were causing me too much consternation."

He frowned. "Why?"

"Because they seem to be more than a map of Mammoth Cave."

Guilt pricked him. A guilt he didn't understand.

She crossed to the table, her skirts sweeping the floor, and carefully unfurled the pages. The smaller drawing he'd done of the cave and its surrounding land lay on top. She pointed to the $X$ he'd marked to indicate her family's property. "What is this?"

He angled himself toward the table without moving his feet. "I believe that shows the location of your daddy's landholding."

She scowled briefly, then moved her finger to another $X$. "And this one?"

"Um . . . without my notes I can't be sure, but I believe that's the Barbee farm."

She slid her finger across the cave to the opposite side and stopped on a thickly penned $X$. She skewered him with a questioning look.

He gulped. He didn't need his notes to remember that one. "The Minyards' place."

She released the pages, and they rolled together on their own with a whispering *thwip*. Her brow puckered into lines of confusion. "None of those farms are part of Mammoth Cave. Why are they on your map?"

"They aren't." He hurried forward and snapped the pages flat. He placed the largest drawing on top and held the edges down with his palms. "See?"

She shook her head slowly. "Devlin, you aren't being honest with me. Your drawing of the cave is incredible. I could follow the tunnels in my mind. Every twist and turn and narrowing of the passages is there on paper. It's truly amazing, and I want to be impressed with your ability. Selfishly, I want to feel as if I played a small role in making the scope and breadth of Mammoth Cave come alive for hundreds of people who've never been here."

Tingles broke across his scalp. The prick of guilt became a stab.

"But all I can think is . . . why? Why are these other places marked, too?"

With the shutters closed to passersby, they could sit at the table and talk. He pulled out a chair and gestured for her to sit. After a moment's pause she perched on the seat, and he slid into another chair. He stacked his arms on the table and leaned in, watching the lamplight dance on the gold flecks in her brown eyes.

"Reb, if I tell you everything, will you listen without interrupting? Will you withhold judgment until you've heard it all?"

The slightest grin twitched at the corners of her mouth. "This isn't going to involve asparagus, is it?"

Her question made no sense, but the bit of teasing in her eyes encouraged him. He bantered back, "Not unless it grows wild in the hills."

She sucked in her lower lip for a moment and then nodded. "All right. I'll listen."

# Thirty-Four

*Rebekah*

As Devlin's explanation lengthened, Rebekah's ears began to ring. A sharp, high-pitched hum of tension. She stared at him, at the single dimple winking occasionally in his left cheek, the fervent furrow of his brow, the shimmer in his blue eyes. She'd gazed into his handsome face dozens of times since his arrival at the cave estate, and the fascination she experienced from the beginning still captured her, but in the back of her mind she felt as though she were looking at a stranger. How could he have so thoroughly deceived her?

"So you see, the entire state of Kentucky would benefit if the government took over the operation of Mammoth Cave. The hotel and grounds would no longer be merely a retreat for the wealthy but a place where people from all social stations could come and get a glimpse of the beauty and magnificence existing both on the surface and beneath these hills."

He shifted in his chair, his gaze lowering to the table briefly before meeting hers again. A nervous smile quivered on his lips. "I'm finished. I'm sure you have questions."

Yes, she did. She took a slow breath, willing the shrill ring to vacate her head so she could think clearly. "I don't understand how you can say the entire state would benefit if this land became the government's instead of the people's who live here. The cave has an owner. He would sacrifice his property."

"He would be adequately compensated. And no longer tied to the massive responsibility."

"And you want those of us who live near the estate to leave our homes. How can that be best for us?"

Devlin winced. "I know it's difficult to consider. Change—packing up and moving on—is intimidating. But think of what waits outside of these hills, Reb. Houses with running water. Electric lights instead of smelly coal oil lamps. No more cooking over an open flame in a fireplace or growing your own food. Instead, you could walk into a grocer's store or butcher shop and buy anything you need, from loaves of bread to dressed chickens."

"I like Mama's homemade bread baked right there in the little hole Daddy made beside the hearth. And dressing out a chicken isn't so hard."

He frowned. "Cities have libraries and museums open to anyone who wishes to frequent them. Not to mention the schools. Including colleges. Many of them accept female students, too, so think of the opportunities you and your sisters would have."

Desire struck with such force it stole her breath for a moment. She chased away the intense longing with a harsh laugh. "Colleges aren't free to the public. How could my daddy afford to send us to college? He can barely afford to keep us in shoes."

Devlin nodded, fervency brightening his eyes. "That's exactly right. On that small patch of ground, he'll never earn enough to provide anything beyond the most rudimentary education for you or Cissy or any of the others. But with the money your family receives from selling your land, you could—"

The ringing increased, stirred by Devlin's eager tone. She clapped her hands over her ears.

He grabbed her wrists and pulled her arms down. "Reb, you love books. Wouldn't you like to earn a degree in library science or education? You could work with books every day. You could encourage others to love books as much as you do."

How could he have tapped into the secret desire of her heart? She wriggled free of his grasp and hugged herself. "Sure I love to read. It's a fine way to learn about faraway places and people who are different from the ones I see every day." Oh, to share her love of learning with others, to see their faces light the way the little girls' did when she read them tales of dragons and princesses and castles. Then a remembrance of Andy's face, pinched with hurt as she ordered him to get lost and let her read in peace, flooded her.

She smacked the table with her open palm, forcing her thoughts back to Devlin and his talk of college. "No stack of books, no matter how high, could be more important to me than the land my great-granddaddy came all the way from Scotland to claim."

Devlin blew out a mighty sigh. "Reb, I think you're cheating yourself."

"And I think you're trying to cheat the folks who live in this hollow. I think you're trying to take away their most precious possessions, and for what? For the government? I thought the government was supposed to be for the people, not the other way around."

He stood and clomped to the door and back. He stopped in front of her and glared down for several tense seconds, his back stiff and his lips pressed so tightly their rosy pink turned white. Then, in a movement so quick she blinked in surprise, he crouched in front of her and took her hands.

"I'm not just thinking of the good of the people in the hollow and the good of the fine state of Kentucky. There's one more reason I want to see Mammoth Cave become a state park. And the reason is purely personal. Can I trust you with it?"

She held her breath. He seemed so stern, so intense, so masculine. A part of her wanted to bask in the strength and purpose he displayed, and the other part wanted to leap from the chair and escape. But his hands held tightly to hers. Her limbs went rigid, as if she'd turned to stone. She wouldn't be able to stand let alone run. She had to stay.

She licked her dry lips and forced the taut muscles in her neck to offer a jerky nod.

He bowed his head for a moment, his eyes slipping closed. Then he met her gaze again. "Like your father, my father is the descendant of immigrants, although my family has been in the country for a decade longer than yours. My great-great-grandfather was born to English colonists in 1776—the very year the Declaration of Independence from England was signed."

Chills broke out over Rebekah's frame. She felt as though she touched a piece of history as she held Devlin's hands.

"My father is a professor at the University of Kentucky. He teaches American history and American politics with a passion beyond description. This country and its betterment have always been of great interest to him because he was taught by his father and his grandfather that being an American is a privilege."

A flutter settled in the center of Rebekah's chest. The ringing in her ears faded. "My granddaddy told my daddy the same thing. Daddy tells us girls to remember how hard my great-granddaddy fought to get to this country and to never take lightly the freedoms and advantages we have here. He's proud of his heritage, but he's also a proud American."

Devlin's lips curved into a sweet smile. "Maybe we have more in common than we first realized."

She offered a tentative smile in reply.

He gave her hands a gentle squeeze and then slipped into the chair, still holding her fingers loosely between his. "My father has aspirations to have a greater impact on America than teaching about its past to young men and women. He wants to become part of the nation's history by serving as a senator. He intends to vie for a seat in the 1910 election. The competition is fierce. He's a Republican in a largely Democratic state, and he's against some popular incumbents. Consequently, he needs an . . . edge."

Suddenly Rebekah understood. She yanked her hands free. "You want to gain control of Mammoth Cave and its surrounding grounds so your father can score points."

His brows came down sharply. "You make it sound as if I'm doing something immoral."

"Aren't you?"

He held out his hands in entreaty. "Reb, there's nothing morally wrong with trying to improve the lot of people's lives."

"There is if you're doing it for yourself instead of for them."

He slumped in the chair, let his head drop back, and stared at the ceiling.

Tension hung like a veil of smoke, making it difficult to draw a full breath. How she disliked the barriers between them. Most of them could never be removed. She couldn't change who she was, a "hills gal," as Tolly called her. Nor could he change who he was, an educated, wealthy city boy. But if they could come to agreement on this one thing, it would be a salve on her wounded heart.

Hesitantly Rebekah reached out and touched his knee with her fingertips. "Devlin?"

He lowered his chin slightly and peered at her through his narrowed eyes. "I listened to you. Now will you listen to me?"

He sat straight in the chair and met her gaze, but he didn't appear happy.

She sighed. "I admire your loyalty to your father. You must love him very much." As much as she loved Daddy.

He nodded. The grim lines around his mouth relaxed a bit.

"Since you love him, it makes sense that you want to do everything you can to help him." How well she understood. She would work here at the estate and hand over her salary forever if need be to help Daddy build his legacy.

He gave another brusque nod.

"But it seems to me, if your father cares about the people who live here, he'd care about how they feel. Instead of sneaking around and trying to find a way to take control of this area, why not ask them if they want the chance at a different kind of life?"

He tipped his head, his mouth pursing into an uncertain scowl.

"America's supposed to be the land of freedom. Give them the freedom to choose."

## Cissy

"Cissy, eyes over here." Mr. Temperance barked the command.

She jerked her attention to him.

"Smile."

She lifted the corners of her mouth.

Mr. Temperance squeezed the bulb on the camera, and the *poof* signaled they were done.

The boy sitting astride Beau's back didn't need help climbing off, so Cissy sneaked another look at the group of young people gathered beneath the cottonwood. Nick was in the middle of them all, and he sure seemed to be having fun talking to the girls who were like mirror reflections of each other. Her stomach hurt.

Mr. Temperance crossed the grass and stopped in front of her, blocking her view. He dipped down and put his hand on her shoulder. "Three more and then we're done. Can you pay attention long enough for three more photographs? Then you can dive in the middle of them and pummel whomever you please."

Her chin quivered. "He ain't noticin' me at all, Mr. Temperance. An' I know why. It's 'cause I don't dress pretty or talk pretty. I was fine for him 'til they came along. But now . . ." She sniffed and swiped her nose with the back of her hand. "I guess you was right about me bein' entertainment to Nick. An' seein' as how there's just one of me, I can't hold a candle to those two."

Mr. Temperance sent a glance over his shoulder and scowled. "I didn't want to be right, Cissy. I hoped your boy might prove me wrong." He patted her shoulder. "Don't let him bother you. If his head can be turned by a pair of supercilious porcelain dolls, he isn't worthy of you."

But she still wanted him. She scuffed her bare foot over the blades of grass. "Yes, sir."

"Chin up, now."

She squared her shoulders and nodded.

"Good girl." He strode to the camera, calling, "Next!"

A teenage boy separated himself from the group and trotted over.

Cissy greeted the guest and smiled the way Mr. Temperance expected, but inside she imagined Real and Reflection coming to sit on Beau. She'd step aside and let Beau give them a good nip. No, two nips. Hard ones. Back where their satin ribbons fluttered. When Mr. Temperance said to smile, she gave him a genuine one. What a fine daydream . . .

But then she reminded herself that if Beau bit anybody again, Mr. Temperance would take the burro to the glue factory. No more little fuzzy-chinned friend named Beauregard. No more money in her pocket. No more chances to win Nick away from the rich girls. It was a bad idea, but she let herself imagine it again. The thought kept a smile on her face.

"All done for today." Mr. Temperance sent a smile over the people still standing around. "Sign up on the board in the office for tomorrow's photography session."

Cissy turned her back on the group and put her arms around Beau's neck. She nuzzled his stiff hide, enjoying his dusty smell. "Let's you an' me head to the barn, fella. I'll get you all brushed down an' tucked in, an' then—"

"Are you finished for the day, Cissy?"

She jolted upright. Nick stood close, hands in his pockets, smiling his warm smile. Something inside of her melted. Then she noticed Real and Reflection a few feet away, smirking. She iced up. "Why do you care?"

His smile dimmed. "I thought you and I had . . . an arrangement."

"I thought so, too." She flashed a glower at the twins. "But I ain't gonna share you with them two."

He glanced at the twins. His eyebrows shot up. "Are you talking about my cousins?"

She gaped at him. He was kin to Real and Reflection? She didn't know whether to laugh or to cry.

"Daphne and Delphinia arrived this morning along with my uncle Rufus, my aunt Twyla, and their brother, Bartholomew. Daph and Delph are a year older than me, and Bart is a year younger than my brother, Lawrence. Our families vacation together every year."

Cissy nibbled the inside of her cheek while worry nibbled at her insides. "So they're stayin' for six weeks, too?"

He grinned. "Only four. Uncle Rufus can't abide country air for longer than that." He chucked her under the chin. "You weren't jealous, were you? You ought to know by now you're my best girl."

The ice dissolved. She hunched her shoulders and giggled. A clearing throat intruded. She shot a look at Mr. Temperance, who watched them with a frown. She giggled again. He'd been so wrong about Nick. She bounded over to him. "Mr. Temperance, Nick an' me are gonna take a walk by the creek. Can I take Beau with me?" Real and Reflection hadn't come near the burro.

Mr. Temperance aimed a short glare at Nick. "Are you sure that's what you want to do?"

Her boss was as prickly as a porcupine facing a wildcat. She covered her mouth to hold back a giggle. "Them two supersilly porcelain dolls? They're Nick's cousins. He says I'm his best girl." She let the giggle escape. "So see? We was both wrong. Ain't it grand?"

Why'd he still look so worried? Cissy stomped her foot and huffed. "Mr. Temperance, can I take Beau with me or not? I'm wastin' time I could be spendin' with Nick."

He flicked his hands at her. "Go on then. I'll leave your pay in Beau's stall. You can collect it there when you return with him."

She gave a happy little hop. "Thank you, Mr. Temperance!" She dashed off.

His voice trailed after her. "Keep that animal between you."

She waved to let him know she heard, but he hadn't needed to tell her such a thing. She already planned to use Beau as a barrier between her and Nick's cousins.

# THIRTY-FIVE

### Devlin

Since he had accepted Cal Adwell's invitation to lunch, Devlin decided it would be wise to attend services at the Good Spring Chapel. He intended to spelunk in the Adwell cave when he'd finished eating, so he chose not to wear a suit. Mother would frown, but she hadn't seen the number of bib overalls over patched white shirts and frayed string ties at the Joppa church last week. His good trousers, shirt, suspenders, and ruby-red silk tie would still put him several steps above most of the men in the congregation when measuring formality.

He located Junior in the barn and asked if Marey was available.

Junior nodded, making his thick brown bangs fall across his eyes. He shoved the strands aside and sauntered to the horse's stall. "You gonna be gone all day, Mr. Bale?"

"I'm not sure. Until midafternoon at least." He snagged a coiled rope from a peg. "May I borrow this, too?"

Junior grunted as he tossed the saddle over Marey's back. "Don't reckon Mr. Vance'd mind as long as you bring it back." He peeked at Devlin from beneath Marey's belly as he tightened the cinch straps. "You've got pretty attached to Marey, haven't you?"

He shrugged. "She's dependable." And Marey didn't plod like old Lightning. He had farther to go this Sunday than last, and he didn't want to chance arriving after the service began. Entering a church service late was very poor form. Devlin tapped his foot in eagerness while Junior scuffed around the animal, checking straps and adjusting the bit.

Finally the youth stepped aside. "Ready to go."

Devlin strapped the satchel containing his necessary tools to the saddle horn, looped the rope over his shoulder as Tolly did in the cave, and climbed into the squeaky leather seat. Once settled, he tossed the stable hand a nickel. The boy caught it, pocketed it, and grinned his thanks. Devlin nodded and aimed Marey for the road.

He'd traveled the county road—what he'd come to call the Hardin Road—so many times he followed it without conscious thought. As he rode in the shade cast by clustering trees, he envisioned the cabins and clearings hidden behind the seemingly impenetrable woods. Every image in his head was picturesque. Peaceful. The perfect park setting. And so many of the properties included caves. Caves with the potential of increasing the scope of Mammoth Cave. A tremble built in his chest.

As he had last Sunday, he fell in with others going the same direction. Among them was the Hardin family. He stayed well behind their wagon. His conversation with Reb weighed heavily on him. Not necessarily because he thought she was right but because their difference of opinion raised such a tremendous mountain between them, robbing them of the slightest chance for friendship. The loss created a greater sadness in the center of his heart than he cared to admit.

Ahead, a white clapboard rectangular building with two doors on the front and a simple sloped roof waited in a small clearing. He reined Marey to a halt and did a double take. Had it not been for the absence of a cemetery, he would have believed he'd somehow found his way back to the Joppa church. The structures were identical.

He clicked his tongue on his teeth, urging Marey into motion. As he drew closer to the yard, he realized there was a cemetery, but the graves were arranged in haphazard rows behind the church rather than beside it. He pulled back on Marey's reins and watched Mr. Hardin assist his wife and children from their wagon. He found himself taken once again by the husband and wife's courtliness despite their humble trappings. Reb came from good stock.

He battled a grin when the two smallest girls ran in unladylike fashion across the yard and darted into the building. Clearly they were familiar and at ease with the place of worship. As he observed Mr. Hardin escort his wife up the steps, Devlin wondered why they hadn't buried their deceased family members in the church graveyard. The plot appeared well cared for and peaceful. Perhaps having their loved ones' resting places nearby gave them a sense of comfort.

He trailed the later arrivals, which included Cal Adwell and an older couple he presumed were his parents, across the patchy grass and up the steps. Like the Joppa church, the sanctuary contained simple wood pews and a small dais and podium, but someone had given the wainscoting a coat of green paint, and the floorboards wore a scuffed covering of white paint. No potbelly stovepipe blocked his view from his position on the back pew.

A middle-aged, balding man wearing a suit with shiny elbows and a fraying lapel circled the room, shaking hands, patting little ones on the head, and speaking congenially. He made his way to the rear of the room, and his gaze fell on Devlin. His face lit, and he approached with his hand extended.

"Well, hello, stranger. Welcome to Good Spring Chapel. I'm Preacher Haynes. It's a real pleasure to have you join us this fine summer mornin'. And just who might you be? Not that it matters. You're welcome here no matter who you are."

"Good morning." Devlin accepted the man's hand, wincing at the preacher's firm grip. "My name is Devlin Bale. It's very nice to be with you and your congregation today."

"Devlin Bale, Devlin Bale . . . Where have I heard that name?" He pinched his chin, his forehead turning into a series of deep furrows. Then he brightened. "Ah yes! My good friend Tolly Sandford told me about you. You're the young man from the university in Lexington who's drafting a map of the big cave."

Somehow it didn't surprise him that Tolly was friends with this white preacher. He smiled and nodded. "Yes, sir, that's me."

Preacher Haynes clamped his hand over Devlin's shoulder and gave a squeeze. "In just a moment we'll start the service, but before we do, would you mind comin' up front an' lettin' me introduce you to the folks o' Good Spring? It's always a treat to have a fresh face among us for Sunday mornin' service."

Be paraded in front of everyone? Including Reb and her family? Devlin started to refuse. But what better opportunity to have his name and face made known to those whose property butted the estate? Being introduced by a minister would remove any seeds of distrust from the people's minds. Reb's question tapped the back door of his mind. *"Why not ask them if they want the chance at a different kind of life?"*

He rose and stepped out of the pew. "Yes, sir. I'd like you to introduce me to the folks of your congregation. And then, if you have time, may I share a word or two?"

"None of them'll leave 'til I give the go-ahead. We've got as much time as we care to take." The preacher planted his hand on Devlin's back, propelling him up the aisle. "So come along, young man, come along."

### Rebekah

"Lookit, Bek, Mr. Bale's here."

Rebekah gave a start at Tabitha's announcement. She sent her gaze in the direction of her sister's pointing finger and spotted Preacher Haynes accompanying Devlin up the aisle to the preaching platform. Daddy and Mama gave her questioning looks, as if she should know the reason for his presence. She shrugged, and they turned their attention to the front.

When the minister stepped onto the platform, the soft conversations taking place in various pews in the room quickly faded. He smiled and boomed, "Good mornin', brothers an' sisters!"

"Good mornin', Preacher Haynes," they recited.

"Is it a good day to be in the house of the Lord?"

"Yes, sir!"

The familiar routine seemed alien with Devlin standing at the edge of the dais, hands clasped loosely in front of him and a half grin bringing out the dimple in his cheek.

Preacher Haynes gestured to Devlin, and Devlin joined him. The preacher put his arm around Devlin's shoulders and beamed at the congregation. "Folks, this here is Devlin Bale, a man who's come all the way from Lexington to spend his summer at Mammoth Cave. Tolly Sandford—you all know Tolly—"

Across the room heads bobbed.

"He tells me Devlin's drawin' up a map of the big cave for his college."

Murmurs rolled through the sanctuary.

"When I greeted Devlin, he asked if he could speak a word or two to us before we get started this mornin'."

Rebekah sucked in a breath and held it.

"So you all give him the same attention you bestow on me." The preacher chuckled. "Or maybe a little better attention from some of you who like to catch a nap durin' the preachin'."

Now chuckles, some self-conscious, rumbled. Rebekah's held breath eased out with her soft laugh, and she nudged Cissy. Only last Sunday she'd had to gently wake Cissy twice when her sister dozed on her shoulder.

Devlin cleared his throat and stood erect, his pose reflecting ease and self-confidence. "As Preacher Haynes indicated, I came to the Mammoth Cave estate to craft a map of the cave's intricate inner workings. I am a cartography student at the University of Kentucky. The map will be my senior project and, hopefully, will help me acquire employment when my studies are complete. But I also have a second reason for spending my summer in your beautiful hollow."

He drew a breath and Rebekah did, too. She gripped her hands in her lap, clutching so tightly they trembled. He was going to do it. He was going to come right out and tell everybody he wanted the government to buy their land. Would they all rise up and ride him out of Good Spring on a rail?

"I believe this hollow and the amazing underground natural structure known as Mammoth Cave shouldn't be selfishly preserved for the enjoyment of a handful of people. I believe folks from all over Kentucky—all over the United States—should be able to come here, breathe in your crisp, clean air, fish in your crystal-clear streams, and experience the wonder of Mammoth Cave."

Rebekah sent a furtive glance across the room. The people were listening, heads tipped, brows furrowed. Curious rather than condemning. But she knew what else he intended to say. How quickly would their expressions change?

"Thus, I'm exploring the possibility of the government assuming owner-ship of the cave and the land surrounding it and making the hollow a state park."

A collective gasp rattled the rafters.

"You're wantin' us to sell out to the government?" The angry blast came from the back corner of the room.

"How much would I get?" The eager question quavered from the front.

Devlin held up his hands. "Folks, I'm not here to make offers or speak on behalf of governmental officials. As I told you earlier, I'm only a college student. But I do plan to visit each of the families in the hollow and gather information to share with those who are in a position to make the land transfer possible. I'm particularly interested in properties with caves."

"So if I don't got a cave on my place, you ain't gonna come callin'?"

Devlin shifted slightly, seeming to search for the speaker. "I—"

Orval Spencer, who was seated in front of Rebekah, bolted to his feet and jammed his beefy finger at Devlin. "You show up on my property, boy, an' you can expect a backside full o' buckshot. Ain't no government man gonna take my land."

Cal stood and aimed a grin at Spencer. "Government'd prob'ly pay a good price, Orval." He nodded at Devlin. "I'll give a listen to your offer, Devlin."

All across the room, voices exploded.

"If the price is right, I'll sure enough give it some consideration."

"Government's already got my taxes. It ain't gonna get anything more'n that from me."

"I might sell off a piece o' my place, but I won't sell my house."

"Why's the government stickin' its nose in our hollow? Ain't there better things to do than bother with us?"

Little Nellie climbed into Rebekah's lap and clung.

Preacher Haynes waved his arms. "Folks, folks, settle yourselves down."

The uproar continued.

"I said shush!"

At the preacher's bellowed command, the hubbub dwindled to a few raspy whispers. He shook his head, gawking at the crowd. "I'm plumb ashamed of you all. This poor boy's probably worryin' about facin' a lynch mob."

Mutters and the shuffle of feet on the floor sounded.

Preacher Haynes turned a glare on Orval Spencer, who still stood with his fists clenched and the back of his neck as red as ripe cherries. "Orval, sit down before you give yourself apoplexy." When Orval plopped into the pew, the preacher put his arm on Devlin's shoulders and offered a weak smile. "Sure am sorry if we all scared you, son. Guess you now know, folks in these parts have some fiery spirits."

Devlin nodded weakly. His shoulders sagged and weariness etched his face.

"Now that we're all good an' awake"—the preacher chuckled—"we'll let Devlin have a seat, an' we'll get the service started."

Devlin stepped off the platform and hurried to the back pew, flicking uncertain glances back and forth as he went. Rebekah tried to catch his eye to give him a smile of encouragement, but he looked past her. Disappointed, she settled Little Nellie beside her and focused on Preacher Haynes.

"Gonna sing a hymn, but before we do, I've got somethin' to say, an' I want every person in this room—you, too, Devlin—to listen close." Fervor gleamed in the preacher's eyes. "If Devlin comes to your door, you give him a welcoming handshake and a respectful ear. You don't have to sell your land if you don't want to, but if I hear tell of even one of you aimin' a shotgun at him or otherwise bringin' him harm, you can expect to face my wrath an' discipline. We're Christians. Christians do what Jesus commanded, to love your neighbor the way you love yourself."

Orval Spencer muttered, "That college boy ain't my neighbor."

Preacher Haynes whirled on the man, his expression so stern Little Nellie latched on to Rebekah again. "Every person who crosses your path, whether family, friend, or foe, is your neighbor, Brother Spencer, an' you'll do well to remember it."

As quickly as it flared, the preacher's vehemence faded. A smile broke across his face, and he bounced his hands, encouraging everyone to stand. "Sing now. 'Immortal, invisible, God only wise . . . ' "

Softly at first, then with growing volume, the people added their voices to the preacher's. Rebekah sang, too, but the words and melody fought their way past a knot in her throat. Devlin meant well. She understood that. But if he persisted with his plans, he might very well tear the hollow apart.

## THIRTY-SIX

*Cissy*

S ee? I toldja this was a good spot to be alone."

Cissy tossed another mushroom into the basket and then peeked over the rim. Half-full already. She'd better slow down. Mama told her to come back to the house when she'd filled it, and she wasn't ready to say good-bye to Nick.

They'd been in her family's cave for more than an hour, and not a soul had come around. The lantern in the middle of the dirt floor sent a soft yellow glow in all directions. Little plump shadows from the mushrooms fell toward the walls, and Cissy's and Nick's shadows—sometimes short and squatty, other times long and thin, depending on how close or far they were from the lantern— moved around the walls like dancers.

Nick had spent his time prowling the small cave, poking at the wall with his penknife, knocking mushrooms loose from their hold, and kicking at rocks. He leaned against an outcropping and shrugged. "Yes, it's private, but it isn't very interesting. This isn't much of a cave compared to Mammoth Cave."

Cissy's clothes weren't much compared to his cousins' wardrobe. Her house wasn't much compared to the hotel. And now her cave wasn't much, either. She balled her fists on her hips. "Well, la-di-da." She imitated Real and Reflection. "I'm sorry it's not much. But I didn't think you came out here to see the cave. Thought you came to see me. Ain't I interestin' enough for ya?"

A grin pulled one side of his lips higher than the other. She loved the way his eyes lit up when he grinned that funny, crooked way. He scuffed toward her, his shadow growing longer and wider on the wall behind him and swallowing hers up. He came so close she had to tip her head back to look into his green eyes.

"You're interesting," he said.

She swallowed, hoping. "Enough?"

He nodded.

She sighed and slid her arms around his neck. "I'm glad."

He eased his hands onto her waist. He glanced out the cave opening and then looked into her eyes again. He licked his lips. "May I kiss you, Cissy?"

She angled her cheek to him.

He shook his head. "Huh-uh. On your mouth."

Heat flooded her. She pushed loose and flounced away, dividing their shadows. "My daddy would skin me. An' then he'd skin you."

"How would he know?"

He wouldn't unless she told. And she wouldn't tell. Even so, her insides went all trembly thinking about letting Nick's lips touch hers. She picked two mushrooms and lobbed them into the basket. "It ain't proper to kiss on the mouth until you're pledged." She reached for another mushroom.

He ambled up behind her. "Who told you that?"

She flicked a frown at him. "Nobody told me. I just know." She gave the mushroom a toss. It hit the rim of the basket and rolled across the ground. She huffed and started toward it.

Nick caught her arm and turned her to face him. "It's not true, you know. That you have to be . . . pledged . . . before kissing on the mouth. I've never been pledged, and I've kissed two girls already."

Her chest went tight. "What girls?"

He shrugged. "Just girls from my school."

"Must be real tarts if they let you kiss 'em."

He laughed. "They aren't tarts."

She gave him a look meant to say, *Yes, they are.*

He shook his head, sighing. "They're my friends, Cissy. Sometimes friends . . . kiss." His thumb moved up and down the inside of her arm. "Have you ever kissed anybody?"

His touch tickled. "No."

"Kissing's fun. I could show you."

She giggled and squirmed free. Her shadow made a funny twirl on the wall. "Huh-uh."

"Why not? Because you're worried I'll think you're a tart?"

Because she didn't know how to do it. He'd kissed two other girls. What if her kissing wasn't as good? She flounced to the opposite side of the cave, folded her arms, and stared at her shadow.

*Scuff, scuff*—his feet crossing the floor. His shadow loomed up and covered hers. She shivered as he slid his hands around her upper arms and pulled her firm against his frame. His cheek tipped against her temple, and her heart started thumping so hard she worried the photograph might get pushed out of her dress.

"Cissy?" His breath was warm on her cheek.

She kept staring at the big, gray, swelling shadow. "Wh-what?"

"I really want to kiss you."

She wanted it, too, but fear of disappointing him made her whole body stiff. She couldn't move.

"Cissy?"

Should she let him kiss her? Just once to know how it felt? Pansy and Burrel had probably kissed by now. And she'd seen Devlin give Bek that kiss on the cheek. Maybe Bek had let him kiss her mouth some other time when nobody was around. The men and women in the magazine serials kissed. Usually right after the man told the woman he loved her.

Cissy jerked free. She whirled around. With the lantern behind him she couldn't see his face very well, but she blurted to his shadowy form, "Do you love me, Nick?"

He didn't answer.

She hung her head, defeated.

Then he took her hand. "Come here, Cissy." He led her to the farthest corner of the cave, away from the opening, away from the lantern, away from the moist places where the mushrooms grew. With every step toward the dark corner, her pulse pounded harder, faster. Then he stopped and let go of her hand. He took hold of her shoulders and turned her sideways facing him.

Her breath came so quick and shallow she thought she would faint. *He's gonna do it. He's gonna kiss me.* But instead he moved backward, away from her. The slightest bit of lantern light flowed between them.

He held his hand toward the wall. "Look."

Confused, she tore her gaze from his face and looked. Her heart banged around inside her chest. She clapped her hand over her mouth. There on the wall deeply carved, crooked letters made a proclamation.

NICK LOVES SISSY

A laugh built behind her hand. So that's what he'd been doing over here while she picked mushrooms.

He said, "Can you read it?"

She nodded.

He aimed that crooked, eye-lighting grin at her. "What do you think?"

The laugh came out. "I think you need to learn how to spell my name."

His eyebrows shot up. He looked at the wall and then at her.

"Cissy starts with a *C*." She held out her hands and he took hold. The shadow of their arms underlined the wonderful words. "But it don't matter. I know it's me." She moved closer, and "Nick loves Sissy" got covered up by their combined shadow. "You know what else I think?"

"What?"

"It'll be all right for you to kiss me now."

### Devlin

Was there a more soothing sound than gently moving water? Devlin didn't believe so. He reclined on a pack, linked his hands over his belly, closed his eyes, and listened.

A faint, irregular *drip-drip* echoed from somewhere ahead, accenting the rhythmic hum of the canoe's nose plowing slowly through the stream and the steady slice of Tolly's oars cutting through water. Behind him a second canoe powered by Lee offered harmony to the sweet melody.

"Devlin, look."

Tolly whispered rather than shouted, but his voice intruded on the cave's song. Devlin frowned, unwilling to break the magic weaving itself around him.

"You's gonna miss 'em if you don' look."

Devlin opened his eyes. The lantern swinging from a hook at the front of the narrow craft highlighted Tolly's grin. The man angled the oars in the water, holding their position, and bobbed his head toward the stream.

"Most I ever seen of 'em. You seen anything like that befo', Mistuh College Boy?"

Devlin rested his fingers on the edge of the canoe and peered overboard. Dozens of fish no larger than his middle finger swam in an intricate ballet. He stared in open-mouthed amazement.

Lee's canoe glided up alongside theirs, and the fish frantically darted beneath the rock shelf at the edge of the stream.

Devlin scowled at the man. "You frightened the fish." He looked longingly toward the place they'd disappeared. He wished he could have caught one and taken it home to show Father.

Lee shrugged. "Sorry, Devlin. I'm goin' on ahead, Tolly. Meetcha at the rock bank."

Tolly waved him on. "That's fine."

Devlin swung one arm toward the rock shelf. "Were the fish white?"

Tolly laughed softly. "'Course they's white. Jus' like the crickets an' spiduhs climbin' aroun' in the cave. You look hard enough down here in the watuh, you'll find white crawfish, too." He took up the oars again and drew them through the water.

Devlin shook his head, imagining the graceful weaving of the little fish through the water. "Why are they white?"

"Why shouldn't they be? Got no cause fo' coluh down here where it's always dark. As fo' them fish, they're blind, too, in case you di'n't notice. Don't even got eyes fo' seein'. Scientists speculate the fishes had eyes a long time ago, but since they di'n't use 'em, their eyes went away." He snorted. "If you ask me, the almighty Creatuh made 'em that way since He knowed they'd spend their lives in the dark an' would have no need fo' seein'."

The man sighed, the release holding the weight of regret. "I've spent some time in this cave wit' no torch or lantern lit. Only black all aroun'. An' it's a lonely feelin', I can tell you. Like you's the only one in the whole world."

He sliced the water again, and the canoe glided forward. "Now I ain't sayin' nothin' bad 'bout folks who spend their lives without seein'." Slice. "There is blind people, you know." Slice. "But them people don't live all alone. They got othuhs around 'em, talkin' to 'em, touchin' 'em." Slice. "That ain't the way it is down here." Slice. "Down here you's all by yo'self in the dark, not a solitary soul to hear yo' voice or speak yo' name." Slice. "I'm tellin' you, Devlin, that's as lonely as lonely can be."

Devlin leaned back again but kept his eyes open, watching the play of the lantern light on the moist cave walls and on the water. Little shimmers of gold danced on the rippling surface of the stream, reminding him of the lamplight shimmering in Reb's eyes. His heart twisted, and the loneliness of which Tolly spoke attacked him with force.

He wished he'd been able to talk to her last Sunday after the church service, but her father had hurried her family out at the preacher's final amen. Then Cal Adwell had ushered him off to his cabin for the rest of the day. Devlin and Tolly left early Monday for the cave. They wouldn't come out again until tomorrow afternoon.

Curiosity warred with worry in the center of his mind. Did she appreciate his honesty? Or had he dismayed her by stirring a hornet's nest?

He sat up with a jolt. "Tolly?"

The canoe rocked precariously. The lantern swayed on its hook, clanking against the pole. Tolly reached for it, and his rapid movement sent one of the oars over the edge of the little craft. Devlin snatched at the length of wood, but it drifted away, carried by the steady flow. Tolly captured the lantern's base and held it. They both remained as still and unmoving as the Appalachian Mountains until the canoe balanced.

Then Tolly raised one eyebrow. "Hope whatevuh it was you needed was worth all that. 'Cause now I only got one oar. Gonna be a lot harduh to make this boat go upstream wit' only one oar."

Devlin cringed. "I'm sorry, Tolly."

The guide shrugged. "Watuh'll carry us backward some but oughta take us to the edge. Then the two o' us can catch hold o' the wall. Lee'll start missin' us an' come huntin'. We'll lash the canoes togethuh an' go on. Might be a while o' waitin', though. Hope you ain't in no hurry."

He wouldn't complain, no matter how long they had to wait, since his foolish action had put them in the predicament.

"While we's driftin', wanna tell me what you was gonna ask?"

He'd never met a more patient soul than Tolly Sandford. "You're friends with Reverend Haynes from the Good Spring church?"

"Ain't nevuh thought o' him as Rev'ren'. He's just Buck to me. Used to swing on scuppernong vines when we was boys an' go wadin' in the creek togethuh. Him an' me, we go way back."

Devlin squirmed. "Did you, um, see him before we set out Monday? Did he, uh, talk to you about . . ."

Tolly chuckled. "Fo' a college boy, you sure havin' trouble spittin' out words. Yep, Buck come to see me Sunday aftuhnoon and tol' me you got folks in his church all wound up. Whole bunch of 'em stayed aroun' aftuh service an' pestered Buck to no end, some frettin' an' some settin' their prices." He shook his head. "What're you up to, boy?"

The canoe bumped against a rock ledge. They both lurched to steady it. Devlin sucked in a breath, scrambling. Cold water filled his gloves. His fingers slid along the slick rocks. On his third attempt he managed to catch a crevice and keep his grip. Tolly clung to a rock shaped like an old man's nose. The canoe stilled. In unison they filled their lungs and released the air.

Devlin started to answer Tolly's question, but he stopped when the older man's brows shot downward into a stern V and he jutted his neck forward, seeming captured by the rock wall. "What is it?"

"Hold on tight."

Devlin dug in his fingers, his pulse thumping in apprehension.

Tolly kept one hand clamped on the rock nose with his thumb in a nostril and pushed his other hand into the gap between two rock ledges. The canoe tried to slide sideways, but Devlin gritted his teeth, dug his knees into the canoe's side, and kept it secure. When Tolly pulled his hand free, he held a canteen. The initials *T S* were scratched into its tin side.

Devlin frowned. "Is that yours?"

"It sure is. But I di'n't put it there."

"Then how—"

"This be the canteen that got took when you, me, an' Reb left our packs in Annetta's Dome."

# THIRTY-SEVEN

*Cissy*

H ere you are, Cissy. I have today's pay ready."

She turned from releasing Beau into his stall and held out her hand. Mr. Temperance dropped the coins into her palm. Two quarters, a dime, a nickel, and a penny. She stared at them, waiting for the tickle in her tummy to strike. Nothing happened. She closed her fingers. The coins were warm from his pocket, but they didn't flood her with warmth. So she squeezed them. Squeezed hard. But happiness didn't flow through her like it used to. She'd even lost her pleasure in earning money.

She sighed. "Thank you, Mr. Temperance."

He cupped her chin and lifted her face. "What's gotten into you this week? Sunday you were nearly euphoric."

She scrunched her nose.

"Overjoyed," he said.

Sunday . . . when Nick carved the most wonderful words in the world on the cave wall and kissed her lips until they felt chapped. She pressed her fingertips to the photograph resting against her heart. Yes, she'd been overjoyed.

"And Monday you were practically giddy."

"Huh?"

The photographer chuckled. "I mean you were so happy you could hardly stand still."

"Oh." That fit, too.

"But Tuesday you arrived with a frown, and you've worn it for three days in a row."

She might never lose her sadness. First she lost Devlin to Reb. Then Pansy to Burrel. And now Nick to . . . who? She must have lost him to someone because after Sunday night, he'd stayed away from her.

Mr. Temperance pulled one of her braids. "Do you want to tell me what's troubling you?"

She hung her head. "It ain't nothin' you can fix." She must be the worst kisser in the whole world for him to change his mind about loving her after he tasted her lips.

"Well, I have an idea."

She angled her head and peeked at him through her eyelashes.

"Take some of the money you've earned and buy yourself something pretty. A new dress or even some hair ribbons. I've never known a girl who didn't get perked up from getting something new."

Cissy chewed her lip. She had enough saved up for the outfit in the catalog. But orders took so long to come. She might fade away from sadness before it got to her. "Where'm I gonna get something new?"

He grinned. "Do you have your money with you?"

She held up her hand. "Just this."

"That probably won't be enough, but I'll lend you extra." He took her shoulders and turned her toward the door. "Let's go, Miss Woeful, and we'll restore you to Miss Sassy."

### Rebekah

Rebekah helped Mrs. Marrett from Jefferson County remove the flannel bloomer she'd donned to protect her silk dress from the "vile elements of the underground." From the time they had boarded the wagon for the two o'clock tour until they emerged from the cave, the woman had delivered a steady stream of complaints punctuated by sharp sniffs that drew her nostrils inward in a very unattractive manner. Now, aboveground, she was still unhappy.

"Such an ungainly costume. Why, it's Bohemian in appearance." She flailed her arm, entangling herself in the fabric. "And wretchedly hot now that

I'm in the sun. Couldn't we have dispensed with this ridiculous uniform in a less sunny place?"

Rebekah gently unwound the twisted sleeve and slipped it free. "I brought you to this sunny spot because you said you were cold when we were in the cave."

"I was cold in the cave, young"—she flicked a tight-lipped glare over Rebekah's clothes and sniffed—"woman. That is no longer the case."

Crit ambled over. "You 'bout got her unraveled, Reb?"

She suspected he meant the woman's nerves as much as the costume. She almost sniffed. If Mr. Marrett, her husband of more than forty years, hadn't succeeded in calming her during the tour, how could Rebekah be expected to accomplish it? She forced a smile and a stiff nod. "Just about."

"Soon as you's done, we can head back to the hotel." He sauntered up the rise.

Mrs. Marrett sniffed. "Insufferable man. Exceedingly officious. Give his kind an ounce of authority, and they—"

The only insufferable person in the vicinity was Mrs. Marrett, but Rebekah wouldn't say so. She wadded the bloomers in her hand and headed for the rise. "Come along now, ma'am. The wagon is waiting."

She and Crit deposited the guests at the drop-off point. Mrs. Marrett was still haranguing her husband as the pair walked away. Crit shook his head. "An' there goes the reason I didn't nevuh take a wife. Women." He snorted. "Nobody can grumble an' gripe as good as a woman."

Rebekah could have told him he was being as narrow minded as the wealthy woman from Jefferson County who'd spoken ill of him based on the color of his skin, but then he might accuse her of griping. She grabbed the edge of the seat and leaped to the ground. "See you at supper, Crit."

"Sure thing, Reb. Go ream all that complainin' out o' yo' ears now."

She laughed and waved as the wagon rattled off. Then she headed across the lawn, fingering the tips in her pocket. The bottom of her coin can was filling up again. Daddy would be pleased when she told him about the fifty-cent piece Mr. Marrett gave her when she escorted his wife to the wagon. He probably would have paid more if she'd lost Mrs. Marrett in the cave. Giggling, she tossed the large coin in the air and caught it again as she made her to way to her cabin.

She topped the rise leading to the staff cabins and stopped, frowning. A woman stood on the edge of Rebekah's stoop, seemingly trying to peek through the window. None of the guests had ever visited her cabin. The woman was likely trying to find Devlin. The thought made her stomach clench. The temptation to tell the woman Devlin was gone and never coming back poked her, but she wouldn't succumb. She would send her away, though. Her cabin wasn't going to become his meeting place for girls he encountered at the hotel.

Closing her hand tightly around the half dollar, she broke into a trot. The woman turned to face the yard, and Rebekah stopped again, her mouth hanging open. That was no woman. It was Cissy.

Her sister's face lit with a smile. She waved her arm back and forth like a flag. "Hi, Bek!"

Rebekah stumbled forward, unable to believe her eyes. Where had Cissy found such a lovely frock? Rebekah let her gaze rove from the rounded collar to the puffy sleeves ending just below Cissy's elbow in a snug narrow cuff fastened by a pearl button. The ivory blouse puffed, too, with a wide ruffle of lace lying across the bosom, and the waist cinched in before flaring into a matching full skirt that ended at Cissy's bare ankles. She swallowed a giggle. Her sister was barefoot.

Cissy met her at the edge of the porch. She held her arms out and twirled. The skirt flared, and the lace flounce at her chest lifted and fell like a butterfly coming to light. "Whatcha think? Am I purty?"

Rebekah's heart swelled. Cissy had always been pretty with her delicately shaped chin, big blue-green eyes, and thick red-brown hair falling like a curtain down her back. She nodded. "You're . . . exquisite."

"Gonna hafta tell me what that means."

"You're beautiful, Cissy. Truly beautiful."

Cissy beamed and rotated her hips, making the skirt sway. "Thank you, Bek. I've been waitin' for you. To show you my new dress. An' to see if you could pin up my hair—make it look like a real lady's hairstyle."

Rebekah gave a leap onto the stoop and unlocked her door. "I'd be glad to, although if you're going to pass for a lady, you'll need shoes."

Cissy made a face, but she laughed as she followed Rebekah into the cabin. "They didn't have shoes at Hunt's store. Didn't have very many dresses, either, but Mr. Temperance picked this one out. Said it was the most"—she wrinkled her nose and rolled her eyes toward the ceiling, then held up her finger and grinned—"sophisticated one there. That means grown up."

Rebekah paused in clinking the tip money into the can on her bureau. "Did Mr. Temperance buy that for you?"

"Uh-huh. I paid some of it. I had sixty-six cents." She crinkled her nose again, giggling. "Half o' that was s'posed to go to Daddy, but I'll make more tomorrow an' pay him back. Folks line up from here to Lexington to get their photographs made. Good thing, too, 'cause I gotta take money out o' what I've set aside at home an' give it to Mr. Temperance. I owe him a dollar fifty-nine."

Rebekah gaped at Cissy. "Your dress cost a dollar fifty-nine?"

"Nope. Two twenty-five." She simpered and fiddled with the end of her braid. "But it's almost as nice as the ones those Ross twins—Daphne an' Delphinia—wear every day. I'm tellin' you, Bek, it's worth every penny." Smiling, she smoothed her hands on the skirt.

Rebekah shook her head. "I hope so. That's a lot of money."

"I know, but when Nick sees me in this, he's bound to—" Cissy sashayed to the table, then plopped down on one of the chairs. "You gonna pin up my hair or not?"

Her sister's tone changed so quickly Rebekah wondered if she'd suddenly transformed into Mrs. Marrett. "Y-yes, sure, Cissy. Let me get my brush and pins." She gathered the items from her drawer and crossed to the table.

Cissy fingered the edge of Devlin's map, giving it a serious perusal. "What is this?"

"Devlin's map. Don't touch it."

Cissy pulled her hand back but didn't shift her gaze even when Rebekah began unraveling her braids. "How come he keeps it here?"

"This is where he works on it."

Cissy jerked her face toward Rebekah. "In your cabin?"

She nodded. "Turn around and hold still." She didn't add "be quiet," but Cissy must have decided Rebekah needed silence to focus on her hair, because she didn't say another word until Rebekah had finished brushing her long hair and pinning it into a fat bun. She pulled a few tendrils loose to soften the stark style, then led Cissy to the small mirror hanging on the wall.

"Is that more grown up?"

Cissy coiled the tendril dangling from her temple around her finger and smiled smugly at the mirror. "It's sophisticated. Thank you, Bek." She spun and wrapped Rebekah in a hug.

Stunned, Rebekah lost her breath for a moment. She couldn't recall the last time Cissy had hugged her. Certainly not since she turned thirteen and moody. She curled her arms around her sister's slender form, but before she could complete the embrace, Cissy pulled loose and pranced away.

"Can I borrow your shoes? I wanna show Nick my new dress, but I don't reckon I oughta go barefooted. Barefoot ain't very ladylike."

Rebekah shrugged. "As long as I get them back for Sunday so I can wear them to church." She pulled her brown high-top shoes from under her bed and handed them to her sister. "They aren't new, but they'll cover your feet. Do you want some stockings, too?"

Cissy sat down on the end of the bed and pulled on the shoes. "With my dress hanging down so far, nobody'll know I ain't wearin' 'em. Besides, gets too hot with all the layers. This is good enough." She laced them, stood, and took a few experimental steps. "A little too big for me, but I like the heels. My shoes don't got heels. I'm a lot taller now." She straightened and struck a pose. "Do I look older?"

Rebekah nodded. "Fifteen and a half for sure."

Cissy huffed. "I am fifteen an' a half."

Rebekah laughed. "I know. But you look every bit of it—a proper, pretty young lady."

Cissy's smile lit up the room. "Thanks, Bek. I'll bring you your shoes before I go home. Then I can let you know what Nick thought of my new dress an' hairstyle, all right?"

"All right." Rebekah stood on the stoop and watched Cissy depart. Her sister moved in a confident stride, swinging her arms and holding her head at a proud angle. She hoped Nick had the sense to appreciate what he saw. Cissy truly was turning into a lovely young lady.

## Cissy

Cissy ambled the length of the boardwalk from cottage one to cottage twenty and back again, hands linked behind her back, chin held high, picking up her feet so the heels didn't drag and make an awful sound.

Nick had told her his family dined at six thirty each evening. The clock hanging on the lobby wall showed six twenty-two, and her peek into the dining room earned a smile and wink from the host, but the Rosses weren't in there. So she started strolling up and down, up and down, waiting for them to come out. If his eyes didn't pop out of his head when he saw her, she'd go off and leave him alone forever, but she wanted him to see—really see—what he was losing.

The door to cottage eighteen opened, and Real and Reflection came out. Tonight they wore matching gowns the same color as mint leaves and their white kid boots with the heels that reminded Cissy of a lady's corseted waist. Cissy sat on the bench between cottages eight and nine and tucked her scuffed, too-big, brown lace-up shoes under her skirt. She angled her face so she could watch them out of the corner of her eye, her pulse pounding.

They gave her a look-over, but they didn't make snooty faces. As they passed the bench, they chorused, "Good evening, miss."

Cissy smiled and nodded, keeping her face turned aside in case they recognized her. But they reached the corner, turned, and kept going, chatting with each other. They never once looked back.

Cissy swallowed a chortle. Supersilly girls . . .

Door latches clicked, and she jolted. Two couples probably as old as Mama and Daddy stepped onto the boardwalk from cottage seventeen and cottage nineteen at the same time. She stayed in her spot and pretended to examine her fingernails while the grownups greeted each other and then paraded by, the women holding the men's arms and the men tapping the planked boards with canes. The men tipped their hats to her, and Cissy gave them the same smile and nod she'd given Real and Reflection. They went on by just as the twins had.

Her heart pounded hard. Nick should come next. Her mouth felt dry, so she licked her lips. Then she rubbed them so they wouldn't look wet when he saw her. She bounced her foot, realized she was doing it, and stopped. Stood up. Sat down. Stood up again and grabbed the porch post with both hands to keep herself from wiggling.

Finally the door on cottage twenty opened. Two boys, maybe Jessie's age, raced up the boardwalk and around the corner, both of them whooping like Indians on the warpath. Nick came out behind them, shaking his head and muttering. He closed the door and turned, and his gaze fell on her. A smile curved his lips.

He headed straight toward her, his steps eager. "Hello there."

She released the post and moved into his pathway. "Hello, Nick."

He stopped so quickly it looked as if he'd run into a post. His mouth fell open and his eyes went wide.

She giggled. "Yep. It's me. Cissy."

He took a clumsy step backward and looked her up and down the way Real and Reflection had. "You look . . ."

She rocked in place, making her skirt sway. "Sophisticated?"

He huffed. "Different, that's for sure." He slid his hands into his trouser pockets and settled his weight on one leg. "What are you doing here?"

"I was watchin' for you. Haven't seen you all week." She didn't mean to, but her voice went hard. "Thought maybe you was sick . . . or somethin'." She fibbed. She'd seen him playing catch with nets one time and another time coming out of the trees with a fishing pole on his shoulder. But if she acted like she was worried instead of mad, it would probably be better.

"I haven't been sick. Just busy."

"Oh." She tipped her head and fluttered her eyelashes at him. "Well, I ain't doin' nothin' tomorrow after I'm done helpin' Mr. Temperance. I know you like to fish. Maybe we can—"

"I don't think I'm going to have time to go fishing with you tomorrow."

"How 'bout Saturday, then?" She smiled and pinched her skirt, lifted it a little bit, and let it drop. "I'll wear my new dress. You thought it was purty. I could tell."

He sighed. "Listen, Cissy, you're very cute, and we had some fun, but there are a lot of girls here at the hotel. I'd like to spend time with some of them, too. I'm not ready to get stuck on one."

Mad swelled up inside of her, and she couldn't hold it down. "But you said I was your best girl. You wrote on the wall that you loved me. An' you kissed me, Nick." She touched her lips, remembering. Worry chased away the mad. "Is it 'cause I don't kiss good enough? I can do better. Let me show you." She puckered her lips and leaned in.

He eased past her, turning sideways to do it. She turned, too, keeping him in her view. "Let's just say you've shown me everything I want to see, and now it's time to . . . move on."

She stamped Rebekah's shoe against the boardwalk and clenched her fists. "I ain't showed you nothin' yet. But I can, more'n any other girl at this hotel can."

A smirk grew on his face. "You can? Like what?"

She searched her mind for something that would get his attention. "You like Mammoth Cave, don'tcha? Well, I can take you far into the cave—farther than any o' the tours go. All the way to the end where jewels grow on the walls an' gold rains from the ceilin'."

He shook his head. "Nobody's ever said anything about jewels in the cave."

"That's 'cause they don't want the guests to know about it. That's why they don't take you all the way in. But I ain't a guest. I've lived by Mammoth Cave my whole life. So I know."

He waved his hand at her and turned away. "You're making this up."

"Am not. An' I can prove it."

"How?"

She grabbed his hand. "I'll show you."

# THIRTY-EIGHT

*Devlin*

After a hot bath and a good dinner, Devlin's weary body begged for rest. If he slept, he could keep his eyes closed. He welcomed the evening sunlight after his long days with nothing but torches, lanterns, or campfires holding back the thick darkness of the cave, but his eyes seemed unwilling to adapt. By the end of the summer would he be like those sightless fish in the cave stream, unable to see at all?

He pushed the ridiculous thought aside and organized the notes he'd taken during the past week. The lower level had proved the most fascinating thus far. Centuries of dripping water created cities of stalactites and stalagmites. Waterfalls formed layers of lace-like patterns on walls. The tunnels held more twists and sharp turns, one a curving figure eight that crossed and met again. A fascinating area. And complicated to capture on paper.

His fingers itched to get started. He glanced at his pocket watch. Almost eight thirty. Was it too late to work? He shrugged. Rebekah was honest enough to tell him if she thought it too late to let him make use of her table. But he wouldn't know unless he asked. He slid his notebook into his satchel, tossed it over his shoulder, and set out.

Evenings at the Mammoth Cave estate seemed lazy compared to the bustle of daytime and the host of activities available to the guests. As twilight fell, adults—some with babies or toddlers drowsing on their shoulders—lined the railing on the observation deck to watch night creep across the sky. Children chased fireflies on the lawn. Young people gathered in little groups or split into couples to talk softly, laugh, and hold hands while surreptitiously watching the adults. The scene was calm, quiet, relaxed.

Devlin moved through the center of it all, his satchel flapping softly against his hip. The pinpoints of light from fireflies reminded him of the spark from Tolly's flint, and he found himself automatically blinking at each little flash. He chuckled at himself and battled a temptation to try his hand at capturing one of the flickering insects, something he hadn't done in years. But he wasn't a child anymore. He had work to do. Determinedly, he aimed his gaze ahead and lengthened his stride.

The lamp burned on the table in Reb's cabin, and her door stood open, throwing a soft path of yellow over the stoop. Tolly and Lee sat on Tolly's stoop, and Reb stood nearby, probably catching up with one another after their days apart.

He raised his arm and waved. "Hello. May I join you?"

Without a moment's pause Tolly answered. "Come on ovuh, Devlin. We was just talkin' 'bout you."

He trotted to their little circle, keeping his smile intact even though Reb folded her arms over her ribs and turned aside. "I hope you weren't tattling about how I lost your oar."

Tolly laughed, the sound boisterous. "Yep, I was, but not fo' the sake o' tattlin'. Fo' tellin' her how the lost oar led me to my stole canteen." He shook his head. "Still puzzles me how that thing got tucked clear down there. Some-body's almighty comf'table in that big ol' cave."

Lee nodded, his dark eyes wide. "Gots ou'selves a myst'ry in there, that's fo' sure."

Tolly slapped his thighs and rose. "An' we gots ou'selves a tired guide sittin' right here. I tol' Marshel that me an' Lee'd take his tours into the cave tomor-ruh so him an' his helpuh can spend the day wit' their fam'lies. So I's gonna turn in. You young folks enjoy yo' evenin'." He ambled stiff legged into his cabin and closed the door behind him.

Lee rose and sighed. "Guess I'll go see if the fellas've got a card game goin'. I'd ask you to come, Reb, but gamblin' ain't fittin' fo' a lady. Even when we only gamble matches."

Devlin's chest went warm. Being a girl, Reb could have been ignored or, worse, ridiculed by the male guides. But instead they accepted her, looked out for her, treated her with dignity and respect. Until he'd come to this hollow, he'd thought only refined men knew how to treat women well. He'd discovered a different kind of gentleman in these hills. Lowly in some ways, perhaps even backward by some people's standards, but loutish? Not at all. He liked these people.

The realization delivered a pang of remorse. It would hurt him to see them lose their property when the Mammoth Cave estate became a government-owned park. But a sacrifice by a few was sometimes necessary for the good of many. To his aggravation the reminder didn't help.

He patted his satchel and aimed his smile at Reb. "I thought if it wasn't too late, I'd try to get a few notes transferred to the map. But if you'd rather I waited until morning, I understand."

She shrugged and moved in the direction of her cabin. "It's all right. I won't turn in until Cissy comes back." A funny little grin, holding both fondness and envy, teased the corners of her mouth. "She went to find her friend Nick more than two hours ago, and she hasn't returned. Apparently he approved her appearance in her new dress. It shouldn't be much longer, though. She's supposed to be home by dark, and she promised to bring my shoes to me before she left for home."

Devlin, following her, glanced at the sky. Only a few stars had made their presence known, but the moon carved a thick, bold wedge of white in the pale-gray sky. Darkness would descend soon. "She'd better hurry."

Reb nodded. "But you can work while I wait. Go on in." She perched on her stoop and rested her chin in her hands, gazing outward.

He stepped past her and entered the cabin. He opened his satchel and spilled the notebook onto the table. Then he reached to unroll his map. His hand stilled midreach. Where was it? His box of tools and the smaller map roughly marking the site of nearby caves waited on the table, as always, but the large, detailed map of Mammoth Cave was gone. He looked under the table, on each of the chairs, even under Reb's bed. Still no map.

Worry quickly magnified to irritation. She'd made clear how she felt about his second reason for being at the estate. Had she hidden the map out of spite? He stomped to the door and barked her name.

She gave a start. "What's wrong?"

He stared hard at her, searching for signs of duplicity. Only puzzlement showed on her face. His shoulders sagged. Did he really expect her to behave underhandedly? She'd always been honest with him even when he'd wished she wouldn't be. The gentility—the honor—he'd seen in her parents also resided in her.

He hung his head for a moment, ashamed of where his thoughts had taken him. "My map is gone."

She frowned. "It can't be. It was there earlier." She charged into the cabin, straight to the table. She stared for several silent seconds at the empty spot on the table and then turned a slow circle, her gaze sweeping the room. "I don't understand . . . It was right there"—she jerked her palm toward the table—"when I twisted Cissy's hair into a bun. She wanted to look at it, but I wouldn't let her. It was there when I left for dinner."

"Did you see it when you came back?"

"Tolly and Lee were outside talking, and they called me over, so I didn't come in. I didn't even look in." She shook her head. "It's got to be here somewhere."

Devlin stood to the side and waited while she searched the cabin, kneeling to peek under every piece of furniture, shifting items in corners to peer behind. Finally she threw her arms wide and shrugged. "I don't understand. It has simply . . . vanished."

"Did you lock your cabin when you went to dinner?"

She shrugged. "No. I wanted Cissy to be able to get in even if I wasn't here."

He cupped his chin, gnawing his lower lip. If someone had burglarized Reb's cabin, they would have taken things of value. His drawing tools in their carved wooden box would be a more likely choice than a rolled length of paper. Unless they knew what the paper contained and had some reason to gain knowledge of the cave's interior.

He jolted. "Do you suppose that the person who stole Tolly's canteen and the food and torches from the packs has taken the map?"

Her eyes widened. "You mean, you think a stranger—a thief—came into my cabin?" The color faded from her face. She sank onto the edge of her bed. "Oh, my . . ."

Now he'd scared her. Even though his supposition made sense, he wished he'd kept it to himself. But now that the possibility had been stated, he might as well follow it with a warning. "Why don't you check your belongings? Make sure nothing of yours is missing. Just in case."

She rose and staggered to her bureau. She opened the top drawer and pawed through things made of airy fabric—her underclothes. His face heated, and he turned his back, allowing her to search in privacy.

Something clinked, and then the drawer snapped closed. "Everything is exactly the way I left it."

He turned slowly, shaking his head. "Then Lee is right. We have a real mystery."

## Cissy

Cissy shivered. This cave was a lot colder than the one where the mushrooms grew. Probably because it was so much deeper and wider. She held the lantern she'd stolen from the guard after Nick tricked him into leaving his post and inched forward with Devlin's map tucked under her arm.

Nick trudged along behind her with the second lantern. He hadn't said much since they entered the cave, but the deeper they got, the more often his huffs pierced the silence. If she didn't come upon something interesting soon, he might turn around and go back out. And she couldn't let him do that.

Years ago when she was no older than Trudy was now, a girl and boy from the hollow went off somewhere for a whole night. When their folks found out, they made the boy marry the girl. Those two were still married, had two or three children, and seemed happy even though the entire hollow had been plenty upset about the situation when it happened. If she could keep Nick in here all night, Daddy would make him marry up with her. Then she'd get to live in a fine house in the city and wear pretty dresses every day like the one she'd bought at Hunt's store.

Nick might have gotten confused in the past days with so many other girls coming to the estate, but she clung to his claim that she was his best girl. She chanted to herself what he'd carved on the cave wall. Oh, he might fuss a little bit at first when Daddy said they'd have to get married right away, but he'd be grateful later on. Because she'd be the best wife she could be. She knew how after watching Mama with Daddy all these years. They'd be happy. Sure they would.

"Cissy, stop." Nick's voice cracked like a whip. "You haven't shown me anything I didn't already see on the tour. I missed my dinner, I'm getting my good suit dirty, and I'm tired. I'm going back."

She whirled around and affected her sauciest look. "Go ahead an' go back if you're too scared to keep goin'. Big ol' chicken, that's all you are."

His glower seemed evil in the heavy shadows. "I'm not a chicken. I've just not encountered anything good enough to warrant tripping around in the dark."

"Enough, enough!" She blasted the word. It bounced against the walls and repeated, taunting her. "I'm so tired of whatever I offer not bein' enough!" She scurried to the edge of a downhill climb and held Devlin Bale's map over the raw gap. "Go then. But I'm goin' deeper to the place where jewels grow. Gonna pick me so many they weigh me down."

He gaped at her. "You're crazy."

She tossed her head. Several pins popped loose, and strands of hair tumbled over her shoulders. She batted at them with her hand. "Maybe I am, maybe I'm not. But you won't never know because you're too much a chicken to go an' see."

He held out his hand. "Give me the map."

Her heart leaped. Would he lead her deeper into the cave? "Why?"

"So I can use it to get myself out of here."

He couldn't go. Not yet. Not until morning had swallowed up the night. She forced herself to think. A plan formed so easy it made her smile. "All right.

Here." She let go of it, and the roll of paper bounced to the bottom of the gap. She clapped her hand to her cheek and dropped her jaw. "Uh-oh, look what happened. Guess you'll hafta go get it."

"Cissy . . ." He growled her name.

She drew back.

He stomped forward, his lantern swinging, and peered below. He glared at her again. "I ought to throttle you."

She balled her fist on her hip. "That'd be a plumb waste of time. Thought you wanted the map."

He blew out a mighty huff. He walked past her and started down the incline, holding the lantern out with one hand and using his other to steady himself. Cissy chewed her thumbnail, watching him. If he got the map, he'd leave. And she'd never get the chance to show him how good she could be to him.

She scurried after him, her lantern swinging. From the time she was big enough to walk, she'd been climbing in the hills and jumping from boulder to boulder in the streams, so making her way one handed down the rocky, uneven pathway to the lower tunnel didn't challenge her too much. She passed him, wriggling free when he caught her arm, and hurried for the map.

But then her foot slipped inside Bek's too-big shoe. Her leg jolted forward and carried her with it. The lantern bounced once way, shattering, and she bounced the other, landing hard on her bottom three times before she stopped.

"Cissy, are you all right?"

Nick sounded worried now. She glanced up and squinted against the glare of his lantern. "I . . . I think so. But I ain't sure."

He inched closer, bringing the light with him. The map lay just a few feet from her. She pulled with her heels, cringing against the pain in her back, and snatched it up before he could get to it. She hugged the map to her chest.

He knelt in front of her and set the lantern down. "Let me help you."

She crunched the map under her arm before holding out her hands. He lifted her in one hard pull. Pain stabbed her lower back, and she cried out.

"Are you hurt badly?"

She didn't think so. She'd taken tumbles before, some worse than this one.

But she liked the way worry creased his brow. So she grimaced and moaned. "Oh, I'm hurtin'. It's real bad."

He looked her up and down. He grimaced, too. "I don't think I can carry you out of here."

She wouldn't let him. At least not yet. "I can walk. But I can't climb. I ain't gonna be able to go back the way we came."

Nick looked at the steep route they'd just taken, then back at her. "I guess I'll have to go by myself."

She gasped. "What about me?"

"You'll have to stay here."

"By myself?"

"Long enough for me to go get you some help."

Real fear smacked her hard, harder than the floor had smacked her bottom. She started to wail. "No, Nick, don't leave me. We only got the one lantern now. I'd be alone in the dark with all the creepy little cave critters." She dropped the map and clung to his suit front. "Don't leave me!"

"Now who's being the chicken?"

"Ni-i-i-ick!" Her wail bounced off the walls and filled the entire space.

He rolled his eyes. "All right, all right, I won't leave you."

She shuddered, ending her tears.

"But I want out of here. Is there another way out?"

She didn't know. But she said, "Yes. Up ahead some."

"Can you find it?"

"Uh-huh. With the lantern. An' the map."

He scooped up the crumpled map and unwadded it. "Which way?"

She frowned at it, pretending she knew what she was doing. One tunnel wove its way north. She tapped it. "This one. It'll take us back to the hotel."

He stared at her for a moment, his eyebrows pulled so tight they formed a caterpillar on his forehead. "Are you sure?"

"Sure I'm sure. You carry the map. I'll carry the lantern." No way she'd let him take that and maybe run off. "This way."

# THIRTY-NINE

*Rebekah*

If she was a person who cursed, she'd be cussing her sister. Rebekah paced outside her cabin, watching the rise for Cissy. Full dark had fallen an hour ago. Devlin could've been hunting for his map, but he hadn't left. He sat on the stoop, elbows on knees, hunched forward, watching the shadows with her. Although she hated to admit it, she appreciated having someone to wait with her.

She stopped and stared hard at the stomped-flat grass pathway where her sister should appear. "Cissy, where are you?" she whispered for the dozenth time.

"Reb, do you think she went on home?"

"No." She closed her eyes and envisioned again her sister's bright countenance, her excitement. Cissy's promise to come back and tell Rebekah what Nick thought about her dress rang in her memory.

"Are you sure?"

"She hugged me, and she promised." Rebekah angled a firm look over her shoulder. "I'm sure."

"Well, it's getting late." Devlin rose and crossed to her. He gazed at the rise, too. "You said her friend's name is Nick?"

"Yes. Nick Ross."

"Hmm . . ." Devlin pinched his chin. The moonlight touched his chiseled features, giving him a severe appearance. "I met the Rosses at dinner a few nights ago. The parents have one cabin, and the boys are staying in another. Would you like me to go see if Cissy is with them?"

"With the boys?"

"Yes."

Her anger flared. "Do you really think my sister would . . . is . . ." She couldn't say it.

Devlin touched her arm. "Reb, they are young and forgetful. If they're inside, they aren't going to notice how dark it's become. They've probably lost track of time. Cissy needs a gentle reminder that it's time to go home."

Her fury fizzled in light of his calm reply. She tried to smile, but her trembling lips refused to cooperate. "I'm sorry."

His smile grew seemingly without effort. "You're worried, and rightfully so. Let me check with the Rosses. If I find Cissy, I'll bring her to you."

"I'll go with you."

He shook his head, the severity creeping over his features again. "You need to be here in case she returns. She'll need to get in to put away your shoes, but with a thief wandering the grounds, you can't leave your door unlocked for her."

Rebekah shivered. "A-all right."

"Go inside and keep watch. I'll be back in a few minutes."

She squared her shoulders. "With a repentant Cissy."

He squeezed her upper arm, a kind gesture that touched her deeply. "That's the way to think."

She stood on the lawn until he crested the rise, turned around, and waved. Then she closed herself in the cabin. She pulled the table away from the window so she could stand close to the glass, where she had a good view of the rise. She held her eyes open as long as possible between blinks, unwilling to miss the first sighting of Cissy. In between blinks she prayed. Minutes passed slowly, but she stayed in place.

When her muscles were beginning to ache from holding her stiff position, she finally spotted a shadow creep over the edge of the rise and grow until it became the shape of a man. Her pulse hiccuped—Devlin. Even in the scant light she knew his sturdy, broad-shouldered form. But where was the second shadow? Where was Cissy?

She darted out the door and met Devlin halfway between the cabin and the rise. "She wasn't with Nick?"

"No, I didn't find her."

She blew out a huff and stomped her foot. "Oh, that girl! She probably forgot all about her promise to come talk to me and went on home—and with my shoes on her feet! Just wait until I see her next. She's going to hear—"

"Reb." Devlin's sharp tone silenced her.

She looked into his stern face. Fear descended. "What is it?"

"The Rosses said they haven't seen her at all."

Rebekah drew back, confused.

"Furthermore, Nick is missing. He didn't meet his family for dinner, and they haven't seen him all evening. They're concerned, too."

Anger swooped in again. She clenched her fists and shook her head. "Cissy is the most spoiled, selfish, thoughtless person I know. She and Nick are probably together somewhere completely unmindful of the worry they're causing. I don't care if she is fifteen years old. I hope Daddy takes a stick to her."

"Do you have any idea where they might have gone? Mr. Ross is ready to start searching. He's particularly worried they might have gone into the woods and lost their way."

"It's unlikely they're lost if they're together. Cissy is familiar with the entire area and could find her way even in the dark. It's more likely they're enjoying themselves and aren't ready to come back." Troublesome thoughts descended. She grabbed Devlin's sleeve. "I need to find them. Cissy . . . sometimes she doesn't think."

He patted her hand. "She's very fond of that little burro the photographer uses. And the barn would be private. Would you like me to go look there?"

"It's a good place to start." Rebekah jutted her chin. "But I'm going with you. Let me lock my door, and—"

"Rebekah Hardin, is that you?"

She released a squeal and Devlin jerked. They both spun toward an approaching dark form. She called, "Wh-who is that?"

"It's me—Doyle Spencer."

She heaved a sigh of relief at the familiar name. She knew Doyle well. He guarded the cave opening from four in the afternoon until midnight, and members of his family attended Good Spring Chapel. The idea of a thief creeping around the cave and grounds was making her far too jumpy.

Doyle stepped close and whipped off his hat, bringing his face into view. A wide, knowing smile created a slash in his dark whiskers. "You look like you seen a ghost. Or maybe you just didn't want nobody to see you out with . . ." He waggled his eyebrows.

Her defenses rose. "I have nothing to hide, Doyle. Devlin was keeping me company while I waited for my sister."

"Sure, sure." He bounced his hat lightly against his thigh and continued to grin. "Glad to see somebody up. Need to leave a message for Tolly." He jammed his thumb toward the dark cabin. "I'd tell him myself but looks like he's sleeping already."

"Yes, he went in quite awhile ago. But I'll give him a message in the morning."

"Good." The man yawned. "It probably ain't nothin' important, but about seven this evenin' I heard a rustle in the bushes 'round the cave openin'. I went to check, an' o' course there was nothin', but when I got back to the openin', somebody'd took off with both my lanterns."

Rebekah gaped at the man. "That was hours ago. You're just now telling someone?"

"Well, now, how was I s'posed to say somethin' earlier? Couldn't leave the openin' 'til Horace showed up to spell me. Took me twice as long to walk here since I didn't have no lantern to guide me. That road's as black as pitch at night with all the trees throwin' shade at it." He snorted and slapped his hat onto his head. "Prob'ly just some fool kids playin' a prank, but I'm s'posed to report any unusual happenin's. If those lanterns don't turn up, I hope Mr. Janin don't take the new ones out o' my pay. Headin' for home now." He ambled off, muttering.

Rebekah's thoughts raced—a missing map, a missing sister, missing lanterns . . . Her pulse thrummed so rapidly that dizziness assailed her. She reached out and caught Devlin's arm to steady herself and found him staring at her with wonder blooming across his face.

"Reb, is it possible . . ."

A sick feeling flooded her stomach. Cissy wanted so much to be important, to impress people. It all made sense now. She nodded. "Cissy took your map and then took Nick Ross into Mammoth Cave."

## Devlin

Devlin stood a few yards from the cave's entrance, unneeded but too intrigued to leave. How could Mr. and Mrs. Hardin be so brave? The poor couple had been rousted from their home in the middle of the night after lying awake in worry over their daughter. Now, as dawn approached, they faced the prospect of another child wandering in the cave that had stolen their son. Yet they stood stalwart and quiet as Tolly readied himself to search. In contrast, the Rosses fumed and threatened serious consequences if their son emerged with so much as a scratch. Festus and Nell Hardin intrigued him. Almost as much as their daughter.

Reb strode by, bent forward with the weight of a pack. Devlin reached out and stopped her. "Let me take that for you."

She looked haggard, ten years older than the last time he'd seen her, but she shook her head. "No. Tolly asked me to get the torches. I'll do it."

He stepped aside and let her pass, shaking his head in wonder. While Reb handed off the pack to Tolly, Mrs. Ross released a mournful shriek and buried her face in her husband's chest. On the other side of the opening, Nell Hardin leaned against Festus. Her face was white and drawn in the lantern light, but she didn't make a sound.

Reb moved determinedly toward the supply wagon. Devlin fell in step with her. Whether she wanted his help or not, he intended to give it. He rasped, "The Rosses ought to be ashamed of themselves. Her caterwauling, his threats . . . It's embarrassing."

She gave him a confused look. "They're scared, Devlin. Tolly and others searched the entire estate grounds and the woods surrounding it. There's no hint of Nick or Cissy anywhere. The only place left to look is the cave. It's so big and full of dangers for two young people who aren't familiar with its passageways. Of course they're going to carry on in ways that seem inappropriate. Fear will do that to people."

He held his hand toward her parents. "Your folks have reason to be afraid, too—even more than the Rosses, considering what happened to your brother. But they aren't carrying on. Look at them." Her gaze followed his direction, and the tenderness that crept across her features caused a lump to fill his throat. "They're strong, Reb."

She nodded slowly, her braid shifting gently with the movement and picking up gold from the lanterns hanging on the wagon's side. "Yes. Because they know who gives strength to the weak."

He crunched his eyebrows, puzzled.

A soft smile appeared on her face, erasing a bit of her weariness. "It's from Isaiah, one of Daddy's favorites verses. 'He giveth power to the faint; and to them that have no might he increaseth strength.' Daddy relies on God when he needs Him. He's leaning heavily on God now, and he's encouraging Mama to do the same." The worry crept in again. "I hope Mama remembers—"

"Reb! Bring me those bandages an' such now. I's ready to go in."

She jerked away from the wagon and ran to Tolly. Devlin trotted on her heels. She handed off the smaller pack and helped Tolly adjust his load. With the pack of torches, another of food, ropes, ax, canteens, and a medical bag hanging from his shoulders, back, and belt, he was as weighted down as a pack mule.

She nibbled her lip. "Won't you let me go with you, Tolly? I could help you."

"Nuh-uh, an' don't be askin' again. One Hardin in that cave is enough."

Reb hung her head, and Devlin automatically stepped forward and gripped her arm, hoping she found some comfort in his touch.

She gave him a weak smile and then reached for Tolly's hand. "My prayers go with you."

"I'll be countin' on that, Reb."

Mr. Ross crowded in. "Stop talking and get in there. We've wasted enough time waiting for him to return on his own. Who knows how far he's gone, what

shape he's in by now after so many hours?" He pointed at Tolly, his face con-
torting. "You had better bring out my son, Sandford, or—"

Devlin stepped between the men. "Mr. Sandford is doing you a favor,
Ross, risking his life to chase down your boy—a boy who should have had the
sense not to go in that cave in the first place. Instead of threatening Tolly, you
should be thanking him."

The man curled his lip. "I'll thank him when he's been successful." He
returned to his weeping wife.

Tolly and Reb said their good-byes, and then Tolly, with a torch held high,
moved into the gaping maw.

Reb gazed after him, her shoulders square and her eyes dry. Devlin's heart
ached for her, and his admiration for her expanded. Mrs. Ross's wails pierced
the gray predawn. Mr. Ross continued to mutter, occasionally inserting a
mild expletive. Devlin stared at them, baffled. They were wealthy people,
powerful by society's standards. Yet they appeared helpless against a hard-
ship. If trial came his way, would he dissolve like the Rosses or stand firm like
the Hardins?

*"He giveth power to the faint,"* Reb had told him. Devlin knew that "He"
was God. But why would God bestow anything on him when he'd never given
Him any part of himself? If tragedy befell him or his family, Devlin feared he
would behave as shamefully as the Rosses.

Reb pulled in a long breath and turned, aiming her steps toward her
parents.

He caught her hand and said quietly, "Reb?"

"Yes?"

"This source of inner strength you and your parents have . . . Will you tell
me how to access it?"

In the flicker of lantern light, he witnessed her eyes brighten with a blur of
tears. Her lips curved into the sweetest, most tender, most joyful smile he'd ever
seen. She squeezed his hand. "Let Daddy tell you. He's the one who taught
me."

Remorse smote him. How could he be so selfish? He jerked his hand
away. "I shouldn't bother you or your father at a time like this. Not while

you're worried about your sister and he's comforting your mother. They must be half-sick with worry."

She caught his hand again and pulled gently yet with determination. "My daddy would say God prepared the way for 'such a time as this.'"

A comment Tolly made weeks ago crept from the recesses of Devlin's memory. *"He knowed we'd be here on this very day an' time . . ."* Other memories surfaced, of moments when his soul seemed to yearn for something. Or Someone. He'd pushed those feelings aside, but in that moment Devlin wanted nothing more than to answer the mysterious call on his heart. A sweet spiral of longing, of pieces coming together, coiled through his middle. The pull on his heart was more intense than Reb's insistent tug on his hand.

Her smile embraced him with a gentle warmth. "Trust me, Devlin. He'll welcome the chance to introduce you to his Source of strength. Talk to him. Yes?"

## FORTY

*Tolly*

Tolly took his time. Those folks waiting for word on their children wanted him to hurry, and he understood their need. But going too fast might mean missing something important. Going too fast might put him in danger, cause him injury. And then how would he be any help at all to those two wandering in here? So he bowed under the weight of his load, sweeping the torch slowly back and forth, searching for clues to Cissy and Nick's whereabouts.

Fool youngsters. Fool Doyle Spencer for not shooting a warning shot in the air the way guards were supposed to if something unusual happened. He wouldn't fuss too much at the young people. They were impetuous, curious, hadn't quite grown into their sense yet. He was mostly upset with Doyle. Tolly couldn't shuck the notion that Doyle had ignored his instructions because they'd been given by a black man.

Most of the Spencers in the hills were good-hearted folks, but that Orval Spencer carried some real prejudices against anybody different from him. And he'd passed those feelings on to his sons. Why the man wanted to leave his boys with a legacy of hate, Tolly would never understand. Pappy's voice whispered from the caverns of Tolly's memory. *"Jesus Hisself tol' us to treat othuhs the way we wants to be treated. So you don' hold on to grudges, Tolly. Don' speak ill o' folks even if you think they deserve it. Be willin' to fo'give. Allus 'member it's yo' callin' as a followuh o' Christ to be Jesus wit' skin on."*

Tolly murmured, "I 'member, Pappy." If his father could forgive the man who'd kept him bound in slavery, Tolly could surely forgive one thickheaded hills man for holding the color of his skin against him.

The torch's flame lit something on the cave floor, something small and thin. Tolly moved the source of light slowly and released a happy gasp. Two hairpins shimmered on the rock floor. He pinched them up and examined them close. They were still clean, hardly a speck of dust marring the squiggly pieces of metal. Which meant the pins hadn't been here long. Hadn't Reb told him how she'd fixed up Cissy's hair all pretty? These pins had to have come from that girl's head.

He dropped the pins in his pocket and thought for a few minutes. From this spot they could go farther into the main level, or they could've taken the natural stairway named the Corkscrew to a lower level. Going forward would be the easier route. He took a few forward steps, scanning the floor for more pins, scuffs in the dirt, anything. Nothing out of the ordinary presented itself.

With his load balanced he eased to the edge of the winding rock stairway and held the torch over the ragged opening. No other hairpins winked in the light, but a small rectangle—was it paper?—lay against a boulder halfway down. Tolly slipped the packs from his shoulders and made his way down the rocky pathway to the rectangle. He picked it up and turned it over. His pulse gave a leap. He held an image of Nick, Cissy, and the little burro Cissy called Beauregard.

He released a snort of consternation. Of course they'd take the hard route instead of the easy one. But at least he knew which way to search. Tolly secured his torch in a gap to free up his hands, then clambered to the top. One pack at a time, he carried the items to the bottom. It took him three trips, but once he had everything transported, he loaded himself up again, yanked the torch loose, and drew in a deep breath.

"Lawd in heaven, lead me to them fool young uns. An' let 'em be all right."

## Rebekah

Rebekah sat cross legged on the ground just outside the cave's gaping entrance. A circle of lantern light fell on Devlin's and her parents' faces, showing Daddy's fervency and Devlin's attentiveness. Mama kept her head low, her eyes closed, and Rebekah could only surmise her mother was praying—for Cissy, for Nick, for Tolly, and for Devlin.

While Daddy patiently, steadfastly explained the difference between knowing about God and becoming one of His children, a truth she'd learned years earlier, her mind drifted backward in time. She committed to memory the sweet time with Cissy, Devlin's steady presence during the ride to her cabin to alert her parents and his continued support during the long wait, Tolly's unhesitating agreement to go in after the pair of wanderers, and Mama's quietness.

Knowing that Mama was reliving the agonizing hours when they'd waited for Tolly to find Andy, Rebekah marveled at how calmly Mama sat—no tears, no wild wailing. Instead, she reflected a quiet peace and trust beyond anything Rebekah had witnessed since Andy's death. Had Daddy's and her prayers helped Mama regain her joy and faith? And if Mama could lose her deep sorrow after burying her son, shouldn't Rebekah be able to lose her guilt?

Hotel guests and people from the hollow gathered on the grass in the moonlight. Word of misfortune always spread quickly in the small community. She sensed some had arrived out of curiosity, others out of concern, and still more because they hungered for excitement. Their muttered voices provided a constant background hum, but at her husband's insistence, Mrs. Ross had finally stopped her noisy weeping.

He'd stated loudly enough for Rebekah to overhear, "You're making a spectacle of us, Genevieve." So she'd quieted but not with the kind of peace Mama exhibited. She continued to snuffle and press a handkerchief to her nose while gazing woefully at her husband, who stood grim faced and seemingly distanced from his wife's distress.

Even though Devlin was right about the indignity of their behavior, her heart ached for Nick's mother and father. They only wanted their son returned to them. Just as she and her parents wanted Cissy back with them again.

She bowed her head and closed her eyes, lapsing into prayer again. She'd repeated the same prayer so many times it formed effortlessly. *Dear God, let Cissy and Nick be safe. Let Tolly find them alive and bring them out whole.* As she prayed, she became aware of Daddy praying, too, aloud but whisper soft.

"Our dear, lovin' Father an' Lord, while You keep watch over our Cissy an' guide her safely out again, I thank You for usin' her calamity to open Devlin's heart to his need for You. Thank You that he's met His Savior."

Rebekah's heart leaped. She opened her eyes and stared at Devlin. Tears slid from beneath his closed eyelids and crept past the stubble on his cheeks, the rivulets of moisture showing silver in the lantern's glow. Tears flooded her eyes, too, and she bit down on her lip to hold back a cry of joy.

"Thank You that He's no longer in the dark," Daddy continued, "but stands secure in the light o' Your presence. You use all things for our good an' Your glory, so I praise You for this long night o' waitin' that brought about so much eternal good. Amen."

"Amen," Devlin echoed.

Devlin and Daddy clasped hands, a silent thank-you passing between them, and Rebekah feared her heart would burst looking upon the two men she loved most in the world celebrating together.

Then Mama said softly, "Do you reckon Tolly's come upon the children yet?"

Devlin released Daddy and took Mama's hand instead. "I'll pray they've been found and are on their way to you now." He bowed his head.

Mama, Daddy, and Rebekah joined him.

### Cissy

Cissy woke to a darkness so black she thought she floated in nothingness. She sucked in a sharp breath, and powdery dust filled her nostrils. She coughed and sat up. Something slid down her body, and then something rustled close by. She shrieked. The sound repeated itself, and she imagined a host of evil spirits swooping around her. Instinctively, she coiled her arms over her head and shrieked again.

"Shut up, Cissy." Nick's sharp voice cut through the black.

She groped for him and found something soft, empty—his jacket? She let go of it and continued sweeping her hands through the blackness until her fingers encountered his arm. She clung even though he squirmed. "Light the lantern again, Nick, please, please." It had been sending out a dim but comforting patch of light when they drifted to sleep.

"I can't. We don't have any matches. It's likely out of fuel anyway."

She whimpered, holding tightly. "Why're you so mad?"

His huff blasted. "Why wouldn't I be? We're stuck here in the dark. Nobody knows where we are. We don't have food or water." He wrenched his arm and she lost her hold.

"Nick!" Cissy pawed the air. Nothing. She bent her knees and wrapped her arms around her legs. She rocked herself, whimpering. Fear put a bitter taste in her mouth, so bitter she wanted to gag. Her heart pounded so hard she thought it would explode. Her lungs forgot how to hold air, so her breath came in short little puffs.

Is this how Andy felt before he died in the cave? Why hadn't she thought about Andy before dragging Nick in here?

Because she never thought about anybody but herself, ever.

Terror rose up and came out in a wail. "I don't wanna die. Ohhhh, I don't wanna die."

"Will you shut up!" Nick's voice grated through the blackness and echoed, *Shut up! Shut up!*

She hugged herself harder. "Stop bein' so mean! You want the last words you ever say to anybody in this world to be 'shut up'?"

*Shut up?*

*Shut up?*

The echoes died. Silence fell. A long silence. A tension-filled silence.

Cissy gulped. "N-Nick?"

"What?"

She nearly collapsed from the relief of knowing he was still there. Even if she couldn't see him, even if she couldn't touch him, she needed to know he was there. She licked her dry lips, swallowed bile, and whispered, "I . . . I'm scared."

"Just shut up, Cissy."

"But—"

"I said to shut up!"

And that's when she knew he wasn't mad. He was scared. Just as scared as she was. Because he thought they were going to die in this cave, too.

Sadness deeper than any she'd known before filled her. She was going to die before she got a chance to grow up. Just like Andy had died before he became a man. Mama had nearly mourned herself to death when Andy died. But Andy had never been the kind of trouble Cissy was. Mama probably wouldn't care as much. And it was purely awful to know that death was coming and that people probably wouldn't even care.

She buried her face against her upraised knees and cried.

# Forty-One

*Tolly*

Tolly's eyelids scraped over his dry eyes. It'd feel so good to keep his eyes closed. But he dragged them open again and squinted against the glaring torchlight.

He was closing in on them. He knew it because he'd heard a girl screech and a boy holler. They were still far ahead or tucked around a bend, out of the reach of his torch. But a little bit ago they'd been alive and bellowing, and that gave him enough hope to keep going forward, no matter how bad his tired body ached or how much his sore eyes wanted to close.

The tunnel narrowed, and his bulky torch pack caught on the wall. With a grunt he stopped and let it fall to the floor. He stared at it, frowning, making himself think. He'd need the rest of those torches to find his way out to daylight, but if he tucked one or two in the smaller pack with the food and blankets, they should give him the light he needed to get himself back to the big pack. Just in case, he slipped the coil of rope from his shoulders and tied one end to the pack. Tied it good and tight with a knot his pappy'd taught him so it wouldn't come loose. Then he draped the coil over his arm. He'd release the rope as he went. If his torch gave out, he could follow the rope back to his pack. Old Tolly Sandford wouldn't get himself trapped in this cave. Pappy had taught him better.

He heaved a sigh of relief as he moved steadily forward, peering beneath the torch as far as the light allowed. Every few steps he called out, "Cissy? Nick? Cissy? Nick?" Between hollers he focused hard and listened for a response.

Up ahead a Y greeted him. He groaned. "Lawd, I's had enough o' havin' to guess which way to go an' guessin' wrong. Cain't You jus' tell me this time instead o' makin' me hunt one way, come up empty, an' hafta to go back an' start ovuh? I's old an' tired."

He jammed the torch into the left passageway, chewing his lip. Then he thrust it into the right one, waiting for the Lord to answer. Out of the corner of his left eye, he caught a flicker of light. His pulse gave a leap, and he aimed his attention into the tunnel.

"Is that you, Cissy?" He bellowed as loud as his weary lungs allowed.

And from the right-hand tunnel drifted a weak voice. "It's me. I'm here."

Then two voices started calling, one on top of the other, their echoes making it sound like a whole town was trapped in the cave. "Here! Here! We're in here! Help! We're here!"

Tolly stood for a moment, confused. If the youngsters were in the right tunnel, who'd been holding up a torch or lantern in the left one? He shook his head. He must've imagined it. Either way, he'd come to save those lost youngsters, and they sure wanted saving.

He called out, "Keep a-yellin'! I's comin'!"

## Cissy

"Here! We're here! We're here!" Cissy's throat hurt so bad she wanted to stop yelling and start crying, but she made herself continue.

Nick yelled, too, and he'd grabbed hold of her arm. He held so tightly his fingers pinched her, but she didn't care. She wasn't alone anymore. Nick was there, and Tolly—she was sure that had been Tolly's voice—was coming. They'd be saved!

A little glow of light showed far up the tunnel, coming closer, closer. Nick jumped up, pulling Cissy with him. She held on to Nick as the ball of fire got bigger, brighter until finally she had to squint because it was so bright it hurt her eyes. But nothing had ever hurt so good as that light. She burst into tears.

The torch lit up Tolly's face and showed his big smile, and then he was laughing. "Now what're all you cryin' fo'?" He wedged the torch into a little crack in the wall, then stood grinning at her.

Cissy couldn't stop blubbering. She jerked loose from Nick and burrowed into Tolly's shirt front. "I was so scared. I thought for sure we was gonna die in here an' get put under the ground forever."

Tolly's chest rumbled with his chuckle. "Dyin' ain't nothin' to fear when heaven's waitin'."

"Heaven ain't waitin' for me." Cissy held Tolly's jacket in her fists and used it to cover her face. "If I came to those pearly gates, they'd shut 'em an' tell me to go away."

"How come?"

" 'Cause I'm not a good girl like my sisters."

He pulled her loose but kept hold of her arms. "Now that's the silliest thing I evuh done heard, an' lemme tell you, I heard plenty o' silliness in my life. Ain't nobody walkin' around on this earth who's good enough. We don't gotta be good. We just gotta be fo'given."

Cissy's chin wobbled. "I ain't forgiven, neither."

"Why not?"

"I . . . I ain't never asked."

"Well, then, maybe you oughta."

Yes, maybe she ought to. She rubbed her eyes and then her nose. She sniffed hard.

Tolly patted her shoulder. "You done wit' that fo' now?"

For now. But she needed to do some thinking. She nodded.

"All right then, lemme give you a look-ovuh, see if you's all right."

Cissy stood still, sniffling, while he examined her and then Nick. When he was done, he put his hands on his hips and shook his head at them.

"A few scrapes an' bruises, an' yo' mamas're gonna have a time gettin' them clothes clean again, but all things considered, you look mighty fine. You hungry?"

Nick nodded. "Yes, sir."

Cissy's stomach was spinning. "I just wanna go home." Once she got there, she'd never leave again. That is, if Mama and Daddy would let her come home. After all her shenanigans, they might figure they'd rather not put up with her anymore. Tears threatened.

Tolly unhooked canteens from his shoulders and handed them over. "We'll getcha home, but it be a long walk to the entrance, an' you's gonna need yo' strength. Take yo'selves a drink to start. Now sip it slow."

The cool water felt so good on her throat. She tipped the canteen upside down to hurry the flow.

"Here now. Di'n't I say sip slow? Don't do no guzzlin', or you's likely to give it back."

Cissy lowered the canteen and wiped her lips with the back of her hand. "Sorry, Tolly. But that's the sweetest water I've ever tasted."

Nick must have thought so, too, because he raised his canteen again and again.

"How 'bout a san'wich?"

Nick nodded eagerly. "Yes. That sounds fine."

Tolly opened his pack and began digging around. "Once you've done ate a san'wich, Nick, I'd be obliged if you'd carry that blanket back out."

Nick gave a start. "What blanket?"

Cissy shook her head. "We don't have no blanket, Tolly. All we brought with us was Devlin's map." She searched the ground around them. "Where'd it go?" Her gaze fell on a moth-eaten blanket lying close to the wall. Chills broke over her. "That blanket . . . it wasn't here when we laid down to rest."

Tolly frowned at her. "You sure?"

Nick nodded. "We only brought a map. Cissy had a hold of it when she fell asleep, but there wasn't any blanket. We would have used it. It's cold in here."

"Then where . . ." Tolly's gaze roved the area, his brow all crunched.

When she woke up, she'd felt something slide off her. It must have been the blanket. Which meant somebody had come up on them while they were asleep and put that blanket on her. Her body went cold, then hot, then cold again. She started to shiver.

Tolly shrugged, the motion stiff. "Well, now, ain't that a puzzle. We'll take it out anyway. It don't belong down here." He pushed napkin-wrapped packages toward them. He smiled, but it looked weak. "Eat these san'wiches now. When you's done, I'll get you two out o' here."

Cissy ignored the sandwich. "Without Devlin's map? He's gonna be madder'n mad if I don't bring it back to him."

"Girl, I cain't be worryin' ovuh no piece o' papuh when—" He closed his lips tight. His nostrils flared and his eyes closed. Then he opened his eyes. "Hurry an' eat. Yo' mamas are eager to see you again."

Cissy's heart ignited with hope. "My mama?"

Tolly frowned. "'Course yo' mama. An' yo' daddy, too."

She grabbed a sandwich. "I'll hurry, Tolly."

## Tolly

Tolly paced while Cissy and Nick ate two sandwiches each and drank more from the canteens. As tired as he was, he ought to be sitting, resting up for the trek out, but he couldn't sit still. An uneasy feeling had hold of him. Something wasn't right. He wanted to get these two out as quickly as he could.

"We're all done, Tolly." Cissy brought him the crumpled napkins. "Can we go now?"

He nodded, urgency making his movements jerky. "Shove them napkins in my pack. Nick, toss that blanket ovuh yo' shoulduh an' take the torch now—gonna let you carry it." His hands were shaking. He might drop it. "Stay right close to me now, both o' you, y'hear?" He shrugged the food pack onto his back, grunting a bit as the weight bit into his shoulders. He looped the rope over his arm and aimed a wobbly grin at the pair. "All right. Let's go."

With the torch behind him, his shadow led the way. He followed the line of his rope to the place where the Y began, and then he stopped so suddenly that Cissy bumped into him. He flapped his hand toward the youngsters. "Nick, gimme that torch."

The boy handed it over, and Tolly swept it from side to side, his heart thudding worse than natives pounding on war drums.

"What's wrong, Tolly?" Cissy sounded fretful.

If he told her, she'd have good reason to be afraid. "Nothin', girl. Just thinkin' fo' a minute is all."

But no amount of thinking would answer the questions roaring through his mind. His big pack—the one with all the torches—wasn't where he'd left it. And the end of the rope, cut clean through with a knife, now curled around the corner into the opening of the second tunnel. Drag marks—from his pack?—marred the dirt floor.

"Here, boy." He gave Nick the torch again and then picked up the fraying end of the rope and slowly wound it into a coil on his arm. The two torches he'd carried with him wouldn't be enough to take them all the way out of the cave. He searched his mind for a shorter way of reaching the entry. Whether tiredness stole it from him or it didn't exist, he couldn't say for sure, but he couldn't think of a shortcut.

*All right, Lawd, what'm I s'posed to do now? 'Less You gimme a miracle, make these last two torches burn longuh'n any of 'em have evuh burned befo', all three o' us is gonna be lost in the dark soon.*

A gentle breeze eased through the tunnel, making the fire at the end of the torch perform a short dance. Tolly stared at the flickering flame, frowning. How'd wind get into the cave? He jerked his face toward the breeze. Just a whisper, but it was there. Far ahead in the tunnel, a tiny pinprick of light glimmered and then dimmed. A mournful groan filled his ears. Or maybe filled his soul. Chills broke out all over him.

Nick stepped close to Tolly, so close the heat from the torch scorched his cheek. "Which way?"

*I's trustin' You, Lawd.* Tolly took the torch and pointed at the left-hand branch of the Y. "This way. Stay close."

## FORTY-TWO

*Devlin*

Devlin helped the hotel cook hand out sandwiches and cookies for the second time that day to the folks scattered on the grassy rise outside the cave opening. He hoped the contents of the baskets would stretch to serve everyone at this dinner hour.

As the day had progressed, more and more people arrived until they stretched all the way to the road and reached the edge of the woods. It seemed the entire hollow and half of the hotel's guests now waited for Tolly, Cissy, and Nick to emerge from the cave. And only a handful of people had brought food with them.

Brother Neville sat near the right side of the entry with the Rosses, who slumped on chairs carried out by hotel staff members. Preacher Haynes joined the Hardins on the left, all of them crowded together on the quilt Rebekah had retrieved from her bed in her cabin. Two camps had formed — the hills folks clustered around the Hardins and the hotel guests around the Rosses. Those in the Hardin camp brought quilts and settled themselves on the colorful squares the way people did for picnics. Hotel guests stood on the grass or sat in the transport wagons that the guides had parked under the trees.

Children—a mix of hills and hotel youngsters—chased each other up and down the road or through the trees, their laughter ringing until adults intervened and hushed them. Their play stopped for a short amount of time and then began again. Devlin ducked aside when two little boys raced by. Why didn't someone take the whole lot of youngsters to the grassy area behind the hotel cottages and organize games for them? They were creating tension with their unconcerned behavior, but expecting them to simply sit for hours on end seemed unreasonable.

He handed the last of the food to a group near the road, then carried the empty basket to Mr. Cooper. "Did everyone get something to eat?"

"Everyone who wanted something." The cook heaved a sigh. "I don't know the Rosses at all, but the Hardins are good people. They don't deserve this worry. I wish there was more I could do."

"You've done plenty by keeping them fed out here, but if you'd like a suggestion . . ."

"What's that?"

Devlin shared his idea about taking the children elsewhere for activities.

Mr. Cooper nodded. "I'll get some of the dining room staff together and send them down for the youngsters. I don't need all of them in the dining room anyway with most of the guests here at the cave."

"Thanks." Devlin gave the big man a pat on the shoulder.

"You're welcome. At times like this a fellow needs to feel useful." The cook offered a sad smile, then ambled off, his head low.

Devlin made his way through the throng to the Hardins. As a hotel guest, he probably belonged in the Rosses' camp, but he couldn't stay away from Reb's family. Just as he'd witnessed a dozen times over the last, long hours, Reb's parents and the preacher bowed with their heads close together, their eyes closed and lips moving. Praying. Devlin didn't know a lot about prayer, but he couldn't resist adding his own.

*Dear God, grant them their request.*

Reb sat opposite her parents. Her littlest sister slept in her arms, and the second youngest lay with her head on Reb's leg, also sleeping. The other girls sat in a tight circle, fidgeting, whispering, flicking hopeful looks toward the opening and then slouching low again. His heart went out to all of them. Like Mr. Cooper, he wished he could do more to help.

He crouched next to Reb. "Want me to take her? Your arms must be tired."

A weary smile creased her face. "They are. But I want to hold Nellie. The way I can't hold Cissy right now." Tears winked in her eyes, but she blinked several times, and the moisture cleared.

If he couldn't hold Little Nellie, he'd hold Reb. He slipped onto the grass behind her. "Lean on me then. It'll help."

She hesitated, blinking at him uncertainly, but after a moment she relaxed against his chest. As much as he wanted to, he didn't encircle her with his arms. Instead, he braced his palms on the grass, angled himself to better bear her weight, and sat quietly.

Soon two wagons rattled down the hill, and the dining room's servers invited the children to go to the hotel for games and refreshments. Parents released the restive youngsters with murmurs of thanks, and a relieved hush settled over the crowd.

An hour crept by. Little Nellie and Trudy awakened from their naps grumpy and groggy, and Mr. Hardin asked Della to take her sisters up the hill to join the games. The girls left, the youngest ones eager and the older ones casting worried looks over their shoulders as they went.

Reb continued to lean lightly against Devlin's chest for several minutes after the girls departed, and for a moment he wondered if she had drifted off to sleep. After their sleepless night and long day, he wouldn't blame her. But then she heaved a delicate sigh and stood.

"Mama, Daddy, I'm going to walk up to the road and back—stretch my legs. All right?"

The couple nodded in unison.

Devlin started to rise, but Reb shook her head. "I need a few minutes alone, Devlin."

Disappointed, he sank back down. He watched her weave between the groups, pausing now and then apparently to answer questions. She reached the road and paced the distance of twenty yards up, back, and up again. With each step her spine grew straighter, her head higher, and by the time she made her way back to the quilt, she seemed to have thrown off a good portion of her weariness.

As she settled beside him, he couldn't resist asking, "Tapping into your Source of strength?"

A smile curved her lips. It was answer enough.

Another hour passed, and night birds began their soulful songs. The air cooled as the sun eased behind the trees. Mr. Cooper came down and announced to the parents that the children were in the hotel dining room enjoying a snack. He promised to keep them there, safe and entertained, until their folks were ready to retrieve them. "No matter how late the hour," he finished before trudging back up the hill.

"I hope the young uns don't end up spendin' the whole night in the dinin' room," a woman seated close to the Hardins said.

The man sharing her quilt snorted. "Better up there than down here. 'Specially if Tolly don't find 'em alive. The young uns shouldn't oughta see—"

"Shh!" the woman hissed but not before Mrs. Hardin's face went white.

Mr. Hardin pulled his wife close to his side. She rested her head on his shoulder, pressing her fist to her mouth. Their minister leaned in and spoke softly to them, and Reb scooted across the quilt to take her mother's hand.

Devlin remained a bit apart, wanting to offer some kind of comfort, but what? Helplessness weighed heavily on him. He clenched his fists, battling the urge to grab one of the lanterns burning at the edge of the entry and charge inside to find those young people himself.

He started to rise, but a faint cry cut through the evening shadows and stopped him midmotion.

"Mama!"

Half the women in the gathering lifted their heads, searching the area.

"Mama! Mama, Daddy!"

The Hardins bolted upright. Rebekah leaped up and stood alert, her body quivering. All three of them turned their gazes toward the cave opening. Devlin stood, too, staring into the cave's dark entry and searching for a glimmer of torchlight.

People all across the lawn were sitting up or pushing to their feet, their murmurs forming a low rumble.

"Mama! Daddy!"

The voice was louder now, strangled as if emerging on a sob, but it wasn't coming from the cave. Mr. and Mrs. Hardin scrambled to their feet, looking around with both hope and uncertainty etched into their features.

Mrs. Hardin called out, "Cissy?"

And Cissy burst from the bushes with Nick close behind her. They came to a startled halt, staring open mouthed at the crowd. Then a thunderous cheer rose, and the Rosses and Hardins raced across the ground to capture their children in hugs.

The crowd surged forward, surrounding the happy families. Devlin got jostled along with the throng and pushed up tight against Reb's back. The happiness exploding through him had to come out. He wrapped his arms around her middle from behind. She curled her arms over his, nestled her head into the curve of his neck, and they rocked while laughter and chatter filled the air. Nell Hardin rained kisses on Cissy's dirty face, and the girl clung to her parents as if she'd never let go.

"Mama, Daddy, I'm so happy to see you. Can't hardly believe you're here after I was so wicked." Cissy blubbered out the words, pressing her cheek to her mother's neck and then her father's chest. "I'm sorry. I love you, Daddy. I love you, Mama. Do you still love me?"

Mr. Hardin caught Cissy's tear-filled face between his hands and gazed down at her with tenderness. "No wrongdoin' could make us not love you, gal. We're your mama an' daddy, an' you're our precious Cissy. We'll always love you."

Joy exploded over the girl's dirty face, and then she collapsed against her father again, weeping.

Devlin battled the sting of tears as well. The reunion was so beautiful. It seemed that her time in the cave had awakened the light of repentance and squashed the dark blot of rebellion. He sensed Cissy's attitude and behavior would be changed from now on.

With the young people safely in their parents' arms, the crowd began to thin. Devlin started to leave, too, to give the Hardins some privacy.

Mr. Hardin said, "How'd you come to be in those bushes, gal?"

Devlin's pulse skipped a beat, and he turned back. Caught up in the celebration, he hadn't realized the significance of their arrival from a place other than the cave's entrance. He blurted a question. "Weren't you in the cave?"

Cissy nodded, her eyes wide. "Deep inside, with no lantern or nothin'." She bit her lower lip for a moment, remorse glimmering in her eyes. "Used your map to take us in there."

He'd completely forgotten about the map.

"An' I lost it. You . . . you'll have to start over again."

Oddly, the map wasn't important anymore. He gave Cissy's shoulder a pat. "That's all right. I'm just happy you're safe now."

"Me, too." Her eyes swam with tears, and she gripped her parents again. "It was black as black, an' I thought Nick an' me was gonna die in there. But Tolly found us, an' he led us out through a hole in the ground."

Devlin's flesh broke out in goose pimples. "A hole? You mean another way to get in and out of the cave?"

"Uh-huh. Pretty sure we came out on Spencer land. There was a whole bunch o' stuff lyin' around by the hole—coils an' jugs an' such. Tolly was right upset about it, but when I asked him what was wrong, he said to never mind an' that my folks was waitin' by the big openin'. He tol' me an' Nick which way to go an' promised he'd be right along." She searched the area, confusion pinching her brows. "Ain't he here yet? Where's Tolly?"

Devlin offered a quick smile. "Don't worry, Cissy. I'll find him." He snatched one of the lanterns from near the entrance, tugged his hat low on his head, and set off through the bushes.

### *Tolly*

A pickax was a sorry replacement for a shovel. Tolly grunted as he swung the pointed head into the ground and broke loose another chunk of earth. He rolled it into the opening and pressed it down with his foot. Despite the chill evening air, sweat streamed down his face. He swiped his forehead with his sleeve, then stood for a moment, panting. His muscles ached and tiredness pulled at him. But he couldn't rest. Not until he'd finished.

The torch he'd jammed into the ground began to fizzle. Quick, before it went all the way out, he grabbed the last one from his pack and touched the heads together. The fire flared, glaring against the graying sky. He pushed the unlit end firm into the ground and returned to his ax. He hoped none of the Spencers showed up before he finished the task. They'd be plenty mad about him using those jugs and still parts to help fill the hole. But if they fussed, he just might aim his ax at them instead and suffer the consequences. Fool men anyway.

He raised the pickax high, ready for another swing, when someone burst out of the bushes and hollered, "Tolly, don't!"

Tolly nearly toppled backward. He set his feet wide, held the ax like a sword, and glared at the dark figure hiding behind a lantern's glow. "Who is that hollerin' at me?"

"Me." The man set down a lantern by the hole, and Tolly got a look at his face. Devlin Bale. Relief flooded him. His muscles went limp, and the ax slid from his grip.

Devlin propped his hands on his knees and scanned the rough area where Tolly had spent the last hour whacking at the ground. He scowled. "What are you doing? Why are you covering it up?"

Tolly blinked. "'Cause I gotta. It don't belong here."

Devlin straightened and shot an impatient look at him. "But it was a separate opening, another means of accessing the cave. Do you understand its importance?"

Tolly nodded slowly, too tired to do it fast. "Yep. It let me an' those two foolsome youngstuhs get to daylight." But now it'd served its purpose. It had to go.

Devlin blew out a breath. "That's not what I meant. This could become a second access to the cave. This could open up a whole new tour route to visitors."

Tolly squinted at the college boy. What did they teach these young people in them places of education? "This ain't a natural openin'. Somebody's come along—probably Orval Spencer, seein' how prickly he's been about anybody darin' to step on his property—an' hacked it out, made his own way into the cave. I speculate he was scopin' out a place to set up a corn liquor still unduh the ground. But he's gonna hafta set it up someplace else. I cain't leave this hole here."

"But why not?"

Tolly's weary legs gave out. He collapsed next to the half-filled hole and sagged forward. "Ain't you listened to nothin' I's said the whole time we been togethuh? Mammoth Cave was crafted by the hands of the good Lawd Almighty. He gave it as much care as He did the part o' the world above the ground. Suppose somebody come along up here an' chopped down ever' tree, just hacked 'em all to pieces so they couldn't nevuh grow again. What would happen?"

Devlin bent down on a knee, his brow puckering. "Well, things wouldn't look the same. We wouldn't be able to make use of the wood or fruit that comes from trees. Animals would lose their places of shelter. We wouldn't have shade anymore, and the landscape would be desolate."

Maybe they'd taught him a few things after all. "That's right. That's right. It would upset the balance o' nature, yes?"

Devlin nodded.

Tolly pointed at him. "An' that's exactly what would happen down below if I leave this hole. The balance o' the cave would be all upset. God planned for one openin', Devlin. One." He jammed his finger at the boy, drumming home his point. "We go messin' wit' that, we's gonna change the cave in ways the Creatuh di'n't intend." Tears pricked Tolly's eyes as sorrow weighted his heart. "Just befo' I foun' this hole, I heard the cave moanin', boy. Cryin' like a wounded crittuh. It's gotta be healed o' this jagged wound."

Devlin sat gazing at Tolly for a long time. Long enough for Tolly to gather his strength. He used the ax and pushed himself to his feet. He gripped the tool two handed and raised it over his head.

Devlin leaped up and grabbed the ax's handle.

Tolly glared at him. "Let me be. I don't got patience fo' you an' yo' plans. I got a job to finish."

The college boy shook his head. He tugged the ax away and took a step backward. "Move aside, Tolly. I'll close the hole."

# FORTY-THREE

## *Rebekah*

The last Saturday in August, Rebekah stood aside and watched Daddy tamp the soil around the arched limestone marker etched with her brother's name, the dates of his time on earth, and the scripture Mama chose. Rebekah read the words aloud while the leaves whispered their lullaby and a moist breeze teased her hair. " 'I am the resurrection, and the life: he that believeth in me, though he were dead, yet shall he live.' "

Daddy rose and moved beside her. He laid his arm across her shoulder and pulled her tight against his ribs. "Jesus Himself said it. That means we can trust it. Andy's livin' with Him, an' we'll see him again by an' by."

She fixed her gaze on "yet shall he live." Andy was gone from this earth, but he wasn't gone from her memories. He lived in a place where no harm or sadness would touch him again. And someday they'd be reunited. A tiny thread of peace—of guilt lifting—eased through her heart. Tears blurred her vision, making the words dance. "By and by . . ."

Daddy kissed the crown of her head and released her. He stepped gingerly to the back section of the little graveyard and adjusted Granddaddy's cross. "Can't hardly believe September waits around the corner. Devlin'll be headin' back to Lexington soon. Gonna miss that young man."

So would she. Melancholy tried to sneak in. Over the past two months, she'd sat beside Devlin in Sunday service, watched him absorb Preacher Haynes's teaching. They'd shared hours and countless talks, with him at the table carefully reconstructing his map and her on the stoop of her cabin. The handsome student who had arrived with self-centered ambitions now planned to use his surveying skills to help the people living in the hollow determine and fix the boundaries of their landholdings to protect their property for the next generation.

Pride filled her when she recalled the letter he'd sent to his father claiming he'd come to believe the land would be better preserved by the hands of those who'd built their homes and lived on it. She'd gained a healthy respect for the elder Bale when he replied that he'd come to his own conclusion that relying on a land acquisition to gain favor was the same as manipulation. He still intended to run for the Senate but on his own abilities. The Bales were honorable men.

She suddenly realized Daddy was talking. She pulled herself from her reflections to give him her attention.

"This year Trudy'll be headin' off to school with her sisters. Only Little Nellie'll be left at home all day with your mama. That'll prob'ly seem quiet." He shifted to Grandmama's cross, tightening the ties holding the crossbar in place. "Leastwise until the beginnin' o' the new year." He hummed as he worked, a secretive grin toying on his lips.

Awareness dawned. "Daddy, is Mama . . . expecting?"

A joyous smile burst over his face. He nodded hard enough to dislodge his hat. "She sure is. An' I hope it ain't prideful to hope for a boy this time. Lord knows I love my gals, but havin' a boy to traipse after me again would be a mighty pleasure." His expression turned wistful.

Rebekah darted behind him and wrapped him in a hug. "Congratulations, Daddy! I'll pray with you for a boy." Not to replace Andy. No boy could ever replace Andy. But to bring his own joy and challenges to their family.

He patted her arms. "Thank you, gal. Pray for your mama, too. She ain't as young as she once was, an' she's lost so many." His gaze turned toward the little crosses. "But she's feelin' fine an' says she's certain sure God's gonna let us raise this one. Who am I to question her faith?"

A knot filled her throat. Daddy's and Mama's faith . . . How beautifully they lived it before her and her sisters.

"Gal, I brought you out here 'cause there's somethin' your mama an' me want you to know."

His serious tone captured her full attention. "What is it, Daddy?"

He placed his hand on her shoulder and gazed intently into her eyes. "We don't want to use the money you been earnin' to buy gravestones an' a fence for this spot in the woods."

Disappointment niggled. "Why not?" She'd worked so hard and so long to earn the privilege of building Daddy's legacy.

"'Cause that money can be put to better use on the livin' than o' the already-gone."

Rebekah shook her head, confused.

"Gal, we want you to take the money from the can an' enroll in college."

She drew back. "Daddy, we can't afford—"

He gave her a little shake. "Just listen to me now. You got a good head on your shoulders. You always have. I had me a talk with Devlin awhile back, an' he told me lots o' students work an' pay their way a little at a time."

Tears flooded Rebekah's eyes—tears of longing, tears of uncertainty, even tears of sadness to leave her beloved hollow. "Do . . . do you really want me to go away, Daddy?"

He crushed her to his chest. His chin pressed the top of her head. "If I did what I wanted, you'd stay right here with your mama an' me your whole life. But that'd be plumb selfish." He set her aside and met her watery gaze. "You got somethin' to give, Rebekah. God's got big plans for you. It's time for you to seek 'em."

"But, Daddy, your legacy." She gestured weakly to the plot of ground with its wooden crosses.

He cupped her cheek. "I'm lookin' at my legacy right now, Rebekah. You, who's chosen to live in God-honorin' ways."

She sniffled. "That's because you taught me to honor Him, Daddy. You and Mama taught me—taught all of us girls—faith."

He nodded, his smile tender. "An' don't you see, gal? You acceptin' it, livin' it, teachin' it to the next generation is the best legacy any man could have."

## *Cissy*

Cissy released the burro into his stall with a loving pat on his rump. "There you go now, Beau. Enjoy them oats. I'll . . . I'll . . ." She swallowed hard. She couldn't say she'd see him again. Because her work at the estate was done. Mr. Temperance would pack his photography gear and head out first thing in the morning. Before she started crying over a smelly old burro, she turned and raced out of the barn.

The photographer was folding his camera's stand. The camera and props were already boxed. Her heart gave a flip. Had he forgotten? She dashed to him and grabbed his sleeve. "Mr. Temperance, remember you're gonna have supper with us tonight."

He paused and grinned at her. "You are the pushiest child I've ever met."

She giggled, hunching her shoulders. "Well, you're old. Thought you might've forgot."

He rolled his eyes. He did that a lot when she was around. "Not so old I'd forget a dinner invitation." He patted the box that held his camera. "And, yes, I'm bringing this with me. Was your mother able to remove all the stains from your pretty dress?"

Some of the ground-in dirt from her time in the cave hadn't come out of the ivory linen, but she didn't care. What were a few mars on a dress when her insides felt all clean and shiny, her dark sins erased by God's hand of forgiveness? "No. But I'll stand in the back, an' nobody'll even see the marks."

She nearly wriggled out of her skin with eagerness to surprise her family. She wouldn't be buying a train ticket to the big city. That dream didn't hold a bit of appeal now that she understood how much her mama and daddy loved her. But she'd spent nearly every penny buying her sisters and Mama new dresses to wear for the picture Mr. Temperance intended to take of them. She'd even bought Daddy a new tie since his Sunday suit was plenty good yet. If only—

She grabbed the man's sleeve again. "Mr. Temperance, I gotta ask you somethin'. An' you tell me if you think it's silly."

He chuckled. "If it hatched in your head, it probably is, but go ahead and ask me anyway."

She cupped her hand beside his ear and began to whisper.

## Devlin

Devlin battled melancholy as he drove the little pony cart across the bumpy road to the Hardins' cabin. The hotel photographer sat in the back cradling his camera in his lap and muttering complaints about the rough ride. But Devlin didn't mind the bumps. They were a part of his memories of this place, and since he wouldn't travel this road for a while after tonight, he intended to savor every little jar and jolt.

He turned onto the lane leading to the cabin, and as he cleared the trees, his stomach gave a flip of happiness that rolled every bit of sadness from his being. Because there she was with her hand curled around one of the rough-hewn porch posts, watching, waiting. For him.

*Dear God in heaven, I love this woman . . .*

Reb stepped off the porch and moved across the lawn as he drew the mule to a stop. She appeared to glide, the sweeping skirt of her pale-yellow dress barely gracing the tips of the freshly cut grass.

He pushed his ivy cap to the back of his head and gave her a thorough perusal, whistling through his teeth. "If I'd known this was going to be a formal affair, I would have dressed more appropriately. Reb, you look wonderful."

She fingered the end of her customary braid and glanced down the length of her dress. "Cissy bought it for me, and she insisted I wear it tonight. She has us all decked out like we're going to a banquet." Her gaze flicked to the back of the cart, and she gave a little start. "Oh, Mr. Temperance, I didn't see you there."

The man winked. "No doubt because you have eyes only for the young man holding the reins."

A delightful blush stole across her cheeks.

Hiding a smile, Devlin leaped out of the cart and reached for the photographer's stand. He aimed a grin at Reb. "I think you're about to discover why Cissy wanted you all gussied up. Would you call your family out to the porch? Mr. Temperance needs to catch this image before the sun goes completely behind the trees."

Her mouth dropped open in an O of wonder, and then she turned and darted inside, giving Devlin a glimpse of her bare soles as she went.

He helped the photographer set up his camera while Cissy bossed her family into position on the porch steps. He grinned at the girl's endless stream of excited chatter.

"No, Little Nellie, Daddy can't hold you. You're gonna stand right down here in front where ever'body can see your purty new dress. An' don't suck your thumb! You ain't a baby anymore. Della, quit scrunching your nose. You look like a rabbit eatin' clover. An', Trudy, for goodness' sake, put your skirt down. You think Mr. Temperance an' Devlin need to see your underthings?"

Finally the camera was set, the family was in position, and Mr. Temperance curled his hand around the bulb. "Ready, everyone? All right, look here, smile, and—" He frowned. "Cissy, something's missing."

The girl gave a jolt. "Oh! I forgot!" She broke through the group and clattered into the house.

Mr. Temperance offered Devlin a wry look. "And she accused me of being forgetful."

Devlin chuckled. Cissy would likely always be flighty, but since she'd left her selfishness behind in the cave, the characteristic seemed more endearing than annoying.

Moments later Cissy emerged with a pair of worn brown boots, the laces snarled and broken. She held them hesitantly toward her parents. "Mama an' Daddy, is it all right if Andy's boots are in the picture, too?"

When Mr. Temperance took the photograph, several pairs of eyes were shiny from tears, but Devlin believed the shimmer would add sweetness to the finished image.

Mrs. Hardin bade the girls to change out of their fancy clothes before sitting down to supper. They thundered inside, pushing at one another goodnaturedly. Reb turned to follow them, but Mr. Hardin caught her arm and whispered something to her. She nodded and came down the steps and across the grass, her movement as graceful as a swan floating on a pond. She stopped in front of Devlin with her hands locked behind her back and her head held at a prim angle.

"Before we eat, may I speak with you?" She flicked a look at the photographer and added softly, "Alone?"

Devlin nodded and offered his elbow. She took hold, and they moved together to the side yard where a gap in the trees allowed the evening sun to paint a golden carpet on the grass. She turned her face up to him, her brown eyes shimmering.

"You're going back to Lexington tomorrow?"

How beautiful she looked bathed in pale sunlight, her hair caught in its beguiling braid and her slender fingers resting at her throat. "Yes. I have to take the earliest stage since my train leaves the Lincoln station at noon." His throat went tight. "It's not going to be easy for me to tell you good-bye."

A mysterious half smile curved her rosy lips. "Well, if Daddy has his way, we'll be saying hello again soon."

Devlin's pulse sped into hopeful double beats. "Do you mean he— You— It's true?"

She laughed, the delightful sound creating a web of joy around them. "Yes, I'm going to enroll at the University of Kentucky for their fall semester."

How had she made sense of his stammering? Probably the same way Mother always understood Father's enigmatic statements. Love put them in tune with each other.

"But I'll need your help finding my way around the campus and securing a job."

"Of course. Whatever you need. I'll show you the university, the city of Lexington, the world if you want me to."

She laughed again. "The world? Really?"

He curled his hands around her upper arms, his thumbs tracing light circles on the soft sleeve of her lovely new frock that brought out the flecks of gold in her brown eyes. "It's the least I can do for the woman I love." He'd said it out loud. He held his breath and searched her face for signs of rejection.

She tipped her head. "You love me, Devlin?" Wonder colored her tone.

He nodded, and his breath whooshed out. "I do. I love you, my beautiful hills girl." He leaned forward slightly, his gaze locked on hers. "Does that frighten you?"

A slow smile curved her sweet lips upward. She rested her hands lightly on his waist, her eyes turning moist. "I think it's a good thing. Because I love you, too, city boy."

He pulled her into his arms and pressed his cheek to her warm hair, releasing a sigh of pure bliss. "Ah, then, I won't tell you good-bye this evening. I'll only say"—he drew back slightly and smiled—"see you soon, Reb."

# Letter to the Reader

In April 2014 on our way home from a visit with friends in Cynthiana, Kentucky, the Hubs and I stumbled upon Mammoth Cave National Park. Curious, we decided to investigate, but we arrived too late in the afternoon to tour the cave. So I toured the gift shop instead. I came home with a stack of books and a deep fascination for Mammoth Cave. I had the pleasure of revisiting the cave in May 2015 and experienced the majesty of the United States' longest cave system firsthand.

As Tolly explained to Devlin, slaves mined saltpeter from the cave to manufacture gunpowder. The owners of the land were savvy enough to realize the cave could serve other purposes as well, and in 1816 guides—mostly slaves who had helped retrieve the saltpeter—began taking groups for paid underground tours. Thus the cave was one of America's first tourist attractions, preceded only by Niagara Falls.

In the earliest years, guests were allowed to break delicate crystals from the walls and carry them away as souvenirs or to singe their names into the ceiling using the soot from candles. Fortunately these practices were largely stopped when Dr. John Croghan purchased the property in 1839. It became his goal to preserve the cave while making its wonders available to as many visitors as possible. Croghan's family kept control of the cave for more than eighty-five years.

The first map of Mammoth Cave was drawn by a slave, Stephen Bishop, in 1845. Bishop, a popular guide at the estate, penned the map by memory. The first accurate instrumental survey of the cave system was performed in 1908 by a German geologist and cartographer, Max Kämper, who was guided by Stephen Bishop's great-nephew. (Of course, if Devlin were a real person, he would have been given credit for the first instrumental survey since he arrived at the estate a year ahead of Kämper.)

Many communities of people lived around the cave, carving out their living from the hillsides. A few took advantage of the influx of tourists by inviting people to visit small caves on their properties. Others merely tolerated the constant flow of people.

As the last of the Croghan heirs died, momentum grew to take the cave from private ownership and make it a national park. Wealthy citizens of Kentucky formed the Mammoth Cave National Park Association in 1926 and began accepting donations to purchase farmsteads in the region. Other tracts within the proposed boundaries for the park were acquired by right of eminent domain. Hundreds of people who had called the hills their home for several generations were forcibly relocated in the process of forming Mammoth Cave National Park. The state of Kentucky made the land a gift to the national government, and the park was officially dedicated on July 1, 1941.

The cabins and homesteads of those who once called the area home have been absorbed by the forests with only a few stone foundations or rock fireplaces remaining. The cemeteries, both those near churches and on private family plots, are maintained by the park officials, just as Devlin presumed they would be.

I tried to stay as true to fact as possible, but I'm sure there are places where story won out over accuracy. I ask any Kentucky historians to forgive me for taking creative liberties while I brought my make-believe characters to life. I truly loved my time at Mammoth Cave, one of God's most glorious creations, and I hope you've enjoyed your time in the story world.

May God bless you muchly as you journey with Him,

*Kim*

# Readers Guide

1. In a moment of frustration, Rebekah told her pesky brother to get lost, and the command created a burden of guilt. Have you spoken impulsively and later regretted the words? How did you make amends? How can we keep from creating these kinds of regretful situations?

2. Because Rebekah had been reading when she lost patience with her brother, she punished herself by giving up the pleasure of reading after his death. She also pushed aside her own dreams for the future to see her father's dream to completion. Were these reasonable actions? Why or why not? How would you have advised Rebekah?

3. Nell Hardin wanted her son to have a permanent grave marker to prove that he once lived. Festus Hardin wanted a fence and stone markers so his children and grandchildren would know the names of their ancestors. Both viewed the cemetery as a legacy. How was their legacy similar to the rock altar God instructed Joshua to build as a reminder to the children of Israel? How did it differ? Have you ever considered leaving a legacy? Was it something tangible (able to be held in your hands) or intangible (held in your heart)? Which is of greater value: a tangible legacy or an intangible legacy? Why?

4. Tolly told Rebekah, "Sacrifice is a hon'rable thing unless it's done fo' the wrong reasons." What is a right reason to sacrifice something of value? What is a wrong reason to sacrifice? What did Tolly sacrifice in the story? Was he right or wrong? Why?

5. Devlin wanted to help his father receive credit for turning the Mammoth Cave estate into a state or national park to further his political career. Was this a selfish or selfless goal? Why? Eventually Devlin changed his mind about the government gaining control of Mammoth Cave and the surrounding properties. What brought about the change?

6. Cissy was dissatisfied with her simple, poor lifestyle and longed for excitement and wealth. What were the blessings in Cissy's life that she overlooked? How does satisfaction with one's self make a difference in attitude and action? Why do some young people view what they have as insignificant or lacking? How can we help our children be content rather than always thinking they need something more to be happy?

7. Tolly, speaking of God, told Devlin, "He knowed we'd be here on this very day an' time." Tolly believed God has a plan for every part of creation. Do you believe God is involved in every facet of creation, including you? Take a moment to examine your life and search for God's fingerprints guiding, molding, and protecting you. Give Him thanks for His care and concern for you.

# Acknowledgments

Chester and Rose McCauley—thank you for the invitation to your home that led to my encounter with Mammoth Cave. It was a God incident for sure!

Mom and Daddy—thank you for returning to Kentucky with me to explore the cave and the surrounding areas. What a wonderful time we shared! I treasure the memories.

The staff at Mammoth Cave National Park—thank you for pointing me toward helpful books, letting me examine cemetery documents, and answering my questions. I appreciate your help very much.

Nathan and Mallea—thank you for your willingness to "fill in" as Devlin and Rebekah. You two are so cute. Especially together. Love you both!

Don and my girls—as always, thanks for your continued support and encouragement.

My posse—my cheerleaders, my prayer warriors, my sisters-of-the-heart—thanks for being part of this journey.

Shannon, Amy, Kelly, Julee, Carol, and the entire fiction staff at Water-Brook—thank you for everything you do to help bring these stories to life. You are a blessing to me.

Finally, and most important, God—thank You for being my Light, my Song, my Strength, my Guide. You work all things together for good when we place our lives in Your capable, loving hands. May any praise or glory be reflected directly back to You.

# Visit the Old Order Mennonite community in the Zimmerman Restoration Trilogy!

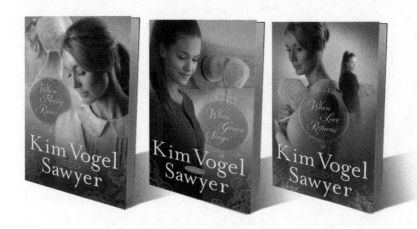

## Revisit history in another Kim Vogel Sawyer novel...

Read an excerpt from these books and more at WaterBrookMultnomah.com!